The Whisper of Dreams

Ben Hennessy

Inspired Quill Publishing

Published by Inspired Quill: July 2014

First Edition

The Whisper of Dreams © 2014 by Ben Hennessy
Contact the author through their website: *www.hennessywrites.com*

Chief Editor: Sara-Jayne Slack
Cover Design by: Jeremy Hanna
Typeset in Minion Pro

Paperback ISBN: 978-1-908600-36-3
eBook ISBN: 978-1-908600-37-0
Print Edition
Printed in the United Kingdom
1 2 3 4 5 6 7 8 9 10

Inspired Quill Publishing, UK
Business Reg. No. 7592847
http://www.inspired-quill.com

Acknowledgements

My family and friends, as ever.

Sara and Inspired Quill for continuing to improve me as a writer with every consecutive step.

And to Madison, for the providing the map readers were requesting.

My test readers: Illy H, Carol O, John P.

Nick Hennessy, who furiously demanded he get a full name acknowledgement this time. Luckily, his help discussing this story means he deserves it.

And the various remarkable minds of Tenaria. You know who you are and why you're important. Thank you all.

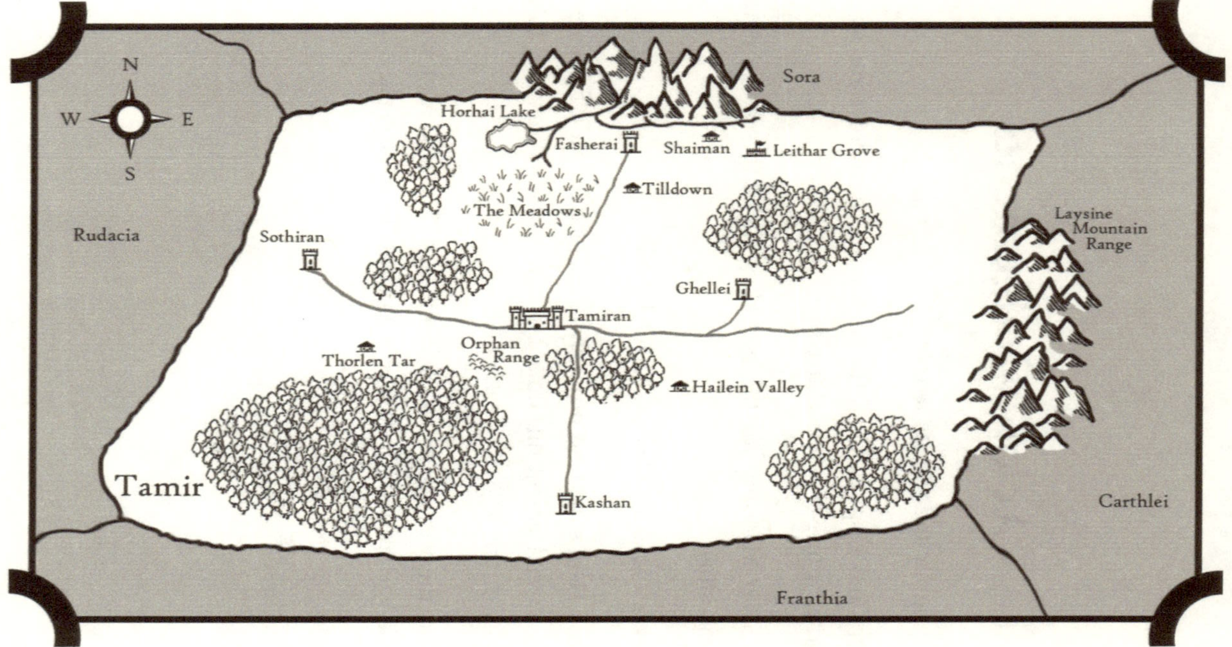

N
W   E
S
Sora
Horhai Lake
Fasherai
Shaiman
Leithar Grove
Tilldown
The Meadows
Rudacia
Sothiran
Ghellei
Laysine Mountain Range
Tamiran
Orphan Range
Thorlen Tar
Hailein Valley
Tamir
Kashan
Franthia
Carthlei

T HE TOWER WAS a monument to solitude. It rose from the ground, up towards the overcast skies, straight and perfect. There were no cracks in the brickwork, no rough edges or decoration. It was devoid of character and lacked evidence that a hand had ever touched it. The door was lacquered wood, belted with a single steel band. A brass ring had been set in its centre, waiting to call for attention. There were no windows except for at the very top, where a dull orange glow emanated from within, a useless lighthouse without a coastline to protect. The tower sat in the bowl of a heavy mountain range, termed by the bordering nations as the *Ethariana Krul*; The Eternal Cage. The peaks of the mountains stabbed at the clouds, colossal claws of the earth for which the tower served as an anchor, giving a sense of perspective.

Within the tower there was no noise. The spiral staircase, lit by the occasional candle which never dripped and never faltered, echoed no sound save for the footsteps of whomever used it. Again there was no sign of a personal touch; a lack of history within except the very ambience of the structure. No portraits hung from the walls. No vases held flowers. No carpet softened the stairs. It was a stifling, claustrophobic place.

A huge room at the top of the tower met the final few steps. Here, at least, were some possessions and furnishings. A broad table upon which sat a neat stack of books, a feathered quill and an ink well. A high-backed chair, cushioned and padded, suggested the desk saw regular use. The walls were lined with shelves containing a variety of jars, scrolls and vials. Books were set in a very meticulous order – the spines announcing the contents were listed alphabetically. An oval rug blending varying shades of red covered most of the stone flooring. The light breaching the only two windows in the tower was created by a heavy fireplace within which logs crackled and spat as flames danced along their surface.

There, against the eastern side of the circular room, stood a bed. Wrapped within a heavy quilt and propped up by pillows was a very old man, gaunt and sickly, with beads of sweat dotting his papery skin. In the glow of the fire he appeared to be made of bronze. Dishevelled hair matched an unkempt beard. His chest rose and fell with a gentle depth that hinted at a peaceful slumber.

Beside the bed was another chair, this one built for comfort. In the chair was a second man. He flicked through a book, reading the pages without ever seeming lost within the words. One leg crossed the other. He held the glasses he wore with one hand, as though they would fall if he released them. They remained in position when he reached down to turn the page, and he would hold them again regardless. His scruffy hair was similar in colour to the bed-ridden man's, and his age was comparable, but he seemed much healthier. He wore a robe of deep maroon which fit his old body to the inch. The fire kept the room warm but he did not sweat beneath the heavy fabric of his garments. He read his book and patiently waited.

Hours passed. Just as the seated man came to the end of his book there was stirring. He looked up, snapping shut the cover of the tome, just as the sleeping man slept no more. Their eyes met.

"Corliani," the newly awoken man murmured, his voice hoarse.

"Tyrrial."

With a yawn, Tyrrial pressed against the mattress beneath him and sought to push himself upright. Suddenly his eyes widened and he yelled out, his right arm faltering.

"Be careful, brother. I would expect that hurt," said Corliani as he folded the arms of his glasses inwards and placed them atop the book in his lap. "You'll need to take it easy for a few weeks."

There was a pause. Tyrrial lifted the quilt and examined himself. His jaw tightened at what he saw there.

"You have been sleeping for almost a month." Interlocking his fingers and leaning forward in his chair, Corliani watched his compatriot. "We have taken it in turns to watch over you and nurse you back to health. Shigasi and I switched places only two days ago. Mubuto was here the week prior to that. We have been very worried, my friend."

"I suspect Shigasi performed the surgery," Tyrrial replied.

"Aye, he did. Such a skilled, steady hand. I would wager he is the finest doctor the world has ever seen. *Will* ever see, for that matter."

Tyrrial smiled. "A few centuries of practice don't hurt, I suppose."

"Would you like some water?"

"Yes, please."

Corliani turned to the jug next to him. Despite the warmth of the room the surface of the jug was dotted with condensation. He filled a cup and handed it over to Tyrrial, who accepted it without a word and took several long swallows. There was a sigh of satisfaction once the water was gone.

"How thoughtful to have cooled it."

With a chuckle Corliani took the cup from him, but gave no reply. Tyrrial lay back against his pillows, gingerly adjusting his position.

Minutes passed. Corliani watched Tyrrial, and Tyrrial watched the fireplace. Smoke poured into the chimney, feeding a labyrinth of vents which ran through the wall itself, designed to heat the stone. Now awake, Tyrrial seemed much less the frail being he had whilst asleep. His amber eyes were alert and his demeanour was proud, despite his current situation.

Eventually he spoke. "Out with it, Corliani. I can hear your thoughts churning."

A single nod. "Very well. What were you doing?"

"Proving my fears correct, it seems." Tyrrial turned his

eyes towards his friend. "The girl almost killed me."

"Had you not chased her across Tamir and murdered her brother, I suspect things would have been rather different."

Tyrrial grunted. "So it *was* her brother."

With a smirk, Corliani continued. "As far as I understand, you slaughtered over two hundred people in Leithar Grove."

"Is that so?" Tyrrial sighed. "Unfortunate. But I suspect an example has been made…?"

"Oh, yes." Corliani nodded once more. "The people of Tamir have been terrified by your little visit. Once the truth came out regarding Prince Remelas' plans to invade Carthlei, there was a national outcry. They're trying to have him removed from succession."

"So I averted a war."

"In a manner of speaking."

Tyrrial reached up to run a hand across his forehead. Corliani produced a handkerchief from the left sleeve of his robe and handed it over. Tyrrial accepted without a word and mopped his face dry.

"What of the girl?" he asked.

"She has gone into hiding."

"She must be dealt with."

"No, she must not." Corliani's words were stern. "You have meddled in Sarene's life enough. Let her be. She is not interested in world domination or in hunting us down. Had you left her alone in the first place, she would most likely be back at her home with her family by now, content to stay in her village. Goodness knows her dealings with the Tamir

Royal House should have put her off politics and military ambition for good."

"If they had started their war the—"

"*If* Tamir had crossed into Carthlei, I would have dealt with it. Tamir is within *my* territory. I am not quite as clueless as you seem to think, my old friend." Corliani paused, taking a deep breath. "As it is, the Tamir army is standing down, Remelas has a deeply unhappy populace to deal with and Sarene is nowhere to be found. You have done enough."

Tyrrial fell silent. He looked down at the wound beneath the quilt again.

"We were scared, Tyrrial," Corliani added. "When we arrived here you were an unconscious, bleeding mess upon the floor. I cannot allow you to risk yourself like that again."

It was true. As angry as Corliani had been to learn of Tyrrial's actions, the fear of losing the man he had called his brother for almost six hundred years had been crippling. He had acted with diligence and care during his time at Tyrrial's side, but alone he had been restless and shaking. He barely slept. He ate little. In his most paranoid moments of the last few decades Corliani had started to doubt whether he loved this calculating, cynical and bad-tempered man any longer, but the idea of losing him had been unbearable. He had felt an ache in his heart during the surgery which had saved his life. Shigasi had removed the blade, all six inches of which had been buried in Tyrrial's side, and sewn him back together. The verdict was that Tyrrial had simply been lucky. For all his power, his experience and skill, he had survived by chance only. If the dagger had struck an inch to either side he wouldn't have made it back to the tower at all.

Tyrrial merely nodded. "Thank you for taking care of me, Corliani. I will share the same sentiments with the others when they arrive. Please inform them that I shall be paying a visit soon."

"Of course. But you should rest, my friend. I will tell them to come to you."

"No," Tyrrial replied. "I need some time to myself. To think on what has transpired. A brush with death is quite a thing to process, brother."

Corliani didn't like the idea, but Tyrrial was not a fool. He would not be babysat or coddled.

"As you wish."

Smiling softly, Tyrrial allowed his head to fall back onto the pillows. "Is there any food?"

"It can be arranged, of course."

"Good. I would greatly enjoy some of your beef casserole."

"Coming right up." Corliani rose from the chair, returning the smile. Some of the tension dropped, and he felt easier than he had in weeks. He turned towards the fireplace, snapping his fingers. A bowl materialised over the fire, already laden with the ingredients needed for his signature dish.

"Corliani?"

He paused, looking at the two bowls now in his hands. "Yes?"

"I meant it. Thank you. From the bottom of my heart."

Chuckling, Corliani shrugged. "We are kin."

"Yes," Tyrrial said behind him. "Yes, we are."

Chapter One

ETHANEI PUSHED AT the door with a gloved hand. The tavern was lively even at this early hour; warmth and conversation washed over him. The drone of voices helped him to leave his issues in the street. He moved towards the bar and waited for the tavern keeper, a thin and wiry man named Ghural, to notice him.

Leaning against the counter he scanned the crowd. About forty people filled the place – not a common occurrence on this side of the village. Every chair was filled and every table surrounded. He saw farmers, traders and merchants, some he'd grown up with and others he'd only seen for the last few years. Thorlen Tar was growing by the summer, and what had been a community of a few dozen families when he was born three decades previously had swelled into a populace of over eight hundred. The status of Tar had been bestowed on the township six years ago. Lord Tharesan, a direct descendant of Thorlen himself, was delighted at the increased prominence his title held. He'd thrown a feast in honour of the township, at which Ethanei had danced with his wife, Clarai, and watched the sunrise with her the next morning, sitting beneath their favourite tree and sharing his last ale.

The memory brought back the image of Clarai's legs wrapped around an old friend of his, and a fresh pang of self-pity took hold. He slapped his hand against the bar top.

"Come on, Ghural! I'm dyin' of thirst over 'ere."

"Be with you in a minute," the tavern owner called back without looking up, as he handed a flagon each to a pair of men he recognised as part of a group which had arrived that evening. They seemed polite, thanking Ghural for the service, but their eyes never stopped moving across the crowd. The rest of their band were commanding the broad table in the centre of the room. One of their number, a tall man who still wore his grey hood pulled up over his face, was leaning back to speak to two other men nearby. They laughed together at something he said.

A tankard, sodden from being freshly dunked, slammed onto the counter before him. Ethanei looked up, realised what had happened, then started fishing in his pocket for coin.

"There you go, you impatient bastard." Ghural grinned. "I'll add it to your tab."

With a chuckle, Ethanei left the coins where they were and reached for his drink. He lifted it, tipped, and swallowed a third of the contents in seconds before giving a long sigh. "Since when did you start givin' tabs?"

"Only for the regulars, like. I know you're good for it."

"Much obliged." He lifted the tankard, nodding across the room. "What's the deal with the grey cloaks over there?"

"Haven't got the slightest. They've spoken to half the room, though. Seem a nice bunch." Ghural nodded to a waiting punter, and stepped off towards the ale casket. "Maybe you can get a drink out of 'em," he called over his shoulder.

Ethanei smiled, taking another pull from his ale. The fresh delivery of alcohol was stirring up what he'd already consumed, and he could feel the dulling effects begin to soak into him again. He glanced across the tavern once more, searching for anyone he knew well enough who happened to have an empty seat next to them.

He recognised several faces. Cullan, a man with a face only his mother could truly love, sat holding court with some of his hired season hands. A successful farmer who was careful with his money, Cullan had a reputation for telling stories and trying to charm ladies through words alone. It must have worked, for he had recently married a girl almost ten summers his junior who was pretty to boot. Ethanei smirked, catching a punch line of something involving a bolting horse. Those at Cullen's table cackled and roared, applauding as the farmer took his seat again.

Beyond them sat the local doctor. The cooper. Shaerer, a skilled carpenter he'd known since a boy, was wedged in between two of his eldest sons. Several more hired workers from the surrounding homesteads. A few who, like him, had been discharged from the army following Prince Remelas's disarmament. One of these, a scary looking chap named Khellien, nodded to him. Ethanei raised his cup in response but, noting the lack of a nearby seat, remained where he was.

Those he didn't recognise ignored him but conversed happily with each other. The ale was flowing and the three barmaids, all daughters of Ghural, slipped and sidestepped between the clientele and the tables with practised ease, gathering empty cups and returning full ones. The eldest and prettiest, Helaina, was working double duty as the waitress. She occasionally disappeared into the back area before returning with plates of food. The dishes were simple in the Duck and Well – mainly cold cuts of meat with bread and cheese – but the cook did a decent mutton stew, and the smell of it mingled with alcohol and people. The crowd itself had a distinctive scent, as men stopped by here straight from their jobs.

Watching Helaina move over to the far corner of the room, where a small booth was tucked against the wall, he saw a spare seat. Helaina handed two plates to those already seated there. They were both hooded. One was slight and wore a deep mauve cloak, her mannerisms and small hands suggesting a young girl, though with her back to the room he couldn't be certain. Opposite her was a hulking brute of a man, a prominent beard visible from beneath the thick cowl he wore. He took the plate, tiny in his giant hand, and gave no sign of gratitude. Helaina moved away, leaving them to eat.

"Another one, my friend!" Ethanei called aloud, before downing the rest of his drink. He wanted a seat, and there was no reason why he couldn't take the free one he'd spotted. The atmosphere was lively and welcoming, and he could be charming enough when he needed to be. Once Ghural had taken his tankard and dunked it, he moved across the room. Drips of golden yellow liquid dotted his path, and he managed to keep himself stable as he passed through the crowd. He exchanged brief greetings with Khellien, clasping him on the shoulder and cracking a quick joke. His eyes met with one of the grey cloaked men, who nodded to him. Ethanei responded in kind.

Reaching the booth, Ethanei raised his tankard in greeting. A small amount spilt from the rim but, luckily, landed on his trouser leg rather than on the table. The mauve-cloaked youngster – definitely a girl – offered him a courteous smile. The man with her continued eating.

"Evening, folks," Ethanei said. "I notice there's an empty space here, and I was wonderin' if I could put meself down for a while?"

The girl looked at her companion. The man finished chewing before digging his fork back into his stew.

"No."

Ethanei laughed. "Come on, friend. There's no need to be rude. I'm simply looking for somewhere to rest me bones for a while."

"There are plenty of other chairs in the room," the man replied, lifting a piece of mutton to his mouth.

"Aye, but they're all taken. I don't mean to impose, but I would truly appreciate the chance to sit with you until another seat's free." He grinned, gesturing to the space on the bench making up the booth. "I'd carry it away but it appears to come as a package. I doubt I could pull you along with me."

The girl brought her hand to her mouth, covering a smile. Her huge companion regarded him for the first time, chewing. The revealed eyes were *hard*. Ethanei brought his tankard to his lips to cover his faltering smile.

Eventually the man exchanged looks with the girl. She nodded cautiously at him.

"Fine," he said. "Go ahead."

"Much obliged," said Ethanei. He made to sit himself next to the girl, noting the greater space afforded there. The man spoke again, dipping a piece of bread around the bottom of his bowl.

"Next to me."

Pausing, half crouched, Ethanei smiled once more. "O'course. Wouldn't want to seem rude, eh. Name's Ethanei." He slid across the edge of the table and sat on the bench next to the man, who paid him no attention. The situation struck him as quite unusual, and he chuckled. The ale was really starting to hit him again and he placed his hands on the table to prop himself up, straightening his back.

"So what brings you both to Thorlen?" Ethanei waved a gloved hand across his face before speaking again. "Sorry. Thorlen *Tar*. Keep forgetting that. Wait..." Fixing a stare on the massive stranger, he leaned forward. "Do I know you?"

The man pushed his bowl to the side before wiping his mouth between thick fingers. He reached for his own ale. "Just passing through."

"Oh right. That's a shame. Quite a nice town, this is. Growing by the year." Ethanei gestured over his shoulder with a thumb. "See this? Everyone 'ere talking and laughing.

Ale flowing. It's a sense of community, y'know? Even with new faces migrating by the season, we've kept that community. Its *togetherness*." He slurred the final syllables, but made up for it with a proud grin. He saw the girl smile in kind.

"Seems so," was all the man had to say, sipping his drink.

"I mean, back when I were a lad, this village had maybe a hundred yards of buildings surrounded by fields. I used to be able to walk for 'ours, exploring, and feel like I were the only person in the world. You know that feelin', my friend?"

The man grunted. "I believe I can understand."

"Well, that's good." Ethanei took a long pull from his ale to gather his thread. "But aye, that was then. Nowadays there's places poppin' up all over the land. We got a guesthouse, two taverns, shops, stables… We even got a market on the week's end! People coming in from the other villages 'ere in the west. On account of it being cheaper to set up a stall in Thorlen than in Sothiran." He looked to the young girl, who was watching him quietly. "You ever been to Sothiran, lass?"

She shook her head, placing her hands in her lap.

"Well, it's not nice. Loads of filth everywhere. All the buildings are bloody tarred. The whole place stinks like a tanners and looks like a cemetery. Full of bastards, too." He chortled, rocking back in his seat.

"How many of those have you had?" asked the man, gesturing to the tankard in Ethanei's hand.

"These? Oh, enough. Nothin' wrong with a good drink. I must say, I've picked up a taste for it recently. What with bein' discharged from the army an' all." Ethanei belched.

"Oops. 'Scuse me, my lady." He winked at the girl.

"A shame about the army," said the man. "It left a lot of men without a career."

"You'd prefer if they'd kept us all on?" Raising a brow, Ethanei leaned back forward again. Something on the table soaked through the fabric of his shirt. "He were gonna invade, you know. Take us to war."

"Do not misunderstand me," the stranger replied. "I was referring to the Royal House's decision to recruit them in the first place. The whole plan was flawed from the start."

"Can't argue there," said Ethanei. "But they paid us all off well. Still don't 'ave to take up the shovel or pick *just* yet." He gave another laugh. Despite the hardships and the lack of employment now, he *was* still secure for money. True, if he didn't find himself a job within the next few months he'd end up with nothing in reserve, but it wasn't quite time for that yet. His marriage had fallen apart and some memories had yet to be drowned out with alcohol. He'd heard one merchant, travelling through from the capital city of Tamiran towards Rudacia, claim that the national treasury had bankrupted itself with the pensions paid to so many. There was talk of numbers ranging from a thousand to a *hundred* thousand men. Nobody knew the truth for sure, but the size of the pension paid out to each soldier had been sizable.

"Anyway," Ethanei added, "Can I interest the pair of you in a drink at all? My round. Wouldn't want you to leave Thorlen Tar with the impression we weren't a welcomin' crowd, eh?" He turned before either of them gave him an answer. "Barmaid! Service, if ya please!"

Before anyone responded, there was a commotion behind him. Ethanei turned in his seat, looking to the left. One of the grey cloaks – the one with the hood – had leapt up onto a table and was clapping his hands. The sound bounced around the room, and eventually everyone fell silent.

"Ladies and gentlemen of Tamir! A moment, if you would?"

KANDERIL TURNED. THE man who now commanded the attention of the room was tall and confident. Besides for him and Sarene, the grey cloak was the only other wearing a hood. The edges of the cloak were thickly lined with wolf's fur.

Those around him were watching, calm and expectant. Kanderil waited.

"Thank you," said the man, giving a formal bow. The other grey cloaks had already moved the flagons and tankards out of the way, giving their colleague a clear platform from which to address the tavern.

"Now you kind folk, mostly inhabitants of this fine town, may be wondering who I am. Indeed, who my friends are also." He motioned to those seated at his table. "Perhaps we are a travelling group of minstrels, here to play you a song. All we need are some instruments and you could sing the night away..." He played a note on an imaginary lute, inciting laughter from some of the crowd.

"Regrettably, that isn't the case. Neither are we mercenaries, nor military of any kind. We are simpl—"

"Then why are you wearing swords?" asked a brash voice

from the back. Kanderil noted a bearded man with red cheeks, his hands resting on a bloated stomach.

"Merely for protection," replied the hooded speaker without skipping a beat. "We all know these are tough times. With the nation still simmering with ill feeling over our Prince's actions, it is wise to keep oneself armed when travelling as much as my companions and I do."

The red-faced man nodded, looking at his own group of friends. There were sounds of agreement throughout the tavern.

"And that's the point, my friend. My *friends*. That's why I'm here today, to ask that you lend me your ear for a short time." The man stood straight, his posture commanding, and folded his arms. "My companions and I are sons of Tamir. We've lived in this wonderful nation all our lives, and will continue to do so until we are called from this life and into the next. We're here to remind you that you, too, should share our pride in calling yourselves Tamir."

The crowd applauded, with a few calls of affirmation thrown in. Kanderil listened. He had heard speeches like this countless times before; from bards, merchants and officers in the Kalethi. Usually the words were intended to build a rapport, encouraging the listener to trust – right before the sales pitch was delivered.

"I'm sure many of you have been affected by the actions in Leithar Grove." Immediately the hooded man held up his hands. "Now, I need not remind you of the tragic events which took place there in late summer. I shouldn't have to repeat the name of the man responsible for bringing the wrath of the Four upon our brave soldier's heads. But, for clarity's sake, let us speak it."

"Prince Remelas."

There was a low murmur from those present. Kanderil saw some of the crowd turn to those next to them, muttering in agreement. Ethanei raised his mug, spilling a little of the contents across the floor, offering a toast. Kanderil then turned to Sarene, who met his gaze. She shrugged at him.

"We were deceived, my friends. The man we turned to for leadership, given the frailty of our beloved King Runath, built an army of incredible number with which to bring war and terror back to our lands. He was to send our countrymen into battle across the borders, into lands we have no right to invade. Despite the years of history we have, all the stories and tales of the Four and their infinite wisdom, Remelas was going to use violence on a grand scale to subdue our Carthleid cousins." The hooded man nodded as some of the crowd shared glances. "Yes, Carthlei and Tamir were once a shared nation, did you know that? Our distant history mentions times where we lived as one great clan, sharing our lands and our wealth."

"History…" The speaker wagged a finger, turning a small circle on the broad table. Kanderil noted the sureness of the steps, his movements uninhibited by the limited space. "History is important. Tamir has always been a dignified nation. We have protected our borders against those who would wish us harm, but we have never sought to initiate violence. Ever since the creation of this kingdom we have been governed by a strong sense of justice. Most here will remember the name Aldion, our greatest champion during the clashes with Soralis a little over a century ago."

More nods from the crowd. One drunken man at the bar broke into the first line of the song '*Aldion the Brave*', but was hushed down by the tavern owner. A few laughs broke out, followed by a wry cheer.

The man on the table smiled beneath the hood. "Aye, that Aldion. The man who led our forces to victory and pushed back the Soraliath forces. But did you know he never set foot across the border? I have studied his journals. He wrote '*It is not my place to seek revenge, or to impose my will upon the citizens of other lands. I will fight until I can fight no more, I will give a pint of my blood protecting a square yard of our homeland, but I shall never march across terrain which does not belong to me.*'

"That, my friends, is how we should be remembered. How we should be viewed by our neighbours." He brought his hands together, pointing with loose fingers towards the crowd. "We have long held the respect of Rudacia, of Carthlei and Franthia and further afield yet. But with Remelas' plans we have been weakened in their eyes. We are now viewed with suspicion and fear. Any man which raises an army a hundred thousand strong *must* be held accountable; believe me, my comrades, this is *exactly* how our neighbours see it. They see Remelas as a threat."

Kanderil ground his teeth. He turned in his seat and rested his elbows on the table, cracking his knuckles. When they arrived in Thorley Tar earlier that evening he had intended to wait until later before eating, when the crowd would be thinning out. The tavern owner had refused the suggestion of eating their meal in their room. The people of Thorlen Tar were infatuated with the idea of community, it seemed. But Kanderil had skipped breaking for lunch during their travel here, and Sarene was famished by the time they arrived. He'd relented to her pleading to take an early meal, allowing them to eat with main evening crowd.

Now he was caught in a propaganda display. Thankfully it was directed at the Prince and not the *other* reasons for Tyrrial's visit.

"He's right isn't he, mate," Ethanei said, peering over his shoulder. Kanderil was surprised the drunkard could even focus on him. "Good that someone's got the bollocks to say all this stuff, eh?"

"He speaks well," Kanderil replied.

The hooded man crossed his wrists at his belt and stood straight-backed. "My name is Anaburan. My friends and I make up the Sons of Tamir. We are here for one reason only: to encourage debate and thought. We love every one of you as family, and we want Tamir to be safe. We fear further reprisals against our lands, not only from the Four but also from the bordering nations. We feel that Remelas must step down as the next King, for he represents danger in the eyes of other rulers."

"You should be careful," said a shaven-headed man near the table Anaburan spoke from. "You'll be arrested by the Guard for talkin' like that."

Anaburan smiled, spreading his hands wide. "Since when was a man forbidden from speaking his mind? These aren't the lands of the Cho'Nanj or the Shu'Cha or any of the other northern races. We have no intention of storming the House of Tamir and seeking bloody retribution. I'm not inciting rebellion or pleading for you to take up arms. I'm just speaking out for those of you who cannot speak for yourselves. With enough support, I will seek an audience with Remelas himself to give you a voice, to shine a light on our concerns."

"The Gathire might see things differen—"

"The *Gathire* are another symptom of the paranoia and decay from which our ruling house suffers! To be given such freedoms to terrorise and suppress our people whenever and however they like is a travesty of justice." Anaburan shook his head. "Let the Gathire hunt me down. I will stand against them just as I stand against the Prince. With my head held high and my ideals for a stronger, safer Tamir on my sleeve."

There was a round of applause then, encouraged by the other grey cloaks sitting around Anaburan's table. The atmosphere grew with an excitement which had been missing at the start of the speech. The air tingled with anticipation, a united fervour building to a crescendo.

"These are important times, my brothers," continued Anaburan, his voice matching the heightened state of his audience. "We have to stand up for ourselves, just as we have always done! Whenever those who intended us harm crossed our borders we fought them off, and now we must do the same within our homeland. I'm not asking for your pledge or your sword-arm. I'm asking for no sacrifice. Just lend us your support by *thinking!*" He tapped the side of his hood. "Don't be afraid to think, and don't be afraid to speak your mind! The Four judged us, butchering hundreds of our countrymen, and Remelas' egotistic schemes were responsible. We mustn't be frightened to demand that our Prince answer to those crimes and give penance for the lives lost on his behalf."

He knows how to perform, Kanderil thought to himself. Sarene was watching Anaburan with her chin propped against her palms.

"Come on," he said in a whisper which still rumbled. "We're going back to our room."

Sarene's tawny stare moved to him, and she nodded against her hands before sliding out of the booth. Kanderil tapped Ethanei on the shoulder.

"Excuse me."

"Eh?" The drunk craned his neck around as if he hadn't realised someone sat behind him.

"Excuse me," Kanderil repeated.

"Oh, right. Wait. Don' you wanna hear what he 'as to say?" The words sounded disconnected from the man; a confused slur dragging them out of his mouth. He stood up and slumped against the table. Kanderil stood and eased his way past. Ethanei looked up at him. Kept looking up.

"Oh, wow…"

Kanderil headed for the stairs leading up to their room. Sarene held onto his belt, keeping close. Eyes were turning to him as they often did. The pair had to pass the central table to get to the other side of the room.

Anaburan paused, folding his arms once more. "Do my

words bore you, my large friend?"

Kanderil said nothing. He pushed his way past one seat, stepped through two standing onlookers, and continued moving.

"Do you disagree with my sentiments?" The question was more insistent this time. Kanderil saw the whole crowd looking at him now. He felt Sarene's grip tighten at his back.

"You speak the truth," Kanderil replied without slowing. "We are merely tired."

"Of course. Sleep well." Anaburan's tone was sincere. Kanderil understood the sentiment. The man had brought the crowd this far and didn't wish to spoil the national pride by challenging anyone who seemingly disagreed. He clearly understood where nationalism became fascism.

The sermon started up again behind them as Kanderil climbed the stairs.

SARENE CLOSED THE door behind her. The room she shared with her guardian was a two-cot space with a window, a table and a threadbare throw on the ground. She exhaled sharply, looking across to Kanderil. The giant Hunter viewed the street beyond the window before checking its latch.

"Lock the door."

She did so, before moving to her bed. Sitting upon it, the frame squeaking in response, she tugged off her boots and wriggled her toes. The boots she'd been bought were a shade too small and her feet were often hurting by the evening.

Kanderil pulled back his cowl and offered her a bemused

smirk. "Next time, we wait before eating."

Sarene nodded, smiling. The comment eased her. That speech in the common room had been fascinating, spoken with meaning but carrying an ominous undercurrent which she couldn't quite put her finger on. She presumed that it was her experience at Leithar Grove which made her aware of it. After all, she knew the facts of what had happened. The Prince was not the sinister figure Anaburan made him out to be. He had ambition, this was true, but he hadn't wanted to invade Carthlei to wipe them out. Remelas was not a blood-thirsty ruler.

Kanderil tugged the strings of his jerkin and slid it from his broad shoulders, along with his shirt. His torso fascinated her as it always did: rigid with ugly stacks of muscle, undefined but wholly solid, spotted with scars and marks from years of military service. Sarene watched him sit down on his bed and loosen the straps of his tall moccasins. She followed suit, unclasping her cloak and popping the toggles from her tunic. She kept her undershirt and breeches on as she always did, slipping beneath her blanket and resting her head on the thin pillow.

"We will leave early, at first light." Kanderil lay back, pulling his blanket over him. It was too small, reaching from chest to calf only. "I would like to put some distance between us and these Sons of Tamir."

Sarene nodded, looking up at the ceiling as Kanderil snuffed out the lantern. The room went dark, the faintest of glows from outside reaching the window, casting shadows on the wall beside her.

She and Kanderil had been travelling together for almost five months now, ever since he'd found her in the forests along the highway leading from her village to the capital city of Tamiran. This was only the third time they had stopped in a city since he had pledged to protect her following the events in Leithar Grove. Following the death of her brother, Jared. She grimaced in the gloom, closing her eyes as her thoughts began to wander.

The past season had been hard. Sarene had believed herself capable of handling grief ever since she had been forced to flee her home following a visit by the Gathire, the secretive special wing of Tamir's military. The image of her mother, scarred across both cheeks and bandaged around the face, had kept tears close to the surface for weeks afterwards. Her sense of loss, knowing that she would not see her family again for a long time had clamped to her heart like a heavy rock. It had pulled at her spirit and kept her subdued for long periods.

Jared's death at the hands of Tyrrial had made a mockery of her assumptions. The pain she felt had all but crippled her. Kanderil was forced to care for her like a child, making her eat and tucking her into her bedding at night. He would walk beside her at all times, even going to the trouble of purchasing a horse to carry her while he led them from place to place. Sarene barely remembered those early days. She had never cried so much and even now, with the summer long since ended and winter on the horizon, thoughts of Jared brought more sorrow than joy. She felt guilt; it was her unique position within the world which had led Jared to his death.

Had it not been for her immunity to the powers of the Four, he would still be alive today.

A tear ran from her eye, passing her temple and trickling into her hair. She sniffed as quietly as she could. Kanderil did not respond, though he surely recognised the sound by now. He'd heard it most nights.

The other two involved in that fateful night had left. Prince Remelas returned to Tamiran. He offered sanctuary for Sarene's family, but she did not yet know whether they had accepted. Following the attack and the ensuing revelation of his plans to raise an army to invade Carthlei for resources and land, there had been an uprising of ill-feeling towards the House of Tamir. The future of the royal family was in doubt. The King of Tamir had taken ill and was near death, reportedly losing himself to madness. Few now trusted Remelas, blaming him for Tyrrial's retribution. Anaburan and the Sons of Tamir had been proof of how far that feeling ran away from the capital.

She could understand Remelas's departure – it would have been stranger had he stayed with her. But Spasmodic, the odd little creation of Tyrrial who had decided to accompany her along her bizarre journey, had not been seen since she had left Leithar Grove. It had mumbled something about wanting to see more of the world and, one morning, had simply disappeared. Amplified by the loss of her home and the death of her brother, she'd experienced a distinct sense of abandonment. The creature had quickly become a fixture of her life, offering a degree of protection Kanderil could not. The Hunter had a deep sense of justice which did not permit him to kill; while Sarene hated violence, Spasmodic had no such restraint, and had ensured that none could touch her.

But now it, too, was gone. All she had was Kanderil, who had been her rock. He hadn't once questioned his responsibility as her guardian and never made her feel like a burden. Even if he could be grumpy and strict at times, it was never without reason, and he *had* kept her safe. That much was never in doubt.

A floorboard creaked outside their door as someone made their way to another room. She heard Kanderil stir at the noise and turned her head, seeing a shadow move past the thin strip of light at the bottom of their door. Then a hinge squeaked and a latch clicked shut. Sarene rested her head back once more.

Sleep claimed her soon after, and her dreams were troubled.

Chapter Two

THE MORNING IN Tamiran was cold, but Prince Remelas stood by the window anyway, staring out over gardens which sat as part of the House of Tamir. Canvas sacks had been tied around many of the plants to protect them from the coming winter, giving the grounds a depressing look. It was as though someone had come and confiscated the colour, putting it to rest until the sunshine returned once more.

Remelas watched the street which ran parallel to the eastern wall of the gardens. There, he saw carts being pushed back and forth, shop fronts being set up and people moving to and fro, ready to start their business for the day. With most of the city still asleep there wasn't the general hum of the capital's populace in the background, and he could hear voices in the crisp air. He couldn't make them out but their presence comforted him. They were his people. They resided in his city, and they were citizens of his father's kingdom.

His kingdom now.

The news of his father's passing had come as no surprise. King Runath had been gravely ill for several weeks, lingering between death and madness. He had spent much of the past week calling for his servant Phurell, a man who had worked as the King's aid for almost three decades before his death nine summers previous. Runath had barely eaten. The thin soup his wife, Queen Syllaine, had spoon-fed him dribbled down his chin into his grey, wiry beard. Weakened by illness and fever he ended up a ghoulish figure lying in his chambers, sallow skinned and skeletal. Withered into a shell of the large, powerful man Remelas had grown up idolising.

Now he was at peace. Remelas was the King of Tamir.

Remelas turned his head at the firm knock, tightening the belt of his robe.

"Come."

The heavy door swung inwards and a man entered. Tall and bald, he wore a long black coat buttoned from his waist to his throat, trimmed with white. The man's face was marred by an ugly scar which ran from his mouth to his temple. The left eyelid drooped down, giving him a curious appearance.

"Chalimer," Remelas said. To his own ears he sounded weary. "How may I help you?"

The Justicar of the Gathire gave a deep bow. "On the contrary, your Highness. I have come to offer my deepest condolences for your loss, and to put myself at your disposal. The Gathire will do everything it can to ease your burdens at this time."

"My thanks. I will keep that in mind."

Chalimer stood straight, one hand held behind his back. "Very good, sir. With your permission, I will make the arrangements for the more formal matters of the King's passing."

Remelas stepped away from the window. The room was luxurious, befitting a member of the royal family. He crossed a beautiful rug of soft fur to a hand-carved camphorwood desk, decorated with a varnished panel surface. He sat down in a cushioned chair and leaned back. With a gesture to the identical seat opposite, he invited Chalimer to join him.

"Do you consider me a friend, Chalimer?" asked Remelas after pouring himself a cup of water from a pitcher beside him. He offered it to his guest, who refused before answering.

"Of course, we have known each other for eight summers, sir. We have conducted official business for two of those, ever since I became Justicar. You are an intelligent man with ambition. I admire that in a ruler."

"I did not mean as a ruler, Chalimer. Do you consider us to have a personal friendship?"

A nod. "I do."

Draining his cup and putting it aside, Remelas continued. "I must ask a favour of you, then. I have few friends left these days, and my request may cause some… controversy. But it is necessary at this time."

Chalimer placed his elbows on the armrests of his seat, laying his fingertips against each other to form a point. "Whatever you need."

"Who knows of my father's death?"

"The attending physician. The Queen, of course. Two aides and the Prime Guide, Thusana."

"One of the aides informed you?"

"Yes, sir. The news was not given to any other. It is customary for the succeeding ruler to give the official announcement to the House."

"I know that," Remelas said, irritated. "I've known that ever since he became ill."

"My apologies, your Highness. I meant no offense." Chalimer's voice was neutral.

Remelas understood the man opposite was simply underlining the proper protocol. He exhaled, releasing his annoyance.

"None taken." The new King of Tamir paused. "I want you to ensure that nobody else learns of my father's passing."

"Of course. For how long?"

"Until I say so."

Chalimer took this information without a change in his calm demeanour. "I see. May I speak freely?"

"Always."

"Are you sure that is wise? With the general populace already concerned by the return of the Four to our lands, delaying the announcement of King Runath's death may amplify feelings of deception should the truth be discovered."

"I did warn you that my decision was controversial." Remelas rubbed his palms together. "Can you keep the news contained?"

"Without question, sir – with one exception."

"Which is?"

"Queen Syllaine. I do not possess the authority to ensure her silence. Nor would I presume to make any attempt to do so."

Remelas nodded, running a hand through his wavy locks. "I will speak to my mother."

Chalimer bowed his head. There was a pause. Remelas brought a fist to his mouth, thinking. Chalimer watched him.

Eventually the King spoke. "Do you understand why I am asking this of you?"

"You do not wish to bring additional disharmony to the people of Tamir during these difficult times."

Remelas smiled. The words were expertly delivered, hinting at the true nature of the problem. "Exactly."

"I would only suggest that you do not delay for too long. The traditional passing of the deceased in Tamiran Square is widely expected due to your father's accomplishments during his reign. Any visible decomposition would be questioned."

"Let us hope the royal physician is trained in embalming, then." Remelas sighed. "There are ways to delay a corpse's rot."

"You intend to wait for some time, then." The observation was that of a patient man. Remelas met the Justicar's gaze.

"As long as it takes."

KANDERIL WOKE BEFORE Sarene. Outside the window, the birdsong was audible but scarce; most had left for the coming winter. He rose and moved to look through the shutters before gathering his clothes, dressing himself with care.

He looked over his ward as he tied his jerkin in place. She slept soundly, as she often did in the mornings. It was only the start of her slumber which seemed troublesome.

Kanderil pulled his moccasins on without tying them in place, not wishing to sit back down on the bed and cause the rickety frame to make a noise.

While threading his belt into place and tucking the knife against his hip, he decided against waking Sarene. This was the first bed she'd had for almost five weeks and they had a long trek south to a distant cabin where he intended for them to spend the winter. There would be one more stop in a town along the way, in Ghiaran Tar, to pick up enough provisions for the season. Then they would shut themselves away from the world.

Kanderil was looking forward to it.

Moving to the door, Kanderil paused. He placed his ear against the wood. Then he frowned. With one hand on the hilt of his dagger he slowly turned the handle and opened the door.

Standing in the corridor, resting against a wall, was one of the grey-cloaked men from last night. The man offered a smile.

Kanderil closed the door behind him and locked it from the outside. He then slid the key back under the door. His eyes never left the grey cloak.

"Anaburan wants to talk to you," the man said.

"What for?"

"No idea." The grey cloak shrugged, stepping away from the wall. "He's waiting for you downstairs. I think he's got breakfast ready."

Kanderil considered refusing, but there was little point.

Nodding once he moved after the stranger, who walked ahead of him.

"A little early for that cloak, no?" Kanderil observed.

"It's more of a uniform," the man said with a shrug.

"So you *are* on official business."

"You'd have to ask Anaburan about that."

THEY DESCENDED THE stairs. As the common area came into view Kanderil saw Anaburan reclining in a seat beside the central table from which he had given his lecture the previous night. The man's cloak was folded and placed on the table, and now without the hood Kanderil saw him to be a handsome man with thinning hair cropped close to his head. A plate of dried fruits lay on the table and he held half a prune in his hand. Looking up as Kanderil appeared, he gave a warm smile.

"Good morning," he said in that same confident voice he had used the night before. "Take a seat, Kanderil." Anaburan gestured to the chair opposite.

Kanderil obliged, adjusting the chair so he could rest his elbows on the table. He leaned forward, enclosing a hand over a fist before resting his chin upon them. "How do you know my name?" he asked.

"Straight to the point, eh?" Anaburan chuckled. He slid the plate before him towards the Hunter. "Please, feel free. It's quite good. Dried, of course, but enjoyable nonetheless."

Kanderil selected a piece of apricot and inspected it as he spoke. "Answer my question." He placed the fruit in his mouth.

Eating the rest of his prune and wiping his hands on a cloth, Anaburan shrugged. "Very well. I recognised you from your days in the Kalethi."

"Did we know each other?" Kanderil appraised the man opposite a second time. "I rarely forget a face."

"We weren't colleagues, no. I was once a member of the Tamir Royal Guard. I was present when you picked up your Valour medal years ago. A chap your size tends to stick in the memory."

"So I have been told." Kanderil slid the plate back away from him. "I cannot see why you would want to meet me. At least to the extent of posting a man outside my room."

Anaburan smiled. The gesture seemed genuine. "I retired from the House of Tamir following Remelas's betrayal. I presume from my words last night you understand that I am no longer his biggest supporter."

"There were a few hints," said Kanderil.

"Aye. Well I still have friends in the military, of course. Rumours exploded about the exact nature of Tyrrial's attack, but I am only interested in facts. I seek first-hand accounts and reliable sources. If I am to hold a platform against the Prince then I need to make sure my information is sound."

"Understandable."

"You would not be surprised, then, to learn that several witnesses mentioned the arrival of a gigantic woodsman along with Prince's half-wit brother, Nichai. Said woodsman was taken to see the Prince that very night with a young girl, a Kalethi scout and a hooded figure. Shortly before Tyrrial arrived."

Kanderil gave a lop-sided grin, assessing the room. The other three Sons of Tamir were seated at a separate table, and the one who had escorted him from his room stood by the stairs. All accounted for.

"What are you implying?"

"You were one of the last to speak to Remelas before the tragic events unfolded. I was hoping that you could share some of that conversation with me." Anaburan smiled. Kanderil did not trust what the gesture implied.

"Unless you can prove that I was there that night, then I have no wish to become involved in your personal vendetta against Remelas."

"Come now, Kanderil." The man sat forward in his chair. "How many seven-foot woodsmen with thick beards and chest-length hair carrying bronze-tipped bows can you honestly claim roam this nation? People remember you because you're *rare*. Perhaps the only one of your distinctive size in all of Tamir."

"An interesting observation. But that does not change my stance. I do not want to feed your campaign to topple Remelas from succession."

Anaburan opened his mouth to continue but instead held back. He gave a quick smile and exhaling slowly, he reclined once more and took a deliberate moment to eat another piece of fruit.

"When we march to Tamiran I will not be seeking the Prince's head on a pole, Kanderil. But if I am to make a strong case and seek justice for the hundreds dead at Leithar Grove, ensuring the safety of our nation, then I must know more." Anaburan spread his hands. "I must."

"Sorry to disappoint." Kanderil rolled his shoulders. "Do I have to pay for the fruit now?"

Anaburan sighed. "Listen to me. There are other rumours. I can pay for your information with some of my own."

"Rumours do not concern me. I expect the events of what happened at those barracks are told differently in each corner of Tamir by now. People will talk. Whatever you have to bargain with will become something else by the next moon cycle."

"What if those rumours regard the girl who was with you that night?"

Kanderil thumbed his nose. Anaburan had picked the words carefully. In proposing that the girl now travelling with him, and the one who had been sighted at Leithar Grove were different, Anaburan offered a truce. A way to speak freely without risking Sarene's safety.

"Go on," came the cool reply.

Anaburan cleared his throat, rubbing the pad of his thumb against the inside of his fingers. "The Sons of Tamir are not the only group to have formed recently. We have heard tales that others are starting to appear all over Tamir, all with wildly different intentions. Some want the Prince dead, killed in sacrifice to the Four. Some fools want to follow through with our invasion of neighbouring lands, convinced that Remelas's survival of Tyrrial's wrath is a sure sign that he can succeed." Anaburan shook his head, his expression suggesting *Can you believe that?*

Kanderil's face remained impassive.

"Some are starting to listen to the prophets and sooth-sayers who still chant their mantra about the girl who will change the world. They're starting to think the girl at Leithar Grove and this 'Queen of the World' mentioned in the ramblings of those madmen may be one and the same."

"On what basis?" Kanderil asked.

"She survived."

"So did the Prince. Do people believe he will change the world also?"

Anaburan smiled. "The *people* of Tamir are scared, Kanderil. Those who are willing to try and do something about it are latching onto anything they can put their faith behind. The general populace are terrified that Tyrrial will return, or that the rest of the Four will follow suit and seek to make an example of us all. The prophets are becoming more focused in their words. They say that the girl in question can defy the Four somehow. That she will rise up against them and mankind will dissolve into an era without guidance, plunging us all back into the days of war and violence."

"What do you believe?"

"I think it is nonsense," the leader of the Sons of Tamir said after a pause, clapping his hands together before reaching for another segment of fruit. "But my methods are based in fact. Remelas betrayed us all and he must be held accountable. All I can say is that I believe my cause is just. Those who blame the girl for whatever reason, or fear what she represents, may be just as confident in their actions. That girl's future is uncertain, and some may seek to harm her."

Slow footfalls came from the stairwell, along with a stiff *thunk* which accompanied each step. Kanderil watched Sarene descend into the common area, carrying their belongings. His great sword was making the other sound; too heavy for the slight girl to carry, it was thudding along the wood behind her. His longbow was strapped to her back along with their packs, and she appeared barely able to stand. Sarene reached the ground floor and peered around, her features uncertain.

"Good morning, girl," said Anaburan, placing his hand on his chest and bowing his head. "Can I interest you in some fruit?"

Kanderil stood from his chair and moved over to her. He took his weapons and started to strap them into place against his body. Relieved to be free of the burden she turned her attention to Anaburan.

"Go ahead," he said.

She looked at Kanderil, who nodded. Wary, she moved across the table and selected a segment of apple which she quickly devoured.

"Keeper," Kanderil said aloud. A face appeared from the doorway to the kitchen. "I would like some bread and hard cheese prepared to take with us. Add it to the cost of our room."

"Comin' right up," the tavern owner said, disappearing again.

"Now, you never held up your side of the bargain," Anaburan said. "What can you tell me about that night?"

"I did not agree to trading," said Kanderil, slinging his

pack over his shoulder.

"True, but to walk away with what I offered would be plain rude."

Kanderil heard something gently dragging against the ground, before noting that the straps of his footwear remained untied. He knelt slowly and began to pull the strands into place, securing the moccasins to his shins.

"All I will say is that Remelas *did* intend to take an army across the border. He said as much to me. He also felt what he was doing was right, and that he was securing Tamir's future. He did not seek conquest. Only expansion."

"The two are very similar," said Anaburan. "And you do not tell me anything I did not already know. We have a prominent member of the military already confessing he knew of Remelas's plans months in advance."

"If you were hoping that he confessed his desire to stick babes on spikes and rape every woman in Carthlei, then I cannot help." Kanderil shifted to the other foot. "I am no longer Kalethi, and I am out of the loop in regards to military ambition."

Sarene took another piece of fruit after a gesture of encouragement from Anaburan, who then spoke again. "Why, then, did you meet the Prince in his private chambers?"

"For reasons which have nothing to do with your cause." Kanderil tied off the final strap. "I pride myself on my honesty, Anaburan. I speak plainly."

"I see."

The tavern keeper appeared again with a paper wrap. He placed it on the counter. "One silver and three copper, if you please."

Kanderil moved across, pulling his money pouch free. He fished around for the coin, which he placed on the bar one by one. The tavern keeper gave his thanks and retreated again. Kanderil got the impression that the owner was uncomfortable in his own house, eager to avoid the conversation taking place within it.

Anaburan was watching Sarene, who had stepped back towards the door. She was playing with her hands, her mauve hood pulled up in preparation to leave.

"I apologise if I make you nervous, lass. I merely wished to speak to…" He considered his words. "Is this your daughter, perhaps?"

"My niece," Kanderil said. "Rachia."

"A pleasure to meet you, Rachia. My name is Anaburan."

Sarene bowed her head, giving a warm smile, though her eyes betrayed her uncertainty.

Anaburan chuckled. "A shy one."

"Always has been," Kanderil said. He moved towards the doorway, tucking the food into his bag. "I am sorry I could not be of more help."

"Just answer me one thing, my friend." Anaburan stood from the chair, reaching for his wolf-fur trimmed cloak. "Do you share my view that Remelas should be prevented from ascending the throne?"

Kanderil turned around, assessing the man one last time. Anaburan held himself like a fighter, standing proud and strong. There was no hint, neither from words nor mannerisms, that the man sought power or held ambitions to topple the House of Tamir for personal gain. He came across as strong-willed and sure of his convictions.

"I do not wish to get involved in the politics of your cause," Kanderil said at last. "But I believe that, should you truly act on behalf of the Tamir people, then you should at least be given the right to present your case before the House."

"That is all I ask." Anaburan gave a broad smile. "I will keep you no longer. And remember my words. Tread carefully out there."

Kanderil opened the door and stepped outside, ducking to avoid hitting his head on the frame. Harsh sunlight met him and he squinted. Sarene stepped out after him, tugging on his sleeve. He looked down to her.

She closed the door, then pointed at it, her other hand forming pincers with fingers and thumb to mimic a mouth.

"I will explain later," he replied.

She crossed her arms and gave him a bemused stare, frowning and pulling up one cheek.

"I promise. Right now we need to get going." Kanderil adjusted the strap of his bag and started off down the street. He heard Sarene sigh behind him.

THE PAIR WALKED to the other end of the main street where their horse had been stabled. Sarene pulled her cloak tighter around her. A thin mist had settled during the night and the sharp contrast to the warmth of the tavern brought a shiver. Kanderil had purchased some new clothes for the coming season, and her usual woollen pants and shirt were now supplemented with a pair of leather riding pants and a heavy tunic. A sheep's wool scarf was wrapped around her neck, but it was itchy and she didn't like it much. She *did* like her new boots, though; her old shoes had long since become too thin to afford any protection from either the elements or the ground they covered daily.

Sarene smiled. She enjoyed the clothes because they were comfortable, but they also matched Kanderil's. With her new attire she felt more like his companion rather than his ward. She'd specifically chosen items similar to his in the tailor's shop. Kanderil hadn't commented but he must have noticed. The mauve cloak had stayed, though. There had been a brief argument about swapping it out for something less noticeable, but Sarene had been adamant. The tatty garment was one of the few things she possessed which she'd owned back at her village home, and it would have been terrible to lose it.

The two of them crossed the street as a wagon passed by carrying a dead cow. Sarene wondered why they hadn't simply walked the cow into town before slaughtering it, but she supposed they must have had a reason. The driver tipped his wide-brimmed hat to them and Sarene waved back. One of the wheels was squeaking at a specific point in its rotation and the noise signalled its journey to wherever the carcass would be prepared.

They reached the stable and moved to where Sarene's chestnut mare was waiting, a heavy blanket over its back. The girl placed a hand on its shoulder and patted a greeting. It snorted, scraping a hoof against the ground.

Kanderil pulled a feedbag from the stable wall and shov-elled in a few handfuls of oats from an open barrel before looping the bag over its ears. The sound of crunching accompanied his movements as he slid the blanket clear. Sarene waddled over from the rear wall with her saddle clutched between her forearms and her chest. The weight wasn't a problem but the shape made it awkward to carry. Kanderil took it from her and lifted it over the horse's back while she knelt down to grab for the straps.

"Oh, by the *Four...*" The deep groan made her jump and she whirled around.

A pair of legs kicked out from under a blanket which she'd thought had covered stable equipment. She saw that the legs belonged to someone who'd been sleeping behind an overturned barrel, the legs sprawled over it. It seemed an incredibly uncomfortable position to be in and she stepped forward, trying to see who the flailing limbs belonged to.

"Shit..." they said again, this time alarmed. "Oh, *shhh...* Me back!"

The legs slipped from the barrel. Rolling face-first on the ground the man hooked an arm behind him, trying to reach between his shoulder blades.

"Ahh..."

Sarene moved towards the unfortunate soul writhing on the floor. She knelt down and grasped his upper arm, trying to pull him upright. At her touch the man flinched.

"*Whoa-* oh, soddin' 'ell. You scared the starch outta me." The man chuckled in relief, squinting at her through puffy eyes. Sarene recognised him as the drunk who'd sat with them the previous night. Ethanei. She tugged at his arm again, giving an encouraging smile.

At first he placed his palms flat on the floor under him to rise, but then his expression hardened and he sighed. "Oh… No, don't bother girl. I might as well lay here for a while more. Maybe I'll get lucky and a horse will fall on me." Ethanei went limp, his body crashing into resignation.

Sarene tilted her head, peering at him.

"Must have been quite a night to end up here," said Kanderil from where he was stood fixing the saddle in place.

"You got that right." Ethanei spat. He grimaced, wiped his mouth with a knuckle and then rolled over onto his back. Sarene tried again to pull him upright. The ground here was damp and filthy; spotted with manure.

"Waking up in a stable is a good sign that you should cut back."

"What's the point in that? I'm not here for fun, y'know." He muttered, squinting up at Sarene. "Oh, wait. It's you two."

"I'm surprised you remember us." Kanderil knelt down to thread the last buckle in place. "You were quite loose by the time we left."

"Pah, that's nothing. You should see me when I'm in a good mood." Ethanei sagged. "I might as well just go straight back. At least it'll be warmer."

Sarene shook her head. She lifted her arms over her head, pointing her fingers to make a triangular roof.

"Erm…" Ethanei lifted his head. "What?"

Kanderil glanced over at them. "She's asking about your

home."

"Is she? Oh. I don't have one anymore. Otherwise I wouldn't be sleeping in a bloody stable, would I?"

Sarene frowned and brushed her knees. She straightened, then waited until Ethanei caught her eye. The girl gestured for him to rise, coaxing him off the ground. Eventually he complied, sitting up with a tight hiss and reaching for his back again.

Kanderil made to pull the feedbag from the horse, but paused. "You seem remarkably well dressed for a homeless man."

Laughing, Ethanei brushed at some crusted vomit which stained the front of his jerkin before tugging at his bracers, which had loosened against his wrists. "You call this well-dressed? I'm a state, man."

"You have *clothes,* and they fit you."

"Well I 'aven't been homeless for long." The drunk slouched, hands dropping to his thighs. "About… six hours, I reckon."

Sarene bit her lip and rubbed her upper arm. She could sympathise.

"Your wife kicked you out." Kanderil's words were not a question.

"How'd you know?" Ethanei shot him a venomous stare. "Have you been shaggin' her as well?"

"Why else would you lose your home so suddenly if you had not been made to leave by your spouse?"

The question immediately deflated the man. "Aye, I guess you're right. She's gettin' it off some guy from the fields, yet *I* have to leave my home. Makes sense, don't it…"

"My condolences." Kanderil slipped the feedbag from the horse and stroked its mane. "Come on, lass. We should be going."

Sarene nodded, her scarf scratching at her jaw. She reached down to pat Ethanei on the shoulder and he gave her a thankful nod. It felt wrong leaving him sitting in the dirt but there was little else they could do for him. The specifics of *why* he'd been kicked out of his home was a mystery but, whatever it was, he'd evidently been left crushed by it. The hangover couldn't help, of course – she'd witnessed enough of them with Jared –

(*falling to the floor, blood streaming, as she watched*)

– but that was for Ethanei to deal with. A good breakfast and some fruit juice would help. It was what her father had always suggested.

Kanderil held the reins as she hooked a foot into the stirrup and mounted the mare.

"Where are you going?" Ethanei asked, looking up at them.

"West."

"What for?"

"Why do you ask?" Kanderil countered.

Placing a gloved hand against the dirty stable floor, Ethanei got to his feet. "Listen." His mouth remained open to continue, but he struggled to find the words. With a smirk, he rubbed his unshaven cheek, not realising that his touch was smearing filth across his skin. Sarene and Kanderil exchanged looks.

"I, uh…" He bit off a laugh. "I know this is a bit presumptive, but if I stay 'ere I'm just gonna end up at the tavern drinkin' piss until I run out of money, an' then I really *will* have nothin' left. I got nothin' left to stay for. D'ya mind if I travel with you two for a while? Until you hit the next town or wherever."

"Yes," said Kanderil. "I do."

"Oh." Ethanei threw up his hands. "Just like that, is it?"

"I am sorry, but I dislike travelling with strangers. I have my reasons. It is nothing personal."

"No, of course…" Rubbing his hands together, Ethanei took a deep breath.

Sarene glared at Kanderil, narrowing her eyes. The dismissive tone had been uncalled for. She understood it was the woodsman's nature, but his complete lack of empathy for the situation irritated her. She held up a hand. Both men looked at her. The girl pointed to Kanderil before bringing two fingers in a V to point at her eyes.

"I'm watching."

It started with a thumb jerked towards Ethanei before both hands her laid over her heart. Sarene followed by abruptly pulling two fists apart as through snapping a stick. She then mimicked drinking from a cup, tipping her head back and slowly crossing her eyes, her tongue lolling from the side of her mouth. Sarene paused, waiting.

"Go on," said Kanderil.

Gesturing to Ethanei again she tapped herself on the chest, drew her hand swiftly across her throat… then shook her head. She shrugged, hoping Kanderil understood.

Ethanei wasn't a threat to her. The man was a drunk and, apparently, a failure in love as well. He wasn't armed. He posed no danger unless everything so far was an act to gain their confidence and trust.

But then, for how long must she be forced to live her life assuming that everyone she met was a potential enemy? Glaithe and Nichai had betrayed their confidence, and it seemed that since that time Kanderil had refused to risk letting anyone else do so. But life on the road was so *lonely*. She understood why she had to be careful, but if it meant spending the rest of her life isolated from everyone other than Kanderil – who she adored, but was hardly a great conversationalist – then she wasn't sure just how safe she wanted to be.

"What's she saying?" Ethanei asked.

"She is of the opinion that it would be uncaring to turn you away."

"Do you agree with her?" The question was guarded but hopeful. Sarene smiled at him.

"No."

"Oh."

Sarene slapped her palms together in front of Kanderil's nose, pulling a face at him. He stared at her while he spoke.

"Would you give us a moment, Ethanei?"

"Sure, sure… I don't wanna be a burden, like. I can always travel by meself."

"Just give us a moment," Kanderil repeated. The vagrant nodded, rubbing at his back, and stepped out of the stable. Kanderil leaned in close to her, fingers curling around the saddle's handle.

"You do understand why I am refusing to travel with him, yes?"

Sarene shook her head. She spread her hands, shrugging.

"I cannot trust him. I do not think he is a danger to either of us, but he is a drunkard. If he travels with us then the next time he is in a town where people mention the girl in the soothsayer's ramblings, who can say he will not pipe up and start telling them all about you?"

She scoffed, shaking her head again. Quickly she ran a hand across her face before shrugging, pointing at her eyes.

"I do not understand."

Sarene took a quick breath. There wasn't a great way to sign *recognition* which wouldn't take a dozen guesses to figure out. Eventually she mimicked talking with her hand, pointed back to where Ethanei had walked, and shook her head while pointing at herself.

Then she mimicked talking but this time indicated Kanderil and nodded.

"You think I am more recognisable."

With a firm nod, Sarene gave a crooked smile.

"That much is true. But I am not the one people are hunting."

Another nod, a much broader grin.

Kanderil's face grew tight as he thought of a way to argue out of it, but said nothing further. He grunted, looking to his left through the stable door. She turned in the saddle to do likewise.

Ethanei was standing in the street, trying to wipe dirt

from his face with a muddy glove. The futility of the effort evidently escaping him. He peered up to the grey sky as if he had felt a spot of rain. Then the man belched so loudly he surprised himself.

Kanderil exhaled. "I see your point."

REMELAS ENTERED HIS father's chambers. His mother, Queen Syllaine, sat beside the bed with her hand laid over that of her dead husband. Nobody else was present in the room.

Moving to the bed, the new King of Tamir regarded the body of the former. Runath looked at peace, in stark contrast to his last weeks of life. Dark circles surrounded closed eyes which sunk back into his skull. His skin was papery thin, yellowed like it had been soaked in vinegar. Runath's solid gold Jaithran ring, knotted into his flaxen hair, glinted from the pillow beneath his head. The bedclothes he wore, thick and expensive, enveloped the withered body, making Runath appear smaller than he was. There was a faint odour of medicinal balms in the air.

Syllaine welcomed him with a thin smile. When Remelas had seen her that morning, having been woken from sleep with the news of Runath's passing, she had been crying. Dignified, of course. She had retained her poise. But tears had dripped from her cheeks and her eyes were puffed red.

Now she had composed herself and was given over to silent introspection. He placed a hand on her shoulder and she brushed his wrist with her cheek.

"How are you doing?" he asked, the question hollow.

"Better," she replied with a coarse voice. "I am better." Syllaine paused, glancing at her husband. "I have been expecting this day for some time now."

"We all have," said Remelas. "He is at peace now. We must be thankful for that."

Syllaine pulled her hands back and laid them in her lap, tilting her head to watch her son. "He was a good man. A *strong* man. He was not ill for a day in his life until he caught this fever. Even with his mental lapses he was always in perfect health. To see him stripped down so quickly…" She sighed. "It is such a shame."

"We all loved him dearly," said Remelas in a quiet tone. "He will be sorely missed by every Tamir."

"Indeed." She lifted a handkerchief to dab at her eyes, taking a moment to gather herself. "Have you informed the House?"

Remelas shook his head, reaching for one of the stools at the foot of the bed and sitting down before the Queen. "Not yet."

"Why not? I presumed that was why the others in attendance here had been called away by Chalimer."

Reaching out to take his mother's hands in his own, Remelas bowed his head. "I have something to discuss with you, mother."

Syllaine said nothing, her eyes fixed on her son. The Jaithran feather braided behind her ear – plucked for her by Runath from the wing of a rare Phoenix Hawk – dangled against her collar. During the last Laysenra festival Tamiran had celebrated the Queen's fiftieth summer in style, Runath having organised a grand feast in her honour with the help of both his aides and their youngest son, the Regent Nichai. Even at this age she was still beautiful, with thin features and prominent cheekbones. The shallowest of wrinkles touched the corners of her mouth, giving maturity without drawing from her elegance. He smiled at her, and she returned it.

"I have decided to delay the announcement."

Syllaine's eyes grew tight and her hands stiffened in his grip. "Why?"

"The people of Tamir are still wary, mother. They do not yet fully trust me, and I must make a strong effort to win them over. If we announce this tragic passing then my ascension may cause further unrest."

The hands were withdrawn. "Politics," said the Queen of Tamir.

"It is not that simple," Remelas replied. "I am simply ensuring that we retain the love of the kingdom. What happened in Leithar Grove was a tragedy and despite my best efforts I have not yet made amends for that, and I s—"

"How does one *make amends?*" The voice was stern now, reminiscent of how Syllaine had spoken to her two sons when they misbehaved as children. The sound of it still had the power to make him nervous, but Remelas straightened his back. He had to make her understand and cowering would do him no favours.

"Please, mother. Allow me a few days to think of something. All I need to do is prove to the people that I am sorry and ask their forgiveness. Offering myself to them so that they accept me as their new King."

Sniffing, Syllaine gripped her handkerchief and paused. Remelas could see that her thoughts were conflicted. Of course they were. He understood. This decision had been difficult for him as well.

"It would seem strange that you call for your people to embrace you immediately before announcing the death of your father." she said finally, the words a sigh.

"I will deal with that when we come to it."

"Will you?" Syllaine raised a brow. "Or do you simply *hope* that a solution will present itself?"

Remelas held her gaze and found no quarter given there.

"Mother, please. I understand this may be taxing for you. We both loved father. I do not wish to disrespect him now. His loss pains me just as it pains you."

Syllaine gave a scornful smile, her eyes glimmering with new tears. "If that were the case you would not have him rotting here in secret while you played games with our subjects. They would not mistrust you had you not sought to make a name for yourself."

Remelas sat back, the words catching him off guard. "I..."

"How *dare* you presume to dictate to me how we treat my husband after his death? I have lived with your father for thirty two summers and loved him each day. I have watched him follow in the footsteps of the generations of Tamir kings before him, all focused on the wellbeing of our people and the advancement of our traditions. He was a great man and we hoped *you* would be some day. He would *never* have made this request."

The accusation that Remelas was somehow disrespecting the throne brought a touch of irritation. "I make this request as the new King of Tamir, and I make it for the benefit of the subjects I now rule. The choice is mine to make."

Syllaine rose to her feet and yelled at him, her grief pouring into her words as the facade of control slipped away. "Don't you *ever* talk to me like a pawn, Remelas! It was your arrogance that brought us to this day!"

Remelas blinked at her, stunned. The last sentence was a solid blow. "What…?"

"The wretched plans to take us to war! Don't try and act surprised, boy. You led the Tamir people to mistrust you with your own hand." She reached out to grip his chin between thumb and forefinger, her face screwed up in rage. "You took over your father's responsibilities during his senility and you used it to build an army! Tyrrial came and destroyed hundreds of lives because you dared to challenge him!"

"No, that isn't—" Remelas tried to pull away from her grip, limply pushing at her forearm, but the Queen of Tamir would not be defied.

"You returned from that place in pieces, broken on the inside. Your father and I made every effort to console you, to help you learn from your mistakes. And now at the first sign of power you seek to hide your father's death from the world so you can improve your standing within it?" She let go, standing with her back straight and placing her hands on her hips. The dark clothing she wore added to her appearance and Remelas was at a loss to respond to this powerful woman.

"Perhaps," she said, "you should focus on fixing your standing with your family first. Your brother is lost, and now your father follows him."

"No," Remelas said, rising from his chair. The inclusion of Nichai was hurtful and he could not sit by to listen further. "*No*. Do *not* blame me for Nichai. He sought me out, he came to—"

"He came because he was determined to take part in your accursed plan!" Syllaine cried. "If you had not angered the Four then your brother would be here today! Nichai's loss gravely saddened your father. Now he lies dead before us and you wish to cover it up." She shook her head, stepping backwards to fall into her chair. She placed a hand to her forehead and slumped to the side, the events of the past hours having exhausted her. Remelas stood before her, impotent.

It was a long time before Syllaine spoke again. When she did, the words were cold. "Do not ask me to be silent. Do not betray your father again. Please, Remelas. Accept the situation and handle it with the grace of a King."

Remelas looked down at the body of his father. The stillness of the corpse matched the empty feeling in the chambers. Despite the sunlight streaming through the windows, despite the small fire burning in the corner, despite the candles which still flicked from the previous night, the room felt icy and unforgiving.

The new King of Tamir stepped away and walked towards the door. He opened it and stood there in the frame, his head bowed.

"I will assemble the House."

Remelas made to speak more but he lost his voice. He left the room, footsteps echoing down the hallway.

Chapter Three

"SO HOW LONG have you been mute?"

Sarene frowned at Ethanei, who winced.

"She prefers the term 'silent'," said Kanderil.

The three of them were walking along the road north-west towards Sothiran. The road was well maintained and easily marked against the grassland which bordered it. The road skirted a mild slope which ran away from them to the west, where sparse forests sat like broken fencing. Kanderil planned to turn away from the main road well before they reached the city. They would stop at a village for supplies before sending Ethanei on his way and backtracking south towards the old woodland cabin. They had a few weeks before the winter really set in, and their new travelling partner would only really delay them by a day or two.

"Of course, aye. No offense meant, my girl."

Sarene waved the apology away, smiling. She brought her arms together and rocked them back and forth, cradling an imaginary babe. The horse she led reared its head as her movements tensed its reins.

"That long, huh? Wow." Ethanei rubbed the back of his

neck. "Must have been pretty difficult."

Sarene shrugged, sweeping a hand under the hood of her cloak to push her hair into place.

Kanderil looked across to the drunk. "She can speak as well as most. I find it quite simple to understand her these days." The girl nodded, pleased by the answer.

"Prolly can speak better than me, most cases." Chuckling, Ethanei shook his head. "Maybe I shoulda got you to try with me wife."

Sarene pursed her lips, eventually snapping her fingers. She brought up her shoulders and arms in question, then shoved her hands forward before swinging an imaginary door closed.

Kanderil coughed, managing to hide his amusement. "That was quite blunt."

She poked her tongue at him in reply.

"No, she's right, if she's askin' why I was thrown out of me own home." Ethanei sighed, burying his hands into the pockets of his overcoat. "I dunno. We separated a while ago, before the summer. Things were just gettin' boring, I suppose. I was never at home, always off with the army. I was good at bein' a soldier and… Well, I guess I lost focus on the marriage. She jus' told me one day that she wanted to end it an' see other people."

"So why did you stay?" Kanderil asked.

"I 'ad nowhere else to go when the army disbanded." Ethanei pulled his hand from his pocket, holding a canteen. He unscrewed the cap and took a quick swallow, pulling a face as he did. He exhaled sharply. "Ah, tha's better."

Sarene rolled her eyes.

"Keeps the cold out." The canteen was closed and put away. "Anyways, once I ended up without a career I went back home. I didn't really 'ave anything else. Don't really fancy goin' back to me mother's… An' besides, I'd lived in Thorlen Tar all me life. I was worried about leavin' for good."

"You travelled plenty as a soldier, I am sure." Kanderil paused, grasping a rock which lay in the middle of the road and tossing it onto the grass where it was less of a danger to wagons. "Had you not found somewhere you liked?"

"Oh, aye, but that's not the point, is it?" Ethanei sniffed, wiping his nose on the back of his hand, which in turn was brushed against his jerkin. "I just meant that I felt 'appier in a place where I knew everyone." A short laugh bubbled up. "Well, at least until one of them started knockin' off me wife."

"So why come away now? What was special about last night?"

"Bah. I came home drunk and started saying some 'orrible things to her. Wasn't really nice, so I guess I can understand why she did it." The drunkard sighed, scratching at his stubbled jaw. "I just wish she'd see it from my point of view."

Silence fell on the group. Kanderil left the man to his thoughts. There was plenty which hadn't been said – marriages came with history, and he doubted the confrontation which had led to a night in the stables was solely born of a night's drinking – but that didn't change the situation. Ethanei was homeless, without work and apparently content to sink into his alcohol. Whatever was in that canteen stank; Kanderil had picked up the odour of it from twelve feet away.

They walked for the majority of the day until the clouded sun began to fall. The slope had eased off and the forest was beginning to close in. Kanderil led the others towards the trees, seeking a place to make camp for the night. There were no streams in this area of Tamir, but they did manage to find a small space near an old logging trail, which cut out most of the breeze and provided good protection against being sighted from the main road, which meant they could build a campfire.

SARENE TETHERED HER horse to a sturdy branch, then crouched down in the centre of the designated camp and began to gather sticks into a stacked pile. Kanderil left with his bow to find some supper. Ethanei lay out on the ground, staring up at the sky.

"I guess we're heading to Sothiran, then." He muttered. "Bloody terrible place."

Sarene nodded, remembering his words from the tavern.

"Still, guess I could find work though. Maybe I could enlist in the guard or somethin'."

Taking her bag, Sarene pulled free a small pouch which contained her kindling. Kanderil had taught her to collect small twigs and grass and to store it for the following day, where it would have dried out sufficiently to provide a better spark. She poked this between the sticks and took out her tinderbox.

Ethanei turned his head, looking over at her. "You're quite handy, Rachia. Did your pa teach you that?"

Shaking her head without looking up, Sarene started to strike. Sparks flew into the kindling, and it took several attempts to create an ember.

"Is he not your father? No? Oh."

Sarene leant forward to blow at the small point of heat, encouraging it to grow. A thin stream of smoke began to rise.

"I did wonder. I mean, you're quite a bit smaller. I reckon his kids would be a bit…" He let the thought finish uncompleted. Sarene waved air towards the fresh flames.

The vagrant continued to make small talk, most of which she either nodded or shrugged at. They had travelled plenty that day, and she was too tired to try and mimic her responses to him. She didn't want to appear rude but, as Ethanei sipped at his canteen, she got the impression her input became less and less vital.

Kanderil returned with two rabbits roughly an hour later, when the fire was fully prepared. He sat down and started to prepare them for their skillet, cutting the skin away and filleting the carcasses with an expert hand.

"Want some of this?" asked Ethanei, shaking the canteen above him. Kanderil wiped his hand on the grass before accepting the canteen between thumb and forefinger. He tipped it against his lips, steeling himself against the liquid as Sarene watched.

"That has quite a kick," he said, handing it back. "What is it?"

"No idea," Ethanei said with a laugh. "Ghural makes it in

'is back room. Good for cleaning pots an' muddlin' thoughts." He laughed, closing the cap and holding it to his chest like a security blanket.

They ate their meal just as the moon became visible through the canopy above. Sarene placed her plate beside her and leant back on her hands, staring upwards. The face was only half visible, like a silver cat's eye turned sideways. The radiance filtered through the patchy clouds, creating an exquisite picture in the sky.

"So you ain't her father, Drutheril," Ethanei said as he wiped his mouth of juice from the meat.

"No," Kanderil replied.

"What are you then?"

"I am her uncle."

"Where you off to?"

"We are travelling. Where to is none of your concern."

"Oh, right. O'course, silly of me to pry." Ethanei raised his knees and laid his arms over them, hooking his hands around each other. "Didn't mean to be rude, like."

Sarene had decided she liked Ethanei. Despite his sorry situation and rough demeanour, he was wary of his manners and seemed eager to please. She found Kanderil's continued dismissal of his questions unnecessary. The woodsman caught her gaze. She wrinkled her nose.

"No need to apologise," he said. "I merely owe some money to people I would rather avoid."

Ethanei nodded, his expression sombre. "Oh, right. I can understand that one. Dabbled in a bit of gambling meself while I was in the military. I saw a handful of lads rack up a proper backlog of unpaid debts. One fella turned up with both his legs broken. Well, I say turned up – we actually found him. On account of his legs bein' broken. Weren't like he walked in or nothin'." He paused. "I think I might be a bit tipsy, y'know."

Sarene covered her mouth with her hand, giggling to herself. If she didn't know better she would have said that Kanderil laughed also.

ETHANEI WOKE FIRST the next morning with a fierce headache. Still on his back, he glanced around the campsite and coughed. His nostrils flared at the smell of the ash from the fire but no smoke accompanied it, suggesting it had long since died. The man brought a hand out from under his cloak and wiped at his face before gripping the bridge of his nose, scrunching up his eyes in an effort to relieve the pressure behind his forehead.

With a groan he sat up. Rachia and her uncle were both still asleep.

Sitting cross-legged between them was a figure in a deep green cavalry coat, the tattered hood pulled far over its head. The thin-lipped mouth beneath it was grinning, revealing small pointed teeth.

"*Ahhh!*" Ethanei scrambled to get to his feet, failed, and fell onto his arse. He reached for his dagger which lay just a bit too far away. Drutheril was up already, rising to one knee with his own knife drawn before Ethanei could even call for him to wake.

"Mornin'," said the hooded figure in a cheerful voice.

Drutheril stared at the figure for a moment before muttering, slipping the knife back into its sheath. "I nearly put a blade in your neck."

"Nah, you didn't."

A blur of movement came from Ethanei's left. He flinched as Rachia scrambled from the ground to leap across the dead fire and launch herself into the figure. It caught her full-force, falling backwards with her latched into a tight hug. The figure started giggling, holding its arms out straight.

The figure's hands were dark, curved claws which reflected the morning light.

"Would you get offa me!" it cackled. "People are gonna talk!"

Rachia did not respond at first, but after the figure poked her in the sides with its elbows she relented, crawling off to sit beside them.

"Where have you been?" asked Drutheril. His voice remained calm, his sudden combat readiness replaced with patience.

"Went south," it said, cracking its neck. "Did you know there's a group of people right down the bottom of the world where they just kill each other all the time? No reason for it. They just pick up a sword and stab each other. It's *amazing*."

"Hm. I have heard of no such race nearby."

"I didn't say nearby, did I? I said down the bottom of the world."

Drutheril frowned. "That would be in the Juu'ad lands. It would require months of travel to reach them."

"Yeah. Joo-had. That's the ones."

"Nonsense. It would be impossible to travel there and back within a season."

"Maybe for *you*." Another giggle. "Anyway, who's that?" Ethanei's mouth fell open as the figure extended one of those wicked claws towards him. "If you were lookin' for a replacement me then you got ripped off."

"I, uh…" Ethanei shook his head. "I ain't replacing no-one."

"He is merely travelling with us for a short time, Drutheril replied.

"Come off it, Kanderil. You wouldn't let any old bugger follow the girl about. Don't tell me you're goin' soft." It grinned again, the expression reminding him of a cat toying with a mouse.

"Kanderil…?" Ethanei said aloud.

The woodsman mumbled something beneath his breath which made the figure chuckle.

"Yes. I thought it best to give you a false name, but it appears my intentions have been foiled." Kanderil addressed the figure again. "Thank you."

"Oh, shit off. How was I meant to know? And would you get offa me?!" The hooded man yelled at Rachia, who had grabbed its arm and forced herself close, giving the ensnared elbow another tight squeeze.

"Is she really Rachia?" asked Ethanei, starting to find his voice now the initial fright was fading. He could no longer feel his heart pounding in his chest.

"Who, Sarene?" said the figure. "No, she's called Sarene.

Not Rachia. She can't be Rachia 'cos her name's Sare—"

Rachia, or Sarene, reached up to slam a hand against the figure's mouth. She held it there for a second before jerking it away, pulling a disgusted face. The figure's tongue was still licking air. She wiped her palm on the ground.

Kanderil gave a deep sigh. "This is Spasmodic. A… friend."

"Hello," said Spasmodic, reaching up to pull its hood free. Dreadlocks the colour of strawberries spilled out across its shoulders and cheeks. Its nose was almost a snout, and small eyes peered at him.

"Oh, what the…"

"Hey!" The monster held out a hand. "Watch what you're gonna say, 'cos if you say *demon* then I'm gonna have to kick you in the balls."

Ethanei gaped at the three of them. They seemed to be expecting a negative reaction, but instead he started nodding.

"Wait, that's not what I meant! I mean, yeah, you're funny lookin' but that's not why—" He paused, catching his breath as Spasmodic sniggered. Ethanei snapped his fingers together. "I thought I knew you. You three were at Leithar Grove!"

Kanderil shook his head as Sarene looked to the ground. "No. You are mistaken."

"No, you were. You came in with the Regent. I were working on the gate when you arrived. I *knew* I recognised you from somewhere!" He laughed, clapping his palms together, the sound rebounding through the trees around them. "That was it! I mean, it's tricky to forget a fella your size. I just couldn't place it before. And the de-… the one that's all talons an' red hair, I saw 'im during the fight. I thought he were with Tyrrial at first—"

"Shall we kill 'im?" asked Spasmodic, its eyes narrowing. Ethanei's words caught in his throat and he started to stammer. The creature grinned. "He knows too much."

"We are not killing anybody," Kanderil said, to Ethanei's profound relief. The woodsman fixed a hard gaze on him and leant forward. "Listen to me. Whatever you think you remember, we were not there for the attack. Understand that."

"I can't just forget," Ethanei replied, his words forceful. He bit back the next, composing himself. His frustration at being spoken to like a child weighted his words. "I was there and I know what I saw. When you were running across the courtyard. You three and some other guy."

Sarene looked away. Ethanei continued.

"Look, I dunno what you were doing there but I saw you. No-one stationed at the place was your size, man. And that thing next to you, I saw it kill a guy for grabbing Rachia. Sarene."

"An' what were you doin', matey?" asked Spasmodic, smirking. "Hidin' out somewhere to see all this?"

Ethanei's glared at the creature. "I was tryin' to get a hold of meself after pullin' me dead Captain from under a burning *rock*." He pulled free one of his gloves and raised the hand, revealing horrible, scarred flesh. The skin ran in seams and sunken marks of red and pink.

"Ah, right. Well, at least you weren't bored, eh?"

Sarene thumped the creature, glaring. It sniggered. Ethanei muttered, pulling the glove back on. The cold air felt good against his skin but he didn't want to leave the wounds exposed to these strangers.

"So don't try an' tell me I'm wrong. That night's imprinted in me memory, much as I'd like to get rid of it."

"I need to ask a favour of you then, Ethanei," said Kanderil. "You must not share the news of our travel with anyone. It is important that we are not discovered."

"Are you kiddin'?" Ethanei laughed. "I mean, no offence but you're not exactly inconspicuous. If you're trying to hide then I'd suggest just *stayin'* somewhere, not runnin' around all over the place. People are gonna remember a bloke like you no matter what you try an' do."

Spasmodic sniggered. "Oh, I think I like him. Where'd we get 'im from? Can I have one?"

Ethanei sat back, drawing his cloak around his shoulders and clasping it into place. "If you want me to leave you be then I'll make me own way to the next town. If I don't know where you are then I don't 'ave to lie."

Sarene shook her head then, getting to her feet. She held her hands out, palms forward, and sought to encourage Ethanei to remain where he was. He obeyed, looking up at her, intrigued.

Kanderil did likewise. "It would be best if we separated from him, lass."

Shaking her head again, Sarene held out four fingers before making two of them walk across the air. Her hand turned in a circle, pointing at all four of them, then gestured towards the highway.

"Why?" Kanderil pressed.

She pointed towards Ethanei and performed a motion similar to snapping a twig.

Kanderil knitted his brow. "You still wish to use that same argument?" Sarene responded with a firm nod. The woodsman ground his teeth. "Fine. We will travel together until we reach the next town."

"Oh?" Spasmodic shrugged. "Whatever. What do we do then?"

"Then," Kanderil muttered, rising to his feet, "I try and become invisible."

Ethanei watched the giant walk away, accompanied by the shrill giggle of the creature.

"This is gonna be *great*," it cheered.

"NO! PLEASE, GET-AAAAHHHHH*hhhhh*!"

Fabric tore. The girl fell to the ground, instinctively pulling her arms over her chest. Sobbing, she rolled to the side, tucking her knees up in the foetal position. The dishevelled man standing over her looked back at the two others standing nearby, holding half a dress in his hand.

"Bet this cost a few silver," he laughed. "Reckon we should have saved it for you, Grallis."

One of the other men muttered, shaking his head. "Would you get on with it? I'm hungry."

The girl made a sudden move, seeking to scramble away. Her assailant gave a quick kick to the back of the knee, sending her crashing back to the floor. He dropped next to her, grasping her throat in his filthy fingers, and started to turn her over. His other hand grabbed at her purse, tugging it free from her waist.

"Please," the girl begged, choking the words through her gasps of fear. "Please, don't do this, please, I c—"

She received a harsh slap across the face. "Shaddap. The more you fight the longer it'll take."

"Give her over here, Bak," said the third man. He was a tall, skinny fellow who seemed unable to support his own weight. His eyes bulged out of his head like a toad, and he wet his lips with the edge of his tongue. "I like it when they're fightin'."

"Keep your mouth shut, boy. She don't need to know any names." Bak grabbed the girl around the throat again, the movement callous and without thought. The girl cried out, too broken to speak further. She tried to withdraw, recall the tranquillity and the peace this forest glade had offered only minutes ago, but it was lost to her. Tears flooded down her cheeks as the man's face loomed nearer, whispering in her ear.

"Just relax," Bak hissed, breath stale and sickening. She watched his gaze drift downwards, towards the tear in her dress. He gripped the fabric between grubby fingers. "This won't take long."

The ring of a blade being drawn caused all three men to look around. One by one they saw a figure emerging from the tree line, wearing a black leather coat which ran from shoulders to ankles, buttoned from the neck to the knees. The coat was sleeveless, revealing slim arms ringed with high silver bracers. A hood swelled around the figure's head, revealing nothing but the mouth and chin even in the morning sunshine.

In one hand was a curved short sword of brilliant steel.

The toad-eyed man licked his lips again. "Eh. You're Niallya."

Saying nothing, the newcomer stopped in the centre of the glade. The two men backed off.

"Wait," said Bak, his mouth clamped over his victim's mouth, holding her to the ground. She, too, was staring wide-eyed at the stranger. "Niallya? The merc? *Hah!*"

Grallis pulled his blade out from his belt and faced her. "All she's gonna be is a witness."

"I seen her before," said Toad-eyes. "In a bar in Ghellei. She were drinkin' like no woman I ain't never seen. Wearin' that same coat. Saw some bloke try to buy her a drink and she din't even sit on his lap!"

"Jurai, you are the dumbest boy I ever had the misfortune of ganging with," said Bak. "Women like her don't sit in laps. What's the old saying…?" Bak's face grew stern as he searched for the words. "Fights like a devil, speaks like a whip, ruts like a two copper whore." He started a laugh which the other two joined.

The figure gave a wry grin. "Eloquent."

Her word brought silence. A gentle breeze passed through the glade.

"Well? What ya want?" asked Grallis.

Niallya took three quick, long strides forward. She spun

on her heel and backed into Jurai, her blade held out behind her. It entered his gut. She stepped aside and withdrew before he could make a sound. Bringing the blade up in an arc towards Grallis, the man was only able to parry in time to send the incoming attack skidding up his own sword. She twisted her wrist and knocked the weapon out of his grasp. Grallis managed a step backwards before she whipped her sword around to cleave him through the belly, cutting deep into flesh. He fell, squealing, his internal organs seeping through the wound.

Jurai toppled over between her and Bak, dead as he landed. She was still smiling. Standing sideways to the girl's abductor, the newcomer flicked blood across the distance with a single twirl of her blade. Bak let go of the girl, who immediately started crawling away from him, scratching and kicking against the ground.

"Wait," said Bak, starting to withdraw, crouched and submissive with his sheathed sword catching around his knees. He held his hands out before him. "Wait, now, let's talk it over. I have gold. You want gold? Here." He tugged the pouch from his belt and tossed it over to her. He flinched as it hit her calf, bouncing with a metallic sigh as it fell to the ground. "There, s'all me gold."

"I do not take payment from men who molest girls," she said. At once she was moving, coming for Bak with her blade out beside her, ready to cut.

"Wait!" Bak cried out, retreating – and then tripped. The girl on the floor gripped him behind the knee and he staggered backwards, falling to the ground. Prone now, he continued to plead. "I can make you rich! Rich beyond anything you thought!"

"Not interested." The sword was raised.

"Ple—"

The blade sliced down through his throat, cleaving the windpipe. The word became a thick gurgle. Bak moved both hands to his neck, trying to keep himself together and hold the blood in. It poured through his fingers, seeping into his shirt. He gave a wet gasp, eyes broad with shock.

The girl quickly hurried to his side, her own fear now twisted with malice as she screamed at him, a flurry of blows striking his head and chest. "That's right, you bastard! *You* choke! You're gonna die, ya hear me? You *bastard*! I hate you! You'll rot, you will, and no one will ever care!" The last thing he saw was her face, screwed up in hysterical fury, before his eyes went dull and his hands fell away from the ferocious wound.

Niallya returned to the fallen purse. She picked it up. Then she moved to the other two bodies and quickly searched them, coming away with another small coin sack. These she deposited in a pocket within the seam of her coat. The girl had fallen to sobbing as her rescuer wiped the curved blade on the shirt of the dead Jurai. The boy's eyes were open, staring at nothing.

The figure stood and began to move away. The girl called after her.

"Wait! You saved my life! They would have… would have…"

Niallya did not stop. The girl pushed herself to her feet

and unsteadily scampered after her saviour.

"Please! The purse you t-took… It was mine. He tried to b-bribe you with my money."

"Consider it payment."

The girl stammered again. Niallya paused, glancing over her shoulder.

"I do not bargain with scum." She looked the girl over, her eyes unseen beneath the hood she wore. "I do not give charity to victims, either. Now cover yourself up."

The words were scornful.

The girl watched, stunned to silence as the figure moved back amongst the trees. Alone now with three bodies she turned to face the glade, once so serene, which had become a place of violence and death.

TWO DAYS AFTER Spasmodic's arrival, the group were within sight of the village. The road wound in a lazy path towards the main street, slithering between two hills. Farmland latticed the ground for as far as the eye could see, though little work was taking place. The harvest was long over. The buildings ahead sat beneath the horizon, which framed the scene before it. The village could have been created by the strokes of a brush, touched in by a great hand. The cold snap had passed, but a light drizzle had taken its place. Sarene wiped her hand across the rim of her hood for the umpteenth time, squeezing water from the fabric to prevent it from dripping into her face.

Ethanei, now having run out of alcohol, had become

much less talkative than before. He travelled with them but acted as though he were a passenger, keeping his distance from the others. Sarene knew he was uncomfortable in Spasmodic's presence, and he tried to draw as little attention to himself as possible. The creature, for its part, wasn't being much help – it would tease the vagrant, making cruel jokes about how it could randomly become violent without being able to control itself. Sarene had tried to calm the situation by walking with Ethanei often, tapping him on the shoulder to point out the surrounding countryside and trying to share her enthusiasm for the beauty of the Tamir lands.

Spasmodic had given few details of where it had been. It continued to claim that it had spent time amongst the Juu'ad, though Kanderil denied it were possible. Sarene didn't have much of an idea of the size of the world or how far away the Juu'ad race could be. Her old life in her valley home hadn't required much knowledge about the geography of the lands outside. But from Kanderil's constant refusal to accept the creature's claims, she gathered it must have been awfully far away. Aside from that Spasmodic answered most questions with the term 'investigated,' which seemed to be its new favourite word.

As they neared the first of the buildings Spasmodic looked up at Kanderil.

"Isn't this about the time you tell me to piss off?"

"Not yet," her guardian replied, his eyes fixed straight ahead. Sarene followed his gaze.

A figure on a tall black horse was trotting towards them. Sarene tensed as she recognised the uniform of the man.

Black clothing with white trim, a high collar rising to a clean-shaven jaw.

Gathire.

The four of them stopped as the Agent neared. He wore a wide-brimmed hat which protected his face from the rain. His cloak was tightly pulled around his shoulders, tucked in across the back of the saddle. Tugging on the reins the horse veered slightly, the rider turning in the saddle to face them.

"Greetings," he said with a wry smile. "I am glad I found you."

"What do you want?" Kanderil demanded.

"Where's your mates?" said Spasmodic, offering a wink. "Last time it took five of you. One won't be a challenge."

The Agent held up a hand, chuckling. "Now, now. There is no need for hostility. I understand that you may have your suspicions, but I am not your enemy." The agent reached into the pack hanging from the side of the saddle, producing from it a tightly wrapped scroll. "My name is Ithulae, and I come with news for Sarene."

Wringing her hands together, Sarene stood her ground.

"How did you know where to wait for her?" Kanderil folded his arms over his chest, his expression stern.

"We have our informants in the area. You were seen in Thorlen Tar, Kanderil. It was a good estimate that you would be heading towards Sothiran. This seemed a likely waypoint, and it was a fair guess that the girl would be nearby."

Kanderil did not respond. His features hardened.

"How did you get 'ere from Tamiran in three days?" asked Ethanei. The words came as more of a suggestion than anything, lacking in confidence.

"The Gathire do not reside exclusively in the capital, stranger." Ithulae smirked. "We have eyes all over the country."

"Oh, right. 'Course."

The Agent lifted the scroll, pointing one end at Sarene. "This is getting wet, girl. The ink will smudge."

Sarene took a few hesitant steps forward, unsure of how close she wanted to get. The Gathire still represented a large threat in her mind. It was they who had attacked her family. It was they who sent men to kidnap her from Kanderil. The Gathire were the ones who had worked for the Regent Nichai, forcing them to accept his terms to head to Leithar Grove and ultimately face Tyrrial.

She didn't trust this man one bit.

Spasmodic cackled behind her. "Don't worry, missy. If he tries anythin' I'll tear his heart out."

The Agent scrutinised the creature as she approached. Quickly she snatched the scroll from his grasp and hurried back beside Kanderil.

"Ah. The demon. I expect you will be pleased to know that Prince Remelas has granted you a pardon for the murder of my compatriots."

"I couldn't give a sod about it," Spasmodic fired back. "All they were was practice."

Sarene examined the seal holding the parchment in place. It was a picture of a lion pressed into red wax. She pulled the seal apart before unravelling the scroll, her eyes scanning the contents eagerly.

"I did not know she could read," said Ithulae.

"She is full of surprises." Kanderil placed a hand on her shoulder. "Was there anything else?"

"Only that Prince Remelas has asked me to invite you to visit the House of Tamir, Kanderil."

"What for?"

"I do not know," said the Agent. "My superior simply informed me that I should encourage you to accept. The Prince has need of your counsel."

"I have no ties to the Prince."

"You do now," Ithulae replied, heeling the mount forward to walk past them. "More than you know, it seems." The horse's hooves *clop*ped a steady beat against the ground as the Agent departed, riding back along the road they had just followed.

Spasmodic turned to watch him leave, sneering. "Would anyone protest if I went and killed him? Smug git."

"Leave it," said Kanderil. He looked down to Sarene. She tilted her head back, smiling. Handing the note to Kanderil she waited, eager for him to read the words.

After a moment he handed the scroll back. "Good news for once, lass."

"What is?" Ethanei asked.

"Her family are safe."

"Why? Are they in danger?"

"Not anymore."

Sarene quickly rolled the scroll back up and stuffed it into her bag. The message informed her that her father, refusing to move to the Palace, had instead agreed to be watched over for the sake of his children. Remelas had sent a detachment of guards to be posted to the village. Her mother was also in good health, it claimed, and had fully recovered from the attack by the Gathire five months earlier. This news was a huge relief to Sarene and she patted her bag, barely containing her joy. Her family were safe and well.

It was likely that her mother still carried the scars of that night's interrogation and she was not naive enough to have ever thought they would fade completely. It was nothing she had not already expected. That she had news of her family at all lifted her spirits.

Her smile faltered a little as she walked on into the village, eager to get out of the rain. The others followed behind, Ethanei continuing to ask questions which Kanderil avoided.

There had been no news of the reaction to Jared's death. Sarene did not know how they were coping, or if they blamed her in any way. She knew her family would not hold her responsible, but she could not shake the feeling of guilt she possessed, locked inside her like a parasite. Even now, with the message of their increased safety, she felt tainted by that sense of remorse, that feeling of blame she had pinned to her heart.

Kanderil stepped in front of her, pointing towards the inn. The building was small, with a sign nailed to the wall instead of hanging over the door, and it did not seem spacious enough to contain a full tavern. Many villages offered simple rooms and she suspected this would be no different. Sarene chewed on her upper lip as she stepped inside, the door held open for her.

At least they would be out of the rain.

NIALLYA CLOSED THE door behind her, then locked it. The single-room home was tucked away in the southern area of Ghellei, in one of the many slums. The city was a haven for people like her, attracting a rough crowd of mercenaries, cut-throats and vagabonds. Tamir's main quarry outside of the Laysine Mountains had led to the creation of the town, providing work for those who were unskilled at farming or any other trade. Anyone with money went to the outlying regions, or headed to Tamiran. Here, they just tried to earn enough to leave. The streets were poorly policed and badly lit. *Accidents* happened if one were not careful.

It was perfect.

Aside from a table, two chairs and a bed, the room had no other furnishings. Not even a fireplace. Niallya could hear a muffled argument coming through one of the thin, adjoining walls. Something broke. A woman shrieked in anger.

Kneeling in the centre of the room Niallya pushed at one of the floorboards. The other end of it rose a few inches, and she pulled it free. She dipped a hand through the gap and felt around. There was a *click*. A section of the floor rose by a couple of inches. Niallya slipped her fingers underneath and lifted, the flooring coming up on a horizontal hinge and revealing a ladder.

She climbed down a slim tunnel into the basement. The room wasn't much bigger than the one she had just left.

There were two rolls of bedding on the floor, a table and a chair. Thick, pale candles lit the room. Lying across one of the bedding rolls was the body of a young man, rolled over onto his side, bound and gagged. The air was bad and stale, as it often was. Niallya had left the entrance to the basement open to ventilate the room.

Sitting at the table, writing into a journal, was a man dressed in dark clothing. Ash blonde hair was tied at the nape of his neck. She retrieved the two coin purses from her coat, placed them on the table, and then waited for him to finish. Glaithe was not one to leave a thought half-noted. The nib of the quill scratched at the paper in neat strokes.

Niallya moved to the boy crumpled on the floor as she stood there. The remains of once-expensive clothing hung from his body, now filthy and frayed. The boy's wrists had been scraped raw by the rope drawn tightly around them. She knelt down next to him, placing a hand against his ribs. They rose and fell in thin, regular movements. She could feel his heart beating against her fingertips.

"Sedated again?" she asked.

A few moments later the quill was laid down. Glaithe turned to look at her, hanging one arm over the backrest of the chair.

"Yes. He was crying."

"Did you not ask him to stop?"

"He became hysterical." Glaithe shrugged. "The neighbours may have heard."

Pulling at the boy's shoulder, Niallya studied his sleeping face. There was a fresh bruise against the boy's cheek, joining an assortment of cuts and blushes, old and new. He was thin and gaunt, his cheeks shallow against his jaw.

"Hard to think this used to be royalty," Niallya observed, rising.

"It was difficult to believe when he was in *good* health," Glaithe replied. "I have a theory that Remelas took all the good, positive aspects of their parents, and Nichai there was left with the scraps."

"Perhaps."

Glaithe motioned to the space left open above the ladder. "So? Any news?"

"You were right." Niallya curled her hands around her hips, shifting her weight to her right foot. "These Sons of Tamir are certainly busy. They've spent the day moving to each shop and home, buying goods from the former and giving them to the people. Whoever they are, they're well-funded."

"Bribery is a simple tool." Glaithe waved a hand through the air. "Loyalty is easily bought. You should know that, my dear."

"Cute." Niallya smirked. "Why, then, do these people ask for the citizens to *talk*? Why not inspire them to rise up against the Prince?"

"I would imagine the Sons of Tamir have better plans than a simple rebellion. Such a thing would be difficult to control." Glaithe examined to his journal, leant forward to blow on the drying ink and then closed it. "But if the public supports them in whatever it is they want – an audience with the House, in this case – then they become harder to ignore."

"We shall see."

"We shall do more than that." Glaithe rose from his chair, moving his hands to button the collar of his shirt. "We shall encourage them to succeed."

Niallya tilted her head. "Why?"

"All in good time. Now, I need you to stay here for a while. I wish to go and speak to a few associates of mine." Glaithe pulled his cloak from a hook which had been screwed into the wall beside the ladder. "The boy should be asleep for a few hours yet. He will not disturb you."

"Do you ever reflect on the fact that that despite hiding in a basement in the back streets of Ghellei, you leave to walk around in public as often as you do?"

"Not at all." Glaithe watched her as he tied the cloak in place. She noted that his eyes never strayed from the darkness which hid her face. "I can avoid unwanted attention in the open streets. I cannot do so sitting in the upper room. The guard would not catch me out there and cannot find me down here. Besides, it keeps Nichai out of trouble."

Glaithe nudged the sleeping boy with his foot. Hard. His obvious disdain for the former Regent of Tamir was palpable in his actions and words. Most of the blows Nichai had endured over the past three months had been for discipline.

A few had been for amusement.

"I'll be sure to feed him when he wakes," she said idly. "We wouldn't want the ace in your sleeve to fall out, would we?"

"Now why would I let that happen?" Glaithe moved past her, setting a foot into the first of the slats in the ladder.

"After all, there is *much* more to be gained with him breathing."

"Quite." Niallya glanced over her shoulder. "That must be why you keep him in such good condition."

"He needs to be alive. Not healthy." Glaithe chuckled to himself and started to climb the rungs towards the room above.

Chapter Four

KANDERIL PAID FOR two rooms and led Sarene up the stairs, unlocking the door to the first. Inside was a space less than ten yards square, with only a tiny bed in the corner. There were eight doors on this floor, and Kanderil guessed all the rooms were of an equal size. The common room could barely fit a decent sized hunting party and it was unusual that a village this small would offer so many lodgings. Sarene sat on the bed, the frame creaking and shifting a few inches to one side. She flinched, looking down in alarm.

The woodsman moved to the window and pushed the shutters open. He heard a scraping against the wall as something scaled the building. Spasmodic pulled itself into the room, dropping into a crouch. It was chewing on something.

"What are you eating?" he asked.

It shrugged. "There was a plant."

"Did you check if it was poisonous?"

"I can't talk to it, silly. *I'm* not a plant."

Kanderil left the conversation well alone, glancing

around as Ethanei entered the room. He had a mug of ale with him. Noting the look he received, Ethanei gave a cheerful grin and raised the mug in toast.

Sarene was reading the scroll again, one finger dragging along beneath the words.

"How do you feel?" Kanderil asked.

She nodded a few times, looking up at him. Offered a thumbs-up with a gentle smile.

"How do *you* feel about it?" said Spasmodic. The woodsman turned his gaze to it.

"What do you mean?"

"C'mon. When that bloke turned up you had that arsey look on your face where your face looks like an arse. The one you get when you're all grumpy about summat."

Kanderil said nothing, leaning against the wall behind him. *Observant* was not a term he would readily use to describe Spasmodic, but the words rang true. That the Gathire had been able to find them so easily, so soon after leaving Thorlen Tar, irritated him. They had avoided detection ever since leaving Leithar Grove. He had not doubted the purpose of Sarene travelling with him until now.

Anaburan had recognised him as well, from years earlier. Ethanei, too, placed him at the scene of Tyrrial's return. Three people had been able to identify him within the last few days. That should never have happened. *Wouldn't* have happened, had he not allowed the drunk to tag along with them. Sarene's good intentions were proving an unnecessary hindrance to his main objective, which was keeping the girl from sight.

He thought back to the brief conversation with Sarene about the merits of allowing Ethanei to join them. Even the girl had pointed out that the woodsman was more recognisable by far. It was true. She could blend in with most crowds. Provided nobody tried to strike up a conversation with her, there was nothing about her outward appearance to stick into the memory – save for the mauve cloak she insisted on wearing. She was young, slim, dark haired and pretty. Nothing out of the ordinary.

Kanderil stood at around seven feet in height and carried a huge frame with it. As much as he disregarded the descriptions of him by others, the Hunter had yet to meet a man his size. That was a simple fact. He could shave his beard away or crop his hair to the scalp, but it would do little to help. For all he knew he was the largest man in Tamir. He had travelled at Sarene's side through the capital Tamiran with no difficulties before, but at that time very few people knew of the girl's importance. Now, though, it seemed the word was spreading. The more villages and towns he visited with her the more he would draw attention to her by default.

He grunted. Another reason why he much preferred the forests.

Ethanei cleared his throat. "Um. Something the matter?"

Kanderil lifted his head. Both the vagrant and Sarene were watching him. Spasmodic was apparently dozing, rocking on its heels.

"We need to split up," the woodsman said at last.

Sarene shrugged her shoulders in question, quirking a brow.

"I have become too visible. You can bet that the Gathire will be watching us now. They may not be a threat at this time, but they will want to keep your location noted for future reference." He met Sarene's gaze. "I need to be seen elsewhere."

"Is that it?" Spasmodic opened its eyes. "What happened to your old shtick about being such a wonderful man in the forests?" It leaned forward, turning its head to the side and peering up at Kanderil. "You all of a sudden running away so the bad people won't see you?"

"I *want* the Gathire to see me," Kanderil replied. "I will simply make sure they see me somewhere they were not expecting."

"So what're you gonna do?" Ethanei asked, sipping on his ale.

"Head for Tamiran. I will speak to the Prince and see what he wants. That should be enough to get some attention. From there I will leave alone and meet Sarene and Spasmodic at my original destination."

"Wait, what?" The creature blinked. Kanderil folded his arms, towering over it.

"I need you to travel with Sarene. I will give her a map to lead the way. You make sure she gets there."

Sarene clicked her tongue before raising her hands. She pointed to Spasmodic, then to herself. Then she touched a fingertip beneath her eye. Finally she walked two sets of fingers across the air, one leading the other.

"Leave at nightfall, when the village is dead. Stay off the roads. The place I intend to meet you will be far from any other inhabited place. It should not be difficult to reach without being seen." He wagged a thick finger at her. "And stay out of trouble."

"Why not do that anyway, *with* you?" Ethanei asked.

"Since when did you get to be part of the family?" Spasmodic jeered.

"I used to be a soldier," Ethanei replied. "I have *some* training."

"Heh. Trust me, matey. You ain't got no training for this one." It gestured to Sarene with a wave of its claws. "Sarene turns into a bear when the moon's full. And she shits fire."

Kanderil interrupted them just as Sarene snapped her fingers at the creature, shaking her head. "As I said, I want to be seen in the capital. Throw the Gathire off their tracks. If I am correct, they should be scouting for *me* and assuming Sarene is close by."

"And they aren't going to see you on the way there?"

Kanderil narrowed his eyes. "*That* is where you come in."

Ethanei blinked in much the same manner as Spasmodic had. "What?"

"You are looking for a place to settle. Tamiran is a good a place as any, so if you will accompany me I have an idea to make sure I am not detected entering the city alone."

"Last time you had a wagon there was a great big fight," Spasmodic wheezed. "I wanna come with you instead."

"You will be looking after Sarene," Kanderil repeated.

"Bah. She can look after herself."

Sarene grinned, nodding her head. Her expression provided enough sarcasm to make the creature laugh. Kanderil understood the joke. Whether she was capable of fending for herself or not, she was aware she wouldn't be allowed to try. Not yet.

"For all we know someone will try and take her in the forests." Kanderil watched as the creature thought about this. Then it bounced on its feet, its dreadlocks springing around its shoulders.

"Right-o. I guess I'd have to do summat about that, aye."

"Indeed."

"Well," said Ethanei, draining his mug. "If I'm going to Tamiran then I'd better get a few drinks in. Riding a wagon is thirsty work, y'know. Anyone else?"

GLAITHE STEPPED FROM the shadows, moving across the square. A statue stood in the centre, flanked by two benches. The stone was somewhat worn now, having been erected over a hundred years ago. There was evidence that precious materials had once been used to decorate parts of the figure, but these had long since been stolen.

The cobbles beneath his feet were wet. Glaithe rotated his foot against them as he strode across towards the opposite corner of the square. They weren't slippery. He meandered to a halt, standing in the poorly lit space, and reached into his pocket for a smoke stick. His face lit up over the match, keeping his eyes shut against the flame so as to not blind himself in the night.

Oh, how he *loathed* this city! Tossing the match away,

the former Agent inhaled a drag of bitter smoke which felt heavy in his lungs. Ghellei was a rat's den of the unfortunate and the devious. He knew it to be full of some of the most disgusting and violent people in Tamir. The Gathire had a few informants placed here and acquired plenty of information from those brave or stupid enough to sell it. One would not wish to make a name for themselves as a snitch. Murder was common. The guard were woefully under-manned here, and the job was risky. Plenty of areas were off-limits, even to the authorities. There was often talk in Tamiran of sending out a squad of the military to clear the place out, but short of making the city a garrison then there was little point. The criminals who used Ghellei as a place of operations would simply move elsewhere and be lost from sight. At least here the bastards were all in one place.

Glaithe shook his head. The sooner he could get out of this place the better. He was tired of it. He was tired of hiding, and could hardly wait to put his plans into action. But Glaithe was a professional, and he was patient. The delay would serve to make his success all the sweeter.

He thought of the hovel he now called home. Having to share the tiny space with the snivelling wretch Nichai was almost unbearable. The Regent would cry and sob all the time, having no guts or spine to hold himself with any pride. Ever since Glaithe had forced him into hiding at the request of Tyrrial, Nichai had been a constant irritation. Had he not needed the Regent alive he would have drawn a blade across the boy's throat months ago. The temptation was still great. He instead contented himself with the occasional beating.

When Nichai was returned to Tamiran it was a certainty that Glaithe would become the most wanted man in Tamir. He had no fear, however. By that time he would have earned Tyrrial's favour, and he would be rewarded.

Glaithe could only imagine the kind of rewards gifted by the Four.

Turning, he watched as the three men following him stepped into the square. They approached him with purpose. One of them held a small club in a heavy hand. Glaithe smiled, turning to face them.

"Good evening, my friends." He made sure his voice was proud and unassuming. "A pleasant area for a late stroll, is it not?"

"Aye," said one of the men, a stocky brute with a drooping moustache. He had placed himself at the front of the group. "You could say that." One of the other men with him chuckled.

"Hold on," Glaithe continued, raising a hand. "Didn't I see you in the Horse and Cart a little earlier? Where that man was speaking. The…" He paused for effect, letting them come closer. "The Sons of Tamir, they called themselves. *Very* fine speech."

"All that brotherhood stuff?" The man with the club grinned in the gloom. "He picked the wrong town. Ain't any of that goin' on here."

"A shame," said Glaithe, flicking ash from his smoke stick. "I always liked Ghellei. Now, was there something you wanted?"

"Your money," said the lead man. "I saw that purse you

were flashing around. Looks pretty full."

"My purse?" Glaithe feigned bewilderment. "Why, I couldn't give you my purse. It is all I have."

"Shame." The lead man nodded. The man with the club moved forward, taking two quick strides before swinging the club at Glaithe's head. Glaithe ducked, the attack missing him. He flicked the smoke stick at the face of the lead man, causing him to flinch, waving a hand before his face. The club swinger, now off-balance, stumbled forward. Glaithe used his extended fingers to strike the man's throat, thrusting against the windpipe. The man dropped the club and fell to his knees, choking for air.

Glaithe turned as the third man, so far silent, made his move. He threw a wild punch which Glaithe leaned away from, using the opportunity to aim a straight kick at the assailant's knee. The joint buckled under the blow and the man cried out in pain, dropping to the floor and clutching his leg.

Turning to the one remaining mugger, Glaithe invited him forwards. "You're lucky I am trying to maintain a low profile. Otherwise you and your friends would be dead by now."

The drooping moustache raised and lowered as the brute tensed with anger. "You think a lot of yourself, boy." He surged towards Glaithe, his speed surprising given his stocky frame. Glaithe swayed to the side, drawing his dagger and sweeping it across the man's cheek. The man yelled out, retaliating with a wild backhanded swing of his fist. Glaithe brought both forearms up to block it before hammering his elbow into the man's spine. The brute fell forward, Glaithe looming over him.

"You should have stayed in the tavern," he said, taunting. Then he whipped a vicious kick up at the man's head. The contact was brutal, knocking his victim unconscious.

Glaithe noticed his smoke stick nearby, the tip glowing faintly in the darkness. He picked it up and took a few puffs, bringing the ember back to life. Satisfied, he walked away from the group, left on the ground and trying to gather themselves.

The man with the broken knee, writhing in pain and trying to grit his teeth against his screams, yelled out.

"You're a dead man, ya hear! Nngh… yer… We're gonna find you an' *kill* you!"

"Don't bother," Glaithe called back over his shoulder. "As far as anyone knows, somebody already did!"

AT FIRST LIGHT, Sarene stood outside of the tavern, stamping her feet against the cold. It felt like she was the only person in the world. Nobody else stirred. No markets had been set up beneath the granite sky, where clouds rolled over each other in a steady avalanche of grey. There weren't any open stores. The homes remained silent. She couldn't even hear any birds. There was nothing but her and this little township. It reminded her of a graveyard. She exhaled, her breath visibly rising from her mouth.

She didn't want Kanderil to leave her and travel to the capital. Sarene had taken the woodsman to be the one certainty in her current situation. The thought of not having him at her side was disconcerting. His very presence brought comfort. Still, the reasons for his departure were understandable. He had her best interests at heart, and she agreed that they should make her location a secret again before setting up in the cabin he'd mentioned for the winter. Sarene didn't trust the Gathire at all. The idea that she was being tracked by them made her shiver.

It would also give her a few weeks with Spasmodic. She'd missed the creature, as much as that surprised her. That she had become attached to something which had been originally created to murder her was definitely a little peculiar.

Sarene smiled to herself. That word. *Created*. Another reminder of just how unique her place in the world was. Who else could say they had a friend like Spasmodic? Something which had never been born or raised. Something which had never been a child. The creature was a living weapon. She'd seen that first hand.

Still, Spasmodic was good company, if a little tiresome. It had a very strange way of looking at the world, often loaded with questions about the most mundane of subjects.

A creaking sound came from along the road. Sarene watched a wagon trundle into view, with Kanderil in the driver's seat. Her mare had been joined by another, this one chestnut coloured. Their hooves made little noise on the packed-dirt street. The wagon was flat and rectangular, designed for cargo instead of people.

She waited as it drew near, Kanderil tugging on the reins to pull up before her. He looked down as she ran around to the back of the cart. Kanderil's cloak was laid out across the left side of the trailer, with his bag sitting atop it. She hopped up and crawled over to the far corner, resting her arm against the back of the seats.

"You will have to kneel," Kanderil said, turning his head. "Make sure your knees lay against the cloak. It will be uncomfortable."

She nodded, doing as asked. She pulled up the hood of her cloak as the wagon lurched forward. The wheels started their creak.

"We will hit a small dell which runs through a section of the forest," Kanderil explained. "I am presuming that the Gathire will be tracking us from distance, so unless they follow us along the road we will be unsighted for around a quarter-hour. That is when we will switch. Spasmodic will meet you as soon as we are clear."

"I'm not convinced," said a voice from underneath Kanderil's cloak. "And what d'you 'ave in this bag? Feels like a bloody anvil." Something shifted.

"It will be convincing enough. Nobody will be close enough to inspect you."

"Right. Sure thing." There was a sigh. "Can someone pass me my hipflask? This headache needs some medicine."

Sarene rolled her eyes. She was starting to wonder about Ethanei. He'd drank steadily for the previous afternoon and most of the evening, before stumbling off to bed muttering something about his ex-wife. Apparently a hangover was another excuse to *keep* drinking.

"Cloaks generally do not sip alcohol on their own,"

Kanderil replied. The deadpan delivery caused Sarene to laugh, the sound like a hiccup.

"I'm not a cloak," Ethanei whined.

"You are for the time being. Now be quiet."

THEY FOLLOWED THE trail for an hour or so. Sarene shifted, using her hands to press against the wagon and allow the blood to flow back into her lower legs. Her knees and ankles were aching, but she trusted Kanderil had a reason for asking her to sit like this.

Instead, she focused on the beautiful, late autumn countryside. The forest drifted towards them. She peered down over the side of the trailer as the road sped along beneath the wheels. Flicking her gaze back and forth between the near and far, Sarene noticed how points in the distance hardly seemed to move while milestones on the road swept on by. She didn't understand why things further away seemed to take longer to pass. Thinking about it made her head hurt.

"So you never told me much about yerself, Kanderil." Ethanei's voice made her jump. She'd all but forgotten he was there.

"Correct," Kanderil replied without looking around. "I did not."

"Well? Now's a good time to start." A cough. "I'm all ears."

"I do not share details of my personal life."

"Why not?"

"Personal preference."

"C'mon, man. If we're riding to Tamiran together you

'ave to give me *somethin'*."

"No," Kanderil said. "I do not."

Ethanei blew air between his lips, which against the cloak sounded much ruder than it should have. Sarene grinned.

"Fine," their hidden passenger said. "I'll start. I were born in Thorlen Tar to a woman who worked in the bakery. I never knew me pa. Me ma said he were a rich fella who lived in the town for a bit. I grew up in what you'd call poverty, I suppose. Never 'ad much. I apprenticed in the stables and worked in the fields. Eventually I joined the army 'bout six years ago, before anyone knew about Remelas' plans. Travelled all over the country and learnt to be a soldier. They put me in the cavalry, on account of me knowing 'ow to shoe an 'orse." Ethanei gave a short laugh.

"I were good at it. Ended up trainin' some of the recruits in 'ow to look after their mounts. Didn't see any action, though. Not much call for cavalry up on the borders. Not enough flat ground 'cept down south, and the Franthians ain't caused any trouble for centuries. In the end I were discharged after Leithar Grove, with all that business." The voice became sour then, speaking with obvious distaste. "Came 'ome, lived with me former wife for a few months, found out she were a cheatin' bitch and ended up in your company. Oh, an' I developed a bit of a drinkin' problem along the way."

Ethanei fell silent. Sarene rocked as the wagon hit a divot in the road. The sound of their travel was the only accompaniment. She wasn't sure how to react. The honesty with which the words were spoken was fascinating. In contrast to

Kanderil, who *was* very selective with the information he shared, this man had wrapped up his life story in a couple of minutes.

"I expect you could find work in Tamiran with your experience," said Kanderil.

There was a long pause before Ethanei replied.

"Yeah, prolly."

Sarene stared at Kanderil, hoping he would turn around to catch her eye. He kept his gaze fixed on the road ahead, his long hair swaying in the breeze. Shaking her head, the girl reached over to Ethanei's pack and fumbled around inside. She pushed past the single change of clothes he had to find the hard object she sought. Pulling out the hipflask, she sneaked it under the cloak and patted where she guessed Ethanei's shoulder to be. Fingers tugged the hipflask from her grip, before a hand came out to give her a thumbs-up.

Smiling, Sarene leant back on her crossed ankles.

KANDERIL SAW THE trail he wanted ahead. The forest around them was becoming thicker now. They had just passed a guard post along the road, but nobody had taken notice of them. There was less than a mile to go before they hit the bend in the road leading them through the slimmest section of the trees. He studied the woodland without moving his head, his eyes scanning the pass. No sign of anyone else in the area.

The wagon rolled along. Shadows cast by the dim sunshine hitting the overhead branches rippled across the wagon and its occupants. The road itself started to hiss as wet dirt was pressed by the wheels – here, as the road dipped down between a gentle valley, the rain of the previous day had funnelled into the ground.

Forcing himself to wait until they were a few hundred yards into the trail, Kanderil glanced backwards. The curve in the road lay behind, snaking away to the west, while they headed in a more northerly route. The trees blocked any onlookers from further afield, and the road ahead rose over the nearby crest leading back to the Highway. This section of road, a shortcut towards central Tamir, had been notorious for banditry and it was considered one of the more danger-ous paths to take. The Tamir guard had stationed posts on either side of the forest, making travel much safer in recent years.

Kanderil slowed the horses and turned around in his seat. "Ok, switch. Just like I told you."

Sarene reluctantly pulled the toggle of her cloak and drew the garment from her shoulders. Ethanei wriggled out from beneath cover and took it from her.

"You really think purple is me colour?"

"Just put it on," said Kanderil.

As Sarene hopped from the back of the cart, Ethanei sat where she had been. Instead of sitting on his knees, though, he sat with his lower legs pushed beneath Kanderil's cloak. He pulled Sarene's beloved garment around him, covering as much of his body as he could, and tugged the hood over his head.

"Good thing I 'ad a shave this morning," he muttered. "I

doubt anyone would believe the girl sprouted a beard overnight."

Sarene shook her head as she stepped off the road, watching them from behind the nearest tree.

"Well?" Kanderil asked. "How does he look?"

She narrowed one eye, staring at the wagon. Then she smirked.

"It will only work from distance," Kanderil said. "I am not expecting anyone to come close enough to tell the difference."

"I'm still not convinced," Ethanei complained. "I'm broader in the shoulders than she is."

"You are the same height sitting down. Just try and look small."

"Hah!" Ethanei laughed. "Right, sure. I'll just pull off a few pounds, aye?"

Sarene chewed on a knuckle as Kanderil looked back to her. He offered a smile, hoping the girl found it comforting.

"The creature will find you as soon as we are clear. It has not reported back, so I am guessing that—"

"I'm already here," said Spasmodic, dropping out of the tree above Sarene. She jumped in fright and it giggled at her surprise. "There's some bloke with a thingyscope a couple of miles ahead, but he's too far away to see this. Other than that, your secret's safe." The creature examined Ethanei. "You've dressed up as a little girl before, ain't ya?"

The only reply was a foul curse.

"Get to the point I marked on the map. Make sure nobody sees you." Kanderil levelled his gaze at Spasmodic.

"And keep out of trouble."

"What do you take me for?" Spasmodic replied with a lop-sided grin.

Kanderil frowned, but addressed Sarene. "I will meet you in a little over a fortnight. Stay safe, lass. And stick to the forests as much as possible."

She clicked her tongue, hesitant to wave goodbye. Kanderil nodded to her instead and she returned the gesture.

Then he flicked the reins and the wagon started forward again, Ethanei rocking to the side in her cloak. Sarene watched them leave, absently moving her hand to play with the Kalethi broach pinned to her sleeve.

THE CITY TEEMED with life. People moved like schools of fish, turning and shifting as one through the narrow lanes. Punctuating the air were cries from vendors hawking their wares; hot food, colourful fabrics and hand-made items. The air was pungent with spices of a hundred different types set up in huge woven bowls, all dust and bulbs and seeds. Each stall or store was open faced, entire families manning the place. Small dogs yapped at passers-by, tied to poles or sat in cages. The people spoke in a quick, tonal language, clipped syllables popping like firecrackers.

Cho'Nanshai was the most populous city in all the lands. Almost a half-million people lived here, a race of people known collectively as *Norshai*. Over the generations, citizens of Cho'Nanj had used an affectionate term; *The City Built From Cities*. The description was fitting. Construction took place everywhere, building and expanding and elevating. The national flag of Cho'Nanj hung everywhere, green and white with a prominent red orchid. The Cho'Nanjii were proud and industrious, forming a nation of so many that poverty was irrelevant. The price of goods was low and people could afford to keep themselves and their huge families. If anywhere had followed the teachings of the Four, it was this nation. Nobody lacked a place to live or food to eat. All were welcome at the table come sundown without exception. War was a distant memory. Cho'Nanj was prosperous and focused on progress and trade.

Tyrrial hated it.

He walked the streets, biting down his irritation at the sheer *mass* of people around him. Despite being the only pale-skinned, white-haired man in the market, nobody paid him a second glance. He didn't want them to. The city was like an anthill, swarming with too many bodies that only had a vague sense of what they wanted. They did what was expected of them, as he saw it. They just existed. The Cho'Nanjii lived in a wet climate with streets full of effluence and depression. The laughter he heard struck him as desperate. The smiles were fake. Tyrrial was glad this was not *his* territory.

Stopping by a stall covered with incense sticks, Tyrrial examined the owner, who appeared hidden in a huge bundle of clothing. The stall reeked of some bittersweet stench coming from a pair of burning sticks. There was a hint of jasmine and something else, something unpleasant. Tyrrial shook his head.

"Wake up."

The bundle of clothes didn't move.

"Wake up," he said again, rapping his knuckles on the display. One of the incense sticks fell over.

"Are you done criticising my people?" the bundle of clothes replied.

"I admire the people of the north," Tyrrial said with a smirk. "There are simply too many of them in one place."

A hand appeared, pulling down a satin scarf to reveal a pair of dark almond eyes.

"You should be in bed."

"Please, Shigasi. Spare me the lecture. I've had it several times from Corliani."

Shigasi chuckled, removing the cowl to reveal flawless skin and prominent features. Tyrrial tried to remember the man's appearance before becoming one of the Four; scrawny, awkward, all elbows and knees and large teeth. Shigasi had utilized his powers well, changed his appearance to the fine-looking man he remained today. A vain conceit which none had mocked him for.

"I presume nobody can see you," Shigasi observed.

"You presume correctly. I contemplated wrapping myself up like a corpse, but I prefer my own clothes."

Shigasi chuckled. "Come around here, would you? Take a seat. These cushions are quite comfortable."

Tyrrial raised a brow. "Are they damp?"

"What do you take me for? Of course they're not."

Moving through the slim gap between the incense stall and the table next to it – a cluttered display of trinkets and necklaces – Tyrrial eased himself into the claustrophobic space and sat down in one of the cushions. He relaxed, easing his hips from side to side to make himself comfortable. Reclining against several rolls of fabric, watching the street, he felt a little better. A light drizzle fell from the sombre clouds, *pitpatpit*ering against the canvas sheet above them. The Cho'Nanjii wore hats with a flat board extending out from it, as though balancing a square of wood on their heads.

Shigasi was peeling open a satsuma with his thumbnail. "So what brings you to my part of the world, brother?"

"I came to offer my gratitude for saving my life."

"Think nothing of it. It was Corliani who summoned us to your tower. I merely put you back together."

"Yes, well, the putting back together certainly helped. Your skills as a surgeon remain unsurpassed." Tyrrial took a section of the fruit offered to him.

"I expect any man who had a spare century to study the craft would be just as skilled. It is all relative, I suppose."

"Could you describe my wounds?"

"There was a knife in your flank. Or did you not notice?"

Tyrrial pulled a seed from his mouth. "You don't say."

"A bad joke. My apologies." Shigasi tapped a finger against his chin. "Let's see. The blade was six inches long. It entered your body just below your ribcage. The liver was missed by a hair's breadth. The large intestine *was* perforated, however. We were fortunate enough to reach you before much of the contents could spill into your torso. I closed the hole, stitched the wound and kept the area disinfected. We provided you with watery soup through a tube at first, but after the first week Mubuto discovered you would swallow in sleep. After that we spoon-fed you broth twice a day until you awoke."

"Why not just use your powers to heal me?"

Shigasi smirked. "You know the reason for that as well as I do."

"Humour me."

"Very well. Corliani tried to seal the wound, of course. Before I arrived. It did not work. We concluded that since Sarene inflicted the wound our powers were rendered useless in putting you back together. We had to treat you using traditional methods."

Tyrrial laid a hand on his side, pushing the fabric of his robe against the raised tissue where the knife had entered his body. The skin around the area was senseless. If he pinched the flesh around the wound he could barely feel it.

"You understand, then, that I was correct. The girl *is* a threat."

Raising a hand, Shigasi inclined his head. "Before we get into that, Tyrrial, let us discuss the actions which led to your injury."

"Corliani gave me the lectu—"

"No," Shigasi put in. "That is not good enough. I have my own questions."

Tyrrial sighed. "Very well. If we must."

"Thank you. There is little point admonishing you for charging into Tamir. I am sure Corliani had already gone over the should-nots and why-woulds. The fact remains that you *did* avert a war."

"I am glad you see it that way."

A young *Norshai* woman came towards the stall, sniffing at one of the lit incense sticks. Shigasi waved a hand. The girl scratched her cheek, gazed around, and then departed as though remembering something.

"Corliani sees it that way as well, brother," Shigasi continued. Smoke wafted past his face. "He is an intelligent man. *My* concern is why you did not seek an audience with this Prince Remelas directly. A quiet word and a display of your power would have had the same effect."

"Perhaps," Tyrrial conceded. "But it would not have made such an example. Word has spread, I am sure, to the adjoining nations. Further than that, even. The lands will know not to dare risk our wrath again. I may have ensured peace for another century."

"Be that as it may, your motivation was not so pure, I think."

Tyrrial quirked a brow. "Go on."

"You sought Remelas and Sarene in the same place at the same time. That was not a coincidence."

"I would not try and convince you otherwise."

"You were going to kill the girl."

"Of course."

"Do you still intend to do so?"

Tyrrial sighed. The owner of the neighbouring stall poked a stick into the fabric shelter above him. A stream of water flooded out and splashed across the dirty street.

"She almost killed me, Shigasi."

"Yes, she did. Do you seek revenge?"

"Did you know," Tyrrial replied, "that there are factions in Tamir now seeking her out? To use her as a standard? A banner against us? They seek to hold her as a magical ward against our powers."

"I am informed that some also seek to kill her. To end this mystical threat which some perceive her to be." Shigasi leant back in his cushion. "As *you* do, it seems."

"But why give the people the choice? Why give them another reason to turn on each other?" Tyrrial placed his hands on his thighs and stretched against the cushions. The awkward angle was beginning to irritate his old bones. "All these centuries of peace ever since we walked the earth. No king has ever raised an army like Tamir did. No ruler has openly defied us. But the girl reaches her sixteenth year just as her Prince chooses to invade a neighbouring nation with an army of the like no man has ever seen. Do you believe that is merely happenstance?"

"You see it as fate." Shigasi tossed the satsuma peel away. "You think this has been orchestrated by the stars. I never took you as one to believe superstition, my friend. Especially considering all we know. As for giving the people a choice, that was always our intention. We never demanded obedience. We asked for it."

"Under the threat of extinction," Tyrrial fired back.

"I prefer the term encouragement. Regardless, we do not rule with an iron fist. We do not expect the people to crumble to our whims. Most of them do not even believe in us these days." The *Norshai* laughed. "At least they didn't until you showed up, all fire and ash."

"She is a danger. A danger to us, to her people. Perhaps even to the world, if left unchecked."

"Sarene is a scared little girl. She is hardly a leader of men. For goodness sake, you killed her brother."

"All the more reason for her to seek vengeance against me. Against us."

Shigasi gave a long sigh. Tyrrial watched him. In the many fables of the Four, Shigasi was always referred to as the most benevolent, the most forgiving. In their descriptions of him he was seen as a man who loved his people. Few held the fact that Shigasi was responsible for the single greatest loss of life in the lands, an event renowned in most languages as a ballad named *The Song of Tides,* in any great regard. Over ten thousand men, woman and children lost in a flood which had decimated the eastern coast of the Hunjaiko kingdom. Even Tyrrial had objected at the time.

"If you are going to seek the girl out a second time, that is your choice," Shigasi said. "I will not be a part of it, however."

"I would not have it any other way," Tyrrial replied. "Let me ask you this, however. Should the day ever come where we must walk the lands again. Repeat our teachings. Would you do so?"

Shigasi considered the question. Tyrrial thought he could see a brief spark of enthusiasm in the man's dark eyes. Another potential customer came to the stall and stared at them without any concept of just how powerful they were. Tyrrial and Shigasi stared back. Lips moved. The man jerked, backing away to be caught up in the never ending stream of people.

"Of course," said Shigasi, the words calm and measured.

Chapter Five

THE SQUEAKING OF the wagon's left wheel was beginning to irritate Kanderil.

"Y'know," said Ethanei, who still sat in the cart behind him. "I've been thinking. How are we gonna keep people fooled when we stop to book a room? I'm gonna look like a man in a purple cloak, not a young lass."

"We are not stopping in any towns," Kanderil replied.

"Oh, right. We living rough, then?"

"You were a soldier. I would have expected you to be used to it."

"Aye, I've slept beneath the stars plenty o' times." Ethanei sniffed. "Were just hopin' we could stop off for a pint or two along the way."

Kanderil glanced around at the man, who was rocking from side to side with the stiff movements of the cart. "How much *do* you drink?"

Ethanei grinned at him. "All o' it, usually."

"Why?"

"Why not? S'not like I 'ave much else to look forward to these days. May as well gawk up at life from the bottom of a mug." Ethanei laughed, shaking his head. "Alcohol don't judge. It's other people who judge. Alcohol just makes things seem a bit less bad, y'know?"

"Until the next morning." Kanderil turned to watch the road once more. "When your head pounds and your mouth is dry."

"Ah, but that's just yer body sayin' it wants more."

"It is an addiction."

"Aw, piss off." Ethanei sounded dismissive. His words were strong and confident, suggesting he'd enjoyed more of whatever was in that hipflask. "I ain't exactly robbin' people for money to pay for the stuff. I ain't lost any work over it."

"You have lost your home," Kanderil observed.

"That's different. Weren't due to the drink, were it. Were due to me wife bein' a bloody whore."

"Perhaps if you had been sober these last few months she would have considered taking you back."

For a time there was no answer. Kanderil held the reins as the road began to wind down into a gentle decline. The trail would meet a small bridge in perhaps an hour's time. If they followed the river beneath they would reach a section where the water became quick, funnelling into a stream. There was a cove where they could stay for the night without being observed, as one of the banks became a sharp cliff of a few dozen yards or so. Avoiding the use of a campfire would mean anyone looking at them through a telescope would see little of use. Providing they started off again before first light, nobody should be any the wiser.

"Who're you to criticise me?" Ethanei said quietly behind

him. Kanderil returned from his thoughts.

"Hm?"

"I said who are you to criticise me?" The man's voice was hard. "Talkin' to me like some kinda scum."

"I did not mean to offend you. I merely voiced an opinion."

"Well it sounded like you took me for a fool." Ethanei leant towards him, placing an arm on the front of the cart. Kanderil thought better of asking him to sit back. "I mean, me drinkin' didn't drive her away. Me *career* did. All that time with the army. She didn't like it so I had to make a choice. I were givin' her money, keepin' her in our home. I thought I were doin' something good for me country. And what d'ya know. Turned out I was just a spoke in the wheel of Remelas's grand plans for war." Ethanei spat to the side. "The bastard. It's his fault I lost her. I were lied to and paid the price."

Kanderil said nothing. He understood the man's anger, even if he felt there was a degree of denial in the words. No marriage was ever *helped* by a drinking problem. But the sense of betrayal came out with honesty. It seemed to be a feeling which resounded through the country. Remelas had hidden his plans away and when it had all come out – only due to the slaughter of hundreds of Tamir soldiers – the scale of the plan had shocked the kingdom. *Frightened* it.

Remembering Jared's initial objection when Remelas had told them about his ambitions, Kanderil couldn't resist a chuckle. The boy had been right.

"What you laughin' at?"

"Nothing." Kanderil shook his head. "You simply remind me of someone I once knew."

"Who's that?"

"Sarene's elder brother."

"Oh." Ethanei sat back in his designated spot. "Where is he, then?"

"Tyrrial killed him."

"Oh."

SARENE WALKED THROUGH the woodland, keeping a tight grip on the map. They were heading east. At least, she was pretty sure they were. Probably. Kanderil had taught her how to navigate and she was trying her best. She knew most of the moss on a tree grew on the northern side, and the branches mostly aimed in a southerly direction. She knew the sun rose in the east and set in the west. She had a few others tricks, but mainly she'd just followed Kanderil. Spasmodic likely knew the right way to go, but it seemed content to let her take the lead.

She stepped over a rock and paused, scratching her chin and wanting to take off the annoying scarf. It was too cold for that, though. Sarene missed her cloak. She trusted Kanderil would bring it back but she felt incomplete without it. Still, as part of the plan it would have been rude of her to refuse.

Spasmodic wandered over. "Don't you ever get tired of sodding about in these bloody forests?"

Shrugging, Sarene unfolding the map yet again. She guessed they were coming to the edge of the woods, and would be left with grassland for maybe six miles. They had to cut south-west, walking between two villages which sat along the main road.

"I'm completely bored of it," Spasmodic continued. It yawned to underline the point. "I wish someone *would* find us. Y'know? Just to keep things interesting."

It had been two days since the group had separated. Spasmodic evidently did not find life as interesting as it once had. It had made frequent complaints, muttering about the slow pace and the lack of anything 'fun'. The creature still made jokes, but they lacked any real enthusiasm.

"Did I tell you about the Juu'ad?" it said. Sarene shook her head. It had, but while it was telling stories it at least had a subject it could engage in. She looked up from the map. West was *that* way. She started walking again, side-stepping a stray root.

"Anyway," Spasmodic continued. "I saw this race, right. There were about ten guys, all big lads, oiled up and naked." It walked along beside her, using its claws to gesture and wave. "You'd have liked it."

Sarene gave the creature a rigid stare. It sniggered in response, and she was powerless against the touch of red at her cheeks.

"So!" Spasmodic clapped. "They had this race. And these guys lined up and started runnin'. I ran along with 'em. They couldn't see me, o'course. I was just investigating at this point. They ran across a big ol' field, and then started up this mountain pass. There's loads of mountains down south, pokin' out all rocky and stuff. These ten guys ran until they were out o' sight of the judges or whoever. I guess they were judges. They had weapons and looked like mean bastards."

Sarene tried to picture it. The Juu'ad were famous even in Tamir for their barbaric ways. It was said that they were a cruel, brutal people, their entire culture based on physical strength and martial skill. She'd once heard a story from one of her Elders that the Juu'ad sent all boys away from home for a whole year, purely to train as warriors. Those who survived were accepted as men, and those who died were disowned by their family. She'd been shocked when she heard it, unable to comprehend such a harsh childhood.

"These ten kept runnin', and when they were up the cliffs they started tryin' to kill each other. Whoever was in the lead was in the most danger. If anyone caught up to 'em they'd try and kick him to the ground, or shove him over the cliff. Just really bad, like. I loved it." Spasmodic giggled at the memory, a twitch pulling at its left cheek. "I swear, one guy had his bloody *eye* ripped out. The guy behind just grabbed his face, dug a finger in and yanked." The creature mimicked pulling something apart between its two hands. "Glorious."

Shuddering, Sarene closed her eyes to push the image she conjured away.

"So they kept just kickin' the buggery out of each other. At the end one guy who was nearly as tall as ol' Kanderil was in the lead. He was running back towards the finish line all cocky and sure he was gonna win, when this little bugger came out of nowhere and was sprinting right up behind him. Just as the big guy realised and turned, this little shit just leapt and tackled him to the ground, got up on his knees and pummelled the big guy's face in. Sat there hammerin' on him for a good minute." Spasmodic shook his head, a somewhat malicious grin on its pale features. "An' you know what happened?"

Sarene shook her head, wincing in preparation.

"The big guy stood up, *laughed*, and then leant forward and invited the little guy to keep going! Girly, I ain't ever seen anything so damned *inspiring*. The little guy just gave up. Dropped to the ground and submitted. The big guy turned around and won the race. I laughed so hard I nearly pissed me pants. I reckon they must'a heard me, too, cos they sent some guys out to check." Spasmodic giggled, and as the sound faded away Sarene watched it. The expression it wore was troubling to her and she focused ahead once more, a hand stroking the trunk of a thin tree as they passed.

She didn't want to think about what happened to that search party.

"Speakin' of which, I need to leak meself." Spasmodic turned without missing a step and ambled off behind a tree. Sarene kept walking. She found it odd that the creature, for all its lack of social graces and coarse demeanour, still made the effort of relieving itself in private. Sarene half-expected it to drop its pants where it stood and piss into the wind. Laughing while it did, perhaps.

She chuckled to herself, stepping underneath a cascade of brassy leaves hanging from a dense thicket.

Standing straight once again, Sarene found herself before a dark-haired boy who couldn't have been much older than she. He wore a collection of leathers too large for him, poorly stitched together with thick string.

Sarene stopped in her tracks and stared at him. The boy stared back. Her gaze fell to the crossbow in his hands and he flinched, lowering the weapon. He produced a soft smile which she returned.

"I, uh…" the boy began. "I didn't mean to startle you."

Shaking her head, Sarene brought her hands to her chest. A sudden wave of nerves struck her. She couldn't reply to him, couldn't give him her name or ask what he was doing in the forest. She took a quick breath to compose herself. *Do what you always do.*

Her hand came to her waist and she extended an arm, bowing in greeting. She made sure to dip her head, her hair slipping before her features to give her a few seconds of privacy.

"Get away from her, you shit!"

Sarene snapped upright just in time to see Spasmodic burst through the thicket, springing towards the boy. Its clawed right hand whipped around and connected with the boy's face, sending him crumpling to the floor before he could even cry out. Spasmodic landed over the now unconscious stranger, knelt over him, talons inches away from the exposed neck.

Sarene sprinted forward and aimed a firm kick at Spasmodic's side. Her foot connected with its shoulder and it whirled around, its bloodlust up.

"What are you doin!?" it yelled at her, snarling.

Standing her ground despite the wave of fear which bloomed up to grip her chest, she pointed at the boy on the floor and shook her head before trying to shoo Spasmodic off of him.

"We don't know what he's here for!"

Sarene put her hands on her hips and nodded her head, gesturing for the creature to move aside. For a moment she believed it would ignore her, but then it swore and gnashed its teeth, rolling to the side and rising into a crouch. She hurried forward, dropping to her knees and examining the stranger's face. There was an ugly bruise forming on his temple and a thin trickle of blood dripped into his ear. Despite this, Sarene deemed him lucky. If Spasmodic had used the sharp side of those claws then the boy would have been dead before he'd hit the ground. She shook him by the shoulders, hoping he was simply stunned, but there was no response.

"What's the problem?" asked Spasmodic. "Just leave 'im before he wakes up and tries to cut your throat."

The words were met with a deep frown. Sarene knew it could be insensitive, but it had just knocked a stranger from his feet and into the next Shalith. She exhaled to show her disapproval.

"Look, we can't wait here 'til he wakes up. We've gotta get to that next campsite the big fella marked out on the map. Sittin' around isn't gonna help."

Sarene mulled this over. Spasmodic was right. They still had a plan to follow. But she felt dreadful just leaving the boy unconscious on the forest floor. Especially *this* forest. Kanderil had made a big point of how dangerous it had once been, full of bandits and thieves. Anything could happen.

An idea struck her. She snapped her fingers to get the creature's attention – somehow it had *already* gotten bored and was now digging a hole in the ground with its claws, firing dirt around. It blinked at her.

"What?"

She mimicked hoisting something up over her shoulder, then pointed to the boy.

Spasmodic's laughter cracked like a whip. "You gotta be kidding me."

With a firm nod she repeated the gesture.

"Look, I ain't carrying this arse around with us! It ain't our fault he's on the…"

Sarene pursed her lips.

"Alright, well maybe it *is*, but if he hadn't – Look, Kanderil will be mad as hell if you start dragging strangers around like puppies!"

She shrugged. Kanderil wasn't here. *She* was in charge. The thought gave her the confidence to jab a finger at the boy again.

Spasmodic peered at her, then at the unconscious youngster. It sniffed, thin lips twitching into a smirk. "Oh, heh. I get it… Look, you'll have to help me pick him up, unless you want me to pull him to bits and stick him in your bag."

She nodded, scooting across to hook her hands beneath the boy's underarms.

"And if you tell anyone I did this, I'll bloody murder you." Spasmodic snorted, clumping over towards her. "I'm only doin' this 'cos you're gonna cause a load more fights, y'know."

Without wanting to dwell too much on what the creature meant by *that*, Sarene started the process of lifting the boy upright. He was heavier than he looked.

THEY TRAVELLED FOR another two hours. Sarene had decided that they should make camp early, as they were now moving along the edge of the great forest and she didn't like the idea of travelling across the open plains with Spasmodic carrying a lifeless body. It would leave them a half-day behind schedule, but they would still have time to spare before Kanderil was expected to arrive at the cabin.

Keeping plenty of space between them and the plains, she stopped and held up a hand. The girl wasn't sure if this was a good position to set up for the night, but there were two thick, heavy trees providing shelter and enough space for a fire. The air was chill now and her fingers were like icy shards poking out of her shirt. She rubbed them against each other, enjoying that slight flare of discomfort as the blood began to re-circulate through them. A fire would be sorely welcome.

Spasmodic pulled up next to her, the boy still slung over its shoulder like a dead lamb. Small jade eyes gleamed from between a set of dreadlocks which hung across its face.

"We stoppin' here then?"

Sarene nodded. Spasmodic returned the gesture, throwing its shoulder forward. The boy fell crashing into the dirt, his limbs sprawling out on the ground. Sarene gasped, running forward to roll him into a more comfortable position. Spasmodic giggled.

"It ain't like he's gonna feel it. You weren't carryin' the bugger around." The creature popped a joint with a sharp twist of its spine.

Laying the boy on his back, Sarene swept his dark hair from his eyes. He seemed peaceful in oblivion, his face childishly innocent. His jaw was smooth, though she couldn't tell if that was from choice or from a lack of hair growth. The wound at his temple was red and angry, with a slim scab running through the centre. She resisted the irrational urge to poke it.

"So what now?" asked Spasmodic. "I'm not fetching sticks. You can build your own bloody fire."

Sarene sat back on her crossed ankles. At least there seemed to be an abundance of firewood here. They still had some food in her pack, though Spasmodic didn't eat it. She presumed it was pilfering its own meals from somewhere. The only food it had accepted from her had been oatcakes, back when the two of them and Kanderil had been travelling past the Meadows.

(*in pursuit of Jared before—*)

Sighing, she rose and started collecting sticks of a useful length. She glanced over at Spasmodic, who was studying the boy. It seemed to be sniffing him. Shaking her head, Sarene focused on the task at hand. She wanted a fire up and burning before the night really set in. Through the breaks in the canopy it appeared to be a cloudless sky, and that meant it was going to be a cold night's camping.

Sarene soon returned to drop the sticks down next to Spasmodic, leaning over to drag her bag across the dirt. She retrieved her tinderbox from inside and plucked out the few remaining twigs and leave. Having neglected to refill it during their walk, she would only get one opportunity to achieve a flame before she'd have to try with wet forest debris. The idea was not a welcoming one. She packed the kindling into place and took a deep breath, the tinderbox poised.

"You're meant to blow after it's a bit shiny," Spasmodic offered. It was watching her with keen interest, the boy forgotten.

Focusing on the task, she struck the tinder a few times before an ember caught. With great care, easing the soft kindling into place around it, she blew gently. A flame flickered into life. She nudged at the base of the kindling and pushed it beneath a propped stick. The flame disappeared and she thought it gone. Then a strip of bark started to smoke and, as she crossed her fingers, lit up. She encouraged the fire with further soft breaths.

"Do you need any help?"

Sarene ignored the creature, using a twig to toss the untouched kindling into the budding fire. It ignited. The first of the sticks rippled with flame which licked from the underside and crept towards the centre of the pile.

Satisfied the flames had caught, Sarene sat back and held her hands out. The warmth was faint, but it was enough. She smiled. Small victories like this served as a reminder that she wasn't completely useless after all.

"I'm serious. I can help with the fire now, sweet cheeks. I'm being selfish."

Sarene glanced up. Spasmodic wore a lopsided smirk. She made to retort with a rather primitive gesture when the boy beside them moaned, surprising the two. Sarene's chest tightened. She hadn't considered how to explain that the boy had been carried to the edge of the forest.

"Ow…" the boy said, raising a hand to his head. He checked his fingers, which came away clean. Sitting upright, his eyes were drawn to the fire. Then he noticed Sarene sitting beside it. She realised she was staring at him wide-eyed and she forced herself to relax.

Then he saw Spasmodic, who winked. He jumped up, scrabbling at the ground.

"Oh, shit…!"

Sarene rushed to stand, holding out her palms. She tried gesturing for the boy to remain still. He backpedalled on his hands for a few more feet before realising she was there. The boy looked at the two of them, trying to make the connection between young girl and inhuman devil. She wished she could say something to calm him.

"Think about it this way," Spasmodic said on cue. "If I were gonna eat ya, I'd have done it by now."

"I-I… uh, I don't…"

"Speak up, mate."

"I… Where am I?" The boy half-sat down, still prepared to make a run for it.

Sarene knelt close to him, leaning forward to grab his hand. He watched, dumbstruck, as she gave it a firm shake. She hoped he understood that the gesture was meant to be welcoming. When the contact was broken the boy gawped at his hand like he didn't know what it was for.

"You're in a forest," said Spasmodic.

The boy looked around him to confirm the statement. Spasmodic giggled, swaying on its heels.

"No, really. Haha. I wouldn't lie to you. Well…" It paused. "I mean, I'm not lying this time."

The boy's mouth fell open. Then he focused on Sarene.

"Are you a witch?"

She shook her head, the edges of her mouth twitching upwards.

"But…"

Sarene snapped her fingers, looking at Spasmodic. She pointed to herself then bowed quickly.

"What?"

She repeated the gesture, sweeping her hair from her face, and then rolled her hands at the wrist to encourage it to understand.

"I'm not bloody bowing," it snapped.

Sarene rolled her eyes. She poked herself in the chest with a thumb, then pointed to it. Then she bowed a third time before presenting both hands to the stranger.

"Oh. Err. Right." The creature cleared its throat for longer than was necessary. "This is Sarene. I'm Spasmodic. Who're you?"

Sarene's arms sagged at her side.

"I… uh … My pa calls me Anthon. I mean, my *name* is Anthon."

"Right. Well, nice to meet ya. Are you gonna try and kill her?"

Anthon panicked at the accusatory tone of the question. "What? No! No, I don't have a clue who she is!"

"Are you *suuuuuure*?" Spasmodic ducked its head down between its shoulders, peering at the boy until Sarene reached over to clap her hands together beside its head. It flicked a tongue across its cracked lips, amused.

"By the... What's going on?" Anthon rubbed a hand across his cheek.

"Bein' honest we kinda kidnapped you. On account of me punchin' you in the head. Sorry 'bout that."

"Are you her minion?" the boy asked. Spasmodic responded with a shrill laugh which split the cold air, a plume of steam cascading from its mouth.

"No, mate. She's not a bloody witch. She used to live on a farm."

Anthon fixed his gaze on her. She blushed a little, offering a shrug.

"Why did you bring me here?"

She reached out to point at the lump on the side of his head, offering a second rise of the shoulders to indicate her uncertainty. Her inner dialogue spoke up on her behalf. *Why did I bring him here?*

"She can't talk," said Spasmodic. "Might be best if we clear that one up now."

"Oh." Anthon swallowed. "Uh, am I your prisoner?"

"Well that depends if ol' big eyes over there wants to investigate the contents of your pa—"

Sarene's hard punch cut off the comment. Spasmodic's voice changed octave, making it sound foolish.

"I mean, heh. No, I don't think so. I think she just wanted to make sure you weren't eaten by a bear or summat."

Sarene turned her head to hide her embarrassment. Spasmodic was entirely the wrong person to have around in situations like this. But then, at least it had listened to her. Kanderil would have scared Anthon off before he'd even had the chance to smile at her. Sarene patted at her heart before holding both hands together in a gesture of submission, hoping Anthon would accept the apology.

"I, uh. Thank you. I think." The boy tested his wound once more. "Ngh… you didn't half catch me there, Spasmic."

"Spas*mo*dic." The creature punctuated the syllable with a claw tip.

Sarene moved to the fireside and opened her satchel, rummaging around inside. Kanderil had left her with a half-wheel of cheese, durable enough for the journey but too strong in flavour for her preference, and a black loaf of sour bread baked to a crust which gave a dull thud when she rapped her knuckles against it. Beside this they had a pound of oats in a canvas sack, and tucked beneath this a tiny sugar pouch; Sarene had a sweet tooth, and Kanderil catered to it. She waved the other two over to join her. Anthon's gaze was drawn to the food.

"Is she offering it to me?" he asked.

Sarene nodded her head, smiling. Spasmodic crawled past Anthon to sit on the opposite side of the fire. The lad got to his feet and took several unsteady steps forward and sat down beside her. Sarene got the impression he did so to be further away from the creature rather than any inclination to be near her.

She broke off a piece of bread and used her skinning knife to cut a decent wedge of cheese, handing them both to their guest. Anthon took the food with a nod of thanks before pulling small pieces off, taking his time to chew and swallow each mouthful.

They ate in silence. Spasmodic watched them with a curious expression on its face. With the evening darker now, the forest around them grew drab as the last of the sunlight faded; a coal shading against grey paper. The fire gave the only contrast, and the flames lit up the creature's face. With the vibrant red hair and dark rings around its eyes, the flickering image portrayed a true demonic visage. The boy did not look up during his meal.

When he had finished, Anthon scanned the campsite. Sarene brushed her hands free of crumbs.

"So I'm free to go?" he said at last. Anthon glanced at Spasmodic but then turned to her. With some reluctance, she nodded.

"Okay. I mean, thanks for making sure I was alright, but I ought to be movin' on. I'm heading south."

"For what?" asked Spasmodic.

"I need to get to – I mean, I'm meant to be…" Anthon's voice trailed off. "Nevermind. Do you have my crossbow?"

"Nah. Left it back where we found you. I weren't carrying that around as well, like. You were heavy enough as it was."

Anthon's face dropped. "Oh, *no*…" He shook his head, looking to the ground and driving a fist into his thigh. "Shit."

Sarene reached out to tug at his shirt, taking it as a good sign that he did not flinch. She brought her hands up to mimic firing it – making a point of aiming the imaginary bolt at Spasmodic, which made the thing laugh – before shrugging in question, turning her hands to aim the palms at the sky.

"My crossbow? It's all I have to catch food with." He muttered. "I mean, I don't have any money to buy food."

"It's only a crossbow, like," Spasmodic said, furrowing its brow.

"That ain't the point." Anthon hesitated. "Nevermind. I shouldn't talk about it."

Spasmodic chuckled. "Gorgeous, look at who you're hangin' out with here. Whatever your secret is, I promise you it ain't half as interestin' as hers." It waved in Sarene's direction. "I bet you don't even get to kill people."

Anthon's eyes widened, the off-hand comment renewing his concern. "What? You kill people?"

Sarene grabbed his sleeve again. She pointed at Spasmodic, and then tapped her ear while shaking her head.

"I can hear him," said Anthon.

She used both hands to cup her ears.

"You mean *don't* listen to him?"

Sarene nodded, exhaling in relief.

"What I'm tryin' to say is that since you're eatin' dinner with a bloody *demon*," – Spasmodic spat the world with contempt – "Then you're free to tell us your sniffy lil' secret."

Anthon stared at Spasmodic for a long time. Eventually he dropped his hands into his lap, adjusting himself on the floor.

"I guess you're right," he breathed. "Fine. I ran away from home a couple of weeks back. I'm makin' me way south. I need to get to Franthia."

"Franthia? What for? Ain't nothin' in that country 'cept sausages and big dresses."

Sarene gave the creature a steady look. She tried to work out how it could have an opinion on their southern neighbour. The words weren't far from the mark, given what she had heard about the Franthian people.

"It's none of your concern, if you'll forgive me," Anthon replied. "I just need to get there. I think I need to hurry as well before something else like this happens."

"Haha, what? How many times have you been kidnapped?"

Anthon gave a wry smile, the playful tone of the question infectious. Sarene smiled along with him. "I ain't been kidnapped before," he said. "I did run away from a couple of bandits, though. And I walked right past a den of wolves. It was only my crossbow which stopped me from gettin' savaged."

"You never fought off a wolf pack. C'mon." Spasmodic was incredulous.

"I shot one and stood me ground before backin' off," Anthon replied. "My pa was a ranger at one time. He taught me a few things."

Sarene ran two fingers in the air in front of her before pointing at the boy, intending to ask why he had fled his home. Anthon paused to consider the action before responding.

"I didn't run away from them…?"

She shook her head, letting the question drop for now.

"Well, hope you're good at runnin'." Spasmodic grinned, its pointed teeth shimmering through the heat of the fire between the three. "Or find a pointed stick or summat."

"Yeah, I guess. I'll manage." He made to rise. Sarene bit her lip before getting to her feet along with him. Up close, Anthon was a few inches taller. She held up one finger in a request for time, before bending down to retrieve the map from her bag. Then she stood next to the boy, circling the tip of her index digit around the southernmost point of Tamir.

"Uhm… What am I looking at?"

Sarene prodded him in the chest before drawing that same circle across the parchment.

"I, uh… I'm heading past this. I'm going into Franthia itself."

Swallowing her irritation, Sarene tried a different tack. She gestured to the three of them, then pointed to the edge of the forest where she believed they now camped. She then traced her finger south towards where the cabin Kanderil had marked lay, some seven days away.

"That's where you're going?"

A nod.

"So we're here?" He pointed to where her finger trail had begun.

Another nod.

"So why did you bring me west?"

"She doesn't want to be captured by anyone," Spasmodic

offered.

"Who's going to capture her?"

"Why don't you come with us and find out?"

The question came out of nowhere, surprising Sarene as well as Anthon. It still crouched on the floor, picking at its teeth with the tip of a claw. Spasmodic seemed so casual in its approach that she immediately grew suspicious. Why *would* it invite Anthon along with them?

"I'm not sure I want to get involved," said the boy. "Why are people hunting her?"

"Ever hear about the Queen of the World?"

Sarene blinked at the lack of an immediate *no*. The boy was genuinely trying to recall the term and that fact…

Well, it frightened her. Only Spasmodic had ever used it before.

"Wait," Anthon said, giving a cautious smile. "You mean what those crazy old guys yell? I come from Heston Tar. We have a man we call the Rooster, cos he's always crowing in the early morning. He babbles on about some girl who's going to end the world or something."

The creature watched Anthon with a wicked, mischievous sneer. A brief flicker of fear swept over the boy's face before it was dismissed with a disbelieving laugh, the sound as bitter as the evening chill.

"No, you're messin' with me. That old guy talks nonsense. You can't be serious about this."

Spasmodic sniggered, holding up one hand to wriggle the claws, which glowed over the fire like dark marble reflecting sunlight.

"We're goin' to find her," it said.

It took some effort for Sarene to keep her expression neutral. The look in its eye… She could read it perfectly. It was the same as when she first met it. When it declared to Kanderil that it had been created to kill her.

It was playing a game.

"I don't understand," Anthon confessed. "Why are they hunting Sarene, then?"

Spasmodic stood up. There was no slow rise; it was on its feet before either of them could blink. "See, someone started a pretty dirty rumour about poor Sarene here. She was chased out of her village by this guy – probably like your Rooster – who claimed that *she* was the one they'd been jabbering on about. All her villagers got scared and ran her off. So now word's spreadin', and people wanna kill her because they're all frightened little buggers who don't like magic. Like when Tyrrial turned up in those barracks. You heard about that, right?" Anthon nodded. "Someone uses magic to kill a few hundred people and *pffh*." It swung a claw through the air, walking towards Anthon, circling the fire. The youth took a step backwards.

Spasmodic closed in and looped an arm over the taller Anthon's shoulder. "Now she's off to a cabin to meet a fella who can hide her. Big guy, used to be in the military. I'm just her protection. That's why I punched you in the face. Thought you were one of the hunters. Can understand it, right? You show up in a forest with a loaded crossbow. Weren't nothin' personal."

Anthon looked at Sarene, who held his gaze. She was

nervous about where her dangerous companion was going with this.

"Why did you bring me with you, then?" the boy asked. "If you thought I was a threat?"

Spasmodic gave a devious grin. "Questioning. If you *were* a hunter we'd have got some information out of you. Turns out you're a stand-up chap, and that's why you're free to go. *But…*" It jabbed the tip of a claw three times in Sarene's direction. "I think what she's askin' is that if you're travellin' south, and *we're* travellin' south, then you should come with us. For her protection and for your own life story. I mean, if you ran away from home you must be lookin' for some adventures, right?"

Sarene folded her arms across her stomach, giving an idle shrug. She *did* want him to come along. There was something about the boy, something she found herself wanting to get to know. The little she knew of him had similarities to her own life. They'd both run away from home. They'd both had a destination when they left. They were both clearly inexperienced in travelling alone, despite having an idea of how to live off the land. And the way he carried himself. He was clearly nervous and perhaps even scared – especially of Spasmodic, though she couldn't fault him for *that* – but he hadn't fled or whimpered. He'd stood his ground, asked for his freedom and then intended to leave. She admired that.

But now Spasmodic was filling Anthon's head with ideas.

Anthon and Sarene looked at each other for a long time with Spasmodic smiling up at them, the tip of its tongue hooked over its lower lip like a hyena waiting to feed.

"COME ON." ETHANEI cleared his throat. Something made an ugly grating noise which made him grimace. "What were you doing in Leithar Grove?"

"I told you I am not willing to discuss that," Kanderil replied. His surly mood matched the weather.

The rain was gentle, but in the distance there was an ominous rumbling, the sound akin to a titanic boulder sliding along a quarry face. The droplets soaking them through were not yet heavy enough to make much noise on the wagon, but moisture had started to collect in the uneven wood beneath Ethanei's backside. He shifted his weight, tucking some of Sarene's cloak underneath him. The slipping hills were the only horizon. The forest they'd left behind was no longer in sight. Aside from the occasional cottage dotting the landscape there was nothing but grass, the road and the wagon. He saw smoke twirling out from a chimney maybe a half-mile to the north. Ethanei wished they could ride over and join them at the fire.

"No, come on. You ain't spoken five words to me since we started on this trip. If I have to sit here for a bloody week then you can't expect me to just twiddle me thumbs and stay quiet. I enjoy talkin'."

"I've noticed."

"So tell me. Why were you there?"

Kanderil said nothing. Ethanei wiped a hand across his wet nose. The wheels turned and the horses jangled the harness.

"Well?"

"I am not willing to discuss that."

"Oh, for…" Ethanei clapped his hands together. "Alright. Tell me about yourself."

"Would that make you feel better?"

"It'd be a start."

Kanderil shook his head. "I used to be a Sergeant in the Kalethi. I retired almost four years ago. I spend my days now in the forests, living off the land. I dislike the cities and I prefer my own company."

"Never would 'ave guessed."

"If my answer displeases you then perhaps we need not continue our con—"

"No, wait. Kanderil, I'm not your enemy, alright? I'm tryin' to help you here. I've known you for what, four days? I'm sitting here pretendin' to be a little girl 'cos you asked me to." Ethanei drew the cloak around himself, the fabric tight in his grasp now that most of it was scrunched up beneath him. "Just stop talkin' to me like I'm gonna sell off your secrets, yeah?"

Kanderil's jaw tensed. At once Ethanei felt awkward. He put this down to the fact he'd run out of firewater, his canteen having emptied the previous morning. Sober, he found social situations more difficult. He didn't feel uncomfortable as such; he enjoyed getting to know people. But without that kick of alcohol he wasn't quite as open and honest as he knew he could be. There *was* a tension in the air, one which made the journey all the more miserable.

"You are right," Kanderil said at last. "I did not mean to

seem ignorant. I appreciate what you are doing for the girl."

Ethanei believed the words were difficult for the giant to say. He shrugged. "S'alright. I guess there's a reason for all the secrecy. I mean, it's not every day someone has a pet demon, right?"

To his surprise, Kanderil chuckled. "Aye. I suppose so."

"Anyway, I won't ask questions about her no more. But about yourself. You ain't wearin' a ring in your hair. I'm guessin you never marrie—"

Something *clunk*ed. The wagon started vibrating, the wood making an awful racket. Ethanei whirled around, placing his hands on the side of the trailer and looking over. The right wheel was wobbling precariously. The horses snorted as Kanderil pulled on the reins, calling for them to stop.

The wheel caught and toppled over onto the ground.

The wagon lurched and Ethanei tried to hold himself in place, but his back legs were sent up over his head. He flipped into the air, his body folding up on himself, and almost landed on his head in the wet road. His lower back slammed into the ground, sending a jolt up his spine and emptying his lungs.

"Oof!"

Kanderil dismounted and walked around the back of the wagon, crouching down to inspect the exposed axel. "Are you ok?" he asked.

Ethanei moved all of his limbs to make sure they were working. He nodded, trying to catch his breath. He was embarrassed at being thrown from the cart by something as simple as a lost wheel, but Kanderil did not make any mention of it.

The woodsman grunted. "The axel detached. The pressure on the wheel must have broken the peg holding it in place." He got to his feet, looking down the road before taking a few steps back. He bent over to pick up a splintered piece of wood.

Getting to his feet with a wince, Ethanei pressed a hand to the small of his back. "Bugger me… Can you fix it?"

"I think so. It will take a little time. I need to fashion a makeshift peg and pound the axel back into its fixing. I suspect the rivet hole is worn down."

"Right."

The rain kept falling. Ethanei swore. His hands were covered in gritty dirt from the road, he was soaked through and he sorely needed a drink.

Kanderil reached into the back of the trailer and pulled out his huge longsword. Ethanei was still astounded by the size of it, unable to think of any way in which fighting with such a weapon would be practical, except for scything down opponents in the same way one swung an axe.

But then, he wouldn't wish to face Kanderil in combat. No, sir.

The woodsman thumped the rear end of the trailer. He then took a step back, raised the sword, and sent a sweeping cut into the planks. The blade wedged deep into the wood. Kanderil levered the blade until a section cracked and came away, rolling to the floor.

"What are you doing?" Ethanei asked, curious.

"I need wood for the peg," Kanderil replied. He picked up the wood, placed it against the wheel, and nodded. He returned the sword to the rear of the wagon and drew his knife.

"You may as well get comfortable. This could take an hour at least."

"Yeah. I'll walk around for a bit I think. Back's killin' me." Ethanei took a few steps, looking back towards the woodsman. "Hey… Those people who're watching us. Won't they be able to tell I'm not a young lass by now?"

"Either they will or they won't," Kanderil replied, whittling the section of wood in his hand. "No point worrying about it now. If it makes you feel better you can sit on the floor and try to look feminine."

Ethanei laughed into the rain as another growl of thunder passed overhead. "A joke? Who woulda known."

Kanderil smirked. "By the way. You were about to ask if I had ever been married."

"Aye, before I was dumped on my face."

"The answer is no."

Ethanei stood there, considering the best way to respond. In the end all he could think of was, "Any reason?"

"I had my career."

"Ah. Yeah, I can relate to that one," said Ethanei as he reflected upon his own choices and the effects on his marriage to Clarai. He moved around to the opposite side of the wagon and reached for his knapsack in search of something to eat.

Clarai. Oh, how he'd ruined *that* one.

THE TWO MEN watched the sheep in the field before them. In this weather most were huddled up together. The thunder spooked them. A few strays wandered about by themselves, but for the most part they were a unit. Justan knew that the woolly coats they were famed for would keep them well enough protected from the elements, but they still came together on a fierce afternoon.

The man leaning back on the fence beside him, Porun, spat to the side. He was using a length of twig to pick between his teeth. Justan puffed on a pipe, resting against the same fence, the embers flaring as he sucked in a great mouthful of thick smoke. He was sensible enough to keep the pipe slightly angled, away from the rain. Damp tobacco was useless tobacco, after all.

"'Ere," said Porun, pointing towards the sheep with his twig. "What d'you reckon they think about all day?"

"Who?" Justan replied mildly.

"Them sheep."

Justan thought about the question. He'd wondered himself. At least, he used to. Nowadays they were just stock to him, no different than a pile of hay or a plank of wood. He made his living rearing them, shearing them and herding them to market from time to time.

"Why d'you ask?" he replied, the final word coming out with an *R. Arsk.*

"I suppose you're better'n anyone else to know. You been lookin' after these sheep most o'yer life." The delivery of the explanation was lazy; bored, even. Porun never looked at him once, instead persevering with his teeth-cleaning.

Justan took another go on his pipe, blowing out smoke as he answered. "I s'pose they just think 'bout what they want next. If they wanna eat. If they wanna piss. If they're cold. If they're randy."

Porun nodded once, chewing the answer over. There was a full minute's silence before he spoke again.

"No, like. I mean, what d'they *think* about."

Justan coughed. "Y'mean thinkin'? Like we do?" *Loike.*

"Aye."

"Well." Justan glanced skyward as the wind picked up. The storm was blowing over and they were lucky it hadn't settled in. He'd lived in this small hamlet all his life, and he knew how the weather worked. Less than an hour until it'd all be dry again. Dry and cold. The cold didn't bother him; he was a heavy-set man who was used to life outdoors.

"Well," he said again. "I don't know if they can. They don't talk, do they."

"Dog's don't talk," Porun pointed out. "An' I reckon they think."

"Aye, but dogs are more brighter, ain't they. You couldn' teach a sheep t'round up other sheep. That's proof right there." *Roight.*

"Your yapper's a bright ol' dog, all right." Chuckling to himself, Porun glanced over his shoulder.

Justan turned his head, watching the slim path leading towards their collection of a dozen or so homes. A horse was approaching at speed. The two men didn't move. As the rider came closer Justan saw that he wore a deep crimson sash across his clothing.

"Is that 'im?" asked Porun.

Nodding, Justan stood. "Aye, that's 'im. Reckon we'd best get over t' birds."

Porun swung a leg over the fence, making a noise along with the exertion of effort, and dropped down beside him. They walked towards Justan's home as the rider slowed, the horse snorting. Its tail flicked back and forth as it took several steps sideways, its body no longer matching its urge to run.

The rider stepped down from the horse, holding its reins. "Do you two ever do any work?" he asked, catching his breath.

"Not on days like this," Justan replied, fumbling in his pocket for a key. "Nowt to do, is there."

"Should join us for a chat sometime," Porun put in. The rider smiled. He was a good twenty summers younger than the two men. Justan liked him. He was good-natured and had a sense of humour about him.

"So you'll be needin' your birds, then," said Justan as he moved past. His shed stood bolted onto the side of his house. It was a gift from the boy's benefactor, a chap he'd never met himself. Justan had been given the shed and five gold on top just for a bit of storage work. He placed the key into the single bolt-lock and pulled the door outward, bracing himself for the smell.

Revealed to the world was a stack of a dozen cages, each containing a pigeon. They sat cooing and clucking at each other, heads making an inquisitive jerk whenever they focused on something new. Justan's appearance excited them, and a few started to flap their wings. The cages were spacious but still restrictive enough to hamper flight. They were also, for the most part, covered in bird shit. Justan cleaned them out once in a while, but he hadn't bothered recently.

"Which one you need?"

"Thorlen Tar."

The shepherd nodded, leaning down and picking up one of the cages by a string handle. The pigeon within cooed as it was brought outside.

"Got yer note?"

"Writing it now," the boy replied. He was kneeling down with a scrap of parchment across his knee, scribbling with a length of graphite. Leaning over to satisfy his own curiosity, Justan took a look at the words as they appeared.

SARENE ALONE – SPLIT SE OF YOU – NOT SEEN E –
LOCATION UNKNOWN

The message meant nothing to him. The boy rolled the note as Justan took the bird out of the cage, holding it firmly in his strong hands, then pushed the missive into the small leather binding around the bird's leg.

"Now you go right 'ome," Porun said with a straight delivery. "Don't be mopin' about with no tarts, y'hear?"

Justan laughed, the sound low and hoarse. He tossed the bird outside and into the air where it flapped hard, fighting to gain altitude. Soon the pigeon was off, heading west, sailing through the miserable skies towards its destination.

The boy closed the door, pinching the bridge of his nose.

"You really ought to clean that out," he said with distaste.

"Aye. I'll get right on that tomorrow."

This time it was Porun's turn to laugh as Justan locked the door. *Leaving 'em to their thoughts*, he mused with a shake of the head.

Chapter Six

NICHAI STARED AT nothing. He was on his side, on the floor, in the dark. His wrists hurt. He'd learnt long ago that the binds holding him were inescapable. There would certainly be scars to prove it. A rumble came from his stomach but he had also learned to ignore this. Food came when it was given. Not when it was required.

He wanted to die, but he couldn't kill himself.

There was no indication of time in this hole in the ground. Nichai never saw the sunrise or the night draw in. There was sometimes light filtering through the floorboards but it was weak and from an unknown source. It could be the sun, or it could be the fireplace or a candle. Glaithe came and went but rarely spoke to him. The hooded woman would check on him from time to time, but in the same way that he once checked on the family dog, Bounder, when it was in its final days. She just came to see if the Regent of Tamir was breathing or not.

He stank, too. Nobody had washed him since they had arrived. The idea of a bath was wondrous to him, but he was scared of the contact which would come with it. Glaithe was a terrible person. Once considered a friend, the former Gathire Agent had taken to beating him from time to time. He was sure his nose had been broken at one stage, and the left side of his chest ached if he laid on it.

The betrayal was the worst part. He'd liked Glaithe, having judged him to be a truly dependable man. Nichai had *admired* him. And now Nichai was entirely at the mercy of that same man; a captor who was dreadful and evil and cold.

Cold. It was awfully cold in this basement.

Nichai thought of his past life, as he often did. The tears began to fall, but he did not sob. He knew that he cried a lot and that his father would disapprove, but he couldn't help it. There couldn't be anything worse in the world than his current situation. The images of his old luxury and wealth during his time as Regent haunted him. The sunny afternoons spent walking the gardens. The delicious food which he was afforded every single day. The money. The clothes. Everything he had taken for granted but had never revelled in. He was loved by the people who found enjoyment in his friendly, approachable manner. He was loved by his brother, Remelas, with whom he shared a very close relationship.

Remelas.

Nichai knew he was still alive. Glaithe had mentioned it several times, along with his plans for Nichai. What those plans entailed he could not tell, but he felt it was something big. There was a lot of planning, and Glaithe spent a lot of time at the desk beside him, writing letters and reading leather-bound tomes. There was also a lot of money stashed behind the desk in a cubby hole dug from the earthen wall. The hooded woman brought it in steadily. Where *she* got it, he had no idea.

The door above swung, the hinges groaning, and then closed again. A key turned a lock. Footsteps walked across the floor, muffled at first and then becoming clearer as they neared the entrance to the basement. Nichai recognised the sound of the bolt being pulled and then light came through, down the ladder and into the hole. Nichai squinted against it, looking up.

Glaithe dropped past the last couple of steps. The man stood there in the gloom, pulling back his hood and removing his gloves. After tucking them into his pocket he pulled a strip of matches and sparked one, the light causing Nichai to close his eyes. When he opened them again three candles had been lit and Glaithe stood before the desk.

Nichai flinched as the other man opened a drawer. That drawer meant *bad things*. Nichai was terrified of *bad things* now. Glaithe pulled out the dark bottle and the cloth. The hard, medicinal scent of the knockout liquid relaxed him somewhat. It wasn't the small, dark billy club which Glaithe used to torment him.

It was the knockout liquid. At least when Nichai slept he wasn't suffering.

Turning, Glaithe fixed his gaze on the Regent. Nichai didn't dare look back so he closed his eyes. He only opened them when he heard Glaithe kneel down beside him.

"You have a choice," he said. "Listen to me, Nichai."

Nichai said nothing.

"Nichai. Look at me." A hand on his shoulder. Nichai obeyed through fear. He didn't want a beating.

"You have a choice," Glaithe said again. "I have some news for you. How you react will dictate whether or not I put you to sleep. If you behave, I will give you some food. If you do *not* behave, then you will receive nothing until tomorrow evening. Understand?" He inspected the bottle, as though reading the label for the first time. Nichai disliked the act. They both knew full well what it was for.

Nichai nodded once, not committing to either answer. He *was* hungry.

Glaithe spoke. "Your father is dead. Remelas announced it yesterday."

The words were spoken so calmly that they didn't register at first.

"You... You're lying," Nichai whispered. His captor smiled.

"Nichai, my boy. Why would I lie? The King's death makes my life easier. Now all I have to do is deal with your brother."

Nichai met Glaithe's eyes for the first time in weeks. He was terrified of angering the man, but this news stirred him. Glaithe's expression gave no sign of deception.

Runath was dead. He would never again see his father.

He would never say goodbye.

The sense of loss lasted only seconds. All at once it came out, and Nichai *screamed.*

The Regent of Tamir screamed with fury and hatred, his eyes bulging and his throat tearing. He gnashed his teeth and ripped at his bonds, feeling new blood flow. He roared with such vehemence that he felt as though the muscles of his stomach would break apart and his neck would rupture. He fought to break free even as Glaithe clamped the cloth over his face and the bitter air of the sleeping liquid filled his lungs. Even as his vision faded he still fought, his self-pity igniting, the seed of loathing within him erupting like a barn fire.

He flailed and kicked and writhed until he fell to darkness, the image of his father dissipating into oblivion.

THE RAIN HAD eased by the next afternoon. Sarene, Anthon and Spasmodic were within a couple of miles of the next forest. The plains were flat here, winding between several huge plots of farmland. Occasionally they would pass a length of fencing, between which sheep and cows and goats would graze at the slim pickings poking out from the hard ground. Spasmodic would watch the animals, his attention entirely devoted to them in the same way a child would stare at a bowl of sugar candy.

Sarene flicked her gaze up to Anthon for a few seconds before looking away again. She wished she had her hood.

The creature's words had worked. That morning Anthon had agreed to join them, having had the night to think it over. Now assured that he was in no danger, it turned out that Anthon had a positive, self-assured nature. He spoke with modesty, polite and courteous while shedding the initial shyness he had shown. Spasmodic had been picking on him for the first few hours, but Anthon was quick-witted with his responses and refused to become a victim. The two of them were already building a rapport, which Sarene was pleased with. Ethanei had been intimidated and Kanderil was simply dismissive, so for someone to meet Spasmodic's abrasive personality with an open mind was something she identified with. She had begun to worry that it was *her* at fault for accepting Spasmodic's acerbic manner and dark humour, as if she were missing something. Now she felt more at ease about herself.

She felt better at having someone her age to travel with, also. Sarene had spent the better part of half a year with men much older than her, and she felt she could be a little more like herself instead of trying to act maturely. It was a breath of fresh air, and she found herself hoping Anthon would stop with them at Kanderil's cabin for a while after they arrived.

Sarene glanced skywards, smirking at the flint-grey clouds. *Don't get ahead of yourself.*

"Something funny?" Anthon asked. She turned her head towards him, shrugging her shoulders. As an afterthought, her mind scrambling for something to reply with, she pointed at him before tapping her temple.

Anthon's face gave a tiny twitch as he read her actions, before grinning. "My lump? Ah, it's fine. It makes me look more interesting that I probably am."

She drew up one cheek and spread her hands in a sign of reluctant agreement, before sniggering. This one he did understand, responding with a laugh which she found most pleasant.

"Say, either of you hungry?" Spasmodic blurted out.

They both turned to look at him. "I didn't think we had much food left," Anthon said.

"I'll get some." It pointed across to a gated field in the distance, where small white-grey blobs were spread across the face of a gentle hill to the west.

Waiting until the creature looked back at them, Sarene walked her fingers before pointing south.

"I'll bring it back, numpty. We don't have to go over there."

"Do you often just go and steal people's livestock?" Anthon asked, the corners of his eyes creased in humour.

"Hah. You have *no* idea."

Sarene shook her head, glancing back the way they had come.

In the distance, a group of riders were moving from east to west at speed. They had veered off the Highway, the horses tearing across open grassland. She brought up a hand to shield her eyes from the hard, pale light from above. There was a touch of reddish fabric at each one's chest. Whoever they were, they weren't Gathire.

"Should we be worried?" Anthon asked behind her. She shook her head, not wanting to alarm him.

Spasmodic spat to the side. "Maybe they want a sheep too," he said.

Sarene turned and started heading south once more. She reached out to grab Spasmodic's coat as she did, twisting the material at his shoulder to tighten her grip. The creature giggled, stumbling along with her. A faint aroma of unclean flesh touched her before the breeze picked up again. Spasmodic could *really* use a bath.

The three of them kept a brisk walk. Sarene guessed they would make it to the tree line ahead within the hour, after which they could take a break. Occasionally she would look behind her. The horses had slowed and were now cantering, close together.

"I'm gettin' a sheep once you're in the forest," said Spasmodic. "Then you two can get to know each other a bit betterrRR*Roowww!*"

Sarene twisted the coat until the collar bit into Spasmodic's neck. It shrugged her loose, tearing itself away, before firing off a dazzling laugh.

Anthon gave a noiseless chuckle, exhaling through his nose and looking away. Sarene pinched herself to keep from blushing. Spasmodic's words hadn't even been that bad – her instant reaction had probably spoken more. She looked back again to hide her grimace.

The riders had stopped.

"Look, if you want me to go have a chat with 'em, just say so." Spasmodic turned around. "Won't take a few minutes."

"Do you know what the people hunting you look like?" asked Anthon.

"Two arms, two legs, a head."

"That narrows it down."

"At least we don't worry about cripples."

Sarene encouraged them both to continue walking with a wave of her hands. Another gust of wind blew her hair across her face and ruffled her scarf, making her chin itch. She rubbed her palm across her jaw with the same movement which swept her hair away.

They only managed to walk for another minute before Anthon spoke up.

"Uh. They're coming this way."

The three of them stopped. The riders were indeed heading in their direction. As they came closer Sarene made out four people. The reddish fabric turned out to be a sash draped from right shoulder to left hip. She glanced back to the southern forest. It was too far away for them to make it in time.

"Reckon they'll split a sheep with us?" said Spasmodic with a grin.

"Are we going to stand here?" Anthon asked, a touch of concern in the words.

Sarene indicated the lack of options around them, unsure of what else to suggest.

"It's only four," Spasmodic replied.

"Four is more than three."

"Heh. You don't think much of me yet, do ya." Spasmodic rolled its shoulders and twisted its neck around to produce an audible *click*, before falling to a crouch. It leant forward, resting on one hand and pulling forward its hood with the other.

Sarene recognised the pose. She felt a little better.

The riders bore down on them. They did not draw weapons.

Anthon stepped beside her, standing his ground. Though he had lost his crossbow, there was a short-blade dagger in his hand. Sarene accepted the gesture, inspired the boy's courage.

As the group came near the lead rider pulled up. The horse slowed, stamping its feet and breathing heavily into the cold air. The rider walked the beast ahead while the other three stayed behind, forming a line.

"You there," the lead rider said, wheeling his mount around to the side. "What is your name?" He addressed Sarene directly. She glanced at Spasmodic, unable to respond.

"Who's askin'?" it said.

The rider glanced at the creature. His eyes grew wide as he noticed the claws splayed wide on the ground.

"*You…*"

"Hah, me? Who's *me*, cockend?"

"The devil that travels with the girl. Which makes her Sarene."

"You're about one word away from me rippin' your throat out, matey." Spasmodic bent at the elbow, bringing its upper body lower to the ground."

"Touch me and Kanderil dies."

Sarene's' chest tightened at the mention of Kanderil. Clapping her hands to gain the rider's attention she shook her head.

"It's true," the man continued, tugging at his sash. "He is in the custody of the Dedicant. After some… encouragement, he gave us your position. Come with us, Sarene, we will let him live."

It couldn't be true. Sarene shook her head a second time. It *couldn't* be. Kanderil would never allow himself to be captured. He was too strong, too skilled.

"Do you have any proof?" asked Anthon with a resolve which caused the rider's brow to rise.

"And who are you, whelp?"

"Kanderil is my father."

"Hah!" The rider threw his head back and laughed. The others behind him joined in. One of the horses snorted. "Kanderil has no sons. Do not test me."

"None that you know of," said Anthon.

"Must have been a runt of a woman," one of the riders at the back called. "Look at him. Barely half the giant's size."

Spasmodic stood up, walking forward. Sarene reached out to grasp his shoulder. The creature turned to look at her, its emerald eyes gleaming from the darkness afforded by its hood.

If the man was telling the truth, then Kanderil's life was in her hands. The decision she made now was vital. She had no idea who these men were nor why they wanted her, but she couldn't just brush it off. How had they known where to look for her? How did they know Kanderil's name, or the fact that he had no sons?

They had even known about Spasmodic, who hadn't even been *with* them for the last three months. Was that possible, without having acquired the information first-hand from her guardian?

The breeze picked up, whipping at her clothes and making her eyes water. She bit her lip, watching the crimson sashes rippling in the same wind.

"We do not have time to waste," the man said. "Come

with us now."

"Alright," said Spasmodic. Winking at her, it took a step backwards. "Go on, missy. Can't keep the nice gentleman waitin'."

Blinking, Sarene stared at the creature.

"Are you serious?" Anthon asked.

"Heh. Nah."

Spasmodic lunged forward, leaping for the first rider. Dreadful talons came around to meet at the man's throat, all but decapitating him before he could even make a sound. His body was dead long before it hit the ground – by which time Spasmodic had vaulted off of the horse's saddle and was in amongst the other three, who were yelling in terror.

Claws lashed, dreadlocks flew and coat-tails spun.

The riders were dead in seconds.

Anthon gasped, stepping back. The grass was now splattered with viscera and gore to match the crimson fabric strewn amongst it. Spasmodic sauntered back towards them, flicking its hands to the side. The smooth surface of the claws spat blood in dotted streams. Three of the horses bolted, but Spasmodic reached out and wrapped a wrist around one of the free reins, shoving a body out of the saddle. The wind hissed and the horse whinnied in fear. A crow cawed, shrill, in the distance.

Sarene felt acid rising from her stomach and she turned, dropped to her knees and vomited. The liquid burnt her throat and stung her gums. Taking several deep breaths to ensure that no more was to come she wiped her hand across her mouth, a strand of yellowish saliva formed as she pulled away.

She'd seen death before – more than anyone her age should have to see – but this was callous. There was no fight, no defence. The men had been torn to pieces before they'd even drawn a blade.

"Oi," Spasmodic said behind her. "Don't go all squeamish now. They were gonna take you."

"I… Did that just happen?" Anthon said, alarmed. "How did you move so fast?"

"I dunno. I just do."

"You killed them!"

"That usually happens when bits of them fall out."

"I mean…" Anthon sought for the right word as Sarene wiped her hand on the grass. "*Shit!*"

"Thaaaat's the spirit."

The dank odour of blood permeated the air now. Sarene closed her eyes against it, holding a fist to her mouth. Eventually she couldn't stand it any longer and she got up, hurrying south towards the forest, away from the scene of death she dare not look back to. Somebody spoke but she didn't pay attention to the words, which were lost in the wind. All she wanted was to get away.

Sarene's mind exploded with a flurry of images as she marched. This was it. This was her life now; isolation and violence. Tears stung her eyes, no longer a result of the lashing wind. Spasmodic's actions were a reminder that things would never be normal again. People she had never met would continue hunting her, and her companions would keep fighting them off. Jared was dead as a result. She'd lost her family too, and even the news that they were being protected had been replaced with the fear that Kanderil was in danger.

It was never going to end. Not until she was either locked away for good… or she was as dead as those four nameless men she now sought to leave behind.

A few minutes passed before she heard a horse approaching. Anthon pulled up his mount beside her.

"Hop on," he said, his expression stern. The animal tossed its head from side to side with its ears pressed flat, and he reached down to pat the beast's flank.

Sarene shook her head, wiping her sleeve across her eyes. She realised she must look a mess but she didn't care. Anthon would leave anyway. It was only a matter of time before she'd be alone again.

"Come on. We'll make better time." Offering his hand, Anthon forced a smile. With further gentle coaxing Sarene accepted it, placing a foot in the stirrup as he pulled her upwards. She slipped into the saddle behind him and wrapped her arms around his waist, laying her head on his back.

There was no self-consciousness anymore. There were bigger issues than simply making a fool of herself. A new group were in pursuit. Kanderil might be in danger.

No. Her guardian *had* to be safe. She couldn't bear the alternative.

Anthon kicked the horse on and they picked up pace. She closed her eyes, holding on tightly and hoping against hope that he would ride forever, taking her away and leaving this dreadful land and its people behind.

THEY REACHED THE forest soon afterwards. Anthon slowed their mount to a walk as they moved between the trees, which were sparse and widely spread. Beneath them the ground was a collection of packed dirt, mulch and rocks, with sickly looking plants floundering in the muted sunlight. Tall trees, white-barked and patchy, reached skywards with thin branches streaming out like cobwebs.

The horse was a fine animal, taking the weight of the pair without much effort. It was no longer spooked, and obeyed Anthon's commands. The boy was a good rider, his control of the animal confident. Sarene watched the passing scenery, her head still laid against Anthon's back. Her cheeks had dried and she, like the gelding, had calmed during the ride.

"Psst," came a voice from above. She looked up to see Spasmodic sitting in the bough of a tree. It waved down at them.

"How did you get up there?" Anthon asked.

"Never you mind, nosey."

Sarene glared at the creature. It craned its neck, peering down at her.

"Stopped cryin' yet, chicken?" it asked, dropping down to the ground and landing easily, despite having fallen at least fifteen feet.

Gripping the rear of the saddle with both hands, Sarene swung her leg around to slip to the floor. She stormed towards the creature, who laughed at her.

"Look," it said, raising its hands. "Before you shove me or kick me or do something else sweetly violent, don't you start thinkin' I ain't thought about this."

Shaking, Sarene halted in front of it.

"C'mon, girly. You think Kanderil would have been kidnapped by those idiots?" It laughed that high-pitched laugh. "Even if he had, you think he'd have spilled? The guy talks about as much as *you* do. If they put his bollocks in a vice, he'd probably just grunt. He's been gone for what, three days? They ain't gonna capture him, carry him off somewhere, torture him and then send out a group of blokes to pick you up that quickly. He's a boring bugger, but he ain't a wimp."

Biting her tongue, Sarene turned away, tugging hard at a thumb. What Spasmodic had done was vicious. Effortlessly murdering four men like it had was frightening. But it was defending her from more would-be kidnappers, something it had always sought to do. She was scared for Kanderil and she wanted to know for sure that he was safe. Shaking her head again she turned and strode back towards the horse, resolute.

"So what do we do now?" asked Anthon.

"Dunno. Are you stickin' around, kid?"

Sarene stared up at Anthon, brushing hair behind her ear. Their gaze met. She was too upset to offer any fake expression and her eyes were open and honest. He gave her a smile and leaned forward on the saddle, folding his arms across the pommel.

"I'm getting the feeling that there's more to this than either of you are letting on."

Placing a hand on the saddle, Sarene pursed her lips at the words.

"Maaaybe," cooed Spasmodic. "But then there'd be no mystery otherwise, would there?"

"Who's Kanderil?"

"A bloke we know. Big bugger. He's helping protect her as well." The creature wiggled its claws at Sarene.

"And you think he's safe?"

"Hah. Trust me, if you met the guy?" The creature pulled up its hood. "He's fine. Now if you're stayin', I'm gonna have a look around to make sure there's no more of them kidnappers nearby." It held the hood up from its face, pinching the fabric between two deadly tips.

Anthon sat up straight once more. "Are we still going south, Sarene?"

A firm nod was his reply.

"Alright. Hop on."

Sarene did as obliged, clambering back up behind Anthon. This time she did not cling to him, instead placing one hand behind her to grip the saddle. Glancing across at Spasmodic, she started gesturing to indicate it should be back soon.

The creature was already gone.

A CARRIAGE ROLLED down the dark street, illuminated by the lamp which hung from a pole attached to its roof, pulled by two horses which had long since passed their prime. The wheels lacked any suspension, so the ride would be uncomfortable at best.

Niallya stepped from a doorway and into the street as it passed. Her black clothing and broad hood lent her a wraith-like appearance; a figure from stories told to misbehaving children. As ever, her curved blade was prominently displayed at her hip. Ghellei knew her by now. The inhabitants of this stinking town were wary in her presence. When she first arrived some six years ago, she was regarded as easy meat. She'd been picked on and insulted by the predominantly male underground, the criminals and outlaws she sought to work with. They had soon learned that Niallya was not a woman to be crossed.

Maiming those who laid an unwanted hand on you was a strong deterrent.

Nowadays only those who saw her as an equal earned her respect and those who had her respect were allowed certain liberties. Niallya was not unreasonable, and the kind of banter her associates took part in came with the reputation she had picked up. She was not without a sense of humour. It was simply that fools irritated her.

Like the one standing at the front door of the gambling den. A tall, boorish thug of a man named Thurm. The bully's thick arms were covered with tattoos of varying quality. Tattoos were rare in Tamir, and Thurm felt it made him more intimidating. Niallya always thought they made him appear in need of a bath.

Looking up as Niallya approached, Thurm's face lit up into a frightful sneer. The gesture made him look more idiotic than threatening.

"Evenin', girl. Come to say 'ello, eh?"

"Not to you," Niallya replied, heading straight for the door. She held out a hand to push it open, but her entrance was barred when one of those ink-scarred arms pressed across the doorway.

"Aww. That's not very nice, is it?"

With her hood arching as far over her head as it did, Niallya could not see the man's face at this tight proximity. She didn't need to. The words came next to her ear, which suggested Thurm was leaning down towards her. The foul breath which tickled her nostrils hinted that he was still smiling.

"Do you want something, Thurm?"

"Well, now. That's an offer I can't refuse."

Niallya gave a pointed sigh. "Do you want something that doesn't involve a childish joke about sex, for once?"

The den's bouncer gave a low, rumbling laugh. That breath assailed her senses. "Who said anything about a joke? What say you and me take a walk down that alley there, and you can give me five minutes o' personal time." A coarse finger trailed down her bare arm. "You wouldn't even need to take yer hood off."

By the *Four*, this man was insufferable. Though Thurm had been crude towards her many times, this was the first instance he'd dared to touch her. Niallya turned a half-step to break the thug's contact with her skin. She raised a hand to point across the street.

"That alley there?" she asked.

"Aye, that's what I was thinkin'."

Giving a throaty laugh, Niallya looked down to the man's crotch, where there was already a distinct bulge. Despite her revulsion she laid a hand against Thurm's upper leg, drawing her touch slowly towards his swelling.

"Why trouble ourselves?" she said. "I'm sure you would want your friends to *see* me in action. Why not let me tend to you right here…"

"Well." Thurm's response slithered like an eel. He coughed. "Whatever you think best, girl."

Niallya moved her hand to his groin, pressed her palm against him and then *twisted* with all her might, digging her fingertips into the arrangement of soft and hard flesh. Something slid against her knuckle, something she was certain wasn't meant to move in *that* direction.

The bouncer could only freeze, his entire body becoming rigid. His breath escaped in tiny gasps, as though scared that any further movement would increase the mind-numbing pain which had quite literally gripped him.

"The only reason you're alive now is because of Kraye," Niallya whispered. "If you *ever* touch me again you'll discover what it's like to swallow your own testicles."

Thurm didn't respond until she rotated her hand a few degrees more, at which point there was a taut, hasty nod. Her grip released as she moved to push open the door, revealing the sound of drunken laughter and rolling dice.

"You *bitch!*" Thurm roared after her even as he fell to his knees. "I'll have you one day! Y'can swear on it! Even if I—"

The noise was cut off by the door slamming behind her. Niallya moved for the stairs, giving a brief glance over the den.

Under Tamir law, organised gambling was illegal. It was too corrupt and almost impossible to regulate. Casual gambling was allowed, though – a game of dice between a group of friends was seen as a common pastime. The general way of utilising this loophole was to set up a tavern and use the claim that all the tables just happened to be playing a friendly round of six-drop. The added bonus was that the gamblers were likely too sloshed by the end of the night to notice they were being fleeced.

This main room was dark, smoky and claustrophobic. Hunting trophies had been nailed to the walls, animals which may have once been something to display but were now tattered, mouldy shapes of skin and stuffing. Three of the five tables were running games, the playing area scattered with drinks and coin. All the customers were men, and each of them had an air of poverty about them, dressed in shabby clothing with unkempt hair. Gambling dens often attracted the dregs of any city, those looking to make a quick bit of coin with the least amount of effort.

A dreadful-looking woman leaned over the counter, wiping a dirty cloth around without enthusiasm. It took a few moments to realise that she couldn't have been much older than Niallya, but the weight of her situation was aging her terribly. Her blouse was unbuttoned to reveal a heavy bosom, propped up with a corset underneath.

Niallya ascended to the upper floor where Kraye would be waiting.

A SEVERE LOOKING man opened the door for her. Niallya stepped into a room which contrasted drastically with the den, moving between two more burly thugs who flanked the inside of the doorway. A broad desk dominated the room, the thing much bigger than it needed to be for the quill and ledgers upon it. Two empty seats were on the side of the desk closest to her, small and simple but well made. A wide window ran across of the wall to her right, looking out onto the murky street. Four curved lanterns lit the room. A wolfskin rug lay across the floor, the condition much better than the hunting trophies downstairs. It was clean, lacking any sign of wear.

In one corner a man worked at an easel. A large canvas had been turned into a picture of Ghellei's abandoned church, which had once been used as a place to worship the Four. The artwork was good. Great, even. With the tip of a brush tapping at a grey-blue section of sky, darkening the edge of a cloud, the man spoke with academic eloquence.

"Niallya. Please, make yourself at home."

Standing in the centre of the room, Niallya placed her hands behind her back and waited as the man worked. He wore a fine silk shirt of clean white, beneath suspenders holding his loose-fitting grey slacks in place. Niallya noted a matching jacket hanging from a hook behind the easel.

"Can I interest you in a drink, my dear?"

"No. Thank you."

A nod. The brush dabbed a little longer. Eventually he stepped backwards, sighing. Looking around to Niallya he gestured with his palette towards the canvas.

"What do you think?"

"You are skilled."

"Oh, I know *that*. I meant what do you think of the picture? What does it *say* to you?" The man's greying hair, long but combed back tightly against the scalp, matched his squared jaw and bushy moustache. His spectacles caught one of the lamps and flared up, hiding his eyes behind shining glass.

Niallya scrutinised the painting. "I'm no art critic, but I do appreciate the realism of your work. The scale seems consistent and the colours blend well."

The artist turned to the picture, as if searching for the truth in her words. Eventually he nodded, satisfied.

Allowing a faint smile, Niallya waited as the brush and palette were put away.

Kraye, the most powerful man in Ghellei, moved to a cabinet on the left wall, from which he produced a dark clay bottle.

"Now. To what do I owe the pleasure of this visit?"

"I'm looking for someone," said Niallya. "A man named Heiran. I believe he's somewhere in Ghellei."

"Yes, I know him. Hell of an eye, can handle a crossbow better than most." Kraye poured himself a measure of amber liquid which carried the strong aroma of whisky. "Why do you need him?"

"I have a job offer for him."

Kraye looked up over his spectacles, re-corking the bottle. "Anything I would be interested in?"

"I doubt it," Niallya replied. "I've been offered a place in a party heading towards the eastern border. There is talk of possible incursions into Tamir territory by Carthlei bandits."

"Rather patriotic for a mercenary group."

"The work is hardly for national security. Carthleid horses are stronger than the Tamir breed. They'll fetch a good price."

"Hm." Kraye placed the bottle on the desk before sipping from his glass. "Seems an awfully long way to go for a few extra silvers on the saddle."

Niallya shrugged. "I am tired of Ghellei. Men like your Thurm can only be taken in small doses."

Chuckling, Kraye nodded. "I can understand. A trim figure like yours must attract all sorts of attention, regardless of what horrors await beneath that cowl."

"The attention bothers me less than the stench," she said in return, glancing over her shoulder at the two men standing watch. Neither of them said anything. *Might as well be statues,* she thought.

Kraye twirled the whiskey around in the glass. "I have work of my own to offer, girl. I like you. You're intelligent, skilled and arrogant. You'd do well working for me."

"I've worked for you in the past," Niallya pointed out.

"Psh. You've extorted a handful of traders and robbed on the Highway for me. I'm talking a *real* job."

"Flattering."

"More than that, my dear." Kraye motioned towards the window with his glass, the liquid within swirling around. "This city is a cesspool. It reeks of corruption and poverty, with the majority of the population barely able to keep a roof over their heads and food on the table. Yet in just under a decade I have enough gold in my coffers to retire by the mountains and buy a mansion full of servants and concubines if I wished it. If I moved to Tamiran I expect I could triple my profits. Should I choose to make the jump, I'll need skilled employees."

"Should you choose to make the jump then seek me out. Until then I prefer to find my own employment. Away from Ghellei, so I will not affect you in any way." This was not the first time she'd been offered a permanent role in the underworld. The idea of spending too long in one place was tiring to her, though. Her two months with Glaithe was already stretching her patience, but the payoff *there* would be more than she could ever gain elsewhere.

One did not turn down an invitation to uphold a contract from the Four.

Kraye nodded. "As you wish. Anyway, what was his name…? Heiran. Why do you need him for your little trip?"

"Our ambushes will be set up along the edges of the Laysine Mountains. A good bowman would give us an advantage amongst so much cover."

"Indeed he would." Kraye sat down in his chair, giving a loud sigh as air puffed out from the cushion beneath him. "Though, I doubt he will want to come along for such a long journey."

Quirking a brow, Niallya inclined her head back. "Why?"

"Heiran suffers from a deep depression. Anger, too. His wife died of lung rot some months back and he fell to pieces. I have offered him work from time to time and he doesn't say a word."

"I want him for his skills. Not his company."

Kraye levelled his gaze at her. The look was disconcerting and she shifted her weight in a subtle gesture of deference. Her reply had been short, and she chided herself for not watching her tone.

"Be that as it may," the gang lord said. "You'll have a time convincing him to go. And the information of his whereabouts will cost you five silvers."

The price was high, but Niallya had come prepared. She felt for the coins in her purse and stepped forward, placing them on the table. Kraye reached over to pick one up for inspection.

"He's in the south-town. Holed up two doors to the right of the blacksmith there; Fuller is the name, I believe. When Heiran isn't running errands for me he spends his days locked up in his room. He is not currently in my employ, so there should be little trouble finding him."

"My thanks, Kraye." Niallya offered a graceful bow.

The grey-haired man sipped at his drink, taking a moment to enjoy the flavour. "You are telling the truth about your reasons for visiting him, aren't you?"

"Of course."

"Then I can expect to hear of a party heading east in the near future...?"

"Within the next ten days." That much was true. There *was* a raiding party leaving Ghellei next week. She'd done her groundwork beforehand.

"Good. I'd like one of the Carthleid horses, should you

find a mark."

"I'll pass that on to the ringleader."

"And whom might that be?"

Niallya smiled, prepared for the question. "The man's name is Kanderil. A former Kalethi gone rogue."

"Kanderil… Can't say I've heard of the man."

"He usually operates out of the south. Tries not to make any one town a home."

"Interesting. Is he in Ghellei?"

"No. We are waiting for word of his movement and will then ride to meet him. He does not like to enter cities already under control, lest he cause any trouble."

Kraye gave an approving look, sipping at the whiskey before hissing between tight lips. "An honourable gesture, if somewhat pointless."

"Quite." Niallya bowed once more. "Forgive me, but I should be going. I would like to speak with Heiran at first light."

"Of course."

As she turned, her footsteps changing from muffled by fur to prominent on wood, one of the guards rapped on the door. The third man posted outside opened it. Niallya paused in the doorway, looking down the staircase.

"One final thing. If Thurm touches me again I will be forced to kill him. Please advise him of this."

Kraye laughed, slapping at the desk. "I'll tell him, but it won't do much good. The lumbering bastard's only good for making sure our customers pay their tabs. He's rather lacking in wit."

"Then I would advise searching for a replacement soon."

"I'll bear that in mind, my dear. Thank you for being so honest with me."

Niallya stepped through the door without another word, descending the stairs and wondering what Thurm's reaction would be when she stepped back onto the street.

Chapter Seven

SARENE SAT BEFORE the campfire, its flames dancing beneath the starless sky. The white bark of the trees around them reflected the fire. Sarene felt claustrophobic. Beyond the ghostly outlines of birch she could see nothing, as though the rest of the world had floated away.

Her eyes were drawn to Anthon by the *clunk* of a plate being shoved into a bag. He had prepared a meal for them after foraging around the nearby area for ingredients. The food had been basic but pleasant. They hadn't shared more than a few words since deciding to camp for the night. Spasmodic was patrolling the area around them to ensure they were safe to grab some sleep. It had been two days since the riders had found them, and the creature was being unexpectedly vigilant.

She huffed. More likely it was just seeking further victims.

Anthon looked up. "Something the matter?"

Shaking her head, Sarene offered a smile.

"You sure? I mean, you haven't really spoken about what happened."

Sarene watched him, waiting. One corner of her mouth creased up.

Turning his head and leaning back, Anthon swore. "Sorry, I mean… I didn't mean anything."

She grinned, shaking her head and inviting him to sit with her. He'd done all the work this evening and Sarene felt a little guilty at not helping. Anthon lowered himself to the ground nearby, crossing his legs. Not *too* close, she noted, but within a distance which seemed companionable.

"What I meant was, y'know. Spasmodic's been chatting away with you, and you've been smiling and moving your hands. I mean gesture—" Anthon laughed then, thumbing his nose. "Look, can I just say talking or do you not like that?"

Sarene gave him a thumbs-up, amused.

"Alright. Good. You've been talking to us, but are you *okay*? You were pretty shaken up when we rode away from those men. I don't think it's something you should just shrug off."

Narrowing her eyes, Sarene studied the boy's face to gauge his meaning. Anthon held up his hands as though he understood this.

"I mean, I'm not saying you *couldn't* shrug it off. I'm not one of these people who thinks all girls are fragile little daisies."

She considered shrugging, just to tease him. Instead she poked her lower lip with her tongue, considering the best way to convey her feelings. He wasn't yet very good at understanding her particular kind of speech. Slowly, Sarene pressed a fingertip to her temple. Then she offered another thumbs up. When Anthon nodded for her to continue, she laid a hand over her heart before lifting her fists to her eyes, scrunching up her face and jarring her shoulders to mimic crying.

Anthon copied her actions, his lips moving as he ran the sentence over. It was cute of him, a sign that he really *wanted* to listen.

"You're upset by it, but you're able to cope," he said at last.

The words were rewarded with a firm nod.

"Whew." That captivating smile. "Glad I got that one."

Sharing a moment of comfortable silence, Sarene inspected her dirty fingernails. She had an abrupt worry that she had been staring, so the girl made a point of not looking back until he spoke again.

Which he did within seconds. "You're tougher than you look"

Sarene raised her head to give him a quizzical glance.

"What I mean is not many people your age could just get on with things." A pause. "How many summers are you, anyway?"

She showed all fingers and thumbs, followed by three fingers on each hand.

"Sixteen?"

A nod.

"I was right then." Anthon grinned. "One younger than me. But what happened was rough, so don't feel bad."

Sarene held up two fingers before her eyes, after which

she curled her hands around her throat and lolled her tongue from the side of her mouth, closing her eyes. She opened them again when she heard Anthon speak.

"Is that your sign for dead people…?"

Another nod.

"Right. So… you saw it coming?"

A shake of the head.

"You… uhm. You've seen dead people before?"

Quickly, Sarene draw a finger across her throat.

"You've seen people being *killed* before."

The response made her think of Jared. Sarene nodded, but this time she didn't feel quite as engaged with the impromptu guessing game. She closed her eyes to push the unpleasant memory away.

"See, you're doing that thing again."

She opened one eye and peered at him.

Anthon pressed his hands into his thighs, considering the next words. "It's kinda like what my pa used to do. He'd talk about stuff and answer my questions, but he'd never really be honest, y'know? He'd only ever give replies which fit the question. He never opened up."

Sarene blinked. They'd only met a few days ago. She felt it a little presumptuous for him to ask her to *open up*. But then again, what would be the harm? She wanted someone to talk to, after all. That's why she'd insisted on bringing Anthon and Ethanei along in the first place.

You've been with Kanderil for too long, she thought to herself.

Carefully, over the next few minutes, Sarene was able to

convey to the boy that she was tired of being chased. She repeated that she'd seen people being killed – with focus she continued gesturing through her mind's image of Jared – and that such events were becoming all too common in her life. Using her map she bounced her finger from forest to forest, emphasising that she'd done nothing but travel for the last few months. Anthon took this all in with no other comment except to clarify her meaning.

She couldn't reveal the *true* nature of her situation. Not yet, at least. This ridiculous notion that she was the Queen of the World would surely just frighten him off.

When she was done, Sarene folded the map and put it away. Anthon tossed another couple of sticks onto the fire, which released dense smoke as the moisture in the wood boiled away. The light dampened briefly before coming back stronger.

"I can't imagine how you might feel," he confessed. "But I appreciate you telling me. I may only be good for cooking the occasional meal, but until we reach your cabin I'll help in any way I can."

Sarene gave a broad smile. The offer was endearing. She remembered how he'd stood next to her when the riders had approached, his small knife in hand. Anthon had made a few self-depreciating comments during the last couple of days about how he was no fighter, but Sarene doubted it. He didn't seem like a coward. He also hadn't seemed nervous during the… well, *fight* was the wrong word. Massacre, perhaps. Whatever it was, this ranger's son had stood his ground when he could have fled.

She reached out to pat him on the knee, bowing her head in thanks. Before he could react Spasmodic appeared beside the fireplace. His sudden presence made her jump, withdrawing her hand back to her lap.

"No one's around. I reckon you're safe." The creature paused, sniffing as it looked from human to human. "Did I interrupt summat?"

Sarene's cheeks flushed. It *hadn't* interrupted anything, but the suggestion made her feel guilty.

"She was telling me what a good job you're making of looking after her," said Anthon without missing a beat.

"Aww." Spasmodic leaned towards her as it dumped itself on the floor beside the fire, scrunching its face up in a mockery of the compliment. "In't that nice."

"So what now?" asked Ethanei.

The wagon rolled along the road leading to the western gate of Tamiran. The immense pale walls which surrounded the city, acting like a barrier to prevent the guts of the capital spilling across the land, had been visible for miles. The red flag of Tamir streamed at the two gate posts, the golden lion roaring in the centre whenever the biting wind revealed it.

"Now we find out if our little ruse has been discovered," Kanderil replied.

They had spent the last week as planned; camping out of sight, away from the Highway and out of the roadside taverns and inns. The extra hour of travel each morning and evening had added a day to their total journey, but that was of no concern. Once the initial unease of being separated from Sarene had passed, Kanderil found that he enjoyed the week. While Ethanei could be irritating at times he was by no means a terrible travelling companion. The vagrant had shared tales about his time in the cavalry, which Kanderil could relate to. In turn he'd found himself talking about events in the Kalethi which he hadn't recalled for years. Now that Ethanei had sobered up for long enough to break free from his hangover, the man revealed a keen sense of humour. Free from his responsibilities to the girl for the time being, Kanderil had relaxed enough to appreciate the wry observations and coarse jokes.

As they approached the western gate Kanderil saw the two guards in their full dress uniform of lacquered breast-plates, red cloaks and plumed helmets. Standing beside one of them was a man attired in the black and silver of the Gathire.

"They are expecting us, at least," said the woodsman.

"Does this mean I can stop pretending to be a little lady now?"

"I see no reason why not."

"Good. I was starting to get self-conscious about me hips, y'know."

Kanderil smiled. Already he could hear the sounds of the city. Shouts and calls blended with the constant pounding of a hammer against wood. An elderly woman wandered out of the gate with a donkey in tow, a young girl sitting on the back of the beast. Kanderil ignored the stare he received from both of them.

Pulling on the reins as they reached the gate, the wagon ground to a halt. The Gathire Agent walked towards them, offering a polite nod of the head which Kanderil did not return.

"Good afternoon, Kanderil. Sarene. My name is Veilen. I have been asked to escort you to the House of Tamir."

"I would have preferred an hour to find some fresh clothing and a bath," Kanderil replied.

"Perhaps afterwards. Remelas is eager to meet you. It has been quite a week, after all." The Agent was staring at the back of the wagon.

"How so?"

Veilen looked up at him. "His ascension."

Ethanei turned around and stared at the Agent. "Ascension? What happened?"

The revelation of the man's face behind the mauve hood produced an expression from the Agent which Kanderil deeply enjoyed.

To his credit, Veilen did not fail in his reply. "You mean you haven't heard of Runath's death? Eight days ago. Remelas announced his passing to the city the next day."

Kanderil's satisfaction was short lived. "We had not heard."

"Bugger me…" Ethanei muttered behind him.

"The coronation was five days ago. You'll be meeting our newly crowned King."

The news changed things. Kanderil had received his message to meet with Remelas before the death of the man's father. The fact that he was still expected – and with apparent urgency – made his summons all the more intriguing.

"Would you mind having someone take care of our wagon?" Kanderil asked. "Driving it through the streets would be a tiresome chore."

"Of course. I will send for someone right away."

Stepping down from the driver's seat, Kanderil moved to the trailer and began gathering his things, strapping his weapons and filthy cloak into place. Ethanei stretched his legs with a deep sigh of relief, hopping over the edge of the cart to stand beside the Agent.

"Sorry," he said, studying Veilen's stoic features. "Were you expectin' someone else?"

"Perhaps."

"Well I'm sad to disappoint, like. Can only offer what I were born with, eh."

"Indeed." Veilen glanced up as Kanderil returned carrying his huge bow. "Is this man of importance? I doubt Remelas would approve of a stranger gracing the steps of the House."

"I'll wipe me shoes," Ethanei fired back, irritated by the man's condescending delivery.

"He travels with me for now."

"I see." The Agent folded his arms behind his back. "I had been informed that Sarene would be travelling with you."

"Not currently," said Kanderil. He stepped past without another word, crossing the threshold into the sprawling, cramped city. His feet sank into the filth covering the cobblestones and his nostrils were assailed by the stench of the wet markets. Already his skin was crawling.

Kanderil *hated* Tamiran.

THE THREE OF them walked along West Junction Road, past the permanent stalls and the various shops and boutiques. The western quarter of the city was not the slum-ridden area of its southern neighbour, but it still had an air of depression. Here and there the terraced homes gave way to a larger construct of some significance. The Tamir National Library was here, a broad building with a domed roof which contained most of the oldest texts still existing in the country. Further along sat one of the University blocks. Each quarter of Tamiran had one block for the teaching of higher education. The West Block's flag was chequered red and white, remarkably spotless considering the foul weather of the last few days. At the front of the block's entrance were two carved gryphons, mythical beasts which had been lauded as possessing both wisdom and power.

Kanderil's mind went to Spasmodic, potentially the only mythical creature in existence, and smiled.

"How's everyone handlin' the news?" Ethanei asked the back of Veilen's head. The Agent glanced over his shoulder before replying. Kanderil noted that the three of them were receiving wary looks from passers-by. The woodsman's size alone would have drawn attention, but the addition of a Gathire brought more than a little suspicion. The Gathire were almost universally distrusted and evidently things had not changed during the last few years.

"As well as can be expected," Veilen replied. "Runath's

passing could not have happened at a more inopportune time. The majority of the people have accepted the coronation of Remelas, as good citizens should, but there have been some demonstrations in the streets from those still sour about Leithar Grove."

"Can't blame 'em."

"Actually, you can. Tamir is experiencing a period of turmoil. The citizens would do well to remember their place and draw together as one. We do not need dissension amongst the public at what must be a very difficult time for the new King and the bereaved Royal Mother."

"Wait a minute. Whaddya mean, *'remember their place'*?" Ethanei stepped forward to catch up to the Agent, but Kanderil held out a hand to hold him back.

"Protesting the tradition of the House of Tamir helps nobody." Veilen glanced to his left at a group of children, who averted their eyes. "And watch your tone with me, stranger."

Kanderil shook his head at Ethanei, who pulled himself free of the huge hand at his shirt.

SHORTLY VEILEN HAILED a carriage which taxied them the rest of the way. They reached the House of Tamir within the hour. After a brief inspection from one of the Royal Guards, the gates opened and the carriage rode along the white gravel path leading to the front entrance, the wheels *crunch*ing the small stones. A servant opened the door to let the occupants out. A huge fountain acted as the focal point for the enclosed area, a stone lion roaring at the sky as water bloomed from its mouth. Around the path were tall hedgerows and evergreen trees which were obviously tended to by a loving hand, all perfect angles and tidy lengths.

Ethanei paused to take in his surroundings, bringing a hand to the back of his neck. "Coo. Not every day a couple o' grunts like us get to see how it looks from this side o' the gate."

"If you will follow me," said Veilen as the driver urged the horses on again, pulling the carriage back towards the gate.

The three of them continued towards the front entrance of the House of Tamir. The steps were hard and smooth. When Kanderil arrived here years earlier for his Valour medal there had been a carpet fitted against each step. He presumed this had been removed to keep the rain from ruining the fabric.

Moving past the thick columns holding the front balcony up over heavy oak doors, Kanderil stepped into the House. The foyer was broad and spotless, pale marble flooring furnished with a heavy maroon rug. Several large paintings of previous generations of the Royal Family were evenly spaced along the walls, each bordered with a golden frame; above these were vast, circular windows. A staircase rose up to a middle balcony which then separated off towards the two main wings of the building. The arched doorways either side of the room were closed.

A butler, resplendent in waistcoat and tailored pants, stepped to meet them, a critical eye running over the two men standing behind the Agent.

"May I help you?" he asked.

Veilen spoke. "The man behind me is Kanderil. He has an appointment with the King."

"Of course. Please wait here." The butler turned and made his way up the majestic staircase, his posture rigid even as he ascended the carpeted steps.

Ethanei hesitantly wandered forward. "Imagine living 'ere," he said.

Kanderil folded his arms. "Nervous?"

"Me? Yeah, a little."

"PERHAPS YOU CAN have a tour while I am meeting with Remelas," said Kanderil.

"Oh, aye. I don't expect I'll be comin' in with you, will I."

"No."

"Right. Well how about it, Gathire? Fancy showin' me 'round?" The vagrant waved a dirty hand towards one of the closed doors.

"I have business elsewhere," Veilen replied calmly.

Sighing, Ethanei walked over to one of the portraits. The clothing and hairstyles suggested several generations had passed since it had been painted. The King sat upon the throne like a bear, all broad shoulders and full beard, surrounded by three children; two daughters and one son. The son was barely a toddler, but he wore the ruby amulet which had been handed down to each successive Prince. The two elder daughters sat with stern faces before their mother, a slender woman with greying hair.

"These things ain't labelled," Ethanei pointed out as he

leaned in closer.

"Do you label paintings of your family?" asked Veilen.

"*My* family couldn't afford paintin's. Who's gonna paint a family livin' out in the sticks?"

"A valid point."

The butler returned, standing at the balcony and looking down at the three guests below.

"King Remelas will see you now."

Veilen turned and offered a crisp bow. "Enjoy your stay in Tamiran, Kanderil." Without a second glance to Ethanei, the Agent made his way back outside. Ethanei muttered something coarse beneath his breath.

THE BUTLER TURNED his head often as he led the two guests into the right wing of the House, as if expecting them to wander off. Not that there was anywhere to become lost. The inner chambers of the House consisted of long corridors with few junctions. Here and there were touches which served as a reminder that this was a *home* as well as the centre of the Tamir government. A potted plant. A sofa beside a veranda door. A small table with a book laid upon it, a mark slipped between the pages, waiting for the reader to return. There was a lack of people, though. Kanderil had presumed the House would be full of servants and staff, but aside from the butler there was nobody to be seen.

Ethanei picked up on this as well. "I've seen more crowding in an antique shop."

"Perhaps the staff remain below stairs," Kanderil offered.

"Yeah, but what 'bout the guards? Surely there'd be some

protection or summat."

"Did you forget the amount of security around the entrance?"

With a shrug, Ethanei sniffed. "Only takes one person to sneak in, like."

The butler stopped before a panelled door, knocking against it three times. A voice came from within, and the butler turned to them.

"The King will see you now, Kanderil. Perhaps your friend would like to wait here." The man extended a hand to present a high-backed chair pushed against the wall.

Ethanei grinned. "Yeah, s'alright. Wouldn't wanna cause a fuss." He moved over to the seat and made a point of brushing it down, as though preparing the cushion for his dirty clothing. The butler endured this with seasoned tolerance.

Kanderil stepped forward as the door opened. He found himself in what appeared to be a meeting chamber. Though not huge, the room was spacious enough for a long table surrounded by eight chairs. A large tapestry pinned to the wall displayed a huge map of the Tamir lands. A small door led to a modest balcony which overlooked the sprawling Royal Gardens. A third closed exit presumably connected this room to the one next door.

The new King of Tamir sat at the table. He seemed utterly fatigued, with eyes which sunk back into his skull and a jawline which hadn't seen a razor for several days. His thick, hazelnut hair was in need of a wash and hung in rat-tails from his scalp. To his left sat Chalimer, the Justicar of the

Gathire, his vulture-like features fixed on the woodsman as he entered the room.

"Kanderil," said Remelas, rising to offer a hand in greeting. Kanderil took it, noting the man's firm grip. "You are a sight for sore eyes, my friend."

"Sore eyes which could use some rest," Kanderil replied. "You look like you have not slept for an age."

Remelas chuckled. "I completely agree, Sergeant, but there has been an awful lot to attend to these past few days."

"I can imagine." A moment's consideration brought a light pause to Kanderil's next words. "Please accept my condolences for your bereavement."

"Thank you. It has been a very trying time for us here at the House. My father was loved by all."

"He was a strong leader," said Kanderil.

"Indeed he was." Remelas exhaled to draw the subject to a close. Kanderil suspected he had exchanged similar words with scores of well-wishers over the past week. The King returned to his seat, gesturing to Kanderil to join him at the table. "How is Sarene?"

"She was fine when last I saw her."

Chalimer raised a brow but said nothing. The man's presence was less than welcome, but it was unsurprising to find him here with them. Kanderil locked eyes with the man, who stared back undaunted before turning to listen to the King speak on.

"I am glad. It must have been a terrible season for her."

"You could say that," Kanderil replied. "She recently received your note, informing her of the guards protecting her family. The girl asked me to convey her thanks."

Remelas bowed his head. "It was the least I could do. I have ensured that Jared's grave will remain untouched during the rebuilding of the barracks."

"I did not know they would be rebuilt."

"Oh, yes. I could not let those ruins serve as a reminder of what Tyrrial did to us. I intend to have the place restored to its former glory by next summer."

Kanderil locked his fingers together and leant forward. The first thought that struck him was that rebuilding a military building in the face of the *reasons* for Tyrrial's violent response was audacious.

What he said was, "A bold move."

"I like to think so."

There was a temporary halt in conversation as Kanderil waited for the King to bring up the reason for his summons. When no such explanation appeared forthcoming, he offered a subject of his own.

"Have you heard of a group named the Sons of Tamir?"

Remelas nodded. "I have been informed of their existence, yes."

"They seek an audience with you."

"So I hear."

"From the speech I overheard their leader give, they seem to be winning over the general public. Have you given any consideration on how to respond?"

A light shake of the head. Remelas sighed. "To be honest with you, Kanderil, I have enough to handle right now within the House. These Sons of Tamir can roam the country as much as they like while they avoid causing trouble, which as much as I understand they are…?" He sought confirmation from Chalimer.

"For now," said the Justicar.

"Should they ever appear at my front gates I will consider granting them an audience. Goodness knows my reputation could use a lift in the eyes of my kingdom. Perhaps a discussion with this new faction will help me to do that."

Kanderil nodded. There was another momentary silence. The King seemed unhurried, and Chalimer said nothing. "Shall we get to business?"

"How do you mean?" Remelas replied.

"You requested my presence."

Chalimer raised a fist to his mouth, clearing his throat. "Actually, it was I who asked you to return to the capital, Sergeant."

Now it was Remelas's turn to raise an eyebrow. "Why?"

"I felt it best for us to have a discussion about Sarene."

Kanderil narrowed his eyes, his jaw drawn tight. "About what, exactly?"

"She is of great importance to the King, Kanderil. I had hoped you would bring her to the capital with you, but it appears you had other plans."

"I dislike being observed by your men," the woodsman growled.

Chalimer leaned back in his seat. "Come now. We are all on the same side. Now that the contract on her has been rescinded, there is no need to fear us."

"You have an unusual way of showing it."

"Excuse me, Kanderil," said Remelas, holding up his hand. "Chalimer, did you insert a message of your own beneath my seal?"

"There was an additional message, yes," the Justicar conceded. "However, if I may be allowed to explain, you will almost certainly agree that it was a necessary deception."

Kanderil grunted, his gaze fixed on the bald-headed man. "I expect Glaithe believed in necessary deceptions too, up until the time he sold the girl out."

Chalimer smiled. "I understand your suspicion, of course. But believe me when I say that you will also understand. You may need me more than you know."

The words reminded Kanderil of the phrase the Agent who had delivered the message used. They served only to irritate him further. He was sick of the secrecy and deceit of factions like the Gathire and of places like Tamiran. It would be easier to get up and walk out, but despite how he felt he still sat in the presence of the King of Tamir. Certain courtesies had to be respected.

Remelas propped his elbows on the table, watching Chalimer. "Explain."

"It is quite simple. Sarene, as much as she or Kanderil here may wish to argue against the point, is a very special individual. Given that the existence of the Four is no longer in doubt, and that Tyrrial's most recent appearance was within our borders, then it would be in Tamir's best interests to know where she is at all times."

"For what purpose?" asked Kanderil through gritted teeth.

Chalimer spread his hands wide, looking directly towards Remelas. "She has already saved your life once before. The time may come when she may have to do so again."

Remelas shook his head. "She was under extreme pressure and took a knife to Tyrrial's flank. There was no grand battle. As far as I remember, it was actually Kanderil's life she fought to protect."

"I understand," said Chalimer. "But consider this. I have received word of a rather well-organised group acting with a great deal of suspicion in the western area of Tamir. They call themselves The Dedicant. We have not yet been able to infiltrate their organisation, but it seems they are placing a *lot* of emphasis on the prophets and their preaching about the girl. The 'Queen of the World', they call her."

"I have heard something similar," said Kanderil. "What is your point?"

"There is circumstantial evidence that they are funded by a man named Methulai. He is one of the wealthiest land barons in the kingdom. As yet we have nothing set in stone, and given his influence and financial support of the House I am hesitant to make accusations towards him. If the rumours prove to be true, however, then this group will enjoy considerable resources. Therefore, I recommend that we have someone looking after Sarene in an official capacity."

"No."

"With all due respect, Kanderil, this is not your decision to make."

"*No*," Kanderil said again. "I have protected her for this long. Judging from your man's response when I pulled up to your gate without her, I can still hide her from the Gathire. I do not need any help hiding her from some rag-tag collection of idiots who have started taking the ramblings of crazed fools as gospel. How much money lines their purses is of no consequence."

Chalimer turned his attention to the King once more. Remelas was listening with a hand across his mouth, deep in thought. "All I recommend is for an additional guardian to be assigned to Sarene, one we can call on when necessary. I will not seek to influence Kanderil's choices in protecting the girl, and the candidate I have in mind will be serve under his command. They will simply act as a go-between between Kanderil and Tamiran, so we know she is safe and well."

"And where you can find her," Kanderil pointed out.

"Of course. You can protest the point as much as you wish, but she *is* unique within Tamir. Perhaps within all the world. Such a rarity should not be forced to hide in the forests, cut off from society."

Kanderil bit off a sharp retort. The arrogance of the request irked him. He felt as though his ability to protect Sarene was being brought into question. Again he locked eyes with Chalimer, and this time the Justicar of the Gathire did not look away. There was a restrained satisfaction in Chalimer's expression which riled Kanderil further.

Remelas removed his hand from his mouth and sighed. "You could have informed me of your idea sooner, Chalimer."

"Forgive me, your Highness, but with so many other matters on your mind I presumed to attend to this personally. After all, the Gathire remain responsible for matters of national security.”

“What do the Assembly think?”

“They agreed with me completely. In fact, they have already provided me with the correct person for the job.”

Remelas frowned. “And who might that be?”

Chalimer sat straight in his chair. “*Orlienn!*”

The door opened. Kanderil briefly saw Ethanei staring at something out of sight. Past him stepped a tall, slender woman in green leather breeches, matching jerkin and brown knee-length boots. Flame-red hair was coarsely chopped in thick, feathered locks around her face. At her belt was a buckle formed in the shape of a stag. She closed the door behind her and stood to attention in the centre of the room, her eyes fixed ahead.

“Allow me to introduce Orlienn. She has been chosen for the task based on her impeccable credentials.”

Kanderil grunted in disbelief. “A ranger?”

“She has served the kingdom for eight years with distinction. There are few better trackers in the land and she knows the wilds of Tamir well. Perhaps even as well as you, Kanderil.” Chalimer spoke the last words with a playful crease at the corner of his mouth.

“She is a ranger,” Kanderil said again. “She can hunt, build camps and carry messages to the authorities. How will that help Sarene?”

Orlienn seemed unmoved by the woodsman’s blunt description of her potential.

Chalimer turned his attention to the giant. "I understand that the Kalethi have a tendency to look down upon the rangers of our forests, but this seemed the most appropriate choice. The rangers have no connections to the Gathire, the Kalethi or the Royal House. She is impartial to all of our various goals and ambitions. Orlienn is dependable, meticulous and takes no unnecessary risks."

Kanderil turned to the King. "Remelas, this is entirely pointless. She will merely get in the way. The fewer people around Sarene, the harder it will be for anybody to track her down."

Remelas rubbed his face. The man seemed to have aged another few summers during the brief meeting. It was difficult to believe he was only in his mid-twenties. "While I have complete faith in your ability to watch Sarene, I am inclined to agree with Chalimer in this instance. There may come a time when the girl needs to be called to the capital."

Clenching his fists, Kanderil leaned forward. "You once told me, back at Leithar Grove, that if I ever required anything from you I need only ask. I ask you now. Do not allow Chalimer to hamper me with this woman."

The reply was weary. "I remember those words well, and the offer stands. But my circumstances have changed. I am the King now, and I have many responsibilities to Tamir. Sarene *is* special, and I see no harm in knowing where she is at any given time."

Kanderil said nothing further, forcing himself to swallow his anger.

Remelas continued. "However, I expect your ranger to do exactly as Kanderil says, Chalimer. If he reports that Orlienn acts with anything less than perfect obedience, I will consider it a personal insult. Considering that *my* seal was used to summon him here."

Chalimer bowed his bald head. "Of course. I have the utmost faith in Orlienn's ability."

"Good." Kanderil turned to Remelas. "If you will excuse me, I must make arrangements of my own."

The King stood and offered his hand again, which Kanderil took. This time the grip was less sure than when he entered. "Look after yourself, Sergeant. I apologise if this meeting has disappointed you. Feel free to stop by before you leave, if you so wish. Perhaps we could enjoy a more civil discussion."

"Aye. Perhaps."

Without looking to Chalimer, fearful that one more smug look would precipitate a regrettable end to the meeting, Kanderil stepped out into the corridor and made his way towards the front entrance. Orlienn followed him, closing the door.

Ethanei stumbled forward out of his seat and hurried along after them. "Who's the redhead?" he called in a voice which echoed along the hallway.

KANDERIL STORMED OUT of the House, marching along the gravel towards the gate. The ranger kept pace with him, falling in a few steps behind. Ethanei was all but jogging to match the larger man's stride.

"Oi, d'you have to go so fast?"

Kanderil did not answer. He remained silent until they were clear of the House. The gate was opened for him by one of the guards on duty. The man offered a salute which only Orlienn returned.

As the House of Tamir was closed off behind them, Kanderil came to a halt. He turned around to Orlienn, his movements deliberate and heavy with purpose. His new companion stood to attention, back straight with her hands held behind her.

"I will tell you right away, lass. I am less than impressed by this ambush. I do not want nor need you with me."

"Understood," said the ranger.

"I will not be slowing my pace or altering my route for you. If you cannot match me then you will be left behind."

"Understood."

"Additionally, the fact that the Gathire selected you to protect Sarene leaves a bad taste in my mouth. I cannot trust you, and I will be watching your every move."

Orlienn nodded. Kanderil shook his head and began to walk along the high street. His investments were being held by a merchant not half an hour from the House. He intended to pick up some money for the coming winter.

Ethanei, still walking briskly to keep up, adjusted the strap of his bag against his shoulder. "So what do we do now?"

"*We* do nothing," Kanderil fired back as two men stepped out of his way. "You are free to go where you please. Find a job here in the capital if you wish."

"Is that it, then? 'Thanks for sitting in me wagon, so long'?" Laughing, Ethanei made another effort to catch up to the woodsman. "C'mon. Let's at least have dinner before we part ways, mate."

Kanderil stopped. The other two did likewise. He took several deep breaths, clenching his fists at his side. He was angry and had every right to be. The Gathire had involved themselves in Sarene's life for the second time, and once again it would be Kanderil's job to make sure they were kept at a safe distance. Now that Remelas had personally approved Orlienn to travel with them, it would be challenging to keep the girl's location hidden. Orlienn could be the most diligent and respectful ranger in the history of Tamir, but when her reports reached Tamiran they could be intercepted and shared by anyone. It didn't matter how good a job Kanderil did now. The secrecy of Sarene's travels would be taken out of his hands.

However, *remaining* angry would help nobody, least of all himself. Kanderil kept his breathing steady, and allowed the taut grip of emotion at the base of his ribs to dissipate. His heart rate slowed and his thoughts began to clear.

Eventually he looked across at Ethanei, who wrung his hands together, producing a rather weak smile.

"Dinner," said Kanderil.

"Aye," said Ethanei with a nod. "The three of us, like. So

I say g'bye and you two can introduce yerselves without any arguments. Think of me as a facility-or."

Kanderil glanced at Orlienn. She stood to attention once again. Whatever else the ranger may turn out to be, she was at least dutiful.

"Fine. What's the worst that could happen?"

Chapter Eight

ANTHON STOOD UP, a green, weed-like plant entwined around his fingers, the roots dripping moist earth.

"This is nutbark. It's not very nice to eat by itself, and if you boil it the water becomes really bitter. But if you slice it up *after* it's been boiled and add it to a stew or broth, it adds a depth to the flavour which is quite tasty. Professional cooks do it in rich people's kitchens."

Sarene nodded as she listened, wearing her best 'interested' expression. Anthon's knowledge of horticulture was astounding. He seemed to know the names of every plant, tree and fungus they walked past. Not only that, but each of them had a use in cooking, crafting, medicine... She'd even learnt that a red berry she'd previously known to be poisonous served as a hair dye for anyone with the daring to actually *use* it.

Spasmodic was less than impressed, however. After several hours of these facts, the creature was at the end of its tether. It pointed towards a cluster of mushrooms growing out of the side of a thick trunk, the caps of which were a dull blue.

"What are they?" it said.

"Those are winterchill toadstoo—"

"Can you eat 'em?"

"No. They'll upset your stomach."

"You can kill people with 'em?"

"Not effectively. They're not deadly in small quantities, so you would have to use a hu—"

"So they're pointless then," Spasmodic hissed.

"Not exactly. If prepared into a paste they make an effective mosquito repellent."

"Do I look like someone who gives a sod about musky-toes?"

"No," Anthon replied. "I am beginning to understand you have very few cares in the world, Spasmodic."

The creature grinned. "Look, mate. Can you just shut up about the bloody forest for a little while?"

The boy nodded, discarding the root in his hand. "Sure. I didn't mean to bore you."

"Yeah. Too much information about the same thingy does my brain in."

Sarene rolled her eyes. She bent down to pick up the nutbark, pointed at it then produced a thumbs-up, accompanied by an enthusiastic smile. Anthon chuckled, pausing to give a regal bow. Sarene giggled, bringing a hand to her mouth.

"How much longer we got 'til we reach this cabin place?" Spasmodic asked, swinging its arms.

Pulling the map from her bag and opening it up, Sarene

pointed to their location as the creature stomped over. If she was correct they should reach the cabin by nightfall the next day. The idea of doing so brought a bittersweet reaction.

Anthon still had not revealed if he would be staying with them or heading on south as originally intended. Sarene enjoyed his company, and she was beginning to believe he shared her sentiment. He often engaged her in conversation and watched intently whenever she signed to him. They made each other laugh and were all but falling over to cook for each other during their breaks in travel. The issue of his departure hadn't been pressed, and it was taking a great deal of restraint to keep from pestering him about his plans.

A spatter of rain swept over them as the breeze kicked up. Through the sparse canopy the clouds were grey and threatening. It was going to be a wet afternoon.

Spasmodic looked up, its countenance changing. Sarene blinked. The weather didn't usually bother it at all. It sniffed.

"I'd hide if I were you," it said.

"What's wrong?" asked Anthon, his voice low.

"Just hide somewhere," the creature replied. It took a few cautious steps forward; then *moved*, disappearing from sight in a heartbeat. Sarene and Anthon exchanged glances before searching for a place to conceal themselves. Sarene pointed towards a collection of undergrowth which had become dense with vines and nettles, then gestured for Anthon to follow.

He grabbed her arm. "Not there. It'll only hide us in from one direction. Come on, follow me."

Anthon led her west, picking a route around the foliage

to prevent making noise when stepping through it. Soon they came to a shallow ditch where a narrow stream trailed through the forest. Anthon lowered himself to the ground and slid down the cold dirt, choosing a section where two trees grew high and proud on the opposite bank. Sarene followed suit, sliding down next to him. They said nothing, taking shallow breaths and making no movement. The atmosphere was tense and the ambience of the woodland smothered them.

A light drizzle started, dripping through the leaves and branches above. Sarene noticed her hand was next to Anthon's, their cold fingers touching. Carefully she moved her hand a couple of inches to the right, breaking the contact.

Was that strange? To fret over their conduct while they were hiding from an unknown menace? Sarene felt the familiar touch of insecurity and she focused on the ground to keep from dwelling on it.

There were people *actively* hunting her and she was more concerned about her fingertips. *That* was ridiculous.

Less than five minutes later Spasmodic reappeared. It looked down at them and grinned.

"All safe now."

"What was it?" asked Anthon as he pulled himself up the bank. He offered his hand to Sarene to help her right herself. She took it and stepped up next to him, letting go as soon as she was stable.

"I had to take a shit," said Spasmodic. The words stunned the girl and she threw her hands up in exasperation.

Anthon laughed. "Really?"

"No, not really," it replied. "There were two more of those guys with the red stripes pokin' around. Was just makin' sure they buggered off."

Sarene drew a finger across her throat before giving a cautious shrug.

"Nah, didn't kill em. If I did that they'd know they were on the right track." The creature wiped its sleeve across its nose, snickering. "Well, their friends would anyway."

Nodding, Anthon sighed. "We should get moving, then. Before they come back."

Spasmodic nodded, taking the lead. "Don't worry so much. Another day and you two can hide in a bed instead of a ditch."

Sarene paced ahead of Anthon to hide the flush of red at her cheeks. She heard the ranger's son give a soft laugh, a sound which made her smile in spite of herself.

THAT EVENING KANDERIL, Ethanei and Orlienn sat in the Bear's Noose, waiting for their food to arrive. The tavern was small, quiet and tucked away in a back street in the southern quarter of Tamiran, having picked up a set of rooms nearby. The smell of varnish and paint suggested the place was either newly constructed or under renovation. It was difficult to tell, though. The interior was squalid, with grim, tattered furnishings and a sticky floor.

Kanderil turned his gaze to Orlienn. The copper-haired ranger hadn't spoken more than a few words during the afternoon while he collected some of his savings and purchased basic supplies. Ethanei seemed fascinated with her, though right now he was much more preoccupied with his ale. They'd been in the place for fifteen minutes and he was well into his third serving.

"So that's how I see it," the vagrant was saying. "Once I've got meself a horse, that is. Hard to be a messenger without one these days."

"Quite," Kanderil replied absently.

"Besides, I can see plenty more o' Tamir that way as well. I knew a messenger once who said he loved it. Ridin' about, free as the wind. Well, as free as you *can* be when they're given a specific place to go. But y'know what I mean."

"You may have to cut down on the alcohol," said Kanderil, looking to the man. Ethanei grinned, raising his mug.

"Aye, but that's a problem for another day. Right now I've been sober for a week. Easy as pie, 'twas. I don't have any worries, me."

An acne-pocked maid stepped through the door to the kitchen, nudging it open with her hip. She brought three steaming plates of food to their table, a robust aroma of spices rising from them. Kanderil's plate was noticeably larger, having ordered a triple serving. His meal was swimming in dark gravy, the mash forming an island in the centre flanked by the meat.

Ethanei whistled, chuckling. "I had wondered how you maintain your trim figure, mate. Now I can see."

Without reply, Kanderil started into his food. The interesting thing about Ethanei's comment was that, since meeting Sarene, Kanderil had *lost* weight. When travelling alone he would easily go through a half-dozen rabbits, pheasants or whatever game was on hand daily. He would exercise often, using the trees and rocks as tools to maintain his muscle mass. Kanderil's size was inherent – he had always been massive – but he recalled his father's warnings that if he did not commit to regular training then the muscle would turn to fat with age, and he would become too obese to do much of use. Years of constant travel kept his stamina high, but over the past two seasons he had started to neglect his other training.

They ate in silence. Despite the disproportionate servings, the three of them finished within minutes of each other. Completely full for the first time in weeks, Kanderil leant back in his chair and took a long swallow of his ale.

"Feel better now?" asked Ethanei. Kanderil nodded, exhaling as he pushed his now-empty cup away. "Good. Maybe now you'll 'ave a drink and loosen up a bit."

"I was never tense," said Kanderil.

Ethanei waved at the maid, pointing at his cup. "Oh really? The way you stormed out of the palace I thought you were going to murder someone."

"That was different. I was irritated by a situation I disagreed with." Kanderil looked to Orlienn. "A situation I still disagree with. But I will adapt regardless."

The ranger placed her hands in her lap. "I apologise if our new relationship troubles you."

"It doesn't trouble me, lass. I doubt you personally sought this assignment."

"That is true. If I had known how strongly you would

object, I may have declined."

Kanderil grunted. "Chalimer would have found someone else. I am annoyed with *his* involvement. Not yours. Providing you do your job and give me no reason to suspect you, we shall get along fine."

Ethanei accepted a fresh ale from the maid with a wink before turning back to the conversation. "Suspect her of what?"

The woodsman wrapped a hand over a fist before pressing them against his jaw, his elbows planted on the table in front of him. "In the summer a man I allowed to accompany me and the girl betrayed us."

"Glaithe," said Orlienn. "I have been informed."

"Then you understand why I am wary. I have no personal dislike of you, but I will be watching you closely and monitoring your actions until I can trust you."

"How long will it take to earn your trust?"

"It is impossible to say."

Orlienn jabbed a thumb towards Ethanei. "How long did it take him?"

"Who said he has my trust?"

Ethanei coughed. "Oh, hey? That hurts, mate. There were me thinkin' we were friends by now."

"I enjoy your company," said Kanderil. "That does not mean I would trust you with Sarene's wellbeing."

"Right. Good to know. At least you're gettin' rid of me tomorrow, then."

Orlienn smiled for the first time since meeting them. "Are you usually this sensitive, Ethanei?"

"Hah." Ethanei shook his head, wiping froth from his upper lip. "I just lost me wife and me home. I guess I'm a bit more emotional than usual."

"My sympathies."

"Gimme a drink and I'll accept 'em." Ethanei grinned, leaning forward towards the ranger. "And, eh. Since I'm in a fragile state, don't you be takin' advantage o' me should I get proper drunk. That would be awful."

Orlienn smirked. "I can assure you that your dignity is safe with me."

Laughing, Ethanei dropped his head so that his forehead rested briefly upon the table. "Two more ales over here!" he roared as he jerked upright again, his hand twirling in the air.

The barkeep, bemused, shuffled over to the ale keg.

GLAITHE KNOCKED ON the warped wood of the door as Niallya stood behind him. The rap of his knuckles rebounded across the street. In this area there were no street poles to light the way. They stood in darkness outside a shadowy building with empty windows.

Lifting a hand to adjust the fold of his sleeve, Glaithe took a step back to examine the building. The front face of the apartment where Heiran lived reminded Glaithe of a wine bottle having been upturned and jammed into a crack far too small for it. The face of the building itself was not flat, swelling around the upper level, the jutting wall propped on two suspect looking beams.

"Well?" asked Niallya, watching him. "We've stood here

for long enough. Heiran is either elsewhere or ignoring us."

Glaithe reached into his coat and pulled out a thin metal strip. "I suppose we invite ourselves inside."

"You're going to simply break in?"

"You weren't?" Stepping close to the door, Glaithe pushed the metal strip between the lock and the door frame. Sliding the strip upwards, he felt something connect on the other side. With a twist of his hands and a nudge of his shoulder, the door swung inwards.

"One would think you've done that before," said Niallya as she stepped past him. Glaithe tucked the strip away and smiled.

"A few times."

He followed the mercenary inside. A steep staircase loomed immediately before them. As soon as Niallya placed her weight on the first step the whole structure creaked. She paused. Glaithe waited, examining the situation. They could not see what lay in wait on the next floor, and should the apartment be occupied there was no chance of making it up the staircase unheard.

Niallya started moving again. Her footfalls kept to the edges of the stairs to avoid placing pressure on their weakest point, but it did little to reduce the noise she made. Glaithe matched her movements. At the least he could make it appear that only one person was ascending.

As they neared the landing above, a man's voice reached them from the sole door, which was built into the right wall and currently standing open.

"Go away," it said.

"We mean you no harm," Glaithe replied.

"I don't care," was the response. The words sounded groggy. "Get outta my home."

There were only three more steps between Niallya and the landing. She moved again. When the stair creaked a throwing knife hurtled out of the room and *thunk*ed into the wall opposite.

"Interesting," she murmured, stopping dead.

"Heiran," called Glaithe. "We have a job offer for you. That is all."

"I'm not interested."

"We can make it worth your while."

"Get outta my *home*!" Something shattered inside the room. Floorboards groaned.

Niallya placed a hand on the hilt of her blade. "Just give us a few moments of your time, Heiran."

The voice paused. Silence in the darkness. Nobody moved. Eventually their answer came. "You aren't Kraye's gang."

"Why do you say that?" asked Glaithe amiably.

"Because he don't send women."

"You are correct," Niallya replied. "We are not with Kraye. Please, allow us to approach and explain why we are here."

Another brief lull. "Are you armed?" called the voice.

"Not yet…" the mercenary said beneath her breath.

"Our weapons are sheathed," Glaithe insisted. "We do not mean you harm."

Nothing.

"May we approach?"

After a long pause the sound of movement bounced through the rickety structure.

"Fine. Come up."

Niallya took the last few steps. Glaithe followed, hearing the sound of a match being struck. He turned the corner after the woman to step into a small fleapit of a room, a newly lit candle on one uneven table illuminating the depressing interior. A blanket was strewn across one corner beside a second door. The sole window had been covered with a thick sheet, preventing any light from getting in. The shattering had been a clay pot which now lay in pieces upon the grimy floor.

Heiran turned from the table to greet them. Dressed in only a pair of cotton pants, his naked torso was marred with dirt and sweat. Lank hair had been tied back to reveal solemn features. Odd, Glaithe thought, that the man's face was clean shaven.

The man picked up a knife from beside the candle. He stared at them with small, suspicious eyes. "Well?"

Glaithe held his hands where they could be seen and wore a broad smile, as though addressing a simpleton. "A pleasure to meet you. My name is Glaithe. This is Niallya."

Heiran looked at the mercenary. "I've heard of you."

"I am flattered."

"Is he your boss?"

"We work together," the former Agent cut in. "She and I are here to offer you a job which will make you rich."

Tapping the flat of the blade against his hip, Heiran

shook his head. "I can't."

"You haven't heard us out yet."

"If you don't work for Kraye, I can't." The man smiled without humour. "I'm exclusive to him, sorta."

"I have already spoken to Kraye," said Niallya. "He is aware that I am looking to hire you."

"Not for anything which will '*make me rich*'," Heiran replied. "Did you tell him that part, girl?"

"No. I did not."

"Well, then. I'm in enough shit with him already, without trying to actually earn some money for myself."

With her hood up it was impossible to read Niallya's expression. Glaithe held out a hand. "Perhaps if you explain we could come to an arrangement."

"Ain't nothing to arrange." Heiran shrugged, kneeling to pick up a mug Glaithe hadn't noticed before. He finished whatever remained inside, throwing the thing aside as he swallowed. The mug clattered against the wooden flooring. "If you got a group to go out smuggling, or pulling up travellers on the highway, then that ain't worth approaching a man throwing knives at you on the stairs. I'm guessing you have bigger plans."

"Where is the harm in earning more money than you're used to?" persisted Niallya.

"You don't get it. If I had enough money I'd up and out of this stinking town. Kraye knows that, so he makes sure I earn just enough to feed meself and pay me owing to the landlord."

"Because of your skills," said Glaithe.

"Aye. Won't lie; I'm better with a crossbow in me hands than most of the scum around here. But that's beside the point. I ain't getting involved. I can't. So kindly turn around and leave, so that I don't have to lie to no one."

"What if I told you you'd never have to deal with Kraye again?" said Glaithe. "I'll give you a sizeable payment up front so you can get out of this dump and move to Tamiran."

"Temptin'," said Heiran, tapping the blade again as he stood. "But it's more complicated than that. It'd be best if you both left." He pointed towards the exit behind them.

"Trust me, Hei—"

"I don't wanna insist." The knife flicked into the air and was caught at the blade. "I'm handy with these as well."

The other door creaked. All three of them turned to regard it. Heiran's eyes widened in horror and he stepped forwards, holding out his free hand.

"No!"

The door swung inwards to reveal a young girl, no more than seven summers old. Long hair hung in clumps around her shoulders. Between grubby hands she held a tatty old bear with dead button-eyes.

Heiran hurried over. "Get back in, girl. I told you not to come out." He tried to usher the child back into the room.

"I thought I heard Mama's voice," she said, rubbing her eye.

"No, not Mama. Go on, get back to bed. I'll be with you soon."

"Wait," said Glaithe. He had to keep the building grin from his face. Covering his mouth with a fist, he coughed once. "Is this your daughter?"

"None of your business," Heiran said in a threatening tone, glancing over his shoulder.

"We can help you. Both of you." Glaithe moved towards the doorway, where the girl was still peering around her father's legs. He knelt down and gave a slow, deliberate wave using only his fingers. "You could say I have some experience caring for young girls in trouble."

"Leave my home. Now."

"I understand why you're afraid, Hei—"

All at once the knife was at Glaithe's neck. The tip pressed against his flesh. He swallowed but did not flinch as his gaze travelled the straight line from blade to arm to face. The girl behind Heiran gripped at the man's knee. Glaithe understood that to continue talking now was risking a mortal wound, but the gamble was worth it. Heiran was the perfect candidate for the job he had in mind.

"I can get the girl out of Ghellei," he said, the words remaining calm. "Permanently. Kraye will never find her."

"I cannot risk it," Heiran replied after a brief consideration. "They'll kill her."

"No," said Glaithe. "They won't. Just listen to my offer. If you still refuse we will leave you in peace and never return."

The tension held for several seconds. There had been no sound behind Glaithe to announce the drawing of Niallya's blade. He hoped she retained her composure. Any sudden movements would put an end to his plans with a single cut.

"I jus'… I don't know *why*, y'know? After all I did, all we been through. Worked me arse off in the army to earn us some coin so we could jus' get outta Thorlen an – Thorlen *Tar*, stupid bloody place – an' make a go of it. Maybe 'ave a kid or two. By the Four, I loves that woman."

Ethanei, now seven cups in, was slumped forward against the table. The eighth cup stood nearby, and Kanderil was waiting for him to knock it over. He'd started this speech over five minutes ago. Whatever Ethanei was revealing had clearly been burning a hole in the man's stomach. As Orlienn reached over to place a hand against the vagrant's forearm Kanderil shook his head, warning against it.

"I mean, Clarai were everythin' I ever wanted. She were funny, sharp as a whip, and beautiful. Damn it, she *is* beautiful, even to this day. When she agreed to wear that feather in her hair for me, big ol' owl feather which took me almost a month to find, I swear I must have smiled for days." Ethanei lifted his hand, flexing the fingers while staring into the palm, as though he could see his memories playing back there.

"I said to her that I'd give her anythin' she wanted. Anythin' at all. I woulda done it, too. Woulda pulled the… the bloody sun outta the sky for her if she'd asked. An' y'know what she said? She said 'Just promise me you'll be there for me.' That's all she wanted. *Me.* My wife just wants me.

"'Course," he added, wilting back in his seat, "After several years that kinda romance dies away. She didn't want me to go to the army, though. I told her, I said, 'But they're payin' more than I can earn on the farms. She were sad that I couldn't be convinced, right up until the day I rode outta the village. She watched me go from the doorway, wavin', and I turned an' waved back just the once. Like it weren't a big deal." He chuckled in bitterness. "I reckon that were the last time Clarai ever really missed me."

"How long were you with the army?" asked Orlienn.

"Six years. Six fuckin' years I spent marchin' around and teaching young lads how to ride in formation. Six years wasted on Remelas and his schemes. Six years, and now I've lost me wife, me king and I'm scarred for life." He gave an irritated tug on one of his gloves. "All for nothing, it were. All for a big load of shite and here I am, sittin' in a tavern with a guy who don't trust me and a girl who don't know me. I'm drunk, and my wife doesn't want anythin' to do with me. Can ye understand why I enjoy a drink now an' then?"

"Ex-wife," said Kanderil.

The abrupt observation struck Ethanei like a hammer blow. He peered at the woodsman with growing anger, the word lighting a fuse.

"What did y'say?"

"Ex-wife. You keep referring to her as your wife."

Ethanei got to his feet, the chair tipping back to clatter against the floor. Evidently the sudden movement wasn't quite anticipated by his equilibrium – the vagrant almost fell over. Sheer force of will kept him upright, swaying as he yelled.

"Y'think that's funny, do ya? You think you're too big for an arse kicking? Makin' mockery of me situation?"

"No, I do not find this funny, lad." Kanderil, who had

now turned to address Ethanei directly, reached over to pick up the man's remaining ale. "This is pitiful. You are taking a sad turn of events and letting them rule you. If you wish to hold Remelas responsible for the failure of your marriage, that is fine. But should you throw the rest of your life away, then the blame will be yours alone."

"So you're judgin' me, eh? Kanderil? Judgin' what I'm doin'?"

"Yes," said Kanderil. "I am. While there is still chance you will listen. With each month that you hide yourself in these cups, the likelihood that you will climb out again reduces." He lifted the mug to his lips and tilted his head back, draining the ale in four swallows.

"You drank me ale, y'bugger!" said Ethanei with needless vehemence; the cry of the addict robbed of his poison.

"I did you a favour."

"I'm not a fuckin' child."

"No, you are not. So stop acting like one."

Ethanei went for Kanderil then, stumbling forward and throwing a wild swing. The Hunter deflected the blow with a large hand, before surging to his feet and gripping Ethanei around the chest, holding him in place. The drunk struggled but was defeated by both brute strength and the certainty of soberness.

"I think it is about time we put you to bed," said Kande-ril.

"Let go'a me!" Ethanei roared, kicking out.

"If you attack me again, I will put you on your arse."

"*Let go'a me!*"

Kanderil did so. Ethanei, now unsupported, whirled around and tried to face the woodsman. In doing so he tripped over his own feet, fell backwards and cracked his head against the upturned chair he'd abandoned moments ago. He sprawled out on the floor, unconscious.

"Oi," said the barman just as the front door to the tavern opened and two more customers stepped in, their attention immediately caught by the prone body decorating the ground. "If he's pissed, get him to his room."

Orlienn stood, moving around the table. "Do you need help with him?"

"No," said Kanderil, reaching down to grip Ethanei's belt. He lifted the vagrant like a satchel, the man's arms and legs dragging along the floorboards. "I will put him to bed. We leave at first light, so get some sleep."

"Very well."

As the woodsman hauled Ethanei upstairs, the newcomers watching him with gaping mouths, he reflected on what had just happened. It was possible the situation could have been handled better. Probable, in fact. He hooked an arm under his burden and hefted the man over his broad shoulder. The stairs protested at the weight.

The worst part was that Ethanei was so drunk it was unlikely he'd even remember the advice Kanderil had offered. The alcohol had encouraged speech; forthright words which painted a picture of a man tortured by regret and guilt. While he'd derided Clarai several times, it was when blind drunk that the truth came out. Ethanei blamed himself.

By this time tomorrow, though, Kanderil would heading

west, back to Sarene. Ethanei would remain here. Whether he sobered up or continued drinking was his choice to make.

Kanderil pushed open the door to Ethanei's room, carrying him to the bunk. After removing his boots and drawing the thin blanket up around his shoulders, the woodsman stepped back. In sleep, Ethanei looked sad. Stripped away of the humour and sarcasm which served him well when awake, there was a certain melancholy about him.

Exiting the room, Kanderil hoped that Ethanei would see that alcohol was not the solution. But the man's future was none of his concern. He had enough responsibilities to deal with.

HEIRAN SAT BACK against the wall, eyes closed. His daughter, whose name was Tillyan, had been sent back to her room. Having decided to listen to Glaithe's proposition, the man was now turning the offer over in his mind. Niallya had remained silent while Glaithe explained what he intended to achieve. She had to hand it to her colleague. He had a way with words, and had described the scheme with flair.

The room was claustrophobic. With only a solitary flame giving them light, the apartment conjured the image of a stone cell in some remote dungeon. Nothing about the place was homely, and she pitied the young girl who lived here. Though, perhaps *lived* was too strong a word. She, like her father, merely existed. Waiting for the next meal, or a change in circumstance which would never come.

Finally, the owner of this dire place spoke up. "What

makes you think you can get away with this plan?"

"I am good at what I do," Glaithe replied in a voice like quicksilver. The confidence he oozed in every action and word was undeterred. Even when the knife had been at his throat, he hadn't backed down.

"That you may be. I'm the one who'll be firin' the bolt."

"You are part of my plan, my friend. I would not have chosen you if I doubted you were up to the task."

"We ain't friends."

With a nod of the head, Glaithe smiled. "Very well. But, hopefully, we will be comrades."

"If I'm caught, I'm dead."

"Niallya will be with you. She is almost as capable as I when it comes to secrecy."

The two mercenaries exchanged looks. There was a smudge of grime across Heiran's chest which looked like a scorch mark in the dim light. "Is that so?"

Clearing her throat, Niallya folded her arms across her stomach. "I will be posing as your wife, carrying a bundle of fabrics. The crossbow will be concealed inside, and you shall be unarmed. Few would suspect a female of being involved. Once you have killed your target, we will calmly evacuate the building and lose ourselves in the crowd."

"There will undoubtedly be a large crowd in Tamiran Square," said Glaithe. "This will impede the guard, but also provide you both with plenty of cover. Niallya will then lead you back to where I will be waiting, with your daughter and a large sack of gold coin."

Heiran rubbed his jaw. "What about Kraye?"

"I will deal with Kraye."

"He'll kill Tillyan. If he finds out I've escaped this boil of a town and made it on my own, he'll take my girl away from me."

"Trust me. You've heard my plans. If I can achieve this, then Kraye will be simplicity itself."

"*Trust* you?" The laugh which Heiran produced was loaded with black humour. "You've asked me to commit murder and treason on our first meeting. And you're asking for trust. D'you see the irony of that?"

"I already trust you."

"Oh, aye?"

"Yes," said Glaithe. "If I did not, I wouldn't have revealed my hand so soon."

"What makes you think I'll accept?"

A bright laugh pierced the gloom of the apartment, and Glaithe spread his hands wide, sweeping fingertips towards the crumbling walls. "Look around you. You're lying in your own filth, earning barely enough to feed your daughter. From the look of your ribs, you're hardly eating three square meals a day. How long have you been doing this?"

Heiran didn't see the funny side. "Long enough."

"Long enough. And how much longer do you think you'll carry on wallowing like a pig? Only, a pig at least gets fed. A pig isn't made to work for its slurry. I'm offering you a way out, and a future for little Tillyan. You'll be a free man again."

"You think mocking my situation is going to win you any favours?"

"No, man," snapped Glaithe, irritation lending power to his words. "I'm telling you exactly how it is. If I had to mollycoddle you and tell you everything was going to be alright then you'd hardly have the stomach for assassination. I'm just being honest. You'll be out of this dump, with gold in your pocket and food in your belly. And you'll never have to worry about Kraye again."

Shifting her weight, Niallya studied the half-naked man opposite. He *looked* like a savage, but there was something more to him. Niallya knew that Heiran was formerly a soldier, and a good one. Word was he'd seen combat and earned the respect of his peers. The tragic passing of his wife had sent him spiralling into a deep depression, forcing him to retire from the army to care for his child.

Tillyan's situation was familiar to her. Stranded in an existence with no prospects.

"If I don't agree, you'll kill me," said Heiran with a sigh of resignation.

The statement brought her attention back to the room. To Glaithe's credit, he didn't falter. "That is not true."

"I'm a lot of things, but I'm not a fool. You've shared too much with me. I'm a liability now. If I don't do what you ask, I'm a dead man."

"I can see why you would suspect such a thing," said Glaithe, shrugging his shoulders. "I'd probably feel the same way were our positions reversed. Which is why we're going to leave now." He reached into a pocket and withdrew a slip of paper. Crossing the room, he left the slip next to the candle, tapping it twice with a finger. "This is my address. I'm a fugitive from the law. Give this paper to the authorities, and I'd be hanged within the week."

Heiran scoffed. He must have understood. The authorities in Ghellei were hard to find, so lacking were their numbers.

"I'm entrusting you with this. You can either turn me over, or you can join me. Call it a leap of faith."

"Kraye wouldn't see it that way. If I went to the authorities he'd assume I was trying to hand him in."

Now it was Glaithe's turn to laugh. "Kraye isn't scared by the guard. He's been openly defying them for years. I doubt he'd be scared by one of his mercs speaking with them. They'd never challenge him, not in his town." Walking towards the door, he waved over his shoulder. "Either come to me with your decision, or do not. I would like to help you, Heiran. But you have to believe me."

Niallya followed him back down the rickety stairs, leaving Heiran to the darkness of his apartment. The man said nothing as they left. Soon they were out in the street, walking back through the dead market, heading for the small shack containing nothing but a basement and an absent Regent. The tang of the air was a pleasing contrast to the cloying of the room they'd departed.

"He was right, wasn't he," she said.

"About killing him?" replied Glaithe. His demeanour was cheerful beneath the silvery moonlight filtering through the unseen clouds.

"Yes. He *is* a risk now."

"Aye. And it'll be a shame to kill him should he turn us

down."

Nodding, Niallya rested one hand against the hilt of her blade. "You suspect he will agree, though."

"Of course, my dear. He's got nothing to lose at this point. Besides, he won't go to the guard. Kraye would kill him and his daughter once he found out. Heiran is on a very tight leash. I expect he'll be with us within the next few days."

"So now we speak to the Sons of Tamir."

"Exactly." Glaithe smirked, inhaling cold air. "Ah, but it is a glorious night!"

Niallya chuckled, her soft voice like a whisper. "You're in a good mood."

He grinned in a way which Niallya found distasteful, and her amusement lessened. The smile suggested more than simple contentment with his plans. "Do not sound so shocked. Why wouldn't I be? Tonight went exactly according to plan, and I am another step closer to the death of King Remelas."

Chapter Nine

K ANDERIL AWOKE JUST as the first rays of sunlight streamed through the window shutters. He allowed himself a few minutes to lie there, enjoying the warmth of the quilt around him even as cold air touched his bare arms. The mattress was surprisingly comfortable, given the poor conditions of the tavern below.

Eventually he got out of bed and walked over to the waiting basin of water. He splashed some of the liquid over his face, where it dripped from his nose and beard. Patting himself dry with a hand-towel, he dressed and shouldered his weapons and satchel.

Downstairs, he found Orlienn already waiting for him. She rose from her chair as his foot left the last step.

"Good morning," she said. Kanderil nodded once. "There is some breakfast available if you wish. I have already eaten."

"I have food," said Kanderil. "I'll eat on the road."

"Very well." She lifted her baldric from the table and slung it over her shoulder. Two small throwing knives were positioned against her chest, with a longer hunting blade sheathed at her hip.

Kanderil appraised her. "I thought rangers used bows."

"My bow is with my horse," Orlienn replied.

"Then why the knives?"

"I am good with them."

Accepting the answer, Kanderil moved to the door. He pushed it open and stepped out into the street, inhaling the chill of the late autumn morning. Then he looked down.

Three young men were standing before him. All of them wore the insignia of the Kalethi; Third Class, meaning they were fresh recruits. Each had flushed faces from standing in the cold. At his appearance they started grinning.

Kanderil exchanged looks with Orlienn as she stepped beside him.

"Sorry to bother you, sir," said one of the recruits, a sandy-haired lad with green eyes. "But we've been waiting here to meet you. I'm Warren, and this is Loreth and Jasper. When we heard we snuck out early to meet you. That is, when we heard you were in town. That is." He sounded nervous, the words lacking confidence.

The woodsman frowned. The action brought an abrupt end to their smiles. "What for?"

The recruit forced a chuckle. "We, err. We were hopin' to talk with you for a little while."

"To hear your story," said Loreth, blurting out the words.

"Story...?" asked Kanderil.

"Yeah. About how you fought Tyrrial."

With a sigh, Kanderil pinched the bridge of his nose. "What are you talking about?"

"Erm," said Warren. "You were the one who saved the Prince. I mean the King. I mean, the Prince when he *was* a King. Remelas."

"The *King* when he was a *Prince*, dummy," sniggered Jasper, prodding his friend in the back. Loreth hissed at them to be quiet.

Ignoring Orlienn's wry smile, Kanderil shook his head. "You are mistaken. I was not there."

"You, uh… You are Kanderil, right?" asked Warren.

"No."

The three recruits looked at each other. Then they all started talking at once.

"But we've heard about you in the barracks—"

"You're the only seven-foot guy the Kalethi had—"

"We were told you'd be here by the Gathire—"

As Kanderil held up his hand, the recruits fell silent. Then he pointed to Jasper. His glare must have spoken volumes, for the boy stared at the floor. "You were told *what* by the Gathire?"

"That the Hero of Leithar Grove was stayin' here. Sir."

Muttering, Kanderil shook his head.

Jasper continued, eager not to be the one to bring this meeting to an unwanted early end. "See, in the Kalethi you're kind of a hero now. We all know what you did. Savin' Remelas and all that. You're the only one to ever get one over on the Four. Now some of us think you're a right champion of Tamir."

"Yeah," said Warren. "That's why we're here. You're a bit of an inspiration, like. Since you learned all your skills with the Kalethi, we want to do the same. So if you had any advice…"

"Yeah, and tips and stuff."

"So we can become as good as you are."

"Famous, too!"

That last remark – from Warren – brought a shove from both his companions. They mumbled under their breath for him to be quiet, then sniggered and hissed at each other like a group of schoolchildren. Every word steamed from their mouths before drifting away in the wintry morning breeze.

"I am not famous," said Kanderil after a brief pause.

"You are in the Kalethi," said Loreth.

The woodsman sighed. "Then here is your advice. Do not believe everything you hear." With that he pushed past them. Orlienn followed, matching him stride for stride as they walked along the narrow street.

"That was uncalled for," she said.

"I did not ask for your opinion," replied Kanderil.

"If those boys are aspiring to follow your lead, then all you did was make fools of them." She gestured back down the alley, where the three recruits were looking at each other, shoulders slumped and heads down. "Look. They're crushed."

"I am not interested."

"No, but *they* were. They've met a real hero and were completely brushed aside."

Kanderil stopped, turning to face the ranger. Orlienn stood still, the soles of her boots clicking a stop against the cobbled street, and met his gaze. "I do not care. The Gathire have been spreading word of my role at Leithar Grove to irritate me, and I will have no part of it. If you wish to ride with me, then you will not pester me further."

Without hesitation, Orlienn bowed her head in acknowledgement. Kanderil started again, heading towards the stables where his carthorses were tethered.

Within twenty-four hours, he had been ambushed twice by the Gathire. Firstly with Orlienn, and now with these immature Kalethi recruits. Chalimer must be laughing somewhere in the city at the thought of Kanderil's face when those three boys met him. He sniffed, pushing the thought aside. Only the image of the Gathire Agent's reaction upon learning Sarene had not travelled with him was of comfort.

But now, with his increasing notoriety and repeated instances of recognition, that successful deception was becoming less and less rewarding.

SARENE ARCHED HER back as she pressed against the muscles either side of her spine, just above her hips. She was exhausted after six days of travel. According to the map, they were roughly in the area of the disused cabin. Spasmodic had gone searching; the creature could cover ground much faster alone, and with luck it would find the cabin much sooner than they could as a group. Kanderil had explained that their intended winter home was deep in the forest and well hidden from travellers.

Anthon took a swig from his canteen. "How long will it take?" he asked, replacing the cap. Sarene shrugged, and he nodded. "Just as I thought."

They'd spent the better part of the morning picking their way through dense foliage, all but kicking through knee-high undergrowth. Plenty of the leaves were nettled, and Sarene was grateful for her new clothes. The boots she wore protected her from the thorny stems, and the leggings were thick enough to defend her from the majority of the leafy stingers. Her old linen trousers and cloth slippers would have been little help. She imagined herself with bloated legs, staggering around the forest. The idea made her grin.

"We're pretty deep here, aye," said Anthon. Exhaling with relief, Sarene stopped stretching and glanced around. They could barely see more than ten yards ahead, surrounded as they were by an army of trunks and branches. The canopy above allowed little of the sky to penetrate, even this late into autumn. Many of the trees had already discarded their leaves, which now covered the ground like a tattered carpet of bronze.

Sarene nodded her agreement. Judging the distances marked on the map had been harder than she'd anticipated. She'd trusted her instincts and the lessons Kanderil had imparted over the past few months, and providing she hadn't miscalculated then the cabin shouldn't be too far away.

Wind whistled through the tops of the trees. Here, the current had to fight to be acknowledged, and only occasionally could be felt against Sarene's skin. She tilted her head back in response to the breeze, which alternately whispered and roared against the woodland. One corner of her mouth pulled up. She skipped forward towards the nearest tree, shrugging off her satchel.

Watching, Anthon took a couple of steps after her. "Where are you going?"

Ignoring him, Sarene placed her foot against the trunk. She took a moment to judge distance, then kicked up and grabbed the lowest branch with both hands. Using her leverage, she walked up the crumbling bark until she was able to wrap a leg around the base of the limb. Satisfied it would hold her weight, she swung herself up to sit there, six feet off the ground. Anthon gathered up her discarded pack, looking up at her.

"Do you want a round of applause?"

She winked before rising carefully to her feet, balancing close to the trunk, one hand pressed against the coarse bark. The tree was enormous, with a substantial core, and a number of long branches grew within easy reach. She started up them, pulling herself higher, always tugging before committing her weight to a bough and assuring her footing before pressing further. It had been too long since she'd climbed a tree purely for fun. As children, she and Jared would often compete to see who dared climb the highest. She usually won, though this had more to do with her slighter frame; the upper branches would creak dangerously when Jared attempted to climb them.

The thought made her smile, and for the first time since Leithar Grove the memory of Jared did not bring her pain. Sarene climbed on, encouraged by this sense of relief, picking her handholds carefully as the limbs began to thin.

"You're pretty high up!" called Anthon. She paused,

looking down, only to find she was easily thirty feet above ground. The ranger's son was no longer visible at the base of the tree. She lifted her head. The view was beautiful, with a crazed labyrinth of branches as far as she could see, like she had climbed inside a gigantic bird's nest. All shades of brown melded into each other, with any gap filled by more wood, more spindly fingers, more cobwebs: a colossal spider of the earth.

Wishing she could call down to Anthon to join her, she instead offered a wave. Either he didn't see it or he ignored her, for there was no response. She leant to the side, seeing if she could find a better vantage point to gain his attention.

"WHADDAYDOINGUPHERE?"

A voice *erupted* beside Sarene's ear, and a jolt of panic dislodged her foot from the branch supporting her. Adrenaline overloaded her senses as she fell, glimpsing a sliver of red and green against the side of the trunk. On instinct she grabbed for it, but caught nothing.

"Oh *shit-*" the voice said, laughing, and Spasmodic surged after her, descending the tree almost as fast as she fell. Twisting, Sarene flailed, desperate for something, *anything*, to slow her freefall. She'd dropped three feet, five feet, seven—

Sarene spread her arms as wide as she could, and her shoulders impacted with a split bough which jarred her spine and sent her breath *whoosh*ing out of her. Her knees took the brunt of the branches' other fork, and she found herself sagging between the two limbs like a living hammock; sore, gasping and frightened, but no longer falling.

Spasmodic swung from a branch above, claws grating against the wood. It cackled, tilting its head to the side. Several of its vibrant red dreadlocks slipped over its shoulder to hang freely, swaying from side to side with every movement.

"Sorry," it said, though the sneer it wore suggested otherwise. "I didn't think you'd freak out."

Catching her breath, Sarene gaped at it in disbelief.

"Still, at least you stopped yerself. You done this before? Flattenin' out like that. I was impressed. Maybe you're part squirrel or something."

She reached for a handhold to pull herself upright. Her heart was pounding and Sarene swallowed hard. She locked eyes with the creature as she grabbed onto a knot in the trunk. It sniggered when she smiled.

Sarene *should* be furious with it, but the exhilaration of the fall was making that difficult. She felt alive and in control for the first time in months.

Carefully she descended the tree, dropping down to Anthon's side. His expression betrayed his concern, and he followed her as she walked away. "By the Four, are you alright?"

She nodded just as Spasmodic landed in a crouch between them, forcing Anthon to swerve. Her shoulder blades ached from the solid impact, but aside from some minor scrapes and developing bruises she was otherwise unharmed.

"Ah, a bit of a drop never hurt anyone," it said. "Anyway, I found the cabin. It's about an hour that way." Spasmodic waved a hand to its left, gesturing vaguely from south to east.

Nodding, still recovering her breath from the exertion of her descent, Sarene beamed at Anthon. The gesture gave him the answer he needed, and he smiled along with her.

"At least you'll have a story for this Kanderil guy."

"Oh man, Kanderil would go nuts if he heard she fell out of a tree," Spasmodic replied with a shrill laugh. Sarene clapped once before pointing directly at the creature, then quickly waved her hands either side of her head, opening her eyes and mouth wide and exhaling hard, producing a throaty *hiss*.

"Pfft. Alright, so *maybe* I had summat to do with it. But yeah, best we don't mention this. He'll just grump at us."

"Whatever you say," said Anthon, holding out Sarene's satchel. She took it with a nod of thanks. "Shall we go and find this cabin? Maybe you'll enjoy climbing onto its roof, too."

THAT AFTERNOON, AS Kanderil and Orlienn led their horses along the Highway west of Tamiran, the rain fell light and straight around them. The wind had died off, giving brief respite to its icy sting. They had ridden hard for most of the morning, so Kanderil called a break to walk the mounts.

Orlienn neglected to wear a hood, instead letting the damp cover her and drip as it wanted. She didn't wipe the wet from her face. Kanderil had not initiated conversation since they'd left the capital, and the ranger observed the lands around them in silence. The cluster of three mountains a few miles south of Tamiran were a prominent feature of the kingdom, isolated and sudden as they were; residents referred to them as the Orphan Range, abandoned by the Laysine mountains far to the east.

To the north were great expanses of forestland, now all but naked in the late autumn, aside from bunches of gold and brown. Beyond which lay the Meadows, the stunning bastion of agriculture which provided much of Tamir's trade exports.

As a two-wheel cart raced past, the driver gave them a cheerful wave. He smiled warmly despite his soaked clothing, which was being spattered by mud fired up by the two spinning wheels. *Ain't it a great day to be outside?*

Kanderil spoke as the sound of the cart faded away behind them. "Why did the Gathire ask you to take this assignment?"

Orlienn glanced over at him. "I presume it has something to do with my record."

"I have never known the Gathire to make such straightforward decisions."

She raised a brow. "Are you well acquainted with them?"

"Only enough to know they are not to be trusted."

"There's that word again." She smiled, bowing her head.

Kanderil shrugged. "It is important to know who I am dealing with. I never questioned Glaithe about his background. Perhaps if I had, I would have seen his betrayal coming."

"If you don't trust the Gathire, then you won't trust any answers I give to your questions." Orlienn transferred the reins of her horse to the other hand, the beast duly clopping to follow behind her. "I could tell you that I'd never spoken to an Agent before three weeks ago, or that I hadn't heard of Sarene until yesterday morning. Both things are true, but would you believe me?"

"No," said Kanderil. "Not yet."

"I thought as much."

They walked on. The light rain quickened and eased in fits and starts without any rhythm. Kanderil could feel the damp seeping in against his right heel. There was a loose stitch somewhere, and the sole no longer protected him against the wet.

Orlienn's inclusion to the group complicated his methods. Where he'd had the sole responsibility for Sarene's safety, now he would be looking over his shoulder. If Chalimer could manoeuvre Remelas into making this decision, what was to say the man wouldn't eventually press to have Orlienn assigned to the Gathire completely? Were Kanderil's judgement called into question at any stage, it was possible the Assembly would seek to have him separated from Sarene. Should that happen, he would have to remove her from Tamir; a choice he had thus far declined to consider. Sarene was already having trouble adjusting to life apart from her family. Taking her to a different nation, with new customs and traditions, would be a tough ask.

"Are you married?"

Looking up, his reflection lost, he focused on Orlienn. She was already watching him.

"No."

She nodded. "Thought so. I doubt any woman would be happy with you sneaking around the forests of Tamir with a young girl."

Kanderil chuckled. "Aye."

"Does it bother you?"

"The question or the lack of a wife?"

"Being alone."

"Why do you ask?"

Orlienn shrugged and returned her gaze to the Highway. There was nothing of interest as far as they could see, save for millions of raindrops falling upon the road, which snaked to the left about a mile ahead. "Chalimer told me that you'd been a recluse for a few years before you met Sarene. I've spent months at a time by myself in the forests, as you might expect." She tapped a finger against her stag belt buckle. "There was never a man who'd offer me a feather, not with so much time spent absent with assignments. There were occasions when I could have used a friend out there."

Kanderil shook his head. "I am comfortable alone. I prefer my own company."

"What made you leave the Kalethi?"

The thought of Jairen Tar came back to him; the burning cottages, bodies strewn across the street like discarded toys. The face of the girl who had died in his arms, eyes open.

"I grew tired of it," he said, stopping. Orlienn drew to a halt also, turning to stand sideways before him, straight-backed. "The horses should have recovered. We can ride." He grabbed the saddle and slipped a foot into the stirrup, pulling himself up. The horse tensed beneath him, bracing itself for the Hunter's great bulk.

The ranger nodded her head, following suit. Her own

climb was much more graceful.

"So that's it," said Anthon, his face drawn tight to conceal the underlying humour. "You're spending the whole winter here."

Still staring at the cabin, Sarene gradually inclined her head. The structure was indeed well hidden from the outside world as Kanderil had promised, in as much as the surrounding forest had reclaimed the building for itself. Branches from the nearest trees had pushed their way into the planks making up the eastern wall, causing part of the roof to fall in. Of the two windows, only one still sported a shutter, which clung on to a single rusty hinge. Vines and lianas had woven around the carcass of the cabin. The door was intact, but the frame was warped and cracked.

Spasmodic pointed towards a section of the dark, shiny leaves which made up the majority of the plant life clambering around the building. "What's that?"

"Poison ivy," replied Anthon.

"Isn't that stuff poisonous?"

"…Yes. It is."

The creature snorted. "Shame." It walked forwards, running a critical gaze over the cabin. Sarene gave a pointed sigh, scratching at her shoulder.

"Look on the bright side," said Anthon, smiling at her. "At least you'll learn a little about carpentry."

She gave him a sideways glance before moving after Spasmodic, who had paused before the entrance. Before she could react, the creature brought up its right leg – then hammered a stiff kick into the wood. The door burst inwards, snapping whatever was holding the latch in place. Sarene choked on her surprise as a squirrel leapt from one of the gaps in the wall, scurrying off into the surrounding woods. She stared wide-eyed as Spasmodic wandered inside.

"What did you do that for?" called Anthon, walking towards the doorframe to check the damage.

"Might have been assassins inside," it said, the words rattling around inside the dilapidated cabin.

Clicking her tongue, Sarene shook her head… then snickered. Another little piece of damage wouldn't really make much difference. The place was a dump. She recalled the claim of Kanderil's friend Fallerin months previous. *He's a lot of things, but a carpenter isn't one of them.*

Sarene hoped this was an exaggeration, otherwise the winter was going to be insufferable.

"There's a fireplace," yelled Spasmodic. "And a cupboard. It's a bit wonky, though."

Stepping inside the cabin, Sarene found little to be pleased with. The floorboards were also uneven and bent, with roots protruding up from the corner beneath the caved roofing. A bed stood in the corner, and while it was in seemingly fair condition, there was nothing to cover the hard wooden slats. A table and three chairs had survived also, but something had nested in one of the upper corners of the room above them and the furniture was covered with bird droppings. The air held the odour of something else; stale and unpleasant.

"The big man sure can pick 'em," Spasmodic said with a grin.

Anthon was kneeling beside the door latch, trying to push the screws back into place without much success. The latch kept falling off, to be caught and replaced. "It's unusual for a traveller's cabin to be this far into the woods. I couldn't see any poaching trails nearby, and there's much easier ways to push south into Franthia."

With a shrug, Sarene walked over to where Spasmodic stood. The creature was staring up at the collapsed section of roofing. As she followed its gaze, it pointed to a collection of twigs and leaves which had been assembled above an exposed support beam.

"Birds," it said solemnly.

Sarene nodded, trying to ascertain whether it was being sarcastic. Spasmodic turned on its heel and walked back outside, its boots *clomp*ing on the dry floorboards. It nudged Anthon off balance as it walked past. The boy wobbled, the door latch falling to the ground. With a sigh he stood up again, dusting his hands.

"I'm guessing we need to tidy up before we sleep to-night," he said.

In response, Sarene knelt down to pick up a long, thin twig. She scurried over to the door and threw it outside, before turning to wink at Anthon. The ranger's son laughed, looking around the ruined cottage.

"Well," he said, slapping his palms together. "It's a start."

The two of them locked eyes for a few seconds, which to Sarene felt a little too long. Then she glanced about her for something to sweep the floor with, ignoring the *snap* as Spasmodic broke something else outside.

THEY WORKED ON restoring the cabin for two days. After fashioning a broom from sticks tied to a branch with one of the many vines, Sarene cleared the interior of debris and dirt while Anthon cut sections of wood with an old felling axe they'd found in a storage cupboard nailed to the outside of the rear wall. Spasmodic had disappeared early on the first day to find some tools, something it said it would have no issues locating. There was, conspicuously, no mention of paying for said tools. A weave covering for the hole in the roof wouldn't provide much protection from the frequent rains, while the broken door and windows did nothing to stop the chill of the nights.

As well as a bag of nails, a hammer and a hacksaw, the creature had also returned with something else.

"What's this?" it asked as it dumped the knapsack of carpentry gear. It was holding out one hand, the palm facing upwards, with the claws flexed around it like some diabolical flower.

Brushing her hands against her tunic, Sarene left the collection of kindling she'd been preparing for the wood cellar and walked over to investigate. Anthon appeared from inside the cabin, his curiosity piqued.

Alive and well in Spasmodic's hand, with both stalk antennae high on its front end, lay a slimy mollusc.

Sarene beckoned Anthon over, waving him forward. The

ranger's son moved close enough to take a look.

"It's a slug," he said.

"What's a slug?"

"Well… that is."

"I thought it was a homeless snail."

Anthon exchanged looks with Sarene. "I suppose that's one way of putting it."

"Slug." Spasmodic chewed the word over. "*Sluuuu-guh.*"

"They're considered pests," Anthon continued. "They can cause havoc with crops and plant life."

"Heh." Spasmodic brought the slug closer to its face, staring with a childish fascination which Sarene found endearing. "So how do I feed it?"

"Feed it?"

"Yeah. You humans keep pets, right? Dogs and cats and… Sheep, I guess." The creature hawked and spat abruptly, the phlegm barely missing Sarene's leg. She dodged to the side, hiccupping in surprise. "I always fancied having a little friend."

Glancing around, Sarene knelt to pick up a small clump of moist leaves from the ground. She reached over to place it into the creature's palm, tucking it next to the slug. Spasmodic snickered, staring at its new companion. The slug, for its part, gave an achingly slow wave of antennae, making no attempt to head for the mulch.

The lack of enthusiasm for Sarene's offering brought a deep frown from Spasmodic. "Go on then. Eat the leaves."

Anthon gave a peculiar grin. "I'm not convinced it takes direction like that."

"Shh. You'll put him off."

The slug continued to do nothing.

Muttering, Spasmodic stomped off towards the cabin. "There's tools and things in the bag. I'm gonna see if I can train him."

Anthon turned his attention to Sarene, his expression matching her own. They were both unsure of exactly what they had just witnessed. Licking her lips, Sarene gave a subtle tap to her temple.

"You don't say," replied Anthon.

After another long pause, the pair of them started to smile. Then they laughed, with the associated guilt of not wanting Spasmodic to hear them. Sarene brought a hand to her mouth and bit down hard on her knuckle, trying to stem her giggling, but it was awfully difficult. Anthon managed to avoid making noise, one hand tight against his jaw, but his eyes creased shut and his shoulders juddered up and down. Sarene made her way towards the tools, focusing her attention elsewhere. They had a few hours before nightfall, and it was important to make a start on repairing the roof.

From within the cabin, she could hear Spasmodic quietly talking to itself. No, not to itself; to the *slug*. Soft, coaxing words designed to form a bond between the two of them.

The idea brought a fresh wave of hilarity which Sarene struggled to control.

THE MAN STEPPED forward and planted the base of the spear into the dusty, cracked ground. Furs and leathers of pale yellow contrasted against the black skin beneath, his torso heavy-set and well defined. At the challenge the lion roared, its terrible maw splitting open. Thirty metres separated human from beast.

Only an oasis far in the distance, green and lush amid the dust and the dirt, and the skeletal remains of a creature which had failed to reach them broke up the otherwise desolate horizon. The sky above was a cloudless blue, bleached by the domineering sun which looked too large to exist without incinerating the world beneath its shimmering glare.

The beast charged.

As it approached the man bent his legs and lowered himself, arms spread wide. He smiled, revealing perfect teeth, and licked his lower lip. The lion's speed was extraordinary, and he was impressed.

The ground between them closed in seconds. At the last second the lion leapt, both forepaws outstretched. The man took the impact at full force, the air expelled from his lungs and the spear falling from his grasp as they crashed against the unforgiving ground. Immediately he rammed his left forearm between the lion's jaws, a heavy steel bracer protecting him from its fangs. The pressure of its bite brought a grunt of pain. He pulled his legs up tight beneath him, rolling back to place his knees against the thing's chest, aware that leaving his belly exposed invited disembowelment from the beast's hind legs. The forelegs around him turned inwards for just a second, the claws carving shallow grooves into his back, before relinquishing as the lion sought to preserve its balance.

Tugging his trapped arm to the left, the man hammered his right fist hard into the beast's temple. The crashing blow stunned the lion for just a moment before it renewed the assault with ferocity. Bracing his shoulders against the earth, the man pushed his knees upwards with all his might, seeking to dislodge the lion enough to reach for his weapon. The lion growled around his forearm, canines grinding against metal, saliva dripping down onto his chest. Fingers scratched at the dirt a few inches too short, an inch too short, fingertips brushing the shaft just enou—

The lion managed to gain purchase, throwing itself forwards again. The beast's weight forced the man to focus on it again, abandoning the spear and instead reaching up to grip the lion's throat. The beast's back legs snapped forward, cutting a wicked gash into his calf. Fuelled by pain, the man cried out as he pushed forward with both huge arms, snapping the lion's head back and placing pressure on its spine. The lion scrambled as its air was cut off, fighting to regain control. After several frantic seconds trying to tear itself free, the lion fell to its side and tried to roll. The man released his grip and kicked away in the opposite direction, creating space between them. As he tumbled to his feet he grasped the spear, bringing it up with both hands.

Again the lion rushed forwards. This time the man brought the base of the spear whipping around to crack against the lion's jaw. Dazed, the lion brought its head down and shook it from side to side, rubbing a paw across its nose. In an instant the spear again whirled and thrust forward, the tip entering the lion's left shoulder. The great predator roared in response, backing away to disengage from the blade.

The black man waited, taking three steps back.

Before him the lion's left foreleg tensed and cramped. It could not compensate in time and pitched forwards, back legs flailing. Within moments both forelegs were paralyzed. The rest of its great body followed within a minute. Then its eyes closed and it lay there, prone and crippled, breath ragged and light.

As the victor took deep lungfuls of air into his broad chest, leaning against the spear, a single pair of hands started to applaud. He turned around to see a white-haired man in a full robe of lavender velvet.

"Impressive," said Tyrrial, walking forward. "You do realise, however, that you had not protected yourself?"

The man nodded. "Without danger there is no challenge, brother."

"Of course not. And without Mubuto, there would be no Four. Remember that the next time you want to pick a fight with a lion."

"The spear tip was laced with a paralyzing agent. As soon as I wounded it, I had won."

"And the rolling around on the floor prior to that…?"

Mubuto offered his hand. Tyrrial took it and the two men embraced. "It is good to see you on your feet again, Tyrrial."

"Yes, yes. I have heard the 'you were lucky' speech from the others."

Standing back, the larger man shrugged. "I would not say lucky. I would say you got exactly what you deserved."

Now it was Tyrrial's turn to laugh. "I knew I could count on you to be blunt with me."

Mubuto walked over to the lion. Kneeling down beside it, he laid a hand against the wound in the beast's shoulder. His lips moved. When the hand withdrew the wound had disappeared, leaving flat skin and undisturbed fur. The lion's breathing became easier, and its tail started to flick from side to side. Mubuto then inspected his own injuries, repeating the healing process.

"Perhaps we could talk somewhere a little less… barren?" said Tyrrial. He gestured around him, one brow raised. "No doubt you are thirsty after your petting session."

Rising to his feet, Mubuto nodded. "Of course. The Orchard?" He dipped two fingers into a small pouch at his belt and retrieved an obsidian stone etched with a single golden rune.

"Wonderful." Tyrrial produced an identical stone from his own pocket, and spoke under his breath.

TYRRIAL SET FOOT onto lush grassland. The cool air was welcome refreshment from the arid heat of the steppes, with clear skies of rich, sapphire blue. Mubuto stood next to him, his great spear lying against a shoulder.

The Orchard, known as *Jantagulanu* in the native dialect, was a beautiful meadow lying at the base of a broad valley which led down towards the Bultha Lakes, a great expanse of water which ebbed out towards the southern oceans. Trees ran for as far as the eye could see, spread thinly and producing many different kinds of fruit. The tribe in control of this area, the Sumnu, kept the Orchard in good order, ensuring the grounds were well maintained and the trees pruned and free of pests. Even now Tyrrial could see a number of locals tending to the Orchard, picking from the trees and placing the fruits into large, shallow wicker bowls.

Replacing the dark stone back inside his pocket, Tyrrial surveyed the area around him. Picturesque and wonderfully positioned at a slant away from the westerly currents, it was a marvel of blues and greens, as though one had stepped inside a glass marble.

"If I didn't know any better," said Mubuto, "I would say this was one of your favourite locations."

Tyrrial smiled, walking towards the nearest tree and reaching towards one of the lower branches. "What makes you say that?" He took hold of a pear and pulled it free, leaves shaking from the gentle *snap* as the fruit's stem gave way.

"It is one of the few you enter without a scowl."

Rubbing the pear against his robe, Tyrrial shrugged his thin shoulders. "This is how the world should be. Man and woman living in complete harmony with the surrounding lands."

Mubuto gave a low, rumbling chuckle. "This area is idyllic. Not everyone else can be as lucky."

"Everyone else should work a little harder." The pear gave a crisp, juicy *crunch* as it was bitten into.

"Such a practical view, my brother."

"Am I so wrong to think that this serenity could be achieved across the lands? Exactly how we intended?"

"Perhaps not." Mubuto laid his spear against the trunk of

the pear tree and stretched his arms, holding his breath. The exhalation which followed was satisfied. "So what can I do for you, Tyrrial?"

"How do you mean?"

"I am presuming you did not come here to watch me wrestle lions."

"No, I did not," Tyrrial admitted. "But that does sound like quite a *good* reason. I shall keep your fondness for pointless risks in mind."

The two of them grew silent. Mubuto lowered himself to the ground, cross legged, and ran his gaze across the Orchard. Tyrrial finished his pear. A young woman dressed in a cotton shift walked by, bowl in hand, inspecting the lower branches for ripe fruit as she moved along the row. She paid no attention to the two legendary figures as she passed only yards from them.

"How are things here in the southern lands?" asked Tyrrial.

Mubuto offered a shrug. "Not much has changed since last we spoke. Aside from the Juu'ad and their internal squabbles, things remain calm."

The smaller of the two nodded. "As ever. I suppose you are grateful for the Juu'ad, for giving you something to keep an eye on."

"I would prefer if they were less antagonistic," the black man replied with a chuckle.

"How do you do it?"

Mubuto quirked a brow. "Do what?"

"The southern lands are the most peaceful. When we

journeyed, these people were savages. How did you usher in such a drastic change?"

"You forget that I am one of these savage people, Tyrrial."

"Oh, do not misunderstand me." Tyrrial tossed the remains of the pear core aside. Nothing landed on the floor. "We've discussed the ancient tribes of the Kunta and the Luthue a hundred times over the centuries, and how progressive they were for their time. But you came from Huuna, one of three glorious cities which thrived on advanced knowledge and study. The rest of these nations were forged in blood and suffering, war and death."

Mubuto remained quiet, watching his companion.

"Where the rest of us walked, of course, there was also endless war. But the northern lands fought for prestige and resources. The east and the west, they were fascinated with territory and power. But here in the south it was always for dominance. Entire civilisations were wiped out in repeated massacres. The tribe with the largest army destroyed their neighbours, until internal revolts splintered these huge war bands into smaller groups and started the whole process again." Tyrrial wagged a finger, a soft smile appearing on his mature features. "But you... You turned it all around with unquestionable success. The southern kingdoms are the safest of all. Despite such heat and limited farmland, you preside over arguably the most prosperous also. So I ask: how? How did you orchestrate these people to such an existence?"

Mubuto mulled over the question, his attention never

leaving Tyrrial. After a pause he spoke.

"There *is* a point to this little history lesson, brother. You are repeating things we are both fully aware of. You also know how I am going to respond, for we have debated my methods many times. So again. What can I do for you?"

"Humour me. How did you do it?"

Mubuto sighed, tilting his head to signify his compliance. "Very well… When our work began, I understood what my people needed. What they could become, so to speak. The southern kingdoms were consumed with tradition and history. Each generation passed on the stories and the tales to the next. At the time, those lessons revolved around the military success or failures between their rivals. If one man lost a brother in battle, he would pass the need for revenge on to his children. It was a never ending cycle of retribution and bloodshed.

"All I did was encourage those who obeyed our directive to shift that legacy of respect for our ancestors to more productive areas. If a man became a great scholar or a woman an acclaimed artist, then *these* were the achievements which should be aspired to by their offspring. Tradition is just as important today as it was all those years ago. The only thing these people, *my* people, changed was how to focus those traditions. Those three great cities became the hub for progression and within a hundred years there were a dozen more. Look at Zembala. I would argue it is the greatest city in the world, and yet when I first arrived it was nothing more than a collection of huts on the outskirts of a swamp, presided over by an obese man with a thirst for diamonds."

"You always make it sound so simple." Tyrrial chuckled softly. "Glossing over the many thousands of warriors you had to overcome."

Mubuto smirked. "That is an entirely different story, and has little bearing on my answer. I suppose I could have tried to rebuild the cultures of these lands from the ground up, but I would have never achieved the results that the southern nations now enjoy."

Holding up one hand, Tyrrial shook his head. "Let us hold my thought for a while longer. There were obstacles for you to overcome. Many tried to kill you once word had spread of your impending arrival."

A nod. "Of course."

"How did you balance the eradication of these hostile forces with the amity of your message?"

"When a chieftain witnesses their army swept out from before them, they are quick to agree to the following lessons of peace."

The two men smiled at each other. A swallow landed a few feet from Mubuto, its head jerking as it studied the larger creatures. The fearsome warrior held out a hand, and the bird hopped up onto his palm without hesitation.

"Do you miss it?" asked Tyrrial.

"I am content with the fruits of my labours."

"I meant the conflict. The application of our will."

Mubuto gave his companion a sideways glance. "Do I miss the killing?"

Tyrrial laughed. "No, brother. Not the death. None of us miss the senseless butchery we undertook in the name of enlightenment. But so long has passed since we journeyed. Look at Tamir. If I had not undertaken the task of subduing Remelas we would have experienced the first full scale invasion of another land in five centuries. It almost cost me my life, but I am glad I intervened. That is the conflict I am talking about. The demonstration of our powers."

"Noble of you." Mubuto laid the tip of a finger against the swallow's head, stroking back along the feathers. The bird shivered, but accepted the contact. "However, do not expect me to believe you were entirely altruistic in your motives. You did what you did because of the girl."

"Perhaps. But her actions vindicated me, I believe. She *is* a threat to us, should she choose to be."

"You killed her brother before her eyes. I would say that provides her with a strong reason which she did not previously have."

"That is beside the point," said Tyrrial shortly. "Let us stay on topic here. Tamir raised an army with the full intent to use it. Who is to say that other nations will not be so bold in the near future?"

"Then we shall deal with it when the time comes," replied Mubuto.

With a soft sigh, Tyrrial spread his hands. "I am guessing that Corliani has not told you, then."

Mubuto raised his hand towards the sky. The swallow flapped and took flight, climbing back into the perfumed air around them. "Told me what?"

"The Carthleid have taken umbrage towards Remelas's plans. Now they know that the Tamir were intended to subjugate them, some are calling for a pre-emptive invasion of their western neighbours."

"Carthlei is going to invade Tamir?"

"Not yet. But it is something we must consider. If not Carthlei, it will be somewhere else eventually."

"The eastern lands belong to Corliani. We must trust his ability to handle the situation."

"Perhaps we can put a stop to this before he has to handle anything." Tyrrial smiled. "Perhaps we can ensure ourselves another five hundred years of peace without worrying about such matters."

Mubuto muttered. "Your fondness for vague implications is grating, my friend. Say what you want to say."

Tyrrial held up a hand… then chuckled. "Forgive me. I am not trying to irritate you. Perhaps it is for the best if we speak together with the others."

Rising from the ground, Mubuto reached for his spear. "Oh, no, you don't. No man travels halfway across the lands to simply suggest we talk elsewhere. What did you come here for, Tyrrial?"

"If the time came to walk once more, spreading our message to humanity. If the time came… Would you?"

A smile gradually appeared on the larger man's face. He glanced across the Orchard, along the rows of trees expertly positioned and tended to, giving the illusion of a living corridor. A rare gust of wind caught the leaves and Mubuto watched as they rustled against each other, whispering their secrets.

"For this to remain as it is? Of course I would."

Tyrrial smiled. "I am glad we can agree, brother."

Chapter Ten

THELLIS RUBBED HIS hands together yet again, before bringing them up to his mouth. He exhaled from the back of his throat, pushing warm air through his fingers. It was cold this evening, painfully so, and he wasn't in the mood for keeping an eye on the ramshackle apartment across the market road.

The sky overhead was clear. After many a night spent stamping his feet and tucking his arms inside his thin jacket, he realised the coming winter was going to be a hard one. All the men working for Kraye kept saying so. Thellis had no reason to disbelieve them. Then again, it was a clever boy such as him who avoided disagreeing with them at all. They were tough people and gave little consideration for the street rats Kraye hired as scouts, watchers and pick pockets. Any of the youngsters who spoke out of turn were liable to get a slap round the head.

Blowing into his hands again with as little success as all previous times, Thellis looked over at the building he'd been assigned to. Nothing happened there. Nobody came or left. Ever. Heiran was a recluse; the man rarely appeared outside except to perform a task for Kraye. There was word amongst the watchers that a young girl lived in the tiny apartment as well. A daughter or something. Gujia had said so one night while they crowded around a coal scuttle fire, keeping warm and sharing what little food Kraye's gang dished out for them. Then again, Gujia had a tendency to lie and make up stories. She thought it would win her friends, but it never worked. It just made her sound like an idiot.

The sound of footsteps brought the lad out of his reflection and Thellis turned his head, peering around the corner of the alley to his right. He saw nothing but a couple of barrels, a broken crate and some refuse. The alley reeked of rotten vegetables and piss. The market was to blame for the former; the late night drunks for the latter. It wouldn't be more than an hour before the taverns kicked out for the night and they all started wandering back to their homes. That was the most dangerous time for a watcher like him. The alley provided an extra route for escape should anyone take offence to his presence.

Movement to his right. A figure, clad in black, strode out across the road. A broad hood concealed their features, but the curved sword sheathed at their side was prominent. They slipped between two of the market stall husks of wood and boarding, heading for Heiran's apartment. The figure – surely a woman, for they were slim of arm and had a smaller stride than a man of the same height – knocked at the door. The sound reverberated around the empty market.

Thellis shuffled to one side and craned his neck to watch for an answer.

Something cold touched the back of his neck. Frozen in place, Thellis felt breath on his cheek. A low, assertive voice spoke.

"You're finished for the night, boy. Take yourself off, and do not tell anyone what you saw."

Blinking, Thellis tried to turn his head to regard the mysterious speaker. The cold at his neck became painful. Sharp.

"If I leave, I'll be given the strap," he said mournfully.

The stranger chuckled under his breath. "Then make your choice. You may leave and face the strap… or stay and welcome death."

The knife pressed harder. A hot trickle ran down the back of his neck. Thellis winced.

"I'll… I'll go."

"A wise decision. Remember my warning. Should I hear that you told tales, your friends will suffer in your place."

Thellis lurched forward, breaking into a run. He sprinted along the edge of the market road, back towards the abandoned shack where the other street rats slept. The blood on his neck was joined by cold sweat which chilled him almost as much as the words he fled from.

GLAITHE SHEATHED HIS knife.

The note had been received that morning. Heiran was in. Evidently the crimes of Prince Remelas weighed heavily on the man's heart. The only demand was that they leave town that same night. Glaithe deduced that Heiran was terrified of being found out.

Kraye ruled this city through more than intelligence and forethought. The gang lord was also an unforgiving man, and made sure everyone knew it.

Across the street, Niallya stepped inside the ramshackle apartment. The door was not closed behind her.

What a find the mercenary had been. Skilled with a sword, cool headed and ambitious, just as he was. Why she insisted on wearing that hood at all times was a mystery. For all he knew she was appallingly scarred about the head, or somehow balding. But then her appearance was trivial, providing she did her job. *That* much she had certainly accomplished.

Over the past three months they'd made enough gold to hire some very capable assassins, should Glaithe have chosen to do so. Mainly from Niallya's efforts of robbing the robbers; crimes against the criminals. He had specified that she take the purses of those already wanted by the law, for the sake of drawing less attention. If a family were killed in their own homes or on the Highway then the guards or, worse, the Gathire would take notice. Few cared for a cut-throat lying dead within the forests.

Continuing that methodology, a famed assassin such as Lhellid the Grim or Fausten Ice-Eyes was not suitable for his needs. Glaithe wanted a complete unknown. Somebody who would not warrant a second glance from passers-by.

Somebody like Heiran.

The widower was perfect. Skilled with a bow, with an obvious dislike of Remelas and the desperation to take such an enormous risk. The combination of fear, solitude and destitution had built a ripe fruit which Glaithe now plucked. It was all falling into place.

He resisted the urge to light a smoke stick. As miniscule a risk as it would be, he didn't want to light up his position to any potential witnesses. Instead he stepped back into the alley, using the shadows to conceal himself. He started to stretch, using the techniques taught by the Gathire. He tensed and eased his muscles in rhythm, twisting his limbs and hooking his arms to loosen the muscles of his shoulders and back, before bending at the waist to stretch his hamstrings and calves. Glaithe remained silent through every one, breathing through his nose and suppressing the natural sighs which accompanied exertion.

STANDING STRAIGHT, GLAITHE looked across the street to see Niallya leading both Heiran and his daughter across the market avenue. Tillyan was all dirty long hair and wide eyes, her stuffed bear dangling from her grip by a flimsy cloth limb. A chilly gust of wind swept across the three of them, and Heiran turned his head against it. Now clothed, he wore a heavy woollen waistcoat over a pale shirt, around which he clutched a threadbare grey cloak. The man's bow was strapped across his back, alongside a quiver.

Niallya stepped into the alley as Glaithe moved from the darkness to meet her.

"Ready?" she asked.

"It'll be easy," Glaithe responded.

"You really do not know Kraye at all, do you."

He smirked. "I imagine I'll know a lot about the man in an hour's time."

"Quite. Try not to get yourself killed. You still owe me a fair amount of money."

"Your compassion is touching." Glaithe nodded to Hei-ran, ignoring the man's cold stare, and pointed back along the alley. "You'll find our wagon back there. He's asleep in the trailer. I'll catch you along the road soon."

Niallya nodded, leading the two refugees down between the buildings while he departed in the opposite direction, following the market road west.

GLAITHE EASED ALONG the back wall of Kraye's mansion. Amidst the grime and muck of Ghellei, a city created of timber and stone, the two-story structure was designed with an architect's finesse and crafted by fine carpenters, each plank and slate lined up to the inch. A modest garden, fenced all around, separated the mansion from the streets; a protective barrier against the common folk. The lawns were well kept, surrounded along the edges of the fence by rosebushes now out of bloom. A gravel path ran from the front entrance to the main gate.

Two men patrolled these gardens. Neither of them saw Glaithe scale over the spike-topped railings nor heard him land on the soft lawn. They didn't notice him hurry, flat-footed, to the mansion wall.

By his timing, he had around eighteen seconds before the next pass of his position.

The distance to the balcony above was around twelve feet. Glaithe was of the opinion that Kraye was conceited enough to keep the only upper balcony to himself; a single door led from it, which he believed to be Kraye's private quarters. The upper balcony was lined with a wooden balustrade. A padded hook attached to a length of rope was wrapped across his shoulder; he pulled this free and jumped, tossing the hook forwards. It slid between two of the balusters before catching hold. Tugging the rope once to be sure, Glaithe pulled himself upwards, threading the slack beneath between the arches of his feet for purchase. Moments later he swung his body over the railing and pulled the rope through the fence, laying down flat.

The guard strolled along the garden below him, passing by without an upwards glance. Glaithe looked out across Ghellei as he waited. In the gloom of the late autumn sky, he saw nothing about the cesspit of a city he would miss.

Alone again Glaithe rose to a crouch, producing a lock-pick from between his teeth. The room beyond was dark. Kraye's schedule meant the gang lord should be in his office at this time. Glaithe felt around inside the lock with the pick until he found the catch. With his tongue poking between his teeth, he tugged on the door handle whilst nudging the catch gently, all the while counting in his head. With six seconds before the next man was due to pass below, the lock tumblers slid into place. Glaithe pushed the door and slipped inside, closing it behind him. Evidently Kraye paid for the mansion to be serviced as well as cleaned, for both the lock and the hinges operated in silence.

He found himself in a bedroom of grand comfort. The bed was huge, pillared and curtained. A heavy quilt sheeted in purple silk lay beneath a mound of pillows, tasselled and stitched in the style of the Western nations. The walls were painted a creamy peach colour, while the floorboards were hidden beneath a vibrant red carpet. A dozen pictures hung from the walls, all painted by the same hand, mainly of landscapes and wide city portraits. Only one stood out, this of a pretty woman with long dark hair and blue eyes, dressed in a frock of deep green. Each painting was framed; each frame was layered in gold leaf, which would have cost some fair coin.

With a dry smirk, Glaithe moved to the portrait of the woman and pulled the frame from its hook to reveal a safe embedded into the wall.

"Much too obvious, Kraye," he whispered aloud before replacing the picture. "I expected more."

Outside, from the corridor, footsteps fell against hard wood. Glaithe remained perfectly still, holding his breath.

The footsteps grew in volume, creaked right outside the door. Then stopped.

Glaithe placed one hand against the hilt of his knife.

Several seconds passed before the footsteps started again, the unknown occupant of the mansion continuing on their way.

Relaxing, Glaithe considered the room. There were several places he could complete the task: the set of drawers beside the bed, covered in bottles of fragrance, shaving materials and tonics; a mirrored dresser standing nearest the door leading further into the mansion. There was a desk with a chair, also. In contrast with the cluttered room, the desk was tidy, with nothing atop it other than a covered ink well and a quill.

The chair tucked under the desk was cushioned and well made. Sturdy. Befitting a man of both Kraye's wealth and size.

The humour of hiding his deposit so close to his victim brought a smile to Glaithe's lips. He moved to the chair, tugging a small sack from his belt. Fingers dipped inside to produce three large gold coins. He checked them over one more time, just to be sure. Each coin had been scarred on one side, a cross within a circle, and then engraved with black paint.

Also within the sack was a small vial. He pulled this free, pulled the stopper with his teeth, and poured a little of the contents onto the first of the coins. The liquid oozed out, drawing tendrils from the edge of the vial when enough had been emptied. Glaithe reached under the chair and stuck the marked coin against the base of the seat.

When this had been repeated for all three coins, Glaithe stood and put away the vial, replacing the sack against his belt.

Nobody who flaunts their wealth in a city like this suffers from paranoia, he thought.

He returned to the exit leading to the balcony. Holding the handle down, he inched the door forwards until he could listen to the grounds below. Both guards wore swords, and both had their scabbards fixed to their waists. The gentle creak of leather announced their positions. Once Glaithe was sure that the next patrolman had walked by, he slid back onto the balcony and closed the door behind him. Ideally he would have locked the door, but there wasn't time and he didn't have the right tools.

Using the hook to lower himself to the ground would take too much time, and unhooking the thing again would be almost impossible. Instead Glaithe coiled the rope around his shoulder, then swung his leg over the balustrade and lowered himself as far as he could. He dropped the remaining distance to the lawn below.

He landed two yards away from a very surprised man holding a match to a smoke stick.

Glaithe ended his life within seconds, pulling a knife and ramming it into the man's eye socket, twisting in one fluid motion. He died without a sound, dropping like wet linen.

"Shit…" murmured Glaithe. He reached down and took the fallen smoke stick from the ground, placing it between his lips. He then ran for the fence, leaping to reach for the top spikes just as the first cry of alarm filled the night air.

NIALLYA HELD THE reins to the wagon as it trundled west along the Highway, beneath stars that glimmered in the deep autumn night like silver flies. Heiran sat beside her, while Tillyan dozed in his lap. The man fussed over his sleeping daughter, checking the blanket pulled up around her shoulders every few minutes and kissing her brow from time to time. The woman couldn't tell if this was a habit born of love, or of nerves. He constantly scanned the terrain around them, as though expecting an ambush. Niallya couldn't blame him.

The road was quiet at such an hour. Only two others had passed them by; both on horseback, both lacking pace. They were tucked up in several layers of heavy clothing to protect against the painful wind. Niallya had yielded, and now wore a black velvet cloak across her shoulders. The cloak was expensive and comfortable, fitting her well.

She smiled at the memory of the woman from whom she'd taken it. The cries of indignation had been most enjoyable.

"Who's in the back?" asked Heiran quietly.

"Nobody," said Niallya. "Just a loose end."

The man chuckled. "This Glaithe is quite the character."

"He is indeed."

"How long have you worked with him?"

"Long enough."

Heiran sighed. "Are you going to be so secretive for the whole journey?"

"I would be glad to talk," the mercenary replied, "but certain subjects are off limits."

"How will that build trust? You have asked me to perform a deed of some magnitude."

Niallya turned her head beneath her cowl, which rustled at the movement. "You accepted of your own free will. And I have not asked you about your personal relationships; nor would I. Should I be caught after the act, I would not want to know any information about you. For your safety and that of your child."

Heiran placed a hand against Tillyan's head, stroking her hair. The girl nuzzled into her father's chest at the touch, drawing the blanker tighter around her.

"Of course," he said. "I understand."

They continued quietly for a few more minutes, the turning of the four wheels on either side liberating them from total silence. Niallya kept her gaze on the road ahead.

The fact that Heiran had a daughter – one he obviously cared for deeply – was an unexpected factor in Glaithe's plan. This wasn't just any assassination; this was regicide. The punishment was execution. The exact method used was unknown, but she imagined it would be suitably awful. Torture by the prison staff was a certainty. If public outrage was great enough, there was a possibility that Heiran's family would be held accountable. He was risking his daughter on the unknown, just to repay a debt. A grudge.

Such hatred was difficult to comprehend. Niallya learned long ago that it was safer to remain distant from those negative feelings. Her own upbringing had been difficult enough. To this day, she suffered nightmares of her father's strap; of his cold hands creeping along her skin in the dead of night, while her mother slept. It would have been easy to give in to resentment and hate. But that would have resolved nothing. Instead she learnt to control her feelings and suppress her fears. Only clear thoughts and a strong resolve could take on anything life produced. And whatever controlled one's existence, be it the Four, the supposed Gods, fate or destiny... well, it certainly had a sense of humour.

"Why are you doing this?"

Niallya looked up. "Pardon?"

Heiran watched the shadows concealing her face. "Why are you risking everything like this?"

"I was wondering the same about you."

"You know why I am."

"I know some of the story. There's more to this than simply getting out of Ghellei."

"You're deflecting."

She smiled. "Yes, I am."

"Sharing the reasons why a mercenary like you is plotting to kill Remelas isn't going to endanger you any further."

Considering this, gently tugging on the reins to steer the two horses back from the edge of the road, Niallya nodded. "I suppose it would not. Very well. I am doing it for the reward."

"From whom?"

"Again, information I should not share. But suffice to say I will reap enough from this task to ensure I need never want for anything in the future."

"Glaithe is wealthy, then?"

A smile. "He is many things, but he is not rich."

"So who's payin' you?"

The sound of a horse racing at speed along the road caused both passengers to turn and look back. A lone figure in dark clothing was pushing a grey mount hard. Niallya passed the reins over to one hand and placed the other on the hilt of her blade. She waited, shrugging off the right shoulder of her cloak. A silver bracer flashed in the moonlight against porcelain skin. As the rider tugged hard on the reins of his horse, the grey tossed its head and dug its hooves into the road, staggering to a halt.

"Heiran, take the reins and head to the forest," said Glaithe. Niallya exhaled, letting go of her blade. "Niallya needs to come with me."

"What happened?" asked Heiran.

"Some idiot tried to mug me as I left the city. I was seen by the guard."

"Seen doing what?"

"Giving him a hug," Glaithe spat in annoyance. "What do you *think*?"

Niallya shook her head, pointing north. "The tree line is almost a mile away. If anyone is on your heels, they'll catch the wagon long before it reaches concealment. Even then, this vehicle won't fit in that area. The woodland is too dense."

Glaithe swore. "Let's make sure we don't screw up, then."

"How many are you expecting?"

"Hard to say. But whatever happens, this wagon needs to keep moving." Glaithe heeled the mount around towards the rear of the wagon, reaching inside to pull free a crossbow and a slim quiver of bolts. "If anyone is following me, we'll make sure they leave empty handed."

"And if you're unsuccessful?" asked Heiran, his voice hard. "I'm left at the mercy of Kraye."

Glaithe shot him a dark glare, a look to match the smothering night. "Then don't get caught."

GLAITHE RODE BACK east for several minutes, with Niallya seated behind him. He pulled up and dismounted at a small bridge built across a shallow river running north to south. Niallya stepped alongside, rubbing her hands together against the cold.

"Sloppy," she said.

"I wasn't expecting one of Kraye's house staff to step outside for a bloody smoke," Glaithe replied. He was calming now, having made it back to the wagon before any pursuers reached him. With a choke point to defend – as narrow an advantage as it was, considering the river was less than ten feet wide – and Niallya beside him, he felt confident he could cope with several assailants.

"What makes you think they've followed you this far?"

"I'd imagine Kraye would be livid to find someone dared to trespass on his property, let alone kill one of his men. I took care to stay out of sight, so if we're lucky they don't know which path to search."

Nodding once, Niallya pulled free her sword. "You do realise we've left Nichai alone with a stranger? One who's agreed to murder his brother?"

Glaithe smiled. "I imagine that would be some conversation."

"Do you trust Heiran enough for that?"

"Unless he has a sudden change of heart towards the House of Tamir, I think we'll be fine." He pulled back the string of his hand-bow – Gathire issue, light and easy to load – before speaking again. "One hour. If nobody shows, we can consider ourselves fortunate."

They waited without speaking. Glaithe paced, rolling his shoulders and flicking his hands, stinging the fingers to encourage circulation. The situation was far from ideal, and the lack of knowledge regarding the men he would be facing was a source of concern. Kraye was known to employ mercenaries and ex-military where possible, and given the recent mass cuts to the Tamir military, this lent the possibility that there would be many with formal combat training available in Ghellei to hire. But at short notice to apprehend a suspected thief? Mobs of regular street thugs were likely. Besides, they had no way of knowing that their mark would be a former Gathire Agent. The two witnesses from the mansions grounds would have seen a single figure fleeing the scene with nothing more than a knife in hand. A common, if rather brave, thief was the most likely culprit.

Time passed. Above, the moon inched across the sky, casting a silvery hue on anything reflective. The bridge was stone and well made, befitting the Highway; the longest single road through Tamir. Nothing stirred; nothing whispered. Glaithe closed his eyes. The stillness of the night enveloped them both; an ethereal black holding them in place within the chill and the hush.

A hush disturbed by the sound of horses.

"Put your blade away," Glaithe said to his companion. After hesitating briefly, Niallya complied.

Six riders approached at speed, four of them holding torches. Glaithe threw back his hood, raising his left arm to flag them down. The right remained concealed by his cloak, which he pulled across to drape over his shoulder.

"Ho! Help, we've been robbed!"

The riders slowed as they approached the bridge. In the torchlight, he identified five men and one woman – though the woman, stout and grim-faced, could easily pass for male, with only her breastplate revealing her gender. All of them were armed. Two of the group pulled free their blades, glaring at Glaithe as he approached.

"Some bastard's stolen my wife's horse!"

One of the group shook his head. "None of our business. Get out of the way."

"But it cost a lot of money! A silver mare, true breeding stock. Goes like the wind. The thief aimed an arrow at my heart and told me to tell *her* to dismount. Something about being chased. A likely story!" Glaithe delivered the words with bitterness, turning his head to spit on the ground.

The group looked at each other. "Chased? By whom?"

"'Krane's men,' he said, as though that meant something. What does it matter? We've been robbed!"

"Why is your wife hiding her face?" called the ugly woman. "And why does she carry a sword?"

"She's been crying," snapped Glaithe. "Allow her some modesty, for goodness sake. And she carries a weapon in case we *get robbed*. As a deterrent. Well… I suppose that didn't work out so well."

"Krane… or Kraye?" asked another, a man with a full beard with humourless eyes, holding a torch high above his head.

"Kraye, Krane, what does it matter? He's stolen a horse which cost me a whole year's wage!"

"That's our man," said the first speaker to the others, before addressing Glaithe directly. "Tell me, you whining fool. Where did he go?"

"Nowhere," replied Glaithe, throwing back his cloak and bringing up his arm. The hand bow clicked, and a bolt smashed through the man's teeth. His head snapped back, and his body slumped to the side. As the five others cried out and drew their weapons, Glaithe pulled free his long knife and threw. The blade hurtled through the air before burying itself in the chest of a second man, who stared at it dumbly.

Niallya was beside him in seconds, her curved blade gleaming against the torches swung back and forth in the confusion. Three of the remaining riders had dismounted by the time she reached them, the one closest to her instead remaining in the saddle, bringing his own crossbow to bear. She threw a vicious cut across the horse's face, causing it to rear up in pain and terror. Leaping to the side to avoid lashing hooves, Niallya rolled back to her feet in time to block a downward sword-sweep from one of the men on foot.

To her right, Glaithe waited as the woman charged him, a hatchet carving a path through the air at head-height. He swayed to the side, the heavy blade missing him by inches, and threw a fist into her jaw. It sent her staggering back but did not drop her. The third footman flanked him, and Glaithe had to dive to the ground to avoid being cleaved through the waist. Before his assailant could react he fired a kick to the man's knees, which buckled and pitched them forward. Glaithe jumped to his feet as the woman approached him again. Without a weapon, he had to wait for an opportunity to disarm her.

That chance never came. The woman suddenly cried out, her eyes growing wide enough for the whites to be clearly visible in the light from the now-scattered torches. Red dribbled from her mouth, before she toppled forwards to reveal Niallya standing behind her, the sword in her hand saturated by glistening liquid. She focused on the man whom Glaithe had kicked. They met at once, swords clashing together, thrusting and parrying back and forth. Glaithe looked across to the rest of Kraye's henchmen; all five others now lay sprawled across the floor, either dead or dying. He grinned. Niallya was proving to be *such* a find.

The final man was well trained, and was holding his own against the opposing mercenary. Glaithe casually walked back to the discarded hand-bow and loaded another bolt. The man had already noticed what Glaithe was doing, and was fighting to keep his focus on the woman.

"Niallya, step back."

"Wait," cried the man in agonising frustration. Niallya blocked one last slash, hopping away. The man brought all his limbs up in a futile effort to protect himself.

"Wait, dammit!"

The bolt entered below his armpit, slipping between his ribs; he fell seconds afterwards, gurgling a final protest.

Niallya wiped her blade on his clothes before sheathing it, looking around the scene of ruin surrounding them. Two of the horses remained at a distance; the others had long since fled.

"So you can fight after all," she said aloud.

"You doubted me all this time?"

"I never believed I would stand with you against six foes. There is a difference."

"One, six or a hundred. All it takes is confidence and a strategy," said Glaithe.

"What do we do with the bodies?"

"Put them under the bridge." Glaithe knelt down to retrieve his knife. The man whose chest it had struck gave an unexpected gasp, then shuddered for a final time. "With the air this cold they shouldn't rot quickly. We may get a half-day or so before anyone notices."

"*Six* bodies?"

"It's better than leaving them lying in the road."

"And the blood?"

Glaithe pointed to the bridge. "Manure. That horse you cut must have emptied its bowels in fright. Drag it over the worst of the stains. Most people tend to avoid shit without investigating further. The drag marks will just look like a wagon caught it."

With a click of the tongue, Niallya knelt down to pick up the fallen hatchet. "Our relationship brings such wonderful tasks." She followed this by walking towards the manure, crouching to scoop up a lump with the squat head. Glaithe chuckled, before turning his attention to the first of the corpses.

THE NEXT MORNING, with the autumn sun filtering through the branches overhead, Orlienn crouched low to the base of a weathered oak. Her slim willow bow was in her hands, an arrow notched to the string. She'd found plenty of signs in the undergrowth suggesting that a warren was nearby. Kanderil was elsewhere in the forest, also hunting.

She reflected on the former Kalethi to whom she'd been assigned. He was a sour man who spoke little and allowed scarce time to *enjoy* the surroundings. The way he'd spoken to the drunk, Ethanei, suggested a man who did not suffer fools. Added to the distain with which he'd treated the three Kalethi recruits… Orlienn wasn't entirely sure she enjoyed Kanderil's company at all. As far as she could tell, all they had in common was a strong dedication to duty and a love of the wilds. Even then, however, the latter came in different ways. Orlienn loved the forests because she enjoyed nature, and wanted to do her part to help and protect it.

Kanderil seemed to prefer them because there were few humans to be found there.

She sighed. Things must have been tough for this Sarene over the past few months, having been stuck with such a cold man. As much as he apparently cared for her safety and his role in it, Orlienn could not imagine that the girl felt much more than a prisoner. She could see him giving out orders and telling Sarene what she could and could not do at any given time. What security was that? Freedom replaced with rules. Protection at the price of liberty. In one so young, such boundaries could be soul destroying.

Orlienn had been lucky, in comparison. Her life had been free of the tragedy and complications of Sarene's. Both her parents were loving, supportive and peaceful. They fully accepted their daughter's decision to follow the path of the Tamir Rangers, and sent her off with their blessing to be apprenticed. Her mentor was a kind soul with a natural skill for both tracking and living off the land, and was widely seen as one of the better rangers in the kingdom. He'd been delighted with her enthusiasm and worked hard to teach her all the skills required to wear the stag buckle as one of the official guardians of the wilds. She'd earned this honour in four short years, and had served for five more with distinction and praise.

Nothing that stood out in her memory held the sadness of Sarene's tale. When Chalimer had spoken during their initial meeting, briefing her on the assignment she'd been tasked with, the story had painted the picture of a girl who had lost much and retained little to look forward to. Sarene had lost her brother, been chased halfway across the nation, and personally experienced one of the greatest atrocities in the last century; the fall of Leithar Grove.

A hare hopped into view. Orlienn cleared her mind and focused her sight down the length of the arrow.

AN HOUR LATER she sat beside a freshly prepared fire with a skinning knife in her hand, preparing one of three hares she'd caught for the skillet. Between the joint hauls, there should be enough meat to last the next couple of days, allowing them to travel without further hunting stops. The wood hissed and crackled beside her as the flames took hold onto the damp fuel.

Kanderil stepped into view soon afterwards, carrying two

hares of his own. The stern-looking giant didn't even acknowledge her as he placed his catch beside hers, before unstrapping his colossal bow from his broad back.

"Only two?" she said idly.

"Yes," replied Kanderil.

"Oh. I thought you would have caught more." She lifted the carcass in her hand as an indication of the extra hare she'd returned with.

The man stepped past her to place the bow beside his saddle. "I did not realise we were in competition." Orlienn gave a bright smile, amused by the sourness of his voice. By the *Four*, he was a miserable man!

"ARE YOU SURE about this?" asked Anthon.

Sarene nodded as she undid the strings of her tunic, pulling the garment free of her torso. Her hair spilled out across her shoulders, the dark strands lying across the white cotton of her undershirt.

"I mean, it's freezing out here."

She unbuttoned the cuffs of the shirt, pulling the fabric up past her forearm. Anthon sighed, removing his overcoat and hanging it from a nearby tree.

"If you insist."

Smiling up at him, Sarene tilted her head to the side. Then she threw a wild right hand towards his face, her fingers extended and her palm flat. Anthon just managed to get his arm up in time to parry the blow. He didn't see her follow up by placing her foot on his thigh and pushing hard.

The movement threw him off balance, and he staggered to the side.

"Whoa!" The boy laughed, shaking his head. "You're really serious about this."

Nodding, Sarene spread her hands in a sign of agreement and winked. She *was* serious. Without Kanderil around to continue her training, it was important to keep on top of things herself. Besides, it would be interesting to spar with a new opponent, one much nearer her size. Kanderil was always careful about not using his prodigious strength to be overbearing, but there was only so much physical training she could do with a man of his stature. Anthon would give her the opportunity to test her offensive abilities.

They each took up a stance, waiting tensely for the other to make a move. Sarene flinched, Anthon did likewise in response, and they both paused again. The two of them grinned at each other, as playfulness started to ebb into contest. Then Anthon moved forward, seeking to grab Sarene's wrist, and Sarene reacted by punching him in the chest.

The session went on for a half-hour before she signalled for a break. Anthon sat down, appearing to understand now why Sarene had suggested they shed parts of their clothing. The exertion was tiring and, despite their breath clearly visible in the afternoon air, they were both sweating. Sarene sat on the hard forest floor, leaning back on her hands and catching her breath. The stillness of the forest was eerie. Her travels with Kanderil had always been accompanied by sounds of insects buzzing and chirping. The whistles and songs of birds flitting from branch to sky. From time to time there would be a rustling through the forest floor, as woodland animals scampered about. But now, with winter almost upon them, there was nothing to suggest anything else in the forest existed except for the three of them.

That *third* emerged from the cabin. Spasmodic wandered to the centre of the small clearing before twisting at the hip, stretching its arms out at its side. A *crack* came from somewhere in its spine and the creature gasped.

"Ohhh, beautiful."

"Good morning?" asked Anthon.

"It's the afternoon, dimwit," Spasmodic replied with a smirk.

"True, but you just woke up."

"So?"

Anthon took a deep breath. "My apologies."

"Yeah, yeah. Anyway, I'm gonna go find some food and show Quicky how to find some as well."

Sarene gave a broad grin. Anthon matched it with his laughter.

"Quicky?"

"Yeah."

"Is that what you've named your…"

Spasmodic giggled. "The slug, yeah. I called him Quicky on account of him not being very fast. It's a joke, y'know?" The creature peered down at his shoulder, where Sarene noted the slug was now perched, unmoving. "Bet nobody's thought of that one before. Heh."

"Definitely not," agreed Anthon.

"So look after her," it said, aiming a claw at Sarene, who poked her tongue out at it. "If she gets kidnapped while I'm gone, I'll probably have to kill you."

"Duly noted." The boy rubbed his hands together, glancing to Sarene. "Try not to get kidnapped."

Sarene brought her hand around to her forehead, providing a lazy salute. With that, Spasmodic wandered off into the forest, mumbling something under its breath with its head turned towards its right shoulder and, presumably, the listening Quicky.

"Well then," said Anthon, turning to face her. "Are we done, or do you want to beat me up some more?"

Arching a brow at his question, Sarene rose to her feet and dusted off her palms on her knees. Anthon did likewise, rolling his head to stretch the muscles of his neck.

"I've been thinking," Anthon said as they began, throwing slaps and low kicks at each other; the attacks lacked bite, but were accurate and by no means soft. "It seems to me like it would be risky to leave you here until Kanderil shows up."

Sarene nodded, focusing on her movements to keep a huge smile from appearing.

"You said he'd be another week or so, right?"

Another nod, before she kicked him in the calf. Anthon winced and stepped back, limping for a moment.

"Ow… But when he's back, you're going to hole up here for the winter, right?"

Holding up three fingers to indicate months, not entirely sure that Anthon would understand, Sarene inclined her head in confirmation.

"Three?"

She rolled her eyes and smiled to herself, dropping her hand and advancing again. A testing slap was easily palmed away.

"I don't think I can stay for the whole winter."

Disappointment crept up on her, but she focused on Anthon's footwork and shoulders. He had a tell where he would drop one arm before coming in with the other for an attack, and it was easy to predict when she would have to defend.

"I mean, this is certainly fun, and I really enjoy your company. Spasmodic's too, for that matter. But I still need to get into Franthia."

Sarene stepped in close, suddenly annoyed. The idea that *he* could just take off and pursue his ambitions struck her as entirely unfair. She reached out for his head, and when he raised his arms to block she hooked her foot around his ankle and shoved, punishing him with the same trick she'd used three times already.

To her surprise, Anthon had prepared himself this time. With his back foot supporting his weight against her shove, he lifted his leg and stepped forward, trapping her foot behind his knee. Off balance, Sarene fell backwards and quickly reached out to grab Anthon's shirt in an effort to remain upright.

All she did was succeed in pulling him over as she fell.

The two of them lay there, Sarene pinned down by Anthon's body, panting from the exercise. Sarene felt uncomfortable at his closeness, with his breath warming her cheeks and his nose inches from her own. But unlike before, she didn't feel the need to get away or make an excuse. He stared down at her, and as their eyes locked, the sadness flowed away just as soon as it had arrived. Her fingers grudgingly allowed his shirt to slip from her grasp.

Anthon flashed a bright smile. "Does this mean I win?"

Sarene bit her lower lip, giving him a nervous smile. Then she slammed her forehead into his nose.

"*Ah*, shit!"

As Anthon rolled off clutching his face, Sarene scrambled to her feet and marched back into the cabin, slamming the door behind her. She ignored Anthon's cries of pain, as well as the ensuing request for her to wait.

Couldn't he see why he should stay around? Was it so hard for him to spend just a few months in her company, instead of going off to other lands to seek… whatever it was he wanted to seek? The fact that he'd essentially rubbed her face in it as well – after all she'd told him about how she was forced to run and hide all the time – was just moronic. How *dare* he do that to her?

Idiot, she thought.

The pitcher of water they'd collected earlier that morning was still half full, and she took a long drink from it. Sated, she slammed the pitcher back onto the table, which wobbled upon impact. Then she ran a hand through her perspiration-damp hair. She grabbed a handful of tresses and tugged hard, wincing at the pain.

Why, then, am I so attracted to him?

Chapter Eleven

ANABURAN LEANED BACK against the door, the handle still in his grasp, and closed his eyes.

It had been another successful night. Here in Rulaph Tar, where the population bordered a little over two thousand, the King's Journey tavern had been packed. It was getting easier with every passing week to fill out whichever hall, inn or drinking house in which the Sons of Tamir decided to give their next sermon. Public opinion was favourable. Tamir wanted a voice with which to address the House.

Anaburan was that voice.

He released the handle and moved further into the room, walking to the window. He could see the western end of the main street, where several audience members he had addressed minutes ago were making their way home. Some spoke to each other or called farewell, as was often a result of the Sons of Tamir holding court. The words Anaburan spoke and the feelings he inspired often led to men and woman treating each other as the big family he claimed them to be. Only in the little ways, of course; through talk, courtesy and manners. But it was enough. A touch of goodwill went a long way in this dark chapter of Tamir's history.

Runath was dead. Remelas was King.

While not unexpected, the death within the monarchy could not have come at a worse time. With Remelas waiting to ascend the throne there remained a chance for the Sons of Tamir to force a public debate or vote. Perhaps to provide another relative with the chance to be crowned King instead, or to set up an interim warden until the matter could be resolved. There was still time to do something about the problem. Remelas' crimes *would* be dealt with.

But *deposing* the King was much more challenging than preventing him from becoming one.

Anaburan moved to the room's single chair and sat down, leaning forward with his elbows on his knees. Both hands were shaking, and Anaburan closed them into fists.

The letter on the table beside him was stamped with the seal of the House of Tamir. Within, the words invited him to speak to the new crowned King. Privately, of course. Behind closed doors. With a retinue of two.

Anaburan glanced over at the satchel hanging from the back of the chair. After a moment, he pulled it up onto his lap and retrieved a small vial from inside. The liquid inside was a revolting brown colour. He pulled the cork and a pungent, acrid smell washed over him. With a grimace he took a tiny sip of the contents, quickly replacing the stopper. The taste made him gag, and he forced himself to take several deep breaths. Then he put the vial back into the bag before taking out a scroll of parchment, a squat bottle of ink and a featherless quill.

Spreading the scroll out on the table, using the bottle to hold the top end in place, he dipped the quill and started to write.

Remelas,

Thank you for your offer. I can admire a man who listens to the will of our people occasionally. Unfortunately I must decline this invitation and instead make one of my own. It is important, I feel, for the Sons of Tamir to hold a public debate in Tamiran Square.

A private conversation will do nothing to ease the fears of my brothers and sisters about the repercussions of Leithar Grove. Instead, it would be better for all citizens of Tamiran to witness our debate and have them recognise that you have appointed me to speak on their behalf. I believe that such an act will go some way to restoring your credibility which, as you well know, has been sorely damaged.

The Sons of Tamir shall arrive in Tamiran a fortnight from now. I trust your good sense will aid you in your response.

Sincerely,

Anaburan

He read over the words. Having been a member of the Royal Guard for several years, he was known to Remelas, and allowed himself a certain liberty with his phrasing. Once satisfied, he lay the quill flat across the ink bottle and blew on the parchment, drying the ink. Then he rolled it up and held it in his hand, tapping the scroll against his forearm. If Remelas accepted the offer, in two weeks Anaburan would be required to give the performance of his life.

After sealing the scroll with wax heated over the candle hanging from the wall, he looked down at his hands again. They had ceased quivering.

A WEEK LATER, Sarene was attempting to use a poorly-made hand plane to smooth down a section of the window shutters. They'd made steady progress on restoring the cabin over the past fortnight. Spasmodic periodically returned from its excursions carrying new tools it had filched from some farmhouse or hamlet. Working several hours a day, she and Anthon had made the place habitable, if not homely. The roof still leaked but only in a couple of places, the huge gap having been filled by a skewed alignment of sawed wood and thatching. The door was back on its hinges, with new fittings screwed into place. The bed had been fixed with new slats once they'd discovered woodworm in the old one, though it still lacked anything soft to make it comfortable. The room was cleared, swept and scrubbed. Now, Sarene was finishing the shutters, which didn't quite fit into the window frame; they jarred at the edge, never closing fully.

Anthon was collecting water for the day. Aside from a short period of sulking after she'd butted him on the nose – thankfully there was no lasting damage, though he had bled a little; a fact which had caused Sarene a great deal of guilt –

they'd continued to enjoy each other's company. During the days they worked on the cabin, cooked and ate together, while Anthon shared stories of his early life and his family. He never said much of his future, which she found strange. Despite the occasional prodding and simple questions through signals and gestures, Anthon was yet to reveal why he wanted to travel into Franthia.

At night they played card games with Jared's deck, which she'd kept since sharing a cabin with him during the summer. Occasionally she would practice her panpipes while Anthon sang. Spasmodic usually found this as an excuse to disappear again, calling it 'dreadful wailing.' On the contrary, Anthon had a fine voice, and she found herself looking forward to the evenings.

Setting down the plane, she stood up to check the shutter against its fitting.

"Interesting."

Sarene spun around to see Kanderil appear from the forest surroundings, stepping into the small glade. Bouncing on her heels, she placed the shutter on the ground – almost dropping it – and ran forward to greet him. Her arms wrapped as far around his waist as they could, and she gripped him into a tight hug. He smelt of perspiration and long travel, but she didn't mind. It was just great to have him back.

"You have been busy, I see." He offered Sarene her folded cloak, which she accepted eagerly. After clutching the garment to her chest she nodded and stepped back.

It was then Sarene noticed another person step out of the

tree line, keeping a respectful distance. The woman was tall and slim, with striking red hair. As their eyes met the stranger offered a warm smile and nodded politely.

"Are you alone?" asked Kanderil. He appraised the cabin they worked to repair in time for his arrival. When Sarene nodded, he muttered. "I told the creature to keep an eye on you. Where is it?"

She shrugged her shoulders, pointing off into the woods. In truth, she had little idea *where* Spasmodic disappeared to when it left the cabin. It would bring things back often, but never revealed what else it had been up to.

Kanderil moved past her, walking towards the cabin. He paused in the doorway to study the structure, tapping against the wall and pulling at the door. Sarene followed along, holding her hands clasped to her chest, hoping that Kanderil would be proud of the work her and Anthon had put in.

"Impressive," he said as he stepped further inside. "I had half expected you to be sleeping under the stars."

Grinning, Sarene gave a modest shrug. Then she turned to the woman, who had walked along with them. Sarene tilted her head and offered her hand.

The woman accepted with a light grip. "My name is Orlienn. You are Sarene, I presume?"

Sarene nodded, withdrawing her hand.

"I have heard plenty about you. It is a pleasure to put a face to the name. A pretty face, too."

Blushing, the girl wrinkled her nose and brought her hands together in thanks.

"Where did you get these building materials?" asked

Kanderil, returning with a saw in his hand. Sarene hooked her claws together and pulled her lips back to reveal her teeth.

"It has been collecting work tools." Kanderil swore under his breath, frowning. "Has there been any point during the last week where you have *not* been alone?"

A noise from the side of the cabin made the Hunter turn. Anthon appeared, carrying a bucket of water, with their canteens strapped across his waist.

"I've been here," he replied – then stopped dead in his tracks, stunned into place by the size of the man before him. A man who lifted the saw to point at him before Sarene could intervene.

"And who are you?"

"Uh… Anthon. Sir."

"What are you doing here?"

"Sarene brought me. We met in the forests north of here."

Dropping the saw, Kanderil laid a hand on Sarene's shoulder, encouraging her to move. "A word in private, lass. Orlienn, check the boy for weapons."

At the order, Sarene started to shake her head, but was given another rough push away from the cabin. Orlienn moved over to Anthon, who placed down the bucket in a hurry before holding out his hands.

"I don't have any weapons. I swear!"

"Just let me search you," said the newcomer, "And that'll be that. I'm not going to hurt you."

Kanderil ushered Sarene out of earshot, manoeuvring

them behind a stout oak tree. She tried to squirm out of his grip but it was pointless. Soon enough he held her steady, leaning in close.

"Why is that boy here?"

Snatching her arm free as he relented, she tapped at her temple before pointing the way she'd just been marched.

"Yes, I noticed the bruising on his face. What of it?"

She hooked her fingers again and made the same signal for Spasmodic, before pointing towards Anthon.

"Spasmodic brought him here?"

She shook her head, tapping her temple again.

"Spasmodic injured him."

A nod.

"How does that account for his presence?"

Chewing her lip, Sarene pondered the best way to answer. She balled her hand into a fist, showing it to Kanderil. Then she knocked herself on the side of the head and fell to the ground. She lay there with eyes closed, making a point of lolling her tongue from the side of her mouth, before peeking to make sure Kanderil was watching. Then she stood up, prickly forest debris sticking to her clothing, and presented the area of the ground which she'd just laid on. To finish she shook her head firmly.

"You did not want to leave him unconscious in the woods."

Delighted that he'd caught her meaning first time, she gave a smile and a thumbs-up.

"That wound on his head is over a week old."

The smile faltered. Sarene gave a hesitant nod.

"So why is he *still* here?"

A sigh. That was a fair question. But how was she expected to answer? By saying that she enjoyed his company? By pointing out that Kanderil wasn't the greatest of conversationalists, and Anthon was more fun? That she found the boy *cute*? Any one of those would just irritate her guardian further. Instead, she crossed her forearms and brought them over her chest.

"He is protecting you?"

Sarene nodded, hair flicking around her jaw.

"While Spasmodic is away doing—"

"Doing bloody important things," said Spasmodic as it landed beside them, having swung down from an overhanging branch. Sarene jumped, startled by the sudden appearance, but Kanderil did not flinch.

"Explain yourself."

"Well, I've got this friend now, y'see. Quicky. I've been teaching him how to do stuff, like hunt and forage an—"

Kanderil growled. "*Quicky?*"

"Yeah. He's right here. Look, say hello." Spasmodic turned sideways to present his left shoulder, to which Quicky still clung. As far as Sarene could tell, it hadn't moved for days.

The sight caused Kanderil to stare in disbelief. He tightened his jaw, eyes narrowed, and Sarene believed he might actually lose his temper. The prospect was not an enjoyable one, and she took an unintentional step back.

"You have been leaving Sarene on her own while you give survival lessons to a *slug*!?"

The statement produced a tight *hnnk* from Sarene, who bit the inside of her cheek in an effort to keep from laughing.

"Yeah," said Spasmodic, sniffing. "Oh, and some blokes with red stripes tried to kidnap her. They're still sniffing around a few miles north. I had to kill a few people. Listen, did you bring any oatcakes? I'm craving 'em."

"Have you lost your senses?" Kanderil persisted, his voice low but the words cracking like ice. "There are men hunting her in the forests and you leave the girl here to..." He couldn't bring himself to finish the sentence, instead closing his eyes and taking a deep breath.

"Don't worry yourself so much," said Spasmodic brightly. "She's been rolling around with that Anthon fella, and not once did he manage to undress her. She takes care of her—"

Sarene's slap across its arm ended the creature's speech, and it sniggered.

"I am glad the two of you find this funny," said Kanderil at last. "Perhaps if these kidnappers show up we can invite them to join the group. At this rate we will have half of Tamir keeping Sarene company." He turned and walked back towards the cabin. Sarene watched him leave, feeling a little guilty. She could understand his annoyance, everything considered – there *were* people in the area seeking her out, after all.

Spasmodic nudged her with its elbow. "That man seriously needs to stick his dingle in something."

Another laugh tore through Sarene's defences, accompanied with flushing cheeks. Shaking her head, she walked out after her guardian with Spasmodic sniggering behind her.

IT TOOK ALMOST an hour for Kanderil to calm down. Satisfied with Spasmodic's assurances that there was no-one else in the forests for a mile in any direction, the huge woodsman contented himself with checking on the work done to restore the cabin. Orlienn did likewise, offering her suggestions on the tasks which still needed to be completed, such as clearing out and repairing the chimney and gathering branches to insulate the rooftop.

Anthon sat with Sarene as she assured him that Kanderil harboured no ill will towards him. Over the days preceding Kanderil's return she had mentioned her protector several times, making sure to point out his stoic demeanour in preparation for when the two finally met. She supposed that Kanderil's great size should have been emphasised. It was easy to forget how intimidating the man could be; when she herself had first laid eyes on him near the Highway, he'd terrified her. Now he no longer scared her, but Kanderil was still *scary*.

At last, Kanderil completed his inspection, towering above the pair with folded arms. Orlienn stood beside him, casting the occasional wary glance to Spasmodic, who was content to sit apart from the group, whispering to Quicky.

"How long do you intend to stay with us?" he asked, eyes fixed on the boy at her side.

"I'm not sure yet," Anthon replied. "I was going to travel into Franthia before the winter sets in."

"That does not leave you much time."

"No, you're right." Anthon shrugged. "I suppose I'll be moving on soon."

Sarene scratched the back of her neck, glancing to the floor.

"How much has she told you?"

"'Scuse me?"

The woodsman nodded to her. "Sarene. How much has she told you about herself?"

"Nothing that I can't keep to myself, sir." Anthon touched his hand over his heart. "I ain't one to gossip."

The answer gave Kanderil pause, but then he nodded. "Very well. See that you stay that way. There is too much at stake here for telling idle stories."

"Understood."

"There is a storm coming in," said Orlienn. She was looking up towards the sky, her hands clasped behind her as though standing to attention. Sarene pursed her lips, watching the woman. The stag buckle at her waist was beautiful, and her eyes were repeatedly drawn to it.

Kanderil nodded. "Aye, seems that way. We should get to work on the final repairs before we shut ourselves off from it."

"I meant for the boy," she continued. "If Anthon leaves today or even tomorrow, he's going to be travelling through a downpour." Orlienn turned her head to look at them. Her eyes caught Sarene's for a second, then focused on Kanderil. "I would suggest he stay with us until it blows over."

Sarene nodded her head several times, encouraging Kanderil to agree. She grabbed a hold of Anthon's sleeve, tugging it. Anthon grinned, looking at her.

"Worried I'm going to catch a chill?"

She clicked her tongue, smiling.

Kanderil observed the pair of them. The moment grew uncomfortable and she lifted a hand to signal for him to speak, when he turned on his heel.

"Fine. You are welcome for a little longer, Anthon. When the weather clears, then we shall make provision to send you out with supplies."

Orlienn hung back, turning her attention to Sarene. The ranger winked at her, and Sarene gave a cautious nod of thanks in return.

"You never said if you had oatcakes," called Spasmodic suddenly. "Quicky's getting hungry."

"Am I right in understanding that Quicky is the slug on your shoulder?" asked Orlienn, turning to face the creature

"Yeah. He gets grumpy when he ain't fed."

"Slugs do not feed on oatcakes."

"This one does. I been introducin' him to lots of different grub."

"I see." Orlienn shook her head and moved back towards the cabin. "No wonder it's dead."

"It's not dead!" Spasmodic yelled as she entered the doorway. "It's just conserving its strength 'til it gets some bloody *oatcakes!*"

NICHAI SAT IN a fog, addled and confused. He'd been dosed too many times recently, and the repeated periods of unconsciousness were doing something to his mind. When

he was awake he felt like he was staring at life from inside a barrel – his eyes never focused to allow him to the surface. Any action he wanted to make, whether it be scratching an itch or adjusting his position to ease his aching body, took a great deal of contemplation before he actually did anything. His thoughts came in solitary bubbles. He knew Glaithe had said something about his father, but he couldn't remember what it was. There was a vague comprehension that he was going to be used in some plan, but for the life of him couldn't begin to understand what it involved. He knew the woman in the hood was called Niallya yet had no memory of ever speaking to her. Everything was disconnected and self-contained.

But he *did* know he was in the back of a wagon. Glaithe, Niallya and another man were sitting in the front. At one point a young girl had been placed in the back beside him. She had settled down to sleep with a blanket around her and a sack of something under her head as a pillow.

He knew this because, at one point in the journey, she'd reached over to gently tug at the cloth sack over his head. Nichai had been bound and gagged, and was too muddled to try and escape or draw attention to himself, despite the feeling of fresh air on his burning skin and the rumbling of movement all around him.

The young girl had stared into his eyes and said nothing. Nichai had stared back. For the first time since Leithar Grove, he connected with another human being who did not wish him harm.

After a few minutes the stranger at the front of the wagon had noticed, and Niallya had reached over to replace the sack. But that moment, that meeting of the eyes, had replayed itself over hundreds of times since.

Now, still in the wagon and covered in a blanket, he stared at nothing while the voices of others continued around him.

"You're sure?" Glaithe was saying.

"I heard it myself," Niallya replied. "Less than a week. It's all anyone was talking about."

"Then I need to get into Tamiran," said the stranger, who Nichai suddenly remembered was named Heiran.

"Soon. I want to confirm for myself that this is happening." The wagon *clunk*ed as something was retrieved from the trailer. Glaithe spoke again, this time closer. "We only have one chance at this, and I do not want to expose the two of you to Tamiran any longer than necessary."

"I am sorry my word is not good enough," said Niallya.

"I trust your judgement, my dear. Allow me to indulge my concerns. This has taken months of planning, and I feel compelled to oversee every single detail."

"Except for when we strike," observed Heiran. "Since you'll be here with your sack-headed friend."

A light chuckle was Heiran's reply. "My friend here requires constant supervision. Besides, once the task is complete then you and I shall never need to speak again. Niallya will provide your payment, and you may take your daughter to start a new life somewhere with my blessing in a location I shall never know."

"Providing we escape arrest following the deed."

"Niallya is remarkably skilled in that area, among others. She will see you safe."

A period of silence. Then Nichai heard movements, and after a brief passage of clinking metal and straining leather, one of the horses departed at a trot. Nichai started to doze; his thoughts running over nothing except his own existence and the incredibly small world he found himself in. The air inside the sack was moist and uncomfortable, and his eyelashes flicked against the coarse fabric every time he opened his eyes.

After a while fingers stroked his neck. The sack was lifted up above his nose, and the gag pulled away. Something pressed to his lips. Nichai opened his mouth without thinking. Bread. He took a small bite and started to chew. His mouth was dry but he was sorely hungry, so he forced himself to swallow. More followed.

"Who is that?" asked Heiran.

"Somebody you do not want to see you," Niallya replied, her voice close to Nichai's face.

"For my own safety again?"

"Once our plan is done, this man will be delivered to the capital. If he can recognise you, it puts us all at risk."

"He's never seen you, then? Or Glaithe?"

"We will never return to Tamiran."

A short, ugly laugh. "Neither will I. Once we're done, I'm taking Tillyan and moving out of the kingdom. Somewhere Kraye will never find us."

"I am glad to hear that."

Nichai allowed himself to be fed further. Once the bread

was finished, a canteen was offered. He took several long swallows, feeling liquid trickle down his chin and onto his shirt. Too soon the canteen was removed and the gag pulled back into place, the sack following seconds afterwards. Nichai sat back, his mind clearing.

He thought of the young girl again. Tillyan, maybe, unless there was more than one child with them. Sable brown hair, with wide, innocent eyes which were much too sad for someone her age. The memory made him think of Sarene and of happier days when he was still the Regent of Tamir. For the first time in what felt like an age, with his belly full and his thirst slaked, Nichai smiled.

If only he hadn't tried to have Sarene brought to him. If only he'd kept his distance.

Nichai closed his eyes, and a tear fell to his cheek.

If only Remelas were here.

KING REMELAS ENTERED his chambers, exhausted. The afternoon had been spent talking to the wealthier citizens of Tamir, who addressed the House for council and rights. He had presided over such matters ever since his father fell ill, but following his ascension to the throne a wave of subjects seeking to take advantage of the new monarch had descended on Tamiran. People looking to win favour, or seek an expansion of territory and assets. Men arguing over the boundaries of their holdings. Others requesting a grant from the treasury to found a new business which was certain to win favour with the people. A few seeking a pardon for a loved one currently being held in jail for petty crime, a mercy which would *win favour* with the people. One woman was looking to be given a post on the Council, following years of diligent service in keeping the many doctors, midwives and surgeons organised and paid for a decade, in a move which was sure to *win favour with the people.*

Almost everything over the last couple of weeks was designed to make Remelas feel he had no choice but to concede. They were daring him to deny their requests, knowing the underlying threat.

Turn me down, and I shall spread word of your failings.

It was getting to the point where the more mundane requests, such as two farmers claiming ownership of a prize-winning pig or a family seeking custody of a house, were a welcome relief. There was no jostling for power in the common men and women. Some simply wanted a fair judgement to help them get on with their lives. One man, covered in mud and soaked through from the passing storm which had continued unabated from the evening before, had stood before the court with his cap dripping in his hands, asking the King for five gold pieces to cover the expense of replacing his turnip crop for the next season, following the fierce summer of this year's harvest which had led to a ruined field. He'd travelled for three days to make the request. Remelas had granted it with delight, ignoring the protests of the House Treasurer.

Tamir was almost bankrupt.

Following the devolvement of the army, severance pay had been granted to thirty one thousand men. Each man received full wage for those three months, plus an extra three months for any who had served for over five years *or* had a wife and child.

Over one and a half million gold, gone in a week. Added to that the expense of Runath's funeral and the construction of his tomb in the Chamber of Kings, deep in the bowels of the House. With summer finished, and Tamir's main trade depending on agriculture, there was nothing coming in to replace that figure.

Remelas had forgone the great ceremony of his coronation. Instead of a grand parade through the streets, he had instead invited the court to be opened to all while the rites of succession were read aloud by the Prime Guide. The turnout was enough to fill the room, but it did not extend to the gated path leading to the front of the House, as was the common response through the ages. The crowd who witnessed the placing of the crown was cool and reserved. King Remelas was the least celebrated monarch in Tamir's history.

The feast had still been prepared in Tamiran Square, if only to give the public *something* to enjoy. That in itself had cost a healthy sum, but—

A knock at the door. Rubbing at his eyes, Remelas turned.

"Enter."

Chalimer entered, closing the door behind him with a *click*. He bowed his head before standing to attention.

"What can I do for you, Justicar? I am extremely tired, and would prefer to be left in peace."

"Of course, your Majesty. My apologies for disturbing

you; I shall be brief."

Remelas nodded, sitting on the end of his great bed. The bed in which his father had died.

"My sources inform me that the Sons of Tamir are on the march. A group of thirty men and women are headed this way from Kashan. Evidently the Sons have a strong communication network, for I have received word that this march is being discussed in several different areas, as far and wide as Sothiran and Fasherai."

Remelas produced a thin smile. "As they promised."

"Indeed. If you wish, I can have them apprehended within the next few days."

"On what charge?"

"Inciting public disorder." Chalimer clasped his hands behind his back. "At this delicate time, such a display could be the tinderbox which sends Tamir into a wave of civil disobedience."

"I believe arresting the men who have spent the last few months talking to thousands of Tamir as brothers and comrades would be just as inflammatory, Chalimer." Remelas raised a brow. "I would have thought you a little smarter than this, my friend."

The Justicar of the Gathire accepted this rebuke with no offense. "I have ways of turning public opinion against them, of course. Circumstances can be provided where the Sons are made to seem a threat to you personally."

"I am sure you could." Remelas stood, moving towards the screen dresser in the corner of the room. His bedclothes were already prepared, draped over a warmed pan.

"It would be preferable to the charade this group of so-called patriots insist upon."

Removing his tunic and kicking free his boots, Remelas reached for the purple silk shirt. "Tell me. Why are you so against a public debate of this nature?"

"Permission to speak freely?"

"Again, you must always speak freely to me."

Chalimer cleared his throat. "Very well. I am afraid that you will lose."

Remelas paused, the buttons of the shirt half-way fastened. The comment was not unkind, but the lack of faith was unsettling. Composing himself, he took a minute to fully dress before walking out from behind the screen.

"You do not think I can satisfy the demands of this Anaburan?"

"Anaburan demands that you be removed from the throne, your Majesty."

"From what you have told me, Anaburan wants to give a voice to the people as well. All I have to do is convince this man that I am not the evil tyrant he seems to think I am. I made a mistake. A grave mistake and one that I will regret for the rest of my life. But a mistake is all. I shall learn from it, be guided by it and be sure to never repeat it." Remelas removed the band holding his hair in place, and shook his head. Thick, curled tendrils of brown fell around his strong jaw. "This public debate will give me the chance to voice all of my thoughts, on a platform which *you* expect to be witnessed by thousands."

"And if you do not win them over?"

Chuckling, Remelas shook his head. "Have a little faith. I am the man who bred the greatest army the world has ever seen beneath the noses of everyone outside the House. Credit me with *some* intelligence."

"I trust you completely," said Chalimer. "You have one of the most creative and intelligent minds I have ever known. However I do not trust the people of Tamir. You will not be addressing a jury of peers. You will be speaking to a large group, favoured by a considerable proportion of the kingdom, who have already passed judgement. Swimming upstream, so to speak."

"A good thing I have always been a strong swimmer, then." Remelas turned to his bed. "Now if you will excuse me, I would like to rest."

Chalimer nodded, reaching for the door handle. "Of course. I shall prepare the welcome of the Sons of Tamir."

"Nothing too strict. This is a debate, not a witch hunt."

The Justicar paused before departing, a crescendo of thunder building in the skies outside the House. "If I had my way, your Majesty, I would have them speaking to you from inside a cage."

Chapter Twelve

T HE NEXT AFTERNOON, with the storm having broken, Kanderil hammered a board into the outside of the chimney to support the chute leading from the cabin. Fortunately the stone fireplace itself was still intact, but encroaching trees had forced themselves into the wooden slats funnelling smoke out of the structure.

Sarene and Anthon had gone exploring to find supplies for his journey, under the protection of Spasmodic. Kanderil insisted on the creature joining them on their little excursion. The girl had convinced him that, while having spent a troubling amount of time alone during the week spent here already, that *she* had never strayed far. He'd relented, and agreed to let her spend an afternoon with the boy providing that Spasmodic accompany them.

Kanderil had questioned the three of them at length about the new crimson sash-wearing threat, learning of their initial confrontation… along with the swift, murderous conclusion. Spasmodic, who rarely gave much information of use, had described that moment with great relish. The two youths had not interjected. From their body language, looking at the floor or their hands with shoulders slumped, Kanderil deduced that it must have been a difficult sight to endure.

Whoever this group were, they were new to Tamir. They weren't Gathire. They definitely weren't Kalethi. They weren't the Tamir guard. The Sons of Tamir wore cloaks. The Seers didn't wear a uniform, and the Guides did not roam the kingdom. Any other group had yet to rise to enough prominence to be known.

Anaburan's words came back to him. His warning of groups searching for the girl of Leithar Grove. The man had been truthful, after all.

This late into the season, making the move to another location was risky. Most other cabins that he knew of would be occupied by now, and the journey could leave them short – not to mention exposed. This new threat was operating in the area. Presumably the group was the same one Chalimer had used as leverage to assign Orlienn to him. Well organised, he'd called them. But that could mean anything. Were they well-trained individuals? Did they have a strong communication network? Were they somehow learning information from official channels?

Kanderil pulled a nail from between his teeth and placed it against the plank. Too many variables.

Variables like Anthon. Having the House of Tamir and, by extension, the Gathire be kept informed of Sarene's whereabouts was one thing. They knew the full story of the girl's importance. But outside of that, few people in the nation could connect Sarene to this ridiculous Queen of the

World nonsense. Keeping her hidden was the best way to keep that situation stable. Anthon was young, and liable to boast about his experience with the girl and her pet demon to impress his peers. Ethanei, too, was unreliable; the man's mouth flapped constantly when drunk.

Then again, whoever this group of sash-wearing kidnappers were, *they'd* worked it all out. But how?

Kanderil hammered the nail harder than necessary. The final strike whacked the edge of his thumb and he hissed in pain.

"Careful," said Orlienn as she walked around the side of the cabin, more makeshift planks in her arms. Her face was dirty and her hands covered in grime. With their travel over, she'd replaced her leather with a heavy sheepskin tunic and a dark skirt, both of which were smattered with dirt. He shook his hand, irritated.

"Thank you for the advice."

"You're welcome." The ranger laid the planks against the wall. "I've cleared out the inside. We'll be able to start a fire without choking ourselves in smoke. How's it coming along here?"

Kanderil looked up at the chute. "Steady. I still need to add a few more nails to the upper reaches of the chute, to keep it close to the wall. Aside from that, it shouldn't take much more work."

"Good. I'll make us some tea, then. Take an hour's break, Kanderil. You've been at this since sunrise."

"I would rather get this finished."

Orlienn smiled. "I thought as much."

"Something wrong with that?"

"Not at all. I'll bring you a mug, though. Just in case you change your mind." She turned and walked the way she'd come, turning the corner without another word.

The ranger was another source of concern. Kanderil picked up a second plank and fished around inside the small pouch of nails as he reflected on her. She did her duty with diligence, completing every task without complaint. But she seemed to hold him in some contempt, with an underlying sarcasm in her manner – the occasional glance or mild quip – which set his teeth on edge.

At least Anthon would be gone by the following evening.

Kanderil pushed these thoughts away and focused on his work, tapping the first nail into the thickest part of the poorly hewn plank.

"I'VE GOT YOU a place to stay for the next few days until the Sons of Tamir turn up," said Glaithe. He descended from his horse and entered the cove, holding a slip of parchment in his hand. "This is the address."

Niallya continued sharpening her blade with a whetstone. "You've been two days."

"Did you miss me?"

"How did you get into Tamiran?"

Glaithe smirked, slipping his bag from his shoulder and unbuckling his knife. "It's remarkably easy, considering I'm supposed to be dead."

Reaching up to take the paper, Heiran brought it close to

his face to read. Tillyan was sitting in his lap; her eyes scanned the page as well, but with the same blank expression she'd worn for the entire journey. Glaithe didn't believe she was able to read the words.

"Is this a house or a room?"

"A small house. More like a hovel, really. Roughly ten yards square and wedged in beside the marketplace."

"Isn't that somewhat public?"

"Yes. You'll blend in with the crowd." Glaithe crouched beside their fire, warming his hands over the flames. "Besides, you'll only be there a few days. Go in, sit tight, and then wait until this meeting takes place. In addition, I have also located where you will take the shot."

Niallya paused, the whetstone held tight against the edge of her sword. "You went into Tamiran Square?"

"Yes," replied Glaithe.

"Is that not dangerous?"

"Probably. But we can hardly have the two of you wander into the square on the day, hoping to find a window to look out from."

With a shrug, the measured grind of stone onto steel continued. "I could have performed the same task."

"You walk around like a wraith, woman. Somebody would have noticed you."

"The hood comes off," she replied.

"Show me."

"Not today."

"Wait a moment," said Heiran, as Tillyan took the paper from him. She studied it intensely while her father spoke.

"How do you even know where Remelas will be during this public debate?"

Glaithe rubbed his hands together, levelling his gaze at the man. Heiran's constant second-guessing of his plans was becoming irritating. "Tamiran Square is traditionally the stage for any such event. The Royal House make their yearly address there. The Laysenra festivities centre there. Coronations take place, new births in the royal family are announced and the Games winners are declared there. I myself was given the bronze horn following my success in the long distance running a few years ago. All major events hosted or centring on the House take place in the Square. It is where the most citizens of Tamiran can gather in once place. I see no reason to believe this will be any different, especially considering that it is due to public opinion that this meeting is happening at all."

"We cannot be certain of where the Prince will be positioned inside the square. A crossbow is only effective within a certain range. If you set us up on the opposite side, the shot will be near impossible to make."

Exhaling slowly, Glaithe forced a smile. "Trust me, Heiran. I am not a fool. There is a set place within the Square where the monarch delivers his speeches. A small stone platform between the two carved lions on the northern side. Where I intend to have you placed is in a storehouse above a section of shops. The distance between you and the King shall be less than seventy yards. Can you make it?"

Heiran nodded. "Providing we don't get another storm, aye."

"I would doubt Remelas would entertain guests outside in a storm," observed Niallya.

Heiran clicked his tongue. "You know what I mean. Yes, I can hit a man from that range."

At that, a wailing started up from behind them. Nichai was struggling against his bonds, the head beneath the sack turning this way and that. Glaithe rose quickly and walked to him, before aiming a solid kick into the young man's ribs. Nichai coughed and shrank into the foetal position, still murmuring.

"I'll be glad to get rid of you, you snivelling wretch," he said, before spitting on the Regent's prone form. He turned to see both Heiran and Tillyan looking at him. The child had grabbed a handful of her father's shirt, peering up at Glaithe with fearful eyes.

"Don't be scared, little one," he said. "This is a bad man."

The girl said nothing, burying her face into Heiran's shoulder.

"So what takes you to Franthia, Anthon?"

Orlienn looked up from her cross-stitching, pressing the needle through the fabric and tugging the red thread through. She had tied her wild red hair back into a tight ponytail, and with her jaw line exposed Sarene felt she had a rather masculine quality.

The boy smiled, offering a shrug in return. He was seated in one of the two chairs which had both been repaired earlier that day. Thankfully, they no longer wobbled precariously when sat upon. "I'm seeking my fortune, is all."

Sarene was in the other chair, taking her time in selecting which card to play in their game of four-match. At this vague reply she clicked her tongue, shaking her head.

"So you say," continued Orlienn. "But what fortune would that be? Some journey for education, others for an apprenticeship. I know one man who left for Carthlei looking for gold in the mountains. There are a lot of possibilities in your words."

"Maybe the mystery is better that the truth," Anthon replied. "Whatever it is, I reckon your journey with Sarene here will be a bit more interesting."

Hearing her name, Sarene glanced up and quirked a brow.

Kanderil, who sat upon the floor on the opposite side of the room to Orlienn, grunted. He was checking the flights of each arrow in his quiver, using a small pair of pliers to tweak the feathers where necessary. "Anyone would think you were on a secret mission."

"Nothing so dramatic, sadly."

Sarene laid a red four and drew from the deck. She winced at the black four revealed. The run of luck with her cards over the last few nights had been abysmal.

Orlienn tapped the crosses on the fabric with the blunt end of the needle. "You could have been great friends with Kanderil, I think. Your dedication to your privacy is admirable."

The remark brought a silent chuckle from Sarene, who nodded her agreement.

"It's like getting piss out a stone," said Spasmodic abruptly. The creature had been in a heap in one corner of the cabin, with its legs drawn beneath it and its arm over its face. With a great yawn it sat up, sniffed, then smacked it lips a few times. "All the time I followed the big bastard around, and he never told me anything. I know more about the princess over there, and she can't even talk."

"I did not realise my personal life was of such importance," said Kanderil.

"You spoke a lot about trust before," said Orlienn calmly. "But without sharing a little about yourself, how can I return in kind?"

The huge woodsman held his arrow up to look along the shaft. Sarene went back to her cards. This line of conversation never led anywhere, so it wasn't worth focusing on. Besides, it was Anthon's last night, and she had other plans in mind. She'd promised herself that after this round of cards she would take a walk with him. Despite all the time they'd spent together these last few weeks, she was nervous. It felt like asking so close to his departure would be obvious. Or, at least, obvious to others. Suspicious, even.

"If you want to know more about me," said Kanderil, "look around you."

Blinking, Sarene glanced up. Spasmodic caught her eye.

"You're old and banged up?" it snickered.

Ignoring the quip, Kanderil continued. "Why else do you think I would know about a cabin far from the travelled pathways of Tamir? The Kalethi would have no reason to patrol this part of the kingdom."

Orlienn smiled. "This was your home."

The Hunter nodded. "I grew up here with my father until my eleventh summer."

Sarene clapped her fingers and thumb beside her ear, before shaking her head and shrugging.

"I did not tell you because it seemed unimportant."

Rolling her eyes with a pointed sigh, the girl placed a card down.

"I would have thought your background would be public knowledge by now," said Anthon. "Through song and verse."

Kanderil locked his steel gaze onto the boy. The look caused him to fidget in his seat and take a keen interest in his cards. "Why, exactly, would that be the case?"

"Well, I mean. You did save the life of the King."

Chuckling softly, Orlienn looked across at the giant. "So word has spread, after all. Those boys in Tamiran were the first of many."

Muttering, Kanderil returned to his work. "I would rather not think about it."

"Does fame disturb you so?"

"It does when I am looking to keep Sarene out of sight."

"How long has it been since you've seen the place?" asked Spasmodic, pushing itself upright and yawning.

"I have not returned since I first left," Kanderil replied, thankful for the change of subject.

"So that means…" The creature poked out its tongue, wincing with the struggle of trying to perform mental arithmetic. "Wait, how old are ya?"

"It has been twenty eight years."

"It must be good to know the place is still standing," said Orlienn, appraising the cabin with renewed interest. "Even despite the damage."

"So you and your old man lived here on your own all that time?" Spasmodic grinned. "No wonder you're such a miserable bugger."

"On the contrary, I spent many happy years here," replied Kanderil. "I learned about the forests and how to live within them."

Anthon laid his hand, revealing four threes and three sevens. Sarene clicked her tongue, throwing down her own cards. One of them skidded across the table and fell to the floor.

"I apologise for being so good," said the boy, laughing at Sarene's withering sneer.

"What time will you be leaving tomorrow, Anthon?" asked Orlienn.

"First light, I suppose. I'm not sure whether to continue through the forests, or head back north to reach the Highway. I don't know how far the trees run for."

"You should be able to clear the forest within the week by heading south west," said Kanderil. "Look on Sarene's map. You should be able to see the most direct path to Franthia."

Sarene reached down to the small pocket stitched into her leggings. She pulled open the flap and reached inside with two fingers, but grasped nothing but fabric. The folded parchment was not there. Confused, she gave a hesitant shrug.

Kanderil frowned. "Where have you put it?"

Another shrug.

"Here," said Orlienn, reaching into the knapsack beside her. "You can look at mine." She withdrew her own hide map and held it out as Anthon crossed the room to take it from her.

"You should be more careful, girl," Kanderil chided. "That map had this location clearly marked."

At a loss to explain where the map had gone, Sarene started checking through her other pockets, before moving to her satchel hanging from the back of the door. Nothing. She'd been extra careful for the reason Kanderil had explained. A thought struck her. She stood up from the chair and clapped her hands. When Anthon turned, she gestured towards the door.

The boy gave a peculiar half-smile. "What for?"

Sarene pointed towards the map in his hands, then offered an imaginary piece of paper to him.

"Isn't it a bit dark to be looking for maps?"

She shook her head, giving a bright smile to hide the fact her confidence was slipping with every second he delayed. To her relief, Anthon nodded and handed Orlienn's map back. "Sure, let's take a quick look."

"Spasmodic will go with you," said Kanderil.

"No I bloody won't," said Spasmodic.

"Yes, you will. For all we know that group are still in the area."

"In the dark? Piss off. Besides, you can't smell what I can smell," it said, turning its head to stare right at Sarene. The hidden meaning in that gaze caused her to wring her hands, before she grabbed Anthon's sleeve and pulled him towards the door.

"I do not care what you *smell*."

"You would if you could smell it."

Sarene grabbed her cloak and scarf before opening the door. When Anthon stepped outside she yanked it closed behind them, ignoring Kanderil's call for them to return.

WRAPPING THE MAUVE cloak around her shoulders, Sarene led them through the darkness of the forest to the spot they'd sat a number of times over the last few days. Following the storms of the previous days, the sky was now clear. Silver radiance shone down like a spotlight through the break in the canopy above, filtered into a vague circle by the opening in the branches overhead. In the centre of this illuminated circle was an overturned log, which they'd rolled into place upon finding the spot away from the cabin. It was still cold, but not as numbingly so as it had been for the middle weeks of autumn.

Sarene sat, smoothing down her cloak, before looking up at Anthon. He paused before her, flicking hair from his brow, giving a warm smile.

"I thought we were looking for your map?"

Tutting, she patted the log beside her. Anthon obliged, moving to sit on the log after checking for rogue shards of bark. When he turned his attention to her, Sarene pointed a finger at him. Then she bounced it once in mid-air and pointed to the sky. Finally she waved.

"Yes, in the morning."

Sarene tapped her chest, the pulled the corners of her mouth down with her thumbs.

"You'll be sad? Why?"

The question made her peer at him from beneath her brow. Either he was being deliberately obtuse, or he hadn't considered the matter at all.

Anthon spread his hands, rocking back on the log. "What can I say? It's been fun, and despite the unusual circumstances, I'm glad you brought me here."

She smiled, pointed at him, gestured back towards the cabin then gave a thumbs up.

"Yes, I like the cabin as well," he said in a response which didn't exactly match what she had meant. Sarene wanted to tell him that she was glad as well. She'd found herself growing more fond of him with each passing day, and the thought of it being over so soon after they'd met was depressing.

After a pause, where she chewed her bottom lip while thinking of how to express her next question, she tapped him on the shoulder and waved towards the cabin a second time, before reaching out to shake his hand. Despite the cold air around them, it was somehow warm to the touch.

"Will I come back?" he asked hesitantly. When Sarene nodded, he shrugged. "I don't know. You said you were only going to be here for the winter. I won't know where you've gone afterwards."

Immediately Sarene mimicked scribbling a note on her hand, before hooking her thumbs together and flapping her fingers as wings.

"You can read and write?"

Rolling her eyes, Sarene nodded.

Anthon laughed. "Yeah, we could write to each other… If Kanderil allows it. He seems quite positive you should be keeping a low profile."

She took a deep breath, snickering, before shaking her head. Kanderil be damned. He may be shutting her off for the winter, but he couldn't keep her buried away forever. Judging from the spreading word of his role in keeping Remelas alive, he wasn't going to be able to keep *himself* hidden, either.

An idea occurred to her. She had nothing to lose by pushing the issue now Anthon would be leaving. She tapped him on the chest – suddenly aware that she'd been edging towards him during their conversation – and then pointed south, in the direction of Franthia. She gave a stern shrug of the shoulders, rolling her hand at the wrist.

Having become accustomed to her signal for a question, he answered correctly. "I told you, I'm seeking my fortune."

Sarene shook her head, inviting him to continue with further hand gestures.

Anthon gave a soft smile. "If I was going to tell you, I'd have done so already."

The reply made Sarene pause. What was so private that he couldn't tell someone he would likely never see again? She nudged him with an elbow. When he met her eyes, she pointed to her mouth. How would she gossip, exactly?

The observation brought a laugh from the boy. "You have a point," he conceded.

Pleased, Sarene folded her arms into her cloak and turned to stare at him. Anthon held off as long as he could, glancing skyward and running a hand through his sandy hair; all the while a smile crept across his handsome features, growing broader with each silent second.

"Alright, fine!" he said with a curse. "Fine. But if you let any of the others know I won't talk to you ever again."

While it was a rather futile threat, Sarene nodded her acceptance.

Anthon took a deep breath. "I'm... going to become a stage actor."

Sarene blinked, her eyes curious.

"It's something I fell in love with ever since my father brought me to a theatre in Sothiran. I saw the play of Melinarak the Lovelorn. The way they told his story through song and drama, with the costumes and everything... Franthia has a great tradition of actors and singers. They say their theatre in Sachain is the greatest in the world, with several shows taking place every day. People flock from all over the lands to go there. I thought maybe they'd take the craft a little more seriously than they do here, where most bards just sit in taverns playing an instrument. So I decided to pack up and leave while my father went on an assignment."

Anthon's eyes, which had lit up during his explanation, dulled. "I've always wanted to do it, but he wanted me to become a ranger like him. He was adamant that actors were all boy-lovers, not real men. He wouldn't let me enrol in the school in Tamiran, so I had to find my own way."

Nodding slowly, Sarene contemplated the words. It would explain why he was so hesitant to share his intentions, if his father had made him feel shameful about it. She laid a hand on his upper arm, and he turned to look at her.

"You don't think it's silly, do you?" The words came out like a statement rather than a question, but there was just enough emphasis on the final two words to betray his fear. Sarene grinned, shaking her head to show she did not. The childlike prompt for reassurance was endearing. Her hand moved to poke him twice over the heart, before giving a thumbs up.

Anthon exhaled in relief. "Good. I'm glad. It's nice to know that I'm not strange."

Their gaze met. Sarene's smile faltered, but in a way which, she hoped, showed her fondness for him. Of *course* it wasn't strange. The fact that he'd hidden this away out of some apprehension for being mocked only endeared him to her further. He had a dream, and he'd taken the leap to follow it, just as she had during the summer. Despite the misgivings of his father, despite the way he perceived this choice he'd made to be somehow wrong or shameful, Anthon had followed his heart.

The boy nodded once, giving a grateful smile.

Sarene's hand was still on his chest.

There had to be some way to show him how she felt. She wanted to encourage him; to let him know that he was a good person, and that he should be proud of his choice. Sarene wanted to tell him that he would be missed. That she *cared* for him, despite the brief time they had spent together.

Panic welled up within her, and she knew that this was the only chance she would get before he left tomorrow. Before he walked away from the cabin to follow his dreams. Her nerves spurred her into action. It was the only way to remove them.

Sarene leant in and pressed her lips against his. The movement took only a second, and during it all her emotions built to a terrifying, exhilarating crescendo. Tension, worry and need. She felt his breath against her cheek and the warmth of his mouth. The connection dispersed all these warring feelings immediately. Time stood still for her, nothing mattering – not the Four, not Jared, not the chill night air or the confines of her situation.

For the first time since Leithar Grove, with her first kiss, she understood what it meant to be truly joyful.

ANTHON PLACED HIS hands against her shoulders and pushed her back.

"Sarene! What… What are you doing?"

At once she could see it on his face. He didn't want this to happen. The firmness of the grip holding her apart from him was evidence enough. He looked stunned. *Offended.* Sarene stared up at him, hopeless, her greatest fears crashing back in like a tidal wave.

"I mean, I like you but I'm going away tomorrow. You shouldn't—"

But the rest of the words were unheard. Sarene pushed herself to her feet, shrugging away his hands, and fled back towards the cabin. The horror of rejection gripped at her chest like fingers of abhorrent steel. Trees rushed past her in darkness now that the canopy above blocked the moonlight once again, and she did not care whether she hit one in her haste. Let an errant branch impale her, for all she cared. Let a root snag her and snap her ankle.

It was pointless. She'd be alone forever. Cast out from society and left in the care of adults who would treat her like a precious, fragile possession, and people her own age who would treat her like a leper.

Anthon called after her. It didn't matter. Forget him. What a *fool* she was.

Reaching the cabin, she opened the door to raised voices.

"I keep telling you, I never said I was here to help!" yelled Spasmodic. It was on its feet opposite Kanderil, who towered over it like a menhir. "You keep making it sound like I'm doing summat wrong but I didn't promise shit."

"You left the girl alone to play with an imaginary friend," Kanderil growled. "Do you remember what these people want to do with her?"

"Ah, sod you," spat the creature. "I'm outta here." It turned on its heel and stormed outside, pushing past Sarene without a glance.

Sarene stood in the doorway, tears spilling down her cheeks. She wanted comfort, but the two who featured most prominently in her life since this horror began were instead arguing about her. She was causing more ill-will without even trying. Aimlessly she reached out to grab Spasmodic behind her, but it was already gone.

Kanderil eyes narrowed as he turned to her. She sniffed, wiping a sleeve against her nose. "Let me guess. He turned you down."

The bitterness of the words staggered her. Sarene stood there, feeling like she'd been slapped. She shook her head, hoping he would see how hurt she was.

Instead, the woodsman continued. "Perhaps if you had not insisted on him being here, you would not be crying now."

The cabin fell to deafening silence. Orlienn clenched her hands but said nothing, still seated beside the fireplace, looking back and forth between the girl and the Hunter as the atmosphere in the cabin grew severe as the autumn night.

Sarene span around and ran back out of the doorway, turning left to avoid Anthon, who she could hear stumbling about in the darkness. Kanderil shouted for her to stop – calling behind, again, always everyone shouting at her to stop – but she sprinted through the forest, her legs thrashing against the plants and bushes, biting with thorns and stingers. She bounced between trunks, stumbling, trying to put as much distance as she could between herself and the cabin.

None of them cared about her. She was just a thing to be protected, placed in a box and locked away. A forced orphan. A damsel in distress. She'd lost her family, her brother and her home. She'd been marched from place to place, witnessed death and endured terror and what was there to show for it? Nothing. Anthon was just humouring her. Everyone was tolerating her. She couldn't fall for anyone; it wouldn't be allowed. Besides, who would take her? She was a mute, a horrible freak. All the names she'd been called as a child by her peers when Jared hadn't been there to defend her. And now, on top of that, she was singled out amongst the world because of a power that was intangible and an importance she never wanted.

It's never going to end. I'm going to be alone forever.

Sarene kept running. The calls had stopped. She didn't doubt for a second that Kanderil was already tracking her. She hoped he never found her. As far as she was concerned, it was over. She didn't want to do this anymore. All she wanted was to go home and be with her family. If needs be she'd make the journey herself.

Only then she'd be endangering them to the wrath of Tyrrial, if he still lived. Or any of the others who were hunting her. There was no way out. She'd have to spend her days hiding, trapped and scared, never knowing who would be the next to try and seize her for their own ends.

Perhaps she could have run away with Anthon, to Franthia. A country where nobody would know who she was. But now that bridge had been burned also. The look on his face when she'd kissed him, now repeating in her mind for the hundredth time already, was an expression of sheer disgust. How could she have been so *stupid* as to think a boy like him – handsome, warm and bright – could ever be attracted to her?

Panting for breath she staggered to a halt, leaning against a tree. The sobs came again and she cried, the rough bark against her cheek, wishing for all her soul that somebody would come and take her away from all of this, to tell her it would be alright.

Someone did come. A hand gripped her throat and pulled her back, where she fell into a tight grasp as an arm encircled her waist. She fought on instinct, snapping her elbow back to strike against a torso. A grunt of pain brushed her ear, and in return the hand left her throat and gripped her hair, tugging to slam her head against the tree beside her. Dazed, she staggered back into the tight grip which now held her upright.

Two more figures stepped into view before her, obscured by strands of hair which had spilled across her face.

"No point gagging her is there?" said one with a hushed laugh.

"Come on, let's get out of here," said another. "Before her friends find us."

A cord of fabric was forced around her face, covering her eyes. She twisted her head this way and that, trying to fight them off, but the blow to her head had sapped her strength. Her assailant lifted her from the ground and carried her into the night.

"SARENE!"

Storming through the woods like a force of nature, Kanderil's eyes scanned every part of the scenery around him. The darkness afforded little assistance but eventually his eyes grew accustomed to the gloom. He searched for any disturbance in the undergrowth; any mark against the trees, which stood silent and knowing. It had been fifteen minutes since the girl fled the cabin, and there was no evidence of where she may be.

"*Sarene!*"

Orlienn matched him stride for stride, almost jogging to keep up. "We will have no luck until sunrise," she said, just as a stone embedded in the ground bashed against her toe. Wincing, she stood still. "Kanderil, this is—"

The Hunter turned around, shaking his head. "She could be in danger. We must find a trail. Now."

The ranger gestured to the forest around them. "We can barely see five feet in front of us. Charging blindly through the night could leave us exposed and far from any tracks which would help us."

Kanderil glanced over his shoulder, running his gaze up a nearby trunk. The bark was intact and harboured no secrets. "Clearly you know nothing of my skills."

"Do you skills involve the ability to see without light?"

"Then we fetch a torch from the cabin."

"We do not *have* any torches. Nor lanterns, nor candles."

"Are all rangers so passive?"

"Are all Kalethi so bull-headed?" Orlienn spat back, before taking a deep breath and composing herself. "My apologies… I speak out of turn. I will fetch two logs from the fire."

A noise from behind them made the two pause, looking south. Somebody was moving towards them. Without another word, Orlienn flattened herself against a tree, a hand on her dagger. Kanderil stood in the clearing, drawing himself to his full height with shoulders squared. They waited as the sounds grew louder, clumsy and without any attempt to conceal their maker.

A figure appeared several yards ahead. Kanderil made to meet them head-on before realising that it was Anthon. The boy gave a smile of relief before stepping towards him.

Orlienn revealed herself, and her sudden appearance made the youth jump.

"By the Four…" he gasped. "You scared me silly."

"What did you do to her?" Kanderil demanded. The hostility of the question brought a look of horror from the boy.

"What? I didn't do anything."

"The state of her when she ran suggests otherwise," said Orlienn. The two adults stood side by side, staring with judgmental eyes.

"No, I…" Anthon sighed, his words quick and nervous. "Look, she kissed me. I pulled away. It's not right – I'm leaving tomorrow, y'know, and I didn't want to give her any wrong ideas."

Kanderil ground the thumb of his right hand into the palm of his left. This is exactly the kind of situation he'd wanted to avoid. Keeping Sarene sheltered and singled out from the world was a necessary position to adopt. It was obvious that the girl was lonely and he was not so insensitive to overlook her eagerness to meet new people. But that added an uncertainty to his plans to keep her safe. He couldn't control developments such as this one, as much as he wanted to.

Anthon may not have intended to upset Sarene, but he had nevertheless. The result was Sarene's flight. Now she had disappeared.

"You think she'd hiding?" Anthon asked.

"I do not know," said Kanderil. "Let us hope she returns soon."

Chapter Thirteen

WITH FIRST LIGHT, Tamir stirred. The subjects of King Remelas made their way from their beds, yawning and foggy, to begin their daily routines. Stalls were laid out in markets and streets. Shepherds walked towards the fields. Parents tended to their children. Tradesmen took stock of their tools and tasks for the day. Every profession, every career, every responsibility. All of it began in that first hour, when there were tasks to be completed. Those fortunate enough to delay rising instead slumbered on, lost in the whisper of dreams, oblivious to the sunshine breaking over the horizon.

Forty miles from Tamiran, the Sons of Tamir resumed their march north, heading directly for the capital. Led by Anaburan they were applauded, cheered and wished well by those they passed. Word had spread that the audience they demanded was soon to be held. All were excited to see what these patriots would say to the King. The expectation was that there would be a huge crowd to witness the debate. Each night the Sons had inspired great discussion, national pride and a great need for justice. The previous three months had met with an unparalleled reception of positivity. Now the Sons, having travelled in small, separate groups, would convene to meet in Tamiran for one of the most important days in the history of the nation.

Three miles outside the great city, Niallya began her own journey with Heiran and Tillyan. They would settle themselves in their temporary home, awaiting the arrival of the Sons of Tamir. The assassination had been discussed in great detail, and the two adults knew their task inside and out. Timing was imperative. Location was paramount. Escape was vital. Not only were their lives at stake, but the result depended greatly on the aftermath. Were they to be discovered upon ending the life of the King, then it would all be for naught. An isolated assassin would be reviled and hated; potentially, Remelas would become a martyr. But to leave Tamir in chaos following an unknown enemy's actions, then the Four's bidding would be completed. With that, Glaithe would step in. Returning Nichai to the House of Tamir would see Tyrrial's instructions followed to the letter. The rewards would surely be wondrous indeed.

Outside of all this, oblivious to the machinations of these others, Kanderil set out with Orlienn to trace the path of Sarene. Having finally accepted that the girl would be impossible to track in the shadows of the night, the Hunter paced the cabin until first light. It was rare indeed that Kanderil felt powerless, and yet those hours had stretched on for a length of time which grated on his patience and gnawed at his restraint. As soon as the very first of the autumn sun's rays lit the sky overhead, he led Orlienn out to pick up the trail.

Anthon had refused to depart for Franthia, instead demanding to join the hunt, but a stern rebuttal from Kanderil had foiled that hope. Instead the boy agreed to wait in the cabin, eager to be sure that Sarene was safe. He blamed himself for her flight, though try as he might he could not see how things could have been different. Refusing the girl's kiss made a fool out of her; to accept it would have made a liar of him.

The creature Spasmodic was nowhere to be found, but it, too, was waiting. It could hardly contain its anticipation. It knew Sarene had been taken, for it had witnessed the kidnappers carry her away through the forest. It harboured no fear for her well-being, however. Predictable as these petty humans were, it did not believe that the girl was in any real danger. In a few days, she would be rescued, and in doing so Spasmodic would sate its need for violence. The Queen of the World would again provide it with another moment, another memory with which to comfort itself in times of agonising, intolerable peace.

Several miles to the north west of the cabin, alone and scared, sat a young girl.

SARENE SURVEYED THE room, continuing to search for anything which could help her. She had been bound at the wrists, her hands behind her, the rope threaded through a rusty iron hoop embedded in the wall. For a long time she had tried to loosen the bolts holding the loop in place, pulling with all her might against the rope; the only give was in the skin of her wrists, which were now raw and painful.

The room appeared to be a cellar. The floor was cold, paved with black slate. A set of stairs led up on the opposite side of the room. The lingering smell of alcohol, faint but sickly sweet, hung in the dry air. The walls were bare, though a few small holes suggested that shelves or racks had once been secured here. A table and a single chair were tucked into one corner of the room; while the chair was plain and undecorated, the table was an ugly monstrosity, carved of lacquered hardwood with grotesque faces at each corner and a confusing mass of circles and symbols along the legs, as though the wood had tried to escape the chisel which had shaped it.

Adjusting her position on the floor, Sarene tried to push herself to her knees. Her arms had been wrenched back and bound close, and after several hours her back ached terribly beneath her shoulder blades.

At first she had been terrified. All her fears whispered to her at once. Surely these men were going to kill her, or sell her to the highest bidder. For a long time she had watched the trap door above the stairs, waiting for somebody to approach with a knife or a leash, coming to seal the deal… whatever that deal may be.

The lack of a window unsettled her also. She disliked closed spaces, and the thought of being kept prisoner underground was nagging at her claustrophobia. As she once had in Porthouse's tunnel, she inhaled through her nose and exhaled through her mouth, calming the rising panic.

Eventually she urged herself to relax. Kanderil had instructed her on more than survival and combat – he also educated her on how to take note of her surroundings in any situation where she found herself isolated. This included situations of captivity, a lesson taught to all Kalethi recruits. With the prior attempts to capture Sarene by various groups, adequate preparation for a time when she could find herself taken hostage was important to the Hunter. His words came back to her, recited in that gruff tone.

Those who would take you prisoner will likely view you as harmless. Use this to your benefit. Look for anything which can be used as either a weapon or a means of escape. Remain calm and focused. Plan your objectives, and approach them one at a time. Be mindful of the routines of your captors. Determine how many there are, and how vigilant. If they watch you at all times, they may fear that your constraints are not sufficient. If they leave you alone, they may underestimate your ability. If they avoid eye contact with you, they may fear your rumoured powers. Look for any advantage, and exploit it as far as you can.

And so Sarene cleared her mind, took several deep breaths, and used the time to note every little detail. The only illumination came from a lantern on the table. The flame within flickered slightly, suggesting a draught somewhere nearby. The sound of occasional footsteps on wood came from above, but they were barely audible through the stone ceiling. Given her presumption that this used to be a wine cellar, it was possible that she was beneath a tavern or inn. She heard no voices, which meant that either her captors were not speaking – which was unlikely – or they had no reason to raise their voice. Perhaps they were confident that their plan, whatever it may be, was an inevitable success.

She had also decided that if these people intended to murder her, they would have done so already. The longer they left her alive, the more likely it became that she was to be used for something. Maybe they were waiting for somebody to arrive.

That meant she had time.

Sarene had discovered a tiny nugget of rust on the ring which held her rope in place. Carefully she had pushed the ring until the small, rigid lump lay against the rope, Now, as she had before stretching her back, she started to grind the rope against the hoop. It would be exhausting work, given her awkward position, and it would take a long time. She felt the very first frayed thread against the base of her thumb. Providing the lump didn't snap off, perhaps she could weaken her bonds sufficiently to loosen them.

A VISITOR ARRIVED long before Sarene could discover the answer to that particular question. The trapdoor opened and booted feet appeared before a heavy cloak, sweeping along the preceding steps. The girl watched as a man descended. He wore a crimson tunic dyed to match the sashes of her abductors, with a matching cloak and heavy gloves. His leggings and boots were both dark, as was his wispy, goat-like beard. His hair was parted at the centre, swept behind both ears in the fashion of the nobles.

Instead of looking at her, the man moved to the table.

Disregarding the chair, he pulled the strap of a small bag from his shoulder and, setting it down, opened the flap and removed several objects one at a time. First was a folded parchment, covered in scratches and tears. Next to this he placed an apple, and then a rolled scroll of paper.

The last item quickened her heartbeat. Light from the lantern reflected against the blade of a knife.

The man nudged each item with the tip of a finger, aligning them to his satisfaction. After this he held his hands behind his back and turned his attention to her, offering a fond smile. Sarene mistrusted the stranger at once. The way he looked at her was exactly how Porthouse, the obese smuggler, had once eyed her; in a manner which suggested he saw her only as a means to great personal gain.

Sarene kept her features neutral, trying to keep both her dislike and her fear concealed.

The man turned at the hip, took a hold of the chair, lifted it with one hand and carried it across the room, setting it down with the backrest turned towards her. It was close enough for Sarene to touch it with her foot, should she have wished. The stranger straddled the chair, folding his arms across the top of the backrest, and leaned forward. His stare made her feel unclean, as though his thoughts saturated her in something nasty. Sarene tried to meet his gaze, but the man's disquieting smile forced her to relent each time she attempted it.

"When I was a child," he said finally in a clear, articulate voice, the words echoing around the stone walls, "I was fascinated with the Four. The stories about them enthralled me, and I would always be the first boy to sit in place, ready for the arrival of my village elders to begin telling the tales selected for that year. My parents would be off with the other adults, dancing and singing and feasting, while I listened to every word. Food would be brought to me, because I would become upset if I was forced to leave the stories for even a minute. Tyrrial, Corliani, Mubuto and Shigasi were my heroes, and my idols. No matter how many times I heard the legends, they never grew old.

"This continued until I was twelve summers old. At that tender age I considered myself an expert on the subject of the Four, and how they had shaped humanity to be better than it once was. The images of war, the description of the poverty and destitution of those dark days when the Four walked the lands, both disgusted and intrigued me." He paused. "Are you familiar with the lessons of the past, my child?"

Sarene gave a hesitant nod, biting her lower lip. The man's speech was curious, and she found it difficult to ignore.

"Good. I'm glad." He tapped a fingernail against the wood of the chair. "It would be ironic, would it not, if you knew nothing of the men you so trouble.

"Anyway, as you are therefore aware, the world was not a very nice place to live. No, not very *nice* at all. The blessings of the Four allowed us to better ourselves. The advancement of civilisation is quite remarkable, if you think about it. Within half a millennia we have progressed from barbarity and despotism to culture and affluence. Nations debate trade and the sharing of technological advances instead of threatening each other with savagery and destruction. Did you know, for example, that standardised education is a concept only three hundred years old? The tools and methods used to teach our children to read and write were only introduced after the Four left. Similarly with our agriculture. The concept of crop rotations and the science behind the health of our very soil came from the advancements of our scholars; a pursuit which had been all but absent during the dark ages. Back then, of course, the intelligent devised cunning ways to murder their fellow man with greater devotion than any other area of advancement. Books were rare; indeed, any kind of record keeping was rare. Few writings remain of those days... save the legends of the Four, which lasted. How could one *not* retain the lessons of these divine beings?"

For a moment, the stranger seemed awed by his own words. *He's managed to astonish himself,* thought Sarene.

"As I grew older I wanted to somehow contribute to these stories. Telling them to the next generation wasn't enough. No, no... I wanted to somehow *expand* upon them. It was my calling to apply the journey of the Four to my own life; to make a difference. I told this to my mother, at age sixteen. And do you know what she said?"

Chuckling, he shook his head. "She said, in a voice tight and dismissive, 'I have no doubt you will make a difference in the world, my boy, but understand one thing: The Four have abandoned us.'

"Can you imagine what that does to a boy, who until that point had grown to believe the Four were amongst us, continuing to guide humanity? I understood *why* she said it, of course. She had recently discovered that my father, her husband, had been sleeping with another woman behind her back. I imagine she was lashing out in anger, since I was soon to depart the nest and leave her alone with him. But what is relevant is that I refused to believe her. I maintained my faith in the Four. I continued with my studies and my plans.

"Here in Tamir, we celebrate the Shalith. Other nations have their own festivals and holidays to pay tribute to the Four, but the continued adherence to their supremacy waned. The Four were becoming a background story, a distant myth, similar to the old Gods or the spirits of the forests and oceans. They were men who had become ghosts, and ghosts reduced to superstition.

"So imagine my surprise when the Seers began to speak of the Four with such consistency." He rose from the chair, and moved towards the table. "All across the kingdom, men who had never met and could hardly be called organised would recite scripture and prophecy with a startling clarity of thought. All the sermons they delivered to any who would listen – every *single* one, girl – shared a remarkable similarity. If you will indulge me, I would like to share one with you." He lifted the scroll from the table and unfurled it. Then he paused.

"Oh, how rude of me. I never introduced myself. My name is Methulai. My associates and I call ourselves the Dedicant."

Sarene remained still. She offered no sign of greeting at his name; to do so would be stupid. Instead she watched him, focusing on the little details, following his movements and mannerisms, trying to paint a picture elaborating on his speech. She recognised a distinct confidence within her captor, but what was its source? Was he deadly in combat? Intelligent? Pious?

Her thoughts were cut short as Methulai began to recite from the scroll in a composed manner.

"And still we ignore the warnings, the tragedy of the past seasons. For there will be a reckoning. A judgement. The ashes shall deliver penance which takes a generation to pass. We have incurred the wrath of the flame, the one who burns, and he will return to illuminate the sins of our lords.

"Unless we act now, brothers and sisters. Unless we join together and match the commandment as was given to our forbearers. We must unite and consign to the one who burns. The Queen of the World" – at this, Methulai glanced up to Sarene – *"is a catalyst for an age of sorrow. Chaos will rule, and war will return. A great war the likes of which no living man, woman or child has ever witnessed. It is written in the stars, in the wind, in the very earth. The ghosts of the past must not be forgotten, for it is they alone who would understand why we must reject her. Fear his coming. For he will arrive without thought and without warning save for this."*

Growing quiet, Methulai rolled the scroll up and tapped it several times against his cheek. Sarene wasn't sure how to react. The words were spoken methodically; lacking any theatrics or emphasis. She had heard these Seers mentioned several times before, but this was the first time she had heard exactly what they had been saying. Catalyst for an age of sorrow? A great war?

The room seemed a little colder.

"I listened to the Seers for a long time. Long before Tyrrial himself returned to make his presence felt within Tamir. How I envy you, Sarene. You were there. You witnessed his very being, delivering judgement upon us. It must have been… Inspiring."

Images of death and horror clawed their way into her mind, and Sarene tried to smother them again.

Methulai placed the scroll back on the table. He then picked up the apple and the knife. He slid the blade through the flesh of the fruit as he approached her. The man took the resulting slice and popped it into his mouth. Chewing, he knelt down beside Sarene and offered another smile as he cut a second segment. This he offered to the girl, who shook her head.

"Come, now. Don't be afraid." He pushed the piece of apple closer, adjusting for her turned head. "Come on." It pressed against her lips, and she could taste the moist sweetness. With something approaching revulsion, she opened her mouth and accepted the offering. He stared at her until she started to chew. "Good girl."

Then he stood, cutting himself one more piece. "I intend to deliver you to Tyrrial myself, as the prophecy dictates. It may take some time before he arrives. As you would imagine, summoning one of the Four is no simple matter." Methulai moved to the desk once again, and gathered the other two items back into the bag. The folded parchment he lifted up and held for her to see. "It was fortunate indeed that this came into my possession. Without it, we may never have had a chance to talk."

Methulai then turned on his heel and moved towards the stairs. "You will be cared for until the time comes for you to depart. I hope, for your sake, that your companions do not seek to snatch you from us. I suspect they will not survive such an undertaking." Heavy footfalls accompanied every step as he departed to the room upstairs.

Sarene watched him leave. When the trapdoor closed she turned her head and spat the half-chewed apple slice to the floor. Immediately she started rubbing her binds against the rusted hoop, the rope making small, coarse scratches against the rough iron. Barely any progress had been made, but she had to do *something* to prevent this man's intention of giving her up to Tyrrial.

KANDERIL KNELT AT the edge of the forest, beside a pile of horse manure. With gloved fingers he lifted a lump the size of an egg.

"Less than twelve hours old," he said, breaking through the fibrous stuff by rotating the pad of his thumb. "The horse grazed on blackberries."

"There were three horses," said Orlienn, stroking the tip of her foot across the dewy grass. The dirt beneath was covered in semi-circular imprints which overlapped each other. "All of them were shoed and were probably here for several hours. They arrived and left by the north west."

The woodsman stood after wiping his hand on the grass. "We can get to our mounts within two hours. Then we ride hard. There is a way station no further than four miles away. That is where we shall begin our search."

Orlienn nodded, moving north towards the farmhouse where they had paid to stable their animals. When Kanderil overtook her, his strides rapid and long, she adjusted her pace to keep up.

He was furious with himself for allowing the girl to run. The words he had said to inspire her flight had been unnecessary. Questions about his past and his mannerisms from both the ranger and the boy, Anthon, had played on his nerves. With Spasmodic's stubborn refusal to take any responsibility for Sarene's welfare in addition, he found himself fighting an uphill battle to maintain a semblance of order and routine.

It was Orlienn who had suggested leaving Sarene alone to take a walk with Anthon, after pointing out the girl's obvious crush. Kanderil had at first refused, reaching for his cloak with the intention of following, but Orlienn had argued that by not allowing Sarene some time alone with Anthon on their last night in each other's company, he could be setting himself up for weeks of resentment. With great reluctance he had conceded the point. Sarene's constant pushing to meet and interact with new people, starting with the drunk Ethanei, was a sign of loneliness even *he* had picked up on.

Then the girl had been turned down for a kiss, and the mistake was there for all to see. Had he followed Sarene, that kiss would never have taken place. Had she left Anthon in the forest where she had found him, she would never have been injured by refusal. Once again, his methods were proved correct.

The fewer people, the better.

And then she had fled through the night in floods of tears. He pursued, but with no light and no method to her flight he had not caught up in time. At daybreak they scouted the surrounding area, finding a collection of footprints beside a tree which had several strands of long, dark hair snagged in the bark. No blood, thankfully. Four sets of tracks led to that point; only three sets departed, with one weighed down as though carrying a heavy burden.

Kanderil increased his pace, jogging along the open fields located between the forest and the Highway. Orlienn kept up with him without breaking a sweat.

HEIRAN SAT IN Tamiran Square with Tillyan on his lap. She was eating a piece of taffy candy he'd bought from one of the sweet shops along the walk from the shack acting as their base of operations in the capital. The child was wrapped in several layers of cloth and wool to protect her from the cold air. She made a loud *chap chap chap* sound as she chewed on the sticky treat, paying no attention to the arms around her waist which never relented their protective grip, ignoring the weight of her father's chin upon her crown.

Across the Square stood the loft from which he would take the shot that would change the kingdom.

Just as Glaithe had said, the storehouse sat above a row

of shops selling ornaments, trinkets and art; Tamiran Square was one of the few places in the capital which could be called scenic, and traditionally the businesses built on its borders sold quality items of aesthetic value. Jewellery. High fashion. Paintings and sketches. It attracted like-minded people, who indulged their passion for the creative arts. During the summer poets and musicians would congregate here, putting on street performances and recitals. It was a fine place to spend an afternoon.

Heiran's eyes remained fixed on the storehouse window.

Glaithe's plan involved setting up on the morning of the confrontation between the King and the Sons of Tamir. Niallya and he would wrap themselves up well, much like he had dressed Tillyan, and then carry a collection of wrapped goods for one of the stores. The two of them would claim to be delivering fabrics and conducting an inventory check to explain their continued presence. Then, they would wait.

Once Remelas began his speech, Heiran would end his life. After this, he and Niallya would make their escape. The back room had a side exit leading to the street on the opposite side. They would then walk away, head back to the apartment where Tillyan would be waiting and lay low until the initial frantic searches for a perpetrator calmed. Niallya would provide the rest of Heiran's gold, and depart to meet with Glaithe.

Heiran and Tillyan would be free to go wherever they pleased.

The man smiled to himself. It sounded so simple.

"Where is the man with the hat on, daddy?" asked Tillyan, craning her neck around to look up at him. She kicked her heels, which bounced against Heiran's shins.

"Which man, darling?"

"The man who came with us. He was always asleep."

"I don't know where he is," replied Heiran. The identity of the stranger Glaithe had brought with him had never been established. From the looks of his clothing and the open wounds on his wrists, the man must have been a captive for weeks. Perhaps months.

Tillyan looked back to her candy. She was sticking and unsticking her fingertips from the taffy, playing with the gummy texture. "I didn't like them being mean to him."

Her father smiled. "Neither did I. But they said he was a nasty man."

"Why?"

"I don't know."

The girl sniffed, reaching up to push the woolly hat back from her eyes. The garment was too large and kept slipping forward to the bridge of her nose. Then she bit into the taffy and gnawed until a piece came away. *Chap chap chap.*

"Close your mouth when you're chewing, princess."

"Bwua ib mawks muh mawwf aw kicki," Tillyan replied. The innocence of the response distorted by taffy and saliva brought a sudden laugh from Heiran, who cuddled his daughter close and rocked back and forth. Tillyan joined in, giggling, the sound again muffled.

This was why he'd agreed to this task. Every reason he needed was right here, in his arms.

THE TRAPDOOR OPENED. Sarene stopped grinding the rope against the iron hoop and shuffled backwards. Her back was on fire and the skin of her wrists was throbbing. She watched as a young boy wearing a red sash over dark clothing descended into the basement. He carried a tray upon which a hunk of break sat solidly next to a rattling bowl.

He seemed nervous in her presence, and as he knelt beside her he almost dropped his charge. Brown soup spilt from the bowl, pooling in one corner of the tray and moistening the bottom of the bread. He winced, and then reached for the spoon. Without words he lifted some of the soup and offered it to Sarene. She peered at it through narrowed eyes.

"It's, uh. It's oxtail," he said as if giving an apology.

Sarene shook her head and tugged on the hoop, indicating she wanted to feed herself.

"Uhm. I can't let you go."

The spoon dripped soup onto Sarene's breeches. She watched it land.

"If you don't eat he'll be mad. Methulai, I mean. He wants you to be happy."

Scoffing, Sarene tugged on her binds again.

"I'm just doing what I'm told, miss. Please."

The fear on his face was obvious. She was under no obligation to help him… despite her stomach rumbling for a couple of hours now. What would they do, force her to eat? Sarene shook her head again, turning away.

The boy swore under his breath and placed the spoon back into the bowl. Then he leaned back, reaching into a pocket to produce a small sliver of wood. He leant forward and to the side, to press the item into her palm.

"This will help you get free," he whispered, his voice wavering. "It's sharp. Don't use it until after somebody comes to change the lantern oil. That means it's night time, and most of the others will be going to sleep. It'll be easier to escape."

Sarene's eyes widened, and she tested the item with her thumb. One side of the wood had something sharp and metallic – like a razor – embedded in it. She tilted her head to the side, frowning at the boy. He dropped his gaze back to the soup, and offered a weak smile.

"Now will you let me feed you?"

After a moment's hesitation, Sarene nodded. He grabbed the spoon and lifted a fresh offering to her lips. She opened her mouth and moved her head forward to take it. The soup was tepid and heavily salted, but not entirely unpleasant.

After several minutes, both the soup and the bread were finished. The boy then offered her a drink from his canteen, which she accepted gratefully. After several long swallows he pulled away and replaced the stopper.

"Remember," he said, picking up the tray with shaking hands. "Don't do anything until the oil is changed." Then he stood, heading for the staircase.

Sarene watched him leave, trying to make sense of what had just happened. Why would one of these people want to help her escape? If these people truly believed her to be a danger to the world, why would the boy risk his own safety by trying to free her? She didn't recognise him as one of the three who had grabbed her in the forest.

With more questions than answers, she sat back. At least she wouldn't have to continue twisting her arms into such a painful position. Thoughtfully, she toyed with the razor in her palm. It was easy to hide in her hand but, if anyone should come to check the rope holding her in place, could be easily spotted if they pulled her fingers open. As a precaution, she inched her shirt back until she reached to lower hem of her leather bracers. With the razor in her fingertips she was just able to slip it into place, leaving just enough to grip again. Then she tugged her shirt back over it and kept her hands still, so as to not dislodge the thing too far out of reach.

The boy had been more than nervous. He'd been *terrified*. What, then, could have spurred him into taking such a great risk? Sarene dwelled on the question, shifting her position on the floor as best she could, the cold of the stone now seeping into her bones and making them ache. She had plenty of time to consider the question.

"NOPE," SAID THE tavern keeper, emptying a basin of filthy dishwater. "Ain't seen any folk matchin' that description." The water pooled on the road, the ground too hard for it to seep away.

"Have any men wearing red sashes passed through over the season?" asked Kanderil. Orlienn now stood with the horses several yards further down the road.

"Might 'ave," the keeper said after considering the new description, shaking the basin to displace any remnants of liquid. "Rings a bell, it does. I couldn't tell you what they were up to though. That is, if they *were* up to anythin'."

"Was anyone else on duty last night who may have seen something?"

The keeper laughed. "Mate, we were all but empty las' night. Two guests and a couple'o drinkers. Had the place closed down well before midnight. Me son helps with the stables an' the general runnin o' the place, but he were off with his missus. No doubt he were too busy fumbling about wi' her to pay attention to any late night riders."

"Where can I find him?" Kanderil asked, his tone emphasising the importance of an answer.

Scratching his head with one hand, the basin hanging from the other, the keeper looked up at the woodsman. "He's fetchin' a sack of oats from one of the nearby barns, so should be back soon. Why's this so important, anyway? They stole summat from ye?"

"Yes."

"Oh, aye? Bastards. Well you're welcome to come in for a drink while ye wait." The man turned and pushed the door to the way station open, stepping inside. When Kanderil did not follow, the man shrugged and let the door swing shut.

Kanderil shook his head, moving a hand to knead at the muscle above his right knee. He winced, digging the tips of his fingers into the joint. "Anything?" he called.

As Orlienn replied the two horses with her lowered their heads to graze at the scant grass. "There are too many tracks to be sure," she said, her voice piercing the deserted area. "At least three horses have passed through carrying more than just a rider, but that doesn't give us much to go on. They could just as easily be weighed down by loaded saddlebags."

Straightening, Kanderil took several steps across the road, turning his attention north. "If they were intending to take the girl south they wouldn't have arrived on the Highway at all. They must be some point north of here. Most likely off the road."

"That's obvious," Orlienn replied. "Most way stations don't take kindly to kidnappers renting rooms. But *where* north? There's nothing out there but farmland and a couple of quarries."

"There's a Shrine," Kanderil suggested.

"As much as we need a solid lead, I doubt the Guides have conspired to get involved," Orlienn said with a humourless laugh. One of the horses raised its head to look at her, and she responded by stroking its sleek neck.

"No, but the Shrine is a destination for many a pilgrimage. If these red-sash bastards are operating in that area, perhaps somebody mentioned it during a visit."

Sighing, the ranger nodded. "It's a start."

"You head out there," said Kanderil, walking towards her. "I will wait for this boy. We will meet at the Kaeshan quarry by sundown."

Orlienn nodded, handing over the reins to the giant's horse. "And if either of us finds anything before then?"

Kanderil met her eyes. Something in his stare must have unsettled her, for she turned away before he could speak.

"Then we regroup, and take her back before the dawn."

HEIRAN RETURNED TO their temporary home, Tillyan wedged against his hip, to find Niallya making a pot of tea. Even here, secluded from the world, the mercenary wore her hood up.

"Do you ever change out of those clothes?" he asked, setting Tillyan down and nudging her towards one corner of the room, where her stuffed bear sat waiting. The tatty thing had toppled over on its side, and the girl snatched it up to clasp against her cheek.

"Of course I do," Niallya replied, stoking the fire with a thin iron rod. "I washed both my coat and myself while you were gone."

"So why the hood?" Heiran moved to an empty chair and sat down, pleased that the place had evidently been cleaned recently; it lacked both the filth and the cloying, pungent stench of his former home.

Niallya paused, holding the poker in her hand. "Must we go through this again?"

"Don't give me that. Either we succeed tomorrow and go our separate ways, or we fail and the reason for concealing your identity is moot." Heiran leaned back, placing both hands behind his head.

"A fair point," the woman said. "However, this is not up for debate. There are few men alive who have seen my face clearly, save those I grew up with or those who have shared my bed."

Heiran glanced to his daughter, who was sat on the floor

playing with her bear. The look was more reactionary than anything else; she wouldn't understand the implications of Niallya's comment. "A roll of the dice for your partners, then."

To his surprise, the mercenary gave a soft laugh. "You could say that."

He sat in silence, watching his daughter, while Niallya finished brewing the pot. A mildly earthy scent filled the air as the leaves released their flavour. When three plain mugs had been filled with the steaming liquid, Niallya produced a tiny cloth sack containing sugar from her bags. She sprinkled this amongst the servings before taking one of the mugs for herself. Heiran called Tillyan over, and scrutinised her while she blew repeatedly on the tea until it had sufficiently cooled.

"Do you know Remelas personally?" asked Niallya.

"Pardon?"

"I have been wondering. There are less risky ways to escape a city than agreeing to do what you're doing. If you had ties to Remelas, your role would make more sense."

The question hung in the air. Heiran sipped at his tea, watching his daughter as she stared into her cup.

"No, I don't know him. My wife did, though."

The girl looked up at him and he ruffled the back of her head. Tillyan produced a broad grin, revealing one missing tooth.

"I see," said the mercenary.

It was then, as he sat back in his chair, that he noticed a wrapped bundle tucked into one corner of the room, along with their cloaks and belongings. Grey fur poked out along one folded edge.

"What is that?" he asked, gesturing with an extended finger.

Niallya's head moved beneath the hood. "A grey cloak with a wolf pelt across the shoulders."

"A bit early to be buying yourself celebratory gifts, isn't it?"

"The cloak is a minor adjustment to our plan."

"Adjustment?" Heiran frowned. "I don't like that word so close to the attempt."

"Do not worry. Your involvement does not change at all."

"Was this Glaithe's idea?"

"No," said Niallya.

"Does he know?"

The mercenary sipped her tea before replying. "I do not need Glaithe's approval for everything I do."

"I see. Will you at least explain to me what it's for?"

She nodded. "The cloak resembles those worn by the Sons of Tamir. Leaving such a garment in the room with your crossbow should divert attention from us during the crucial first hours of our escape."

"That seems awfully convenient." Heiran shook his head. "It's too obvious. They will know it's a set up. No assassin would be stupid enough to leave his cloak behind, especially one as identifiable as *that*."

"We do not need to set up the Sons of Tamir as the culprits. We just need to present the possibility for a short time, while we flee the city. If even one Gathire agent is diverted from the hunt for us, then it shall be a worthwhile ploy." Niallya shrugged her slim shoulders. "Besides, we need something to wrap your crossbow in and such a fine garment will add weight to our guise of tailor's assistants."

Heiran stared at the hooded figure opposite, frustrated at being unable to read her face. She sat in her chair like a phantom, shrouded from his inspections and guarding her manner. He looked over at the cloak again, just as Tillyan tugged on his leggings.

"My tea is still too hot, daddy," she complained. Heiran glanced down at her, reaching for the cup. He took it and blew several times, steam rising over the rim with each breath. As he handed the cup back, he addressed Niallya.

"Do you have plans for tonight?"

The slightest of smirks played on the woman's mouth, the only part that he could see. "Are you asking me to dinner?"

"Hardly," Heiran said with a grin. "I wanted you to keep an eye on my girl."

"Where are you going?"

"I just need a few hours to myself. To prepare, like. Mentally. Y'know?"

"I know. If you wish."

Nodding, he finished his drink. "Thank you. I won't be long. I heard folk talking that the Sons should arrive tomorrow."

"Well then," replied Niallya. "Early to bed for both of us."

Chapter Fourteen

WAKING WITH A start and unable to wipe her eyes, Sarene blinked rapidly to get her bearings. The corner of her mouth was crusty, and there was a small wet spot on her collar where she'd drooled. Her neck throbbed with the ache of her hanging head, and her shoulders weren't much better. She had no idea how long she'd been out, and it took a few seconds for her to remember her predicament. She tugged at her bonds, which were tight as ever.

Somebody came down the stairs, heavy footsteps on each wooden slat. The opening of the trapdoor must have woken her. A heavy-set man with brown hair tied back from his face appeared, carrying an oil lamp and a candle. He wore dark clothing and a crimson sash, just like the others. At the bottom of the stairs he paused. The man then bowed his head, before turning his attention to the lamp on the table.

Was that… respect that he'd shown?

He went about the task of replacing the oil, first blowing out the flame contained within the glass. "Are you hungry?" he asked.

Waiting until the man looked at her, she shook her head. He nodded in return.

"You should get some rest."

At the reminder, Sarene tilted her head to rub the corner of her mouth against her jerkin, wiping away the dry saliva. Then she adjusted her position, pressing against the floor with her heels and tensing the muscles of her legs. The constant cold against her lower body was causing cramps, and she tried to alleviate the tightness as best she could.

The man replaced the oil drum and relit the lantern. Then he approached her. Sarene sat back down, watching him closely. He smiled.

"I just need to check the rope, is all," he explained. With that he reached down for the rusted hoop and pulled it, before doing the same to the binds holding her in place.

At this, he paused, frowning. A shake of the head.

"What do we have here?"

Sarene froze. The razor. Her eyes widened before he reached to prod at her wrist, causing her to wince. He muttered, turning towards the stairs and walking away.

"You've torn yourself to shreds, lass. If that gets infected you'll be in trouble. Let me get something." He marched back up the stairs, calling as he went. "Brack, we got any vinegar up there?"

Her heart racing, Sarene closed her eyes. If he'd noticed the razor, her chances of escape would have been crushed – not to mention that boy would have been horrified to learn of its discovery. Instead this man was worried about her scratch marks. Another person concerned for her well-being. It made no *sense*. Why would they be eager to take such good care of her if they really believed she was such a threat to them?

But then, this one wasn't looking to help her escape. Just to keep her healthy. Perhaps this group were under strict instructions to keep Methulai's gift to Tyrrial in the best possible condition.

The man returned carrying a clear bottle and a small flannel. He moved to Sarene and knelt down as she watched. He had a kind face, rounded at the cheeks, with deep lines around the nose and mouth. Laughter lines. Up close, there was nothing scary about him at all. There were many men just like him back at her village, jolly a—

A searing pain washed up both her arms as he pressed the flannel against her wrists. The bitter tang of vinegar reached her nostrils. Her mouth fell agape and she tried to pull away, succeeding only in scratching herself further against the roughness of the rope.

"Easy girl," the man said, smiling. "It'll keep those wounds clean."

As the initial shock passed, Sarene realised the pain wasn't *quite* as awful as she'd first imagined. She hadn't realised how badly she'd torn her skin. The pain went around every exposed section of her wrists. Perhaps it was for the best that she couldn't see the wounds.

After a few more dabs the man stood, corking the bottle. "There. I'll go over it again later on. But now, like I said. Try and catch a bit o' sleep, aye?" He smiled at her. Sarene wasn't ready to form a bond with her captors just yet, so she looked away as he retreated back up the stairs.

As soon as he was lost from sight, she bent her wrists and started feeling around the hem of her bracers for the edge of the razor. She didn't want to spend any longer in this cellar than she had to. She could feel the small wooden strip against her nail. Carefully, with the tendons of her forearm aching as they were forced to stretch, she pinched the block between two of her fingers.

Then footsteps again. The man was coming back. She let her hands fall slack behind her and watched him approach. He was carrying a folded blanket this time.

"Here," he said. "I'm surprised no-one's done this for you yet." He moved to her and placed the blanket on the floor beside her. "Lift yer arse, if you'd be so kind."

Sarene obliged. The weight of her body against her bound hands was painful – *just like everything else,* she thought – but the temporary annoyance was worth it as he slid the blanket beneath her. When he leaned away she sat down again. The feeling was delicious, with the fabric now insulating her bones against the chill stone floor. She smiled, nodding her thanks in spite of herself.

The man grinned. "Good, eh? I'm glad. Maybe you won't be shiverin' all over the place now." He chuckled, and moved across to the table. He took a hold of the chair and dragged it out, setting it up with the back against the wall, facing her.

It was then she noticed the small book in his hand.

"Don't you mind me," he said, sitting down with a groan. "You just close yer eyes and nod off." Still smiling, the man thumbed through the well-worn pages and settled down against the chair, stretching his legs out and crossing them at the ankles.

Sarene studied him, keeping the disappointment from her face. Then she closed her eyes, shutting herself off from the room. The boy's face came to mind, and she considered the idea that she had been tricked.

How, exactly, was she supposed to cut herself free with a guard posted to her?

HEIRAN SAT ALONE at a table in The Tethered Steed, which he had decided was a ridiculous name for a drinking house considering it stood in a lane barely wide enough for a horse to fit. The place was small, poorly lit and held the odour of something disgusting and repellent, like an army latrine dug into a peat bog. The terrible conditions were acceptable, however, since Heiran wanted to be alone. A small fire burned in one wall, the chimney above sucking the smoke out in drafts which succumbed to the whims of the wind outside. The chimney did its job most of the time.

He took a sip from his cup. Something within him wanted to call for a full pitcher of wine. Perhaps a stronger choice. Brandy would be good. The nerves which had been building for the last few days were reaching a critical point. He was scared.

No, worse; Heiran was terrified.

The matter of pulling the trigger on a crossbow was the easy part. Ending a man's life was something he had done before, and while it bothered him the memory was endurable. Remelas deserved to be punished for his indiscretions.

The mercenary recalled the moment his wife confessed her night of weakness one spring afternoon, five years previous, and the stone chill of betrayal which had filled his heart. The Prince had stopped in their village with his entourage to wait out a passing storm, taking a fancy to a pretty serving girl who happened to be working his inn that evening.

Their marriage had recovered, but was never the same.

Even following her death, Heiran could never fully forgive her. To be the man to kill Remelas was of no consequence. He would be glad to watch the man fall, dead, to the ground.

What swamped Heiran with fear was the impact he would be making. This was more than a man's life. This was creating history. Tamir would be altered by his actions.

Tomorrow, he would change the world.

That concept wouldn't leave him. The weight on his shoulders grew with each hour he dwelt on it. His beautiful daughter would hear the story as she grew up of the day a man ended the life of the King of Tamir, as would all children of the next generation. He would become the monster under the bed. The assassin in the shadows.

If he successfully escaped, his anonymous legacy would be treason.

If he were caught, Heiran would be one of the most reviled figures in Tamir, now and evermore.

Heiran gave a humourless smirk and sipped his watery ale. At the bar, a man who had been slouched on a stool since his arrival suddenly sat up, belched, and rubbed his eyes. Judging by the shabby clothes and days of stubble, the man was no stranger to ale.

"Want another drink?" said the barman, a broad fellow wearing a shirt and overcoat which had been finely made several years ago, but now looked rather depressed.

The patron nodded, blinking a few times to recover his focus. "Yes, friend. I think that'd be a wonderful idea."

As the barman took a tankard from beneath the bar and dunked it into the same piss-poor brew Heiran was drinking, the drunk rubbed his face a few times. There were dark circles around his eyes and he was perspiring. Taking the tankard as it was handed to him, he lifted it and took several long swallows.

"Ugh," he said, wincing as he pulled the drink away. "Did I really drink this pigswill?"

"All afternoon," said the barman. "And it's a family recipe, so watch your tongue."

The drunk mumbled something into his mug. After imbibing some more of the terrible ale, he smacked his lips and glanced around the room. Heiran averted his gaze, not wanting to encourage discussion.

It was too late. "Hey... Don't I know you?"

Heiran chuckled. "Almost certainly not."

Wood scraped on wood as the legs of the stool ground against the floor. The drunk measured his balance, decided he could stand, and then approached. "No, no. I do know. Yeah, you're... uhm..." He clicked the fingers of his free hand together a few times. "Don't tell me, it's on the tip o'me tongue. Heh... Harrrran? Harrin?"

Surprised, Heiran looked up. This time he paid attention,

studying the man. Recognition came like a slap to the face. "Ethanei?"

"Yeah!" Ethanei stumbled forward and deposited himself in the chair opposite. "Yeah, that's right! Corporal in the Tamir Cavalry, I were. Six years. We served together under Farnorn, out the barracks near Sothiran."

The memory came at once. Heiran remembered the seven months he'd served on the western border, shortly before he resigned following the death of his wife. Ethanei had been in charge of ensuring new recruits – of which there had been many at that stage, the first waves of Remelas's mass army – were able to care properly for their mounts. With Heiran being as skilled as he was with the crossbow, he also gave his fair share of training. Ethanei had become something of a friend, following a similar schedule, to share meals and the occasional drink with.

"'Ere," said Ethanei. "Y'don't mind if I sit w'you for a round? I need to find somewhere to sleep tonight, otherwise I'd stick ar—"

"That's fine," said Heiran, regretting the words even as he said them. "I will be leaving soon too."

"Oh, aye. You gettin' up early for the big show as well?"

"Show?"

"Yeah. Those Sons o' Tamir folk. They'll be here tomorrow, so everyone says."

Heiran kept his face neutral. "I can't say I've heard much about it."

"Where have you been, man?" Ethanei scratched an itch at the palm of his gloved hand. "All the city is chatterin' away about nothing else. The Sons are gonna have a big, public debate about Remelas's actions leadin' to the deaths up at Leithar Grove. I reckon we could be sayin' goodbye to our King by sundown."

"Wouldn't that be something."

"Yeah. The bastard. Can you believe what they did to us? I mean, all that secrecy. All the time I thought we're doing our duty an' it turns out Remelas were looking to bring the Four down on top of our heads."

"I heard the stories," said Heiran. "I'd left the army by the time it all came out."

"Oh, yeah. I heard. My condolences, and all that." Ethanei gave an embarrassed cough, distracting himself with his drink. Heiran nodded.

"So what brings you to Tamiran?" he asked. "Surely you didn't travel all this way just to listen to these Sons of Tamir."

"Pah, if only it were that simple. I split up with me wife, cheating bitch that she is, and ended up here lookin' for work." Ethanei grinned. "Were quite the journey, I can tell you."

"Have you found any?"

"Aye, I'm mucking out stables for a few silvers a week. Shit work, if you'll excuse the phrase, but it keeps me fed and watered."

"Just like the horses," Heiran replied.

"Yep. I reckon I prefer the company of the bloody things at this point. A horse generally doesn't ruin your life. At least, providing you don't spook 'em, or get behind one when it's playing silly beggars." The drunkard sniffed. "So what about you?"

"What about me?"

"I thought you lived to the east. Near Ghellei."

"I did." Shrugging his shoulders, watching a small insect fly between them, Heiran smiled. "I fancied a change of scenery."

"Workin'?"

"You could say that."

"Huh." Ethanei held up his empty mug, waving it to catch the tavern owner's attention. The man muttered something beneath his breath, reaching for a fresh container. "Whatever it is must be better than flinging crap around all day. But still, c'mon. What have you been up to?"

"Caring for my daughter, mainly. After my wife passed, my time was taken up with the little'un. Now she's older, we were able to make the move here to the capital." Heiran examined his fingernails to distract himself from the absurdity he felt at the nonsense passing his lips. "I was looking to get her into one of the schools here. Ghellei isn't exactly well known for its education system."

"Aye, shithole of a town, it is." Ethanei laughed. "Well good for you. How old is she now?"

"It was her fourth summer this year."

"Aw, bless. I'm glad. Good to know you're taking care of yourself. Some said…" Ethanei grew quiet, with an expression on his face suggesting he'd spoken a second longer than he should. Heiran watched him as the barman brought over the fresh ale, taking the empty mug. It bought Ethanei a few more seconds.

"Some said what?"

"Oh, nothin'. How long you been in town for?"

Heiran kept his gaze fixed. "Some said what?" he repeated.

Ethanei scratched the back of his head. "Eh… Look, it were just rumours between soldiers. But some said you'd taken your wife's death pretty hard. Y'know?"

"I did. Does that seem strange to you?"

"No, *no*. Of course not, mate. I just, eh… I mean, some said you'd gone a bit mad."

At this Heiran laughed, a full-bellied roar, the likes of which he hadn't experienced in too long. The sound surprised Ethanei, who regarded him with a grimace.

"Mad? No, not mad. No more than any man who suffers the loss of a loved one. I drank for a while and shut myself off from the world. I grieved. Then I moved on. What else should I have done?"

Ethanei offered a weak smile. "I dunno. Like I said, it were just army men chatting. You remember when Ishmai got caught in that tent fire along the border, and burnt most of his hair away? And we all used to say he spent every night cryin' himself t'sleep cos he'd lost his famous blonde locks? Were bollocks, weren't it. But people talk cos there's bugger-all else to do between duties."

Calming himself, Heiran nodded, placing his hand on the table. "I understand. Don't you worry. I'm not offended. Just… amused, I suppose."

The two of them fell silent. Heiran stared at nothing, reflecting on this news.

"You okay?" asked Ethanei. "Like, really? You seem a bit… well, sad."

Heiran forced a smile. "I suppose I am. But then, with the kingdom in the state it's in, who can blame me. Aside from my girl, there's precious little to be happy about these days."

Ethanei spread his arms wide, leaning back in his chair and consequently spilling some of his ale across the floor. "You should come watch the debate tomorrow. I've heard these Sons of Tamir speak. It's pretty inspiring stuff, I can tell you. I felt like a true Tamir again afterwards."

With a crooked smile, Heiran rose from his seat. "Perhaps I'll do just that. Enjoy your evening, my friend."

"Oh aye, I will. I'll do me best to make sure that I'm nice and sleepy before midnight, then up and perky as a fox amongst the chickens come sunrise."

"I'd advise heading to another place, then. That ale wouldn't get you drunk if you dropped the keg on your head."

"I heard that," said the barman, wringing out his damp washcloth over a bucket.

"You look after yourself, Heiran. Who knows, maybe we'll bump into each other again soon."

Heiran turned, heading for the door. "Maybe we will."

THE SUN HAD fallen an hour ago, and the wintery breeze stung the skin. Kanderil ate a slab of bread while his horse rested from the afternoon's ride. The few clouds in the sky sped along across the starry heavens, whisked along in the wind.

The tavern keeper's boy had known nothing. Stammering and gormless, he reacted to the questions as though a wrong answer would earn him a beating. As it was, there was nothing to tell. No riders had been seen nor heard the previous night, at least as far as anyone could recall. Kanderil departed after one final inspection of the road, looking for any clues which could point him in Sarene's direction. The road revealed little.

Orlienn, who now brushed her mount's coat around the tack, had more success with the Shrine but scarce enough to make a certain decision on where to proceed next. It turned out that the red-sash riders had first been mentioned to the Guide towards the start of the autumn, maybe two months ago. The Guide could not say who they represented, other than to mention that they rarely carried weapons and were courteous to those they met. It was unlikely that Sarene's captors were a militaristic faction.

Which left them clutching at straws. Kanderil rubbed the back of his neck in frustration. The two of them were at the edge of the Kaeshan quarry, which fell away several yards before them into an empty pit of jagged rock and broken earth. Once it had been rich with limestone, but had been abandoned at the turn of the decade. The lower depths of the great hole had formed a lake, where on clear days the water shimmered in beautiful turquoise. Now, with no sun to illuminate the quarry, it could have been a gateway to the centre of the earth, where creatures of fairy tale lurked in the darkness.

"There are several small villages in the surrounding areas," said Kanderil. "One of them is a cattle farming community, housing around three hundred people."

Glancing over her shoulder, Orlienn nodded. The brush made a steady *ssshh ssshh* along the gelding's sides. "You think we could find her there?"

"It makes sense that these people have somewhere to go. The likelihood of a group of fanatics collectively living in a small hamlet makes less sense than grouping together amongst a larger commune. It is easier to hide within a village than in a cottage."

"There would be more witnesses," the ranger said.

"True enough."

"What makes you think they're fanatics?"

Kanderil muttered. "Spasmodic murdered at least four of their number. Any sensible group would have learned their lesson, but these kept searching for Sarene."

"So because of that, they become fanatical? Perhaps they are just determined, or devoted to a cause."

"A cause. How righteous it must be to believe in something or someone which advocates the abduction of young girls."

Orlienn sighed. "You're scared for her, aren't you?"

"I am supposed to keep her under my guard."

"No… I mean," she continued, choosing her words carefully. "You've been charging around like a bear with a sore head. It's clear that you're scared of what these people will *do* to her."

Kanderil, grim faced, shook his head. "No. They will not harm her."

Orlienn stopped brushing. "How can you be so sure?"

"It makes no sense to chase the girl down and kidnap her if they did. The dangers were too great. Again, a number of them have already been killed hunting her. If they wanted her dead, they would have done the job in the woods where they found her. They have a purpose for her. It fits the same description of how the Gathire hunted Sarene. Chalimer needed her intact and healthy to satisfy the Regent's curiosity. Tyrrial wanted her dead in response to his own fears. A bandit named Hawk pursued her to get to *me*. But this new group… Their ultimate objective is what concerns m—"

A flurry of movement to one side made Orlienn jump. Kanderil pulled free his huge knife before he remembered the only living thing apart from the Four capable of such speed.

"What are you doing here?" Kanderil asked, Spasmodic now standing before them, its coat rippling into place around its frame.

"I forgot me slug," it said. "Went back to the cabin to fetch it and you'd already buggered off. Anthon's there, chewin' on his nails. I thought you'd need the help."

"Do you have any idea of where we can find her?" asked Orlienn, a hand on her chest. Her quickened breathing announced how badly the creature had scared her.

"Yes, actually." Spasmodic grinned in the darkness.

"Where?" asked Kanderil, his tired body renewed by the two words. He moved towards his waiting mount.

"Wait, wait. Hold yer horses. Well, not literally, you'll break the things."

"*Where?*"

Spasmodic giggled. "Ooh, I like it when you get all demanding."

Standing his ground and rounding on the demonic figure, Kanderil clenched his fists. "Tell me where Sarene is. I do not have time for your games."

"Hey, tell me summat first. When did you last sleep? You look like shit."

Irritation sparked the Hunter's response. "What?"

"When did he last sleep?" Spasmodic asked Orlienn, pointing a thumb at him. "Be honest, like."

"Not at all last night," she replied with hesitation. "So I would say two days."

"Exactly. I know where the girl is, and its four hours easy on these dumb animals of yours. Then you'll have to fight 'em. You should get some kip first, matey."

Kanderil glowered at the creature. "You want me to sleep when we're a half-day's ride away from rescuing her?"

"Look, she's fine. I could smell it. Whatever they've got in mind, they ain't doing horrible stuff to her."

"You were there?" said Orlienn.

"Yeah. She's in an old building that looks a bit like a place I saw in the country south from here. Had a load of old people chanting bollocks and growing flowers, the mental gits."

"You mean the monastery?" said Kanderil in disbelief. "The place was decimated in a fire half a dozen years ago.

There would be nowhere for the group to hide, let alone keep Sarene out of sight."

"Well looks like someone fixed it," said Spasmodic with a sneer. "The place looks pretty tidy. No old people this time, though. S'hardly a fortress, but it's got walls and a ceiling. That pretty much defines a building, dunnit?"

"Why didn't you get her out?"

"Pssh. If playing with those Gathire bastards taught me anything, it's not to jump ahead into the middle of a big bunch of strangers without a little backup."

Kanderil recalled finding Spasmodic lying in the dirt north of the Meadows, bleeding from an atrocious wound deep across its chest following a confrontation with a squad of Agents. Only the quick actions of a total stranger, who turned out to be Glaithe, had saved its life. They subsequently discovered the accelerated healing ability which was part of the creature's bizarre make up. What should have been a crippling injury had all but disappeared within two weeks.

"A sensible choice," he admitted.

"Maybe I'm growin' up. I'm not even a year old yet, remember?" Spasmodic giggled brightly. "Get some sleep, you idiot. I'll be happy to shepherd you off in the right direction once you're ready for a ruckus."

"I'm ready now," insisted Kanderil.

"Well I don't fancy getting one of your arrows in me arse when you yawn."

"I must admit," said Orlienn, her voice a light and graceful comparison to the two others, "that I find myself tired after our journey. While I too wish to rescue Sarene and see her safe, a short rest would be welcome."

Kanderil considered the point. He was convinced he was capable of making the ride and engaging the enemy without delay. Orlienn, however, yawned beside him, and he could not say the same for her.

"Fine," he said. "I'll meet you there by sunrise." He jammed a foot into a stirrup and pulled himself up into his mount's saddle.

"Wait, I thought we were gonna—"

But Spasmodic's reply was cut off, as Kanderil's horse flung its head at the rider's urging. He departed at a trot, not risking a full gallop in the darkness but unable to sit around while Sarene remained in her captor's hands.

MORNING CAME WITH the crowing of caged roosters in the marketplace outside. Niallya opened her eyes. The room she occupied was tiny, even though it contained nothing except her bed. There was a slit in the wall, no more than three inches across and double that high, the only connection to the outside world from this part of the terraced block. She stretched, enjoying the delicious warmth as her muscles expanded. Then she slid out from beneath the blanket and moved to where her folded clothes lay. Her usual attire would be too conspicuous, so along with the wolf-fur cloak she had picked up some plain cotton garments to wear beneath a brown hooded cloak, along with a heavy woollen cowl and scarf to obscure her features. Niallya dressed, then opened the door which sat at the top of the stairs. There was so little space she had to place her foot upon the first step to leave the room.

Descending the short staircase, she found Heiran sitting with his daughter in front of the fire. Tillyan was eating a slice of bread, upon which a boiled egg had been broken up into pieces. Heiran looked up at Niallya, his hand stroking the girl's hair. His face was haggard and drawn.

"Good morning," he offered.

"Good morning," Niallya replied. A similar meal was waiting for her on the table, and she went over to pick it up. "How are you feeling?" She sat in one of the chairs, facing away from the other two so she could lower the scarf from her mouth.

"As well as can be expected." Heiran replied. "Yourself?"

"My bed was adequate."

"Good."

Niallya ate in silence. The bread was stale but of decent quality. She regarded the wrapped cloak they would be taking with them as part of their ruse. Only one bolt lay beside the crossbow inside. It seemed wasteful to bring more. If Heiran missed, there would not be time to reload and try again.

When she was finished, Niallya pulled up her scarf and rose. "I must excuse myself for a few minutes. Will you be ready when I return?"

"Yes."

Nodding she moved to the door, turning the stiff handle and nudging the wood with her shoulder. The street outside was already filled with the early risers of Tamiran. Niallya scanned the area for an outhouse. Surely here in the capital there would be a place befitting a respectable woman such as herself.

HEIRAN SMILED AS he watched Tillyan walk over to her stuffed bear.

"Can we go to the candy shop again?" she asked, turning around to face him. Her mouth spread into a hopeful grin, displaying her child-teeth in two wonky rows. Heiran shook his head, ushering her over towards him. She tottered forward as he rose to one knee, reaching out to place his hands on her tiny shoulders.

"Not today, princess. I've got to do the job I brought us here for. So I'll need you to stay here and be quiet, just like in Ghellei. Okay?"

At the mention of their former home the girl's face sunk into doubt. She nodded several times.

"But this is the last time. When I come back I'll have enough to find a true home for us. And I'll never have to leave you alone again."

With the honest scepticism of the young, Tillyan stared at him from beneath her brow. Heiran ran a thumb across her cheek before propping up her chin with a bent finger.

"Aren't we staying here?" the girl asked.

"No," said Heiran. "We're only here while daddy does his work. When this is over we'll go somewhere safe, out in the countryside. We'll have a new home with plenty of space, and we won't be stuck in the smelly old city any more. And we won't have to hide."

The stuffed bear, hooked around the neck by a skinny elbow, was lifted into a forceful hug. Tillyan swayed where she stood, considering the words.

"Promise?"

"Promise."

The girl smiled, and her father drew her into a fierce embrace. He refused to cry, though tears threatened to spill. There was no option but to make it back safe for his daughter.

"I love you, Tilly."

"I love you too, daddy."

"You'll stay here until I come get you, okay?"

"Okay."

"Good." He released her with considerable effort, fussing her hair and running a hand along her shoulders, before kissing her brow. Finally Heiran tipped her chin up towards him, holding her gaze with his own. "I'll see you soon."

"Bye bye, daddy." She patted him on the cheek before he stood, then made her way to the table and pulled herself up onto one of the chairs. She popped the bear down before her.

"The pitcher is still full, and there's more bread in my bag."

"I'm not hungry yet."

"I meant for later, silly."

"I'm not silly," Tillyan said with a giggle.

A knock at the door signalled Niallya's return. Composing himself, Heiran moved to pick up the wolf-fur cloak and the weapon within, slipping the bolt into a pocket. He wrapped the bundle up in his arms and moved to the door, prodding it with his foot. It opened and Niallya stood in the street, waiting.

"Ready?" she asked.

"Let's go."

Chapter Fifteen

KANDERIL CROUCHED IN the tree line, his bow close to hand beside him, one hand pressed against his right thigh as he massaged the dense muscle. The monastery had indeed been renovated following the fire which had gutted it. The frame remained intact, and the repairs had mostly been constructed by taking stone from the remains of the wall which surrounded the vineyard. Once a place of reverence to nature – as a by-product of their journey, the Four had rendered the concept of individual deities somewhat obsolete in many places throughout the world – the monks had left to start anew elsewhere following the blaze. Kanderil had still been a member of the Kalethi at the time, and there had been no explanation why the monks didn't simply rebuild. As such, the once beautiful gardens fell into disrepair, and the place had been abandoned.

Not any longer. The lands belonged to the kingdom, granted to the monks as a place of historic significance. The fact that it was now occupied and repaired suggested that the construction had taken place with the blessing of the Tamir Council.

"When we have Sarene back, I want you to send a message to Chalimer," Kanderil said aloud, turning his attention to Orlienn. "There must be public records stating who bought these lands."

Orlienn nodded. She had arrived a short time ago with the creature. The latter seemed excited at the prospect of the rescue, fidgeting along beside them. "Very well."

"So what's the plan, big man?" asked Spasmodic. Kanderil surveyed the monastery, taking in the surroundings once more. The new day rose from the far side of the structure, casting long shadows. At least two hundred yards of open ground lay between them and the building. Several tracks led between the building and the Highway to the south, so Kanderil had led them west, circling away from the obvious route. If they had men on watch – and Kanderil had no reason to suspect these people would not – then it would be difficult to make the run without being spotted. That would place Sarene in danger.

Difficult for him and Orlienn, at least. "Can you make it over there without being seen?"

"Probably," said Spasmodic.

"Probably?"

It grinned, leaning in close. "I'm quick, but I can't magically jump there."

"How long would it take?"

"A few seconds."

"To cover that distance?" Orlienn shook her head. "That's impossible."

"Have you not been payin' attention, cherrycheeks? I'm

not one of you."

"It tells the truth," said Kanderil. "I do not know how it moves so fast, but it does." He tugged on his coarse beard a few times before pointing to the stable attached to the southern wall of the building. "Release those horses, making sure they make plenty of noise. Then get up on the roof. When the occupants come out to investigate, hold your position until we arrive."

"And then?" Spasmodic giggled, rocking on its booted heels.

"Then make sure they won't bother us further. But do *not* kill them."

Spasmodic flicked its tongue, rolling its eyes. "Are you kidding me? Even after they stole away the girl, doing sod-knows what to her, you won't let me teach 'em a lesson?"

"If you start killing people, the others will panic. They may take drastic action in response, such as harming Sarene."

"Then they'll just come after her again!" It spat, muttering. "And you reckon *I'm* clueless."

"Sarene is the priority, not your need for violence. I do not care how you take them out. Just keep them alive."

"And if something happens to Sarene?" asked Orlienn, her hazel eyes focused on Kanderil. The woodsman grabbed his huge bow from the ground and started heading west, keeping within the trees.

"We should approach from further along. Providing the group keep their attention on the horses at the east entrance, it will give us a better chance of approaching undetected."

WHEN KANDERIL AND Orlienn were in position, Spasmodic snapped its neck to the side, producing an audible *pop*. Then it moved.

The ground beneath its feet rushed past, several yards covered with each stride. It sped towards the monastery, rising in stature with each heartbeat. Within seconds it was close enough to leap, claws digging into the masonry. It kept close to the wall, peering around the corner and listening. There were voices coming from within, but none were alarmed. It could smell the damp straw of the thatched roof, the stale musk of the horses and the sweat of the humans inside the building.

It could smell Sarene, too. Fainter. She was being concealed somewhere. Somewhere cold.

Spasmodic checked around the corner again. Nothing moved except for the horses, who were mostly chewing. He could hear them. Through the uneven slats of the stable's roof he saw one raise a head, ears high. Spasmodic snickered. Damned right it should be nervous.

If it got carried away during the impending fight and a few lives were lost, then what would Kanderil do? Moan at him? The oversized human understood that Spasmodic was necessary to keeping the girl safe. Safe from harm, anyway…. Little games like this were a different matter.

The creature remembered its speech convincing Anthon to join them. It had realised Sarene's interest in the boy from the very first time she had laid eyes on him. Humans were very aromatic creatures, even if they didn't realise it. Fear and illness were easy to spot, but the subtle ones… All had their own little scents. Lust was one of them, and the concept was hilarious. Humans were the only animal it had encountered so far who went at great lengths to hide their basic needs. The horses in front of it mated because they were in heat. Humans hid it behind gifts, plants and words.

And Anthon had kept the girl occupied for long enough to pay little attention to the amount of time Spasmodic was spending away from her, planning its entertainment.

Horses in front of it.

"Oh yeah," it whispered, suppressing a giggle. Swinging down from the wall and landing in a low crouch, it crawled towards the horses. The stallion which had noticed the creature started to whinny, moving forward. The others – there were nine in total – began to realise that something was wrong, and they fed from each other's growing tension.

Spasmodic stood up straight, tucked its thumb-stumps into its rope belt, and turned around. Then it pulled down its pants and revealed its bare white backside to the horses, shaking its hips.

One of the geldings snorted, kicking its forelegs as it reached the front door of the stable. The other horses started to follow suit, neighing and pawing at the ground.

Beaming, Spasmodic retied its belt and stood straight. Then it moved around to the front of the stable, flicked open the latch, and pulled back the door. Entering the shack housing the beasts it spread its arms wide, claw-tips clicking against the wooden beams keeping each horse in their respective stalls as it walked the length of the structure.

The horses, anxious now, began to pace from side to side. Trapped. One big scare was all it would take.

Spasmodic flicked the locked beam of each stall, allowing the horses to escape. Then it leapt directly upwards, grabbed hold of the ceiling, and thundered a heavy kick into the wood. The shack rocked with the power of it, and the horses bolted. They whinnied and neighed, causing a great racket which brought sounds of alarm from within the monastery. Quickly, Spasmodic pulled itself through a gap over one of the northern stalls and hopped to the thatched roof of the main building, the creature climbing up its southern edge. There it flattened itself out, burying its face in the straw and trying its hardest not to laugh. Men were running out of the building now, trying to grab the horses, but they were too slow.

Always too slow.

KANDERIL RAN, BOW in hand, an arrow notched to the drawstring. Orlienn kept pace with him, but Kanderil gestured for her to overtake him. The ranger was faster on her feet, and it was better for her to arrive unseen even if he did not. All it would take was one errant glance in their direction, and the time they had to get to Sarene would diminish rapidly.

Orlienn reached the western wall of the monastery and crouched low, drawing her short bow. She peered around the corner along the southern wall, where the now-empty stable stood. Voices came from the front of the monastery, too indistinct to make out, as people yelled at each other in confusion. Spasmodic was unseen, but the cries that filled the air were not of terror. Kanderil would have expected a lot more noise if the creature attacked.

A small door, several yards to Orlienn's left, opened. A man wearing a crimson sash stepped outside, saw Kanderil, and called out.

"Someone's he—"

Kanderil released a shaft, hitting the man in the right shoulder. He fell back inside the door, an arm scrabbling for the frame as he tried to maintain balance, crying out in pain. Cursing, Kanderil drew another arrow.

"*Let's have some fun!*" A high-pitched shriek from atop the monastery. Within seconds a man cried out, the yell joined by a second, then a third – a cacophony of strangers unified by their sudden panic.

Orlienn kept the back entrance covered with her bow as Kanderil arrived. A flash of movement at the door and Kanderil flung himself to the ground, a crossbow bolt missing him by several feet.

They had to get to Sarene as quickly as possible.

SARENE LISTENED TO the commotion above. The stout man posted to watch her during the previous night had gone up to investigate. As soon as he had left, she had twisted her hand around to retrieve the wooden strip from her bracer. The razor embedded within it nicked at her skin, but she managed to take the thing into her grip and draw it free. Then she sliced at the bonds holding her. The razor was fresh, and she could feel the rope give way within the first few strikes, frayed strands flicking around her sore wrists.

Another man, this one mean looking and carrying a sword, hurried down the stairs. He took one look at her, and turned to call back up.

"She's secure."

A voice responded with a command, and the man nodded. When he turned back to watch the staircase, Sarene continued cutting. There were more cries of alarm. The people up there were yelling out in shock… no, more than that. *Dread.*

Spasmodic.

The man in the room with her paced back and forth, paying scarce attention to the prisoner. His fingers flexed and tightened around the hilt of the sword. He was visibly sweating, and more than once he lifted a hand to scrape his forehead.

Sarene continued cutting. Feeling the rope loosening against her wrists, she pulled hard. Not quite enough. A few more slices, and then again. A few more, a—

The rope snapped At once the young woman scrambled to her feet, feeling pins and needles in her legs as the blood flowed back into the areas which had been cramping.

The man in front of her noticed the movement a little too early and turned to face her. He brought his sword up before him.

"Stay right there, girl!"

Sarene slapped the flat of the blade with her palm. His stance was not practiced, and he was unable to keep the weapon steady. Stepping in close, Sarene followed with a swift knee which thudded again her captor's groin. He cried out, frozen by the sudden pain.

With a scant moment to measure, Sarene threw her right hand as forcefully as she could, rolling her shoulder forwards. Her fist connected with his temple, and the man staggered over, falling forward awkwardly. Sarene swept up the sword, then brought the hilt crashing down against his cheek. He moaned, curling into a foetal position.

She glanced up the staircase. No visible movement.

Quickly she ascended the steps to find herself in a large room containing a fireplace and several rows of chairs, similar to the Shrine she'd seen in the summer. Behind her a short hallway ran towards the main entrance. Outside she saw a fight going on, at the centre of which was a whirling dervish of red hair and green leather. But between her and Spasmodic were at least six more men in crimson sashes.

That left two more corridors, leading further into the building. She took the one on the left, running forward to find another way out. Kanderil had to be here somewhere. Maybe there was a back entrance somewhere he was covering.

She ran into the corridor, and almost bumped into Methulai, who appeared from one of the adjoining rooms. Their eyes met, and the leader of the Dedicant shook his head rapidly, reaching for her with a shaking hand.

"You can't leave," he said, eyes zealous. "You can't

leave!"

Sarene turned to flee, slipping against the wooden floor, before righting herself and heading along the other corridor towards the door at the very end. There was movement behind her and something brushed her shoulder, but she twisted and continued running. She could make it. Footsteps and more shouts meant she was being pursued, but she could *make* it.

"You have to come with me, Sarene!" Methulai yelled with a disturbing quiver to his voice, as though touched by madness. "You can't leave! The world must be saved!"

She carried on running. The door was only ten yards away. Five yards. She reached out to grab the handle. Instead of slowing, Sarene crashed into the door with her shoulder. It was heavy oak, and did not budge. She grabbed the handle, turned and pulled.

Locked.

Sarene turned about, looking for another escape route. Two more open doorways lead along the corridor, which she'd noticed from the corner of her eye as she ran contained sleeping quarters. Maybe there was a window she could escape through. Sh—

No. Methulai was too close. He descended upon her, his cloak billowing out behind him and his crimson-clad form filling the corridor. He reached out, and Sarene held the sword out in front of her. The cultist slowed, eyeing the blade.

"You wouldn't use that against me, would you...?" he asked with a genuine smile.

A hand grabbed at Methulai's arm, pulling him back. "That demon has almost breached the entrance! We must flee, my Lord!"

Sarene saw that it was the boy who had provided the razor. Her eyes darted from him to Methulai, keeping the sword trained on the latter.

"If we leave the girl to escape, we will doom the world," Methulai replied, shrugging the boy off. "We cannot allow that. She *must* come with us."

Sarene watched as Methulai reached out to grab for her sword. She thrust it as a warning, but the man ignored this, trusting his thick gloves to actually *grip* the blade. The edges cut into the leather protecting his hands, and as he twisted the sword she saw drops of blood trickle out onto the steel. She pushed forward again, and Methulai grimaced in pain… but the devotion to his cause was evident in his eyes.

Methulai shoved the sword aside and aimed a kick at Sarene's leg. She gasped in pain and fell back against the door. He reached with his other hand and grabbed her arm, dragging her forwards with him. Sarene writhed and squirmed, lashing out with every limb. Spasmodic would be here soon. Kanderil had to be nearby. She fought for all she was worth.

"Come on, my Lord!" the youth said again. "If you are caught, then this will all be for nothing."

Methulai shook his head. "No… Not me. The girl." He let go of Sarene's arm, only to grab a handful of her hair. She reached up to grip his wrist with both hands, letting the full weight of her body impede him further as she hung from his arm.

Then she saw the knife in his free hand.

"She cannot leave," said Methulai.

Sarene's vision drew everything into sharp focus. Every detail of Methulai's face, calm and focused as it was, held her complete attention. She saw every bump on his skin, every wrinkle of his clothing, every hair out of place. The slightest change in his demeanour as a decision was made. His pupils contracted.

Methulai threw his arm forward, his hand thumping against Sarene's chest. She thought he'd punched her, but when he stepped back something slid against her ribs, exiting her body.

"Tyrrial's will be done." Methulai turned and hurried down the corridor, pushing past the boy. He was staring at her, his mouth agape. Then he turned and ran, following Methulai back towards the main room.

Sarene stared down at her shirt. There was a tear in the fabric. She tested it with her fingers. At her touch darkness spread through the cotton, like ink through blotting paper. Her fingers came away wet, warm and red.

She looked along the stone corridor, charred black in places. Methulai and the boy were gone.

Alone again…

KANDERIL STEPPED INTO the door-frame just as another red-sash ran towards the exit. The man was ashen faced and wide-eyed, a splash of red dots marking one cheek. He didn't noticed the giant stepping into his path until it was too late.

"Oh *shi—*"

The Hunter grabbed him by the hair and slammed his head into the nearest wall. The red-sash slumped to the ground.

Whatever was happening outside had scared the man witless. Even from here the creature's laughter was audible, piercing the air between the sound of swords and cries of the injured.

Kanderil stepped inside, eyes sweeping across the room. It appeared to be a kitchen area, with cooking pots and utensils stacked into place. A large table sat in the centre of the room.

Heading into the corridor leading away from the opposite side of the kitchen, Kanderil followed it towards the main central room. Two sleeping quarters connected to the wall on his left. He made sure to pass these with care, lest a waiting opponent take him by surprise. None of the rooms were occupied.

A yell, much closer this time. Another cultist ran towards him from the front entrance, brandishing a spear. Again the unfiltered terror on the man's face was alarming. The cultist thrust the iron tip towards Kanderil's heart with a ragged scream. Kanderil only just managed to step aside, tucking the shaft under one arm and yanking his assailant forwards into a straight right-hand. The fist connected with the man's jaw and sent him stumbling into one of the adjoining rooms, where he crashed over a bed and lay still.

"Nicely done," said Orlienn as she appeared from the

kitchen, a throwing knife in her hand. "Do you know what Spasmodic is doing out there?"

"No." Dropping the spear and stepping out into the central room, Kanderil saw a shimmer of movement. Someone was descending through a trapdoor built into one corner. He strode to follow, weaving between the benches which lined the room. A second doorway opened directly to his left, and he glanced up to ensure he wouldn't be ambushed entering the trapdoor.

Sarene. Slumped against the wall at the opposite end of the corridor like a hastily discarded toy.

Kanderil's skin crawled across his body as a chill gripped his nerves and tangled them around the fingers of some unseen spectre. With his stomach tightening into a cruel knot, he kicked the trapdoor shut with his foot and drew free his hunting knife. Another two rooms lay open between him and the girl, and despite his overbearing need to reach Sarene as soon as possible he forced himself to assert the same caution as before; checking that each was unoccupied before passing. Each second of delay twisting further within him. As before, both rooms were empty.

Sprinting the final few yards, Kanderil dropped to his knees and skidded forward in his refusal to reduce his speed. Now crouched over the girl, he saw that she was unconscious, with blood seeping thickly from the right side of her chest. He turned her onto her back, laying her out flat, and then tore the left arm of the girl's shirt to use as a bandage. This he pressed tight against the wound to staunch the bleeding. Sarene's features were pallid, strands of dark hair clinging to her face, and her breath shallow and gurgling in her chest. He pressed two fingers beneath the girl's chin. The pulse was erratic.

Sarene was dying.

Movement behind him heralded Orlienn's arrival. Kanderil didn't bother to acknowledge her as she crouched beside him. She was engaged, just as he, with the girl's condition. Already she was fishing around in a pouch slung against her hip.

"Is there time?"

"The wound is deep," Kanderil replied. "She will not make it back to the cabin."

"Where, then?" she asked, her tone flat, straightening her back to thread the eye of the needle she had just produced.

"If we cannot stop the bleeding, nowhere."

"Hey, what's goin' on?" called Spasmodic from behind them. "None o' these buggers wanna play anymore."

"We could cauterise the wound," said Orlienn. "There's a kettle over a fire in the kitchen. The base would seal the flesh."

"Her lung has been punctured. Fluid is already building. If we seal it in she will drown." Kanderil strove to remain calm. He had witnessed death during his career with the Kalethi, but the sight of Sarene fading before him threatened to tip him over the limit of his composure. He continued to press down on the wound with the cloth, which was already soaked through in his hand.

Spasmodic leaned over them, giving a cautious chuckle. "Come on, stop messin' around. Get her up and we can chase after the others. Find out what they wanted her for!"

"Is she breathing?" asked Orlienn.

"Barely."

The two of them continued to work, for what use it was. Aside from placing pressure on the wound, they did not have the medical knowledge nor the equipment to do much except hope the bleed would clot.

Kanderil was a realist. He'd seen injuries like this before, following battle. The recipient did not survive. It was too much, too great a shock to the system. The girl simply wasn't strong enough.

"But..." Spasmodic said. It gave a brief, nervous giggle. Then it shook its head, dreadlocks bouncing around its shoulders. Blood covered its face and dripped from its clothing. "But she's not meant to get hurt. They said she's gonna change everything. Tell her to get up!"

"*She's dying!*" Kanderil roared, releasing his frustration at the creature as it buzzed around behind them. "I was meant to protect her, and I failed!" He turned back to the girl, checking her pulse again. Still fluttering against the tips of his fingers, as though a butterfly were trying to break through her skin. At the touch blood trickled from the corner of her mouth. Immediately he turned her to her side, so as to open the airway. More liquid spilt; so *dark*.

"She..." Spasmodic laughed. "No, that's not it. That isn't how things end. I've seen it."

"Seen what?" asked Orlienn, glancing round.

But the creature was moving. It knelt down between them. "Let go of 'er."

"Get out of the way," demanded Kanderil. "I need to press down on th—"

Spasmodic reached out with startling speed. Its claws hung less than an inch from Kanderil's throat. "Let go of her. I can get her to that Shrine place. You can't."

"She will not make it," said Kanderil, locking his gaze on Tyrrial's creation.

"She won't fuckin' make it lying on the floor," Spasmodic snarled.

Kanderil glanced down. It was right; Sarene would be dead within minutes if something wasn't done. He nodded, leaning back on the balls of his feet and helping to lift her into Spasmodic's arms. "Press against her chest with this cloth. Move as fast as you can."

Spasmodic nodded, turning – and was gone. Kanderil stared at the ground where a large pool of Sarene's blood filtered into the gaps between the slates, staining the cold stone. He felt the warmth of her blood on his fingers.

"What now?" asked Orlienn, shouldering her bow. The situation had shaken her, and she pressed her hands against her hips to stop them trembling.

"Now we search this place from top to bottom. I want to find out why they brought the girl here." Kanderil stalked back along the corridor, sheathing his knife and leaving sickly-red smears against the hilt. "And if any of these bastards are still alive I will make them wish they were not."

They entered the main chamber. Kanderil directed Orlienn to secure the back entrance, in case any Dedicant sought to circle the building. Then he approached the open main doors.

Before he reached them he could smell it; a rusty tang stronger than Sarene's blood covering his hands. He walked out into the frosty gardens surrounding the building, his footsteps *crunch*ing against the frozen grass.

Kanderil forced himself to study the horrifying scene, committing each detail to memory. Each torn body. Every twisted face. The creature had ripped apart every Dedicant foolish enough to stand before it.

Orlienn appeared behind him, cursed, then choked. Within moments she disappeared back into the building.

He didn't think any less of her for it.

THE CREATURE RAN with the Queen of the World fading in its arms.

Booted feet ate up the open terrain between it and the Shrine, as the creature moved faster than it ever had before. Grass and tree and hill and road were blurs, shimmers of colour without substance. Its face was beaten as its velocity threatened to turn the very wind into a solid, abrasive whole. The feeling was exhilarating; while it had previously pushed itself to sprint at the highest speed it could manage, this was the first time the creature had a reason to do so. There was a need, an importance, which pumped its muscles and snapped its joints that much harder.

The girl flopped, deadweight in its grip, collected up and cradled against its chest. While they were of similar size, the creature carried her with ease. It looked down just long enough to see the ghostly pale flesh masked beneath the blood which had conquered her clothing and skin. The sight brought a gnawing sensation just at the centre of its chest, tight and uncomfortable. A feeling it hadn't experienced before. Something it had no wish to experience now.

It could smell death in the air, and the creature pushed on.

Things weren't supposed to be this way. The circles had shown the coming war.

With a mixture of anguish and rage, it roared at the heavens and forced itself to accelerate.

Chapter Sixteen

SARENE OPENED HER eyes.

She was on her feet and walking forwards. The broad back of another person filled her vision.

Glancing left and right she saw nothing but white; endless *white*. No horizon, no scenery. Impossible. Her mind teased at the word *void*, but that had always conjured an image of darkness and solitude. This was more like a desert. A great expanse of light which never ended.

Beneath her feet, however, was a pathway. The trail she and those around her followed was two dozen yards across, sandy and flat. The footsteps of the man in front left no mark upon the ground.

Still walking, Sarene craned her neck to look over the shoulders in front of her. Ahead a line of people snaked away into the distance. The assortment of individuals was stunning, a variety of builds, heights and skin colours. Most of these strangers wore fashions and hairstyles she had never seen before. To her surprise, animals padded alongside. She saw dogs and cats, wolves, pigs and sheep. She saw one great beast, bigger than anything she had ever seen before, with huge ears and a long nose, its tail swaying. The sight of it took her breath away.

Breath.

Sarene realised she wasn't breathing.

Panic seized her as she tried to inhale but nothing filled her lungs. Her eyes widened. She coughed hard, trying to clear whatever must be blocking her airways. Only when she realised that she felt perfectly fine did she pause, stepping out of the line and standing still. Her chest didn't burn from a lack of air. Sarene waited, counting in her head. After a minute had passed there was still no pain.

The girl looked both ways along the line of strangers. Since joining them in their meandering, a steady flow of others had formed behind her. The line ran in both directions for as far as she could see. There was no entry point. No gate or door. Just people and animals walking along the sandy path; people she had never met.

Curious now, Sarene started walking alongside the line, setting herself a quick pace. She passed an incredible assortment of characters. Men and women, ugly and beautiful, old and young. Children, too. A few figures carried babes. None of them glanced in her direction.

Among them all were the creatures of the lands. Some she recognised, others she did not. She resisted the urge to touch any of them, scared that any contact would somehow jolt them.

She followed, unable to make sense of time. It couldn't have been long before she saw the line's ultimate destination as it curved across to the right, revealing what lay ahead.

A colossal gateway, its oblong frame carved from some unknown green material, towered over the scene. An oasis, the only sign of terrain visible in this barren landscape, curled around it. Sand built in banks where the bottom of the gate met either side of the pathway. A few trees, the trunks seemingly created by stacking conical measures of wood atop each other, hung curved either side of the gate.

Within the gateway stood what appeared to be a mirror. Whenever something stepped through the gate, the mirror rippled and the entrant disappeared. Even at her current distance, she felt a comforting warmth emanating from within, calming her from the moment she set eyes upon it. Sarene smiled. The girl increased her pace, eager to see where this wonderful gateway led.

Several yards to the side of the gate a man stood dressed in a sapphire blue robe. Long, silvery grey hair and beard obscured his face. Sarene guessed he must be very old. The man stared into a perfect sphere which hung in the air, its metallic surface reflecting the line of strangers passing into the gateway. Beneath the sphere, which was around two feet across the centre, ran a thin stream, peculiar in that she could not see where the flow began or led.

As she approached, the man raised his head. Sarene slowed, cautious now. He was the first to take any notice of her presence. She considered making a dash for the gateway, but he was already walking towards it, blocking her path. Sarene stopped, watching his movements intently.

The old man placed both hands behind his back, inspecting the gate. He leant forward as the head of the line stepped through and vanished. Satisfied, the man turned and strolled towards Sarene. She offered a weak smile which he ignored. As the man approached she realised that, behind the mass of hair, he wasn't nearly as old as she'd assumed; his face was clear of wrinkles or blemishes, and his crystal blue eyes sparkled. The colour and depth of his irises were mesmerising and Sarene found it difficult to look away.

Instead of meeting her directly, the man took his time to circle around her, running his gaze up and down her frame. He was a head taller despite his gently stooped posture. Sarene turned on the spot, nervous. At one point the man reached out a hand and snapped his fingers; *click*. Sarene jumped.

"You can see me?" he asked. When Sarene nodded, he smiled. "Remarkable."

Sarene glanced around again at the white desolation of her surroundings, the endless line of man and beast – then saw a huge fish moving *through* the pathway as though it were liquid, the bottle-shaped snout appearing periodically through the sand. It, too, was heading towards the gateway. She gasped, bringing her hand to her mouth.

"You can see *them*, too?" said the man behind her. It took a few seconds for Sarene to realise he was talking to her, and she nodded once more.

The man chuckled. "So it is you. Sarene."

Sarene turned around at the mention of her name, to find herself staring up into those beautiful eyes.

"The Queen of the World."

She shook her head. Not *this* again. She wasn't the Queen

of anything. Sarene tried to change the subject by gesturing around her, sweeping an arm towards the gate, before shrugging her shoulders in question.

"…Pardon?" said the man.

Sarene repeated the gesture, this time pointing directly at the gateway, then walking her fingers in the air towards it. She looked back to the man, who had brought his hand to his chin in thought. He snapped his fingers again.

"Are we playing a game?"

Sarene screwed up her face and held out her hand flat, wavering. *Sort of.*

"I see. It looks awfully fun, but I thought we could perhaps speak of more important matters first."

The answer opened more questions than before. Sarene scratched her head before tapping her temple, then flicked all her fingertips at once, trying to display her confusion.

"Why not just say what you mean for now. That may be easier."

She drew a line across her throat before lifting a finger to her lips.

The man simply grinned. "Silly girl. Of course you can talk."

Sarene blinked. She shook her head cautiously.

"Whatever may have prevented your body from communicating does not apply to your spirit. Just speak."

The words held her still for several moments. The man waited, clasping his hands behind his back. Her lips moved, twitching at first, her tongue flicking over the front of her teeth. She focused on what she wanted to say, holding the words in her mind.

"…I can ta—" said Sarene before she squeaked, her hand slapped over her mouth. She stared at nothing as her mind whirled, trying to believe that the sound had come from *her*.

Her *voice*.

"You never spoke in life, did you?" said the man. She shook her head. "Of course. My apologies… sometimes these little details slip by me. I have so much to remember."

Slowly, Sarene removed her shaking hand from her face.

"I… can talk?"

"Yes. At least, your spirit can. As I said."

"My spirit?" Sarene was stunned at the sound of her words. They were pretty. Light and melodic, just like the songs she played on her pan pipes. Jared's gift had been more appropriate than he could have known.

"Yes. Your spirit. You are dead, are you not?"

That cut through her shock. Sarene gaped at the man. "Dead? I… I don't remember."

"Try," said the man.

Sarene placed a hand on her chest as she tried to recall what had brought her here. She remembered Kanderil and Spasmodic. A cabin. Anthon, the boy who had joined her there. Then some men had come… She was in a cellar… a man with a knife.

Methulai. The image of him filling a cold stone corridor, trapping her, his knife shining in the light cast from the doorway opposite.

"He hurt me," she said, the chilling words her first whisper.

"So you are dead."

"I don't want to be dead," said Sarene. She once again met those ethereal eyes.

"No, I wouldn't expect you to. Come on, let us sit down and discuss your options." He began walking back towards the gate, tucking his hands into his sleeves. Sarene ran a hand through her hair. She still *felt* solid. The strands slipped between her fingers, tickling her skin. The expanse of white nothing stretched away before her.

I'm dead?

A GREAT CRY came from the south of the city. Remelas glanced out of his window as an attendant buttoned the front of his coat; thigh-length and thick weaved, embellished with green thread. He had spent the whole morning preparing. Now, freshly bathed, clean shaven and with his hair trimmed, he regarded himself in the mirror. Remelas was every inch the King of Tamir.

Chalimer stood by the doorway. "That will be Anaburan and his friends arriving."

"No doubt," replied Remelas. "From the sounds of it, they are warmly received."

"My informants say the citizens of Tamiran have been discussing nothing else for over a week. I wouldn't be surprised if they walk to the Square with thousands in their wake."

"Thousands whom I will be happy to address, Justicar." The King tugged at his sleeves as the attendant stepped back.

"I believe my emerald cloak will match this." The attendant nodded and moved to one of the huge cupboards lining the north wall.

"How will you officiate this?" said Chalimer. "I do not for a moment believe you intend to hold a common argument against this man."

"Hardly. I will allow Anaburan to speak first. He must air his grievances and deliver his intentions. I have no doubt he will receive quite the applause when he is done."

"And then?"

"And then I will respond. I wish to know exactly what his assertions are before I speak. The final word will be mine."

"I have always preferred that approach myself," agreed Chalimer. "The last to speak can always counter previous points."

"Indeed." Remelas held his arms at his side as the attendant returned with a magnificent cloak of satin, embedded along the edges with tiny emeralds which glistened in the pale autumn sun. Eventually he presented himself to the Justicar of the Gathire, spreading his arms. "How do I look?"

"Regal," replied Chalimer.

"Good enough."

"I have one request to make about this audience you shall hold."

"Which is?"

"Move to the Tamiran University. Their courtyard is not so much smaller than the Square, and any lost space is made up by the street before it."

"The University?" Remelas shook his head. "No. The Square is central to the city. Moving the discussion to the richer areas may be seen as an insult to the poor."

Chalimer cleared his throat, pacing towards the window. "That as it may be, I feel obliged to remind you that the Gathire are just as responsible for your personal safety as your royal guards. If this *is* a precursor for an attempt on your life, moving location at the last moment will foil any would-be assassins who have already set up position."

Remelas brought himself to his full height as the attendant placed the Tamir Crown upon his head. "Will you cease badgering me about the perils of today's events if I agree?"

"I shall."

"Then make it so. Have word sent to Anaburan informing him of the change of location. And set up your men accordingly."

"I have taken the liberty of doing so already."

Remelas quirked a brow. "Were you so confident of my agreement?"

"As a Gathire, I am confident that all my intentions will be realised."

"An interesting comment to make in my presence."

Chalimer offered a short bow. "The importance of my wishes shall always come second to yours, my King."

Remelas smiled, turning back towards the window and placing his hands against the sill, looking out across his city. "Well then. I intend to win this debate and regain the love of my people."

"And your wish is my command."

SARENE FOLLOWED THE man to his position by the gate. Closer now, she realised just how enormous the opening was. Despite the constant flow of creatures into it, the entrance never seemed crowded. Staring at it for too long hurt her head and she had to look away. She laid a hand against the sturdy tree next to her. The bark was rough and layered, like a pine cone, while the leaves above tapered into spear-points.

She stood waiting for his attention, awkward in the peculiar surroundings and unsure of her place within them. At last the man turned to her. "My name is Feragh. I once lived in the west of the world. Karalos. Have you heard of it?"

Sarene thought for a moment before shaking her head.

The man nodded. "It may be known to you by another name. Karalos was a beautiful place, bordered by the great ocean to the west and sweeping hills to the east. I do miss it so." Feragh smiled. "I watch it sometimes. Through the waters."

The words petered out. Sarene tugged at her hands, unsure of how to respond.

"I expect you have many questions," he said at last.

She nodded.

"Well, go ahead. Why not exercise that voice of yours."

Sarene licked her lips, glancing back to the great line behind her. "…What is this place?" she asked with great hesitation, apprehensive not only about her question but the sounds she made to seek its answer.

"This is where all living things come at the end. It has various names. Heaven. The afterlife. Paradise. When a soul leaves the material plane and departs the body, it ends up here."

Sarene stared at the line, watching the slow wander of the countless beings. "All these people have died."

"Yes. But they are not lost. On the contrary; they have come home."

"What do you mean?"

Feragh raised a hand to point towards the gate, the loose sleeve dangling from his arm. "That entrance leads to rebirth. All souls join as one, together, with no separation or segregation. The resulting energy is also known by many different terms. Magic. The supernatural. Chi, sorcery. Spirituality. A gift or a curse. It is where all the power of the soul comes from, and ultimately where it leads."

"So… what happens to it?" asked Sarene, facing the man again. "I mean, when we die and go through that doorway. Do we just stay there?"

"Not forever. Eventually, all experience many different existences. Sometimes several at once."

The girl blinked.

Smiling, Feragh brought his hands together. "Let me explain it this way. If you were to take a cup of water and pour it into a lake, then the water would be absorbed, would it not? It would be impossible to extract that same glass of water completely."

"I suppose so," offered Sarene.

"But if you filled your cup from the lake, there is always a chance that *some* of your original water would find its way back into the glass. That is very much what happens. When a new soul is created in the world, it is created from the power which lies behind that gateway. And perhaps a tiny part of what you were will be included.

"It is why there are such expressions as 'soul mate', or 'love at first sight'. Oftentimes, they are connected by a previous existence two completely different people may have once shared, in some way." Feragh chuckled. "Perhaps, should one look far enough in history, we were all connected in that way."

"So I have to walk through the gateway," said Sarene. She regarded the way it stood, with no apparent support or foundations. The entrance to the source of everything simply *was*, flanked by a few odd-looking trees and some fine sand.

"Only if you wish to," said Feragh.

Sarene paused. "What else would I do?"

"Go back to your body."

"You said I was dead."

"You are. But you may return to life if you decide to. This time, at least."

Sarene held up a hand, palm outward. "Wait a moment. You said the glass *couldn't* be filled. I mean, that we couldn't go back as a whol-..." She sighed, frustrated at her inability to explain herself. "How can I go back?"

"Let us say you are slightly immortal," said Feragh.

That was absurd. "How can I be a *slightly* immortal?" asked Sarene, her features scrunched up in disbelief.

"In the same way one can be *slightly* injured, or *slightly* awake. There are various degrees of everything. You could not speak in life. Did you ever consider yourself a cripple?"

"No," said Sarene. "Never."

"Well, then. Your body suffered a mortal wound, but your soul is still here. If your body was completely destroyed, or had been somehow torn apart, then your soul would have no choice but to heed the call. And yet, here you are. Are you drawn to the gateway behind you? Do you feel compelled to walk through it?"

The girl faced the entrance, watching more strangers file through to whatever lay beyond. "No," she said again.

"That is because you are immune not only to the power it gives, but also the energy it takes. If you wish to go back to your body, all you need to do is choose."

Sarene clasped her hands together. "Is Jared in there?"

"Jared?"

"My brother. He… died. Three months ago."

"Then yes, Jared will be in there."

She exhaled nothing, the action somehow meaningless without breath. "I suppose I can't see him."

"He would no longer exist in a form you would recognise. But know that he is more than content, wherever he now resides."

Sarene smiled. Some of the weight she had carried since Jared's passing lifted. Not entirely, but enough. She would never see him again, in this life or the next, but the thought of what he once was living on forever in spirit was comforting. "That's nice to know."

Feragh snapped his fingers. Sarene turned around to see

that a stool had appeared behind him. The unusual figure sat down, placing his hands on his knees. She met those euphoric eyes, and he tilted his head.

"You have more questions. I do not need magic to see that."

Sarene grinned. "I have lots of questions."

"Then ask away, my child. Time here does not run parallel to time in the material world. I cannot say how long you have already spent and I could not guess how much longer it will be. You may have been lost to your family and friends for seconds or for days."

That worried her. "Days? Won't they bury me?"

"Why would they do that?"

"Because that's what we do with our dead. In my country, at least."

Feragh laughed sudden, clapping his thigh and rocking forward.

Sarene frowned, surprised by his reaction. "It's not funny, y'know."

The man calmed himself, shaking his head. "My apologies. I forget that you know so little. You have died in the sense that your soul has departed your body. However, your body will function so long as you linger here, awaiting your decision to return or to relinquish it to nature. Your heart will beat and your lungs will draw air. You are immune to all supernatural energies, but even *your* soul was created by the same source of magic. That magic is now acting to repair your body for your return."

"So I can't die?"

"Hm. Let us not get hasty. I did say you were only slightly immortal. You would do well to avoid being decapitated or incinerated, for instance. The soul cannot repair such an absolute fate. I expect you to live to be very old, however."

"If I go back."

"If you go back," agreed Feragh. "Which I hope you choose to do."

The depth of his words, though subtle, resounded through the wasteland of light surrounding them. "Why?" asked Sarene.

Feragh smiled. "Because I would like you to save your world."

Chapter Seventeen

T HE DUSTY STOCKROOM held a dry, musty odour. Filled with reams of fabric, folded materials and crates of strings and thread, barely eight feet of floor could be seen. An ancient mannequin torso, the base of which has been lost, leaned against the back right corner of the room. A barrel full of rolled woven rugs stood next to the door leading back out to the hallway, the variety of colours sticking out resembled an exploding firework which had frozen in place. Every step Niallya or Heiran took *clonk*ed on the wooden flooring, although the sound was otherwise muffled by the clutter around them.

Heiran knelt beside the window, screwing the first arm of the crossbow into place. The weapon was much larger than Niallya had expected, though with the range between them and the target it wasn't wholly surprising. She sat upon a pile of folded cotton sheets, listening to the sounds of life outside. The steady cheer had risen with each passing minute, as the Sons of Tamir approached the Square with, no doubt, an ever-growing following of citizens. It sounded like a parade she had once watched as a child during Shalith, when the men and women of her village and the surrounding areas had dressed up like woodland animals and danced through the streets of her home, giving out candied fruits and small trinkets. Everyone had applauded and cheered, whistled and laughed, without becoming bored or tired of the spectacle. It was one of the better memories she had, and Niallya thought of it often.

From the sheer volume outside, however, this had to be a crowd numbering thousands. The Square would be full, making their job easier. Escape would be simple.

She studied the single bolt lying beside Heiran. It was over three inches in length with narrow flights, headed with a steel tip. Reaching down to grab it, Niallya found it carried a hefty weight in her palm.

"What is this used for?" she asked.

"Big game," said Heiran as he snapped the second arm into place. "Bears. Stags. Mountain lions if you fancy dying young."

Niallya turned the object over in her hand. "I do not know much about such things. Is a heavy bolt accurate?"

"Less than a regular bolt," Heiran admitted. "But at this distance, with only one shot, I need something which'll cause a lot of damage. That will tear through a human pretty well. As long as I hit him in the body and providing he doesn't arrive in full plate armour, he shouldn't be getting back up."

"And if you miss?"

"I'll feel bad for whoever stands next to him."

Niallya smirked, closing her hand around the bolt. A knock rattled the door. The two of them looked first at each other, then towards the entrance where the handle was beginning to turn.

Springing to her feet, Niallya walked forward to obscure the view of Heiran and his crossbow. She forced herself to smile as the owner of the shop downstairs appeared, a tiny woman with mousey blonde hair wrapped into a tight bun. The woman, who had introduced herself as Grenaline, stepped into the room with her hands together.

"My, it's rather dusty in here, isn't it?" she said, peering around.

Niallya nodded. "We brought it all up diggin' around."

Grenaline bowed her head and stepped forwards, apparently oblivious to Niallya backpedalling with her. "Of course, of course. Now, while you were here, I was hoping you could take a message back to Sasa for me. I've seen a couple of rats scurrying about my shop over the past few weeks, and I think they might be nesting somewhere in here, y'see."

"Oh, aye" Niallya replied. "That'll be a problem. We'd need to be doin' summat about that."

"Indeed. I don't want to cause a fuss. I'm not the type to do that, as I'm sure Sasa might have said. I'm happy to have her rent this room for her stock and all. It's as much for her own concern as it is mine, since rats would be chewing up all her lovely materials and doing the Four-knows what in amongst the sheets." She pulled a face expressing her distasteful thoughts. "But still, I have to think about my own business as well, and I can't be having rats sneaking about between the floorboards. It'll put people off if they found out."

Reaching out to lay a hand on the woman's arm, Niallya nodded firmly enough for the motion to be seen from beneath her cowl. "Don't you worry, m'dear. I'll be makin' sure Sasa hears all about 'em, and we'll be back to root the little critters out before y'know it."

"Oh, that's lovely to hear. Wonderful. Can I get anything for either of you? Tea? I'm off out to hear this speech from the King in a moment. The whole city is talking about it, have you heard?"

"Yep, we heard," said Niallya. "Don't you trouble yerself, like. Go on an' get a good view o' the King, before it fills up. We're fine."

"Are y'sure?" Grenaline said, leaning back to look past Niallya. The mercenary noticed a second too late to block her view, turning instead to see Heiran sitting cross-legged on the floor, a scrap of paper in his hand, looking through a box of assorted threads. A decidedly bow-shaped bulge lay on the floor next to him, covered in a buttery yellow sheet embroidered with flowers.

"I'm fine," said Heiran. "Thank you."

"Ah, right. Well then, I'll just be away into the street. If you're done here before I'm back then let yourselves out, won't you? I'll leave the latch on, so you don't need to worry about a key." She waddled off through the door. "A pleasure to meet you both!"

"An' you," said Niallya, herding the woman out of the room. "Enjoy yer day!"

"Same t'you!"

Niallya closed the door, and then took a deep breath.

Behind her, Heiran spoke. "That was quite a convincing accent you put on. Anyone would think you were a country lass from the west."

"Perhaps that was my true speaking voice," said Niallya, turning. "Where did you get that paper from?"

"I found it in this box."

"Fortunate." She moved towards the window to look outside, seeing the trickle of people from less than a half-hour earlier now becoming a flood of bodies, as people positioned themselves in preparation of the coming debate.

"How long, d'you reckon?" asked Heiran, pulling the sheet back from the crossbow.

"Soon," said Niallya.

Minutes passed. More and more of the general public filed into the Square. The day was forgivingly mild, with the skies cloudy but lacking the threat of rain. The Tamir Guard were in amongst the people now, lining the streets, directing groups this way and that. Dotted between them, clad in black and standing immobile amongst the clustering pack, were a handful of Gathire.

A great cheer went up from the south of the Square. There, Niallya saw a group of around thirty people, all wearing great grey cloaks trimmed with fur. The Sons of Tamir had arrived.

"That him?" asked Heiran.

"No. Anaburan."

"He sounds popular."

Niallya said nothing. She watched the Sons move as a unit, the crowd spreading in front of them, allowing them to approach unhindered. At the sides and rear, however, many of the crowd stepped forward to pat shoulders and slap backs, hustling and cajoling to wish these defenders of the people well, encouraging them to provide what had been rumoured for weeks beforehand.

The potential removal of Remelas from the throne.

The mercenary couldn't resist a smile. Depose an unwanted ruler with words, and you became a champion.

Glaithe's method would invoke a wildly differing reaction.

Heiran stood, the weapon left at his feet, primed and ready. He looked out the window – and frowned. "They aren't stopping."

Niallya arched a brow. "Hmm?"

"The Sons of Tamir. They're not stopping."

She turned around to look back out onto the street. Sure enough, the grey cloaks were heading for the north-west corner of the Square, which led towards the richer quarter of Tamiran.

"You think they'll be coming back?" asked Heiran, nervous.

Niallya watched the Tamiran guard. They were directing traffic, and each one herded people in a similar direction. At the central platform itself, where she had expected Remelas to stand, a group of guards were pointing to the north east, after the Sons, after Anaburan. The crowd began to move after them, a great trail of Tamir swept in their wake.

"He's changed venue."

Heiran shook his head. "No. You can't be sure."

"We need to move," said Niallya. "Reset the crossbow and wrap it back up. There isn't much time."

"Time for what?! If he's gonna be somewhere else then we can't go through with this."

"We can and we will. Now hurry!"

THE KING OF Tamir stood ready on the stage in the courtyard of the Tamir University, along West Junction Road. The platform stood only three feet in height, ten square in total, but it was enough. Remelas would be visible to his subjects.

The jade-threaded cloak glimmered in the cold light. His father's crown, his now, adorned his head; the symbol of his regal birth right fit as though it had been created especially for him. Remelas was born for this role and nothing would dissuade him. Not this Anaburan, nor his followers. Not even Tyrrial, the catalyst for his present situation.

Chalimer stood to his left, as the representative of the Gathire. The Justicar scanned the gathering crowd with a severe expression, though his posture remained relaxed. He had tucked his left arm behind his back, bent at the elbow, while his right hand hung against his belt.

To Remelas's right was General Garonal, the head of the Tamir army; at least, what was left of it. A great bear of a man, Garonal towered over the other two men. He'd dressed in full uniform, with the tabard of Tamir covering a chainmail suit of polished steel. The red cloth stood out amongst the emerald green and raven black of the others sharing the stage, the golden lion of Tamir roaring at the centre of his chest.

Queen Syllaine waited patiently at the General's side, clad still in a black dress of mourning with dark furs to keep her slim frame warm. Her hair lay in a thick braid over one shoulder. She watched the citizens of the capital marching towards them with no readable expression, her features retaining a stately grace.

At the head of the approaching mob, which still cheered and called out at a raucous volume, were the Sons of Tamir. Leading them was a man whose eyes were fixed on Remelas himself. The King presumed this to be Anaburan, and he held that gaze with conviction. Let him come with his grandeur. For all his good intentions and his claims to speak for the people, he was still a subject. A man. Nothing more, despite what others may say of his heroic aims.

Remelas took a deep breath to gather his thoughts.

Anaburan may be a champion, but *he* was a King.

As the Sons of Tamir stopped in the centre of the court-yard, a dozen yards between them and their host, the line of guards flanking the four principle figures on the stage stepped forward. They created a line of separation, a solid wall of shields and pikes. The thousands of Tamir swept in around them like sand through an hourglass, streaming through the great University gate to fill all available space within. When no more space was to be found, the people packed the street outside from west to east. Bodies were everywhere Remelas looked, and the air around them was charged with anticipation.

He was the underdog here. That was fine with him.

"King Remelas!" called the central figure within the group of grey cloaks. The voice was commanding, easily identified amongst the huge crowd. As one, the Sons of Tamir formed a horseshoe shape around their leader, the men and women around them stepping back to accommodate them.

The citizens of Tamir hushed gradually, a ripple of silence spreading back along the spectators as they took notice of those ahead. Remelas was reminded of a pebble falling into a pond.

"King Remelas," he said again, audible throughout the courtyard and beyond. "I thank you for the opportunity to speak with you this late autumn day. Your willingness to listen to your subjects is a mark in your favour."

Remelas smiled. "On the contrary, Anaburan. I thank you for rising to the task of presenting yourself here in the capital. I have anticipated this meeting for several weeks. Perhaps you will consider joining me here on the stage, so your supporters can clearly see you?"

Anaburan removed his hood, revealing his balding head and strong features. He folded his arms over his chest. "A kind offer, but I shall remain where I am. Amongst my people. My voice is all that matters; my appearance means nothing."

At that a smattering of encouragement came from the great crowd, barking here and there, the ebb and sway of support not yet wholly restrained. It was an early gesture which Remelas acknowledged with a nod.

"Then tell me, Anaburan. I have heard the rumours of

your intentions here today. Please, enlighten me. What is it you seek?"

"*Get off t'throne!*" yelled a voice from the crowd, and the words set off an eruption of both silencing hisses and jeering laughter from one section of the crowd.

Holding up one hand, Anaburan chuckled. "A phrase I wouldn't have used myself, but a perfect example of why I am necessary. I seek answers, Remelas. Answers for those slain at Leithar Grove. Answers for their mothers and fathers, brothers and sisters, wives and husbands, sons and daughters. Answers for the soldiers who find themselves without work, betrayed by a ruler who would unite them under a banner of conquest without their knowledge. Answers for the Carthleid, who now view us a treacherous neighbour and will surely look to raise an army of their own. Answers for the Franthians, the Soraliath and the Rudacians, who must be wary of this small nation which borders their own; our leader's thirst for bloodshed now revealed. Answers for the Four, who brought judgement upon us with fire and blood. And answers to your people, the Tamir people, who have now lost faith in a King who would lead us to the dark days of old!"

Anaburan's voice rose at the end, matching his conviction. A great roar went up, thousands of voices as one, and the cheer went on for longer than Remelas had expected. He kept his outward feelings measured, neither smiling nor scowling, focusing his attention on Anaburan and paying no heed to those baying for his words.

NIALLYA LED HEIRAN along a back road adjacent to Pride Lane, skirting the great crowd which had assembled in the northwest quarter of the city.

"The only area large enough to house this many people is the University courtyard," said Niallya, re-wrapping the grey cloak in her arms. "We need a vantage point above to take the shot."

Heiran spat to the side before shaking his head. "And sneak in with that many witnesses, hoping someone left a window open in this weather?"

Ignoring him, Niallya considered the few options available. She didn't know Tamiran as well as she knew Ghellei, but she could recall West Junction Road in her mind. The bank of expensive homes surrounding the University were dotted amongst dormitories, but the street exactly opposite the courtyard was a flat row of buildings over two centuries old. A shot from there would be too obvious, chancing capture soon afterwards.

AS THE NOISE died down Anaburan spread his arms. "I have walked our great kingdom for an entire season, speaking with my brothers and sisters who work the fields and mind the stalls. Those with professions and without. Landowners, commoners, both rich and poor. In every town I passed through I gave my case against you, and I have yet to find one dissenting voice who could convince me of anything but your ambition and greed.

"You say you seek expansion for the good of the nation? Our nation has stood just fine for centuries, respected by our neighbours across the border. We were happy, proud and could look each other in the eye without any doubts. Now? We're a fearful, scared people. The Four judged us, Remelas. Who is to say they will not do so again with you as our ruler?

"I ask you one final question. If it had been Garonal, standing there beside you, or Chalimer and his cursed Gathire; if either of them had done what you had done, what would your reaction be? If someone you trusted had built an army behind your back, created a huge force with which to bring war to our lands and those lands nearby, and you had found out *only* after the deaths of several hundred of your subjects. Would you forgive them? Or would you see them cast from their position and punished as traitors?"

Anaburan rose both arms skyward, and the motion coupled with his words brought a final huge *roar* from the Tamir around him. The sheer force of the noise rocked Remelas, as he understood that they were completely with the Sons of Tamir just then. At that moment he truly felt the depth of scorn his populace had for him, and the sensation was stomach-churning.

Remelas grit his teeth and held his hands behind his back, waiting for the crowd to calm, when Chalimer leant in close.

"This is where you win them back," he said, that thin voice as calm as ever. "Remember who you are, your Highness."

Remelas glanced down and to the left. "Do you still doubt me, my friend?"

"No," whispered Chalimer, nodding out towards the crowd. "I doubt them."

Resisting the urge to smile, Remelas took one step forward. The crowd took a long time to hush, carried away by their own enthusiasm.

When they fell quiet once more, the King of Tamir spoke.

NIALLYA POINTED UP towards a flint-grey building stood at the opposite end of a small alleyway leading towards the University. She turned along that road, threading through the scattered onlookers who were content to listen to the debate reverberating along the street in front of the University courtyard. Heiran jogged along behind her, carrying the crossbow he'd wrapped within the wolf-fur lined cloak.

Reaching a panel door set into the wall of the dormitory building, Niallya tested the handle. To her relief it opened without resistance. The hinges were oiled, and the door opened in silence. She stepped in, standing to the side to allow Heiran through after her. The door closed, muffling the voices of those outside.

The pair found themselves in a scullery kitchen; a sterile-looking place with tile flooring and lacquered work surfaces. Pots and pans hung from black hooks protruding from the ceiling. On the opposite side of the room was another door, open, and through that she could see the stairwell. Niallya headed for it, saying nothing, but thankful that the dormitories were kept unlocked for the comings and goings of the various students. Heiran followed.

Out in the hallway a rug muted their footsteps. Niallya noticed the front entrance which led back out onto Pride Lane. They would be able to flee the scene in the correct direction at least.

She led the way up the stairs, keeping flat against the wall. She'd left her sword behind at their apartment, and approaching the upper floor unarmed demanded careful movements. Not that she anticipated much difficulty in dealing with any student residents who may still be present. Niallya hoped that they would be outside by now, amongst the crowd.

The landing at the top of the second flight of stairs led off into three rooms, one of which was at the rear north-facing wall. Providing it had a window, it would afford the perfect opportunity for a shot at Remelas. Niallya covered the ground in three quick steps and opened the door.

Inside she saw a man standing at the window, smoking a pipe and dressed in a quilted gown. He turned to gaze upon her, one eye behind a glass monocle.

"I say, what do you think you—"

Niallya leapt forward, thrusting a heel into the man's stomach. He doubled over, letting out a great *whoof* of air, before she followed up with a violent knee to the jaw which sent him sprawling.

Moving in behind her, Heiran sniffed. He stepped over the fallen man and knelt, pulling the first folds of the cloak from over the disassembled crossbow. "You've done that before."

"Once or twice," said Niallya. "Hurry up."

"YOU MAKE A strong argument," said Remelas, taking a single step forward towards the edge of the stage. The words brought a hush over the crowd, accompanied by hisses and whispers as those gathered quietened each other, eager to hear the response. "I admire your passion, Anaburan. Truly, a man who speaks for the people while seeking no personal gain is to be respected."

He paused, looking out across the sea of faces. The urge to fold his arms across his chest was strong, but he resisted. Any sign of being on the defensive, no matter how small, could undermine his position.

"You say that I am to be held accountable. I have heard the rumours which have been passed through the streets of Tamiran and other cities around my kingdom. In the space of a season, through the words of others, I was transformed from a proud member of the House of Tamir to a... a scheming, bloodthirsty tyrant looking to bring suffering and death to our lands. I no longer enjoy the luxury of reverence which I once took for granted, and which my Father greatly appreciated.

"Am I to be held accountable? The answer to that question is 'yes'."

A murmur ran through the crowd. Anaburan, still central to the group, smiled.

"You say hundreds were killed at Leithar Grove. The exact figure is two hundred and seventeen men and eight women. One hundred and eighty-four soldiers. Twenty two cavalry. Two Gathire. Four Kalethi. Of those, eighteen were officers. Thirteen servants, stable boys and kitchen staff.

"Amongst the survivors were sixty three wounded. Half of those will be unable to work in any job requiring physical labour. Many of the survivors suffered burns to their bodies. Only eighty-three people escaped unharmed, though the mental anguish they endured may last a lifetime.

"I can name every single person present at those barracks on the day of Tyrrial's return. Every name serves as a reminder of the tragedy which, in the basest form, was a consequence of my judgement. I could tell you that I intended to absorb Carthlei into my kingdom with a minimum of bloodshed, but would not expect you to believe me. I could tell you that there was no plan to massacre the Carthleid or raze their cities, and would not expect you to trust my words. The foundation of my standing amongst you has been shattered, and for that I take full responsibility. But please, my people. Even if you refute my every word, allow me the concession of one true fact.

"I lost my brother, Nichai, that day. My mother who stands beside me, your widowed Queen, grieves for an absent son. In addition were those two hundred and twenty five Tamir. There is not a day that goes by where I do not grieve for them equally. Their memory will remain with me until the time of my death, and will guide my hand with every future decision that I make."

Remelas clenched his hands, holding them behind his back. The crowd were muttering to each other. He could read from their expressions that an admission of guilt had not been expected. Anaburan still stared at him, but the smile had faded.

"HOW LONG?" ASKED Niallya.

"A few more minutes," said Heiran, fastening the second arm of the crossbow into place. "I cannot take the shot until the bow is properly prepared. Otherwise I risk the strength of the release being too low, or the bolt firing inaccurately."

"We may not have a few more minutes. Remelas is winding down."

Shaking his head, Heiran hissed air from between his teeth. "I told you this was a bad idea. We're heavily exposed here, without a prepared escape route. Plus we now have a witness." He indicated the unconscious homeowner lying face-down on the floor. The man's monocle had shattered beneath Niallya's attack and tiny shards of glass speckled against his skin.

"We do not know when another opportunity like this will arise."

"This isn't an opportunity, this is suicide."

"Are you able to make the shot?" said Niallya.

"What?"

"I said, are you able to make the shot?"

Heiran swore, leaning to look out of the window. Over the rows and rows of citizens listening to Remelas's speech,

Niallya could see the stage holding four of the most important people in the kingdom. The distance to Remelas was around a hundred and fifty yards.

"Yes. Are you able to get us out of here?"

Niallya said nothing.

"SO WHERE DOES that leave us?"

Remelas walked the stage, back and forth, his gaze running over the mass of spectators. He held his next words, taking the time to reach inside his cloak and withdraw a golden necklace with a huge ruby pendant; the Scion Amulet. He held it up, to where the soft light could strike from the myriad of polished surfaces.

"That leaves us here. Anaburan has spoken, and he has called for me to relinquish the throne. Many of you may agree with him, and for that I do not blame you. This amulet has represented my lineage for centuries, ever since the House of Tamir was first created; a simple mansion overlooking a paddock of cows and sheep. From that grew the greatest city in all the lands, a city within which you now stand. Each past generation of my ancestors handed this amulet on to the first born son of the next. It is not merely a show of wealth or status, as some of you may suppose from such a luxurious item.

"This amulet represents a pledge; that the boy in possession would grow to be the ruler of his people, and would study, train and craft his knowledge and skills to serve his kingdom to the absolute best of his ability.

"I failed in this, and I brought heartbreak to you all. Nothing I can do or say will change that. But if you permit me to remain as your King, understand that I shall pledge every single remaining day I possess to making amends."

Remelas paused, having timed his movements to leave him standing central to those sharing his stage, just as when he started his speech. The Scion Amulet swung gently in his grasp as he exhaled. Not a single noise came from the crowd before him. Time stood still. The cut of the red gemstone rendered his image tenfold.

"I am the last living heir from my father's direct bloodline. If you wish me to stand down, I shall. But know that every monarch who ever stood in the House shall know my failure. Allow me to prove to you that I ca—"

There was a fraction of time in which only his subconscious reacted. The whistle of air, the most imperceptible movement from the edge of his vision. Remelas could do nothing; he didn't realise there was anything to *be* done until the bolt slammed into his neck. Immediately he felt dizzy, and he staggered. A raised hand felt hot warmth spray against his palm, and he couldn't breathe.

The King of Tamir fell back, and he focused on the sky; a view which was filled moments later by the screaming face of his mother. He couldn't hear Syllaine's cries. He couldn't hear anything except his own staggered heartbeat, which hammered like a drum from behind his eyes. Remelas was only vaguely aware of movement around him and tugging at his body.

He realised he was dying, and he wanted to fight for air

and refuse the growing pressure in his chest. Instead, calm amidst the falling chaos around him, the only awareness was his regret.

Now he could never win back the love of his people.

A GREAT ROAR exploded from outside as thousands of voices cried out in shock. Heiran stood straight, the crossbow prepared but the bolt still in his hand. Niallya moved beside him to look through the window.

"He's down!" exclaimed Heiran.

Sure enough, Remelas lay prone on the stage, Syllaine crouched over him. General Garonal was yelling for assistance even as he joined her, forcing both his hands across the King's neck.

"*Arrest those men!*" Chalimer yelled, pointing a bony finger at the Sons of Tamir. Immediately the grey cloaks were surrounded by a ring of men wielding swords, their movements certain and prepared, surely Gathire in plain clothes. The Sons formed a defensive ring around Anaburan, unarmed but set to defend their leader. There was pandemonium as the crowd both dispersed and surged forwards, with some looking to flee the scene while others fought to get a better look at their dying monarch. People ran into each other, shoving their fellow citizens aside and yelling at each other, at the Sons and the King. Niallya heard cries and wails. Even a few cheers.

"Someone else took the shot," said Heiran in disbelief.

"Fortunate for us," said Niallya, drawing the small telescope Glaithe had given her for the mission. She handed it to Heiran. "Get a closer look. We need to know the wound is mortal."

"If they're holding his neck, I'd be surprised if it wasn't," he replied, lifting the scope to his eye. He twisted the lens to adjust the view. "…Yep, I would say he's done for. Whoever fired must have better aim than I. The amount of blood around him means an artery was severed." He lowered the telescope. "Rot in hell, you bastard."

Heiran turned to face Niallya, who thrust a blade into his chest.

She stared out through the window, moving aside, allowing the man to fall to the ground. He clutched at her clothing and she stepped back further. Bloodstains would draw attention she needed to avoid. She focused on the sounds of the crowd and the uproar which the assassination of Remelas had created. Heiran gasped as blood pooled around his body, staining the polished floor, a macabre parallel to his ruler's blood which stained the wooden stage of the University courtyard. Two performances cut short.

Kneeling to retrieve the fallen crossbow, Niallya pulled the bolt from Heiran's dead hand. She then held the latter between her teeth and wound the bow's mechanism into place. It was tough work, with the pinching ache of the wheel against her fingers. Finally she loaded the bolt into place and looked at the unconscious form of the house owner.

She turned him over with her foot, then fired the bolt. At such close range the thing tore through his body and struck the floor beneath him, producing a single muted grunt and a spasm of contracted muscle.

Niallya laid the crossbow beneath Heiran's hand, then pressed the hilt of her knife into the homeowner's. At the last she unfurled the grey cloak used to smuggle the crossbow through the streets and draped it across Heiran's shoulders, tying it in place around his neck while keeping her feet away from the spreading pool of blood beneath him.

The scene complete, Niallya headed at pace for the stairs, forcing herself to calm her breathing.

"REMELAS!"

SYLLAINE'S HAGGARD CRY ripped through the mayhem of the courtyard as the mother held her lifeless son to her chest, rocking back and forth. The Queen was lost to despair, wailing and sobbing. Blood covered her hands and made her black dress glisten.

Turning to face the trapped Sons of Tamir, Chalimer watched the regular guardsmen attempting to remove the onlookers from the scene, pushing back the fascinated men, women and children who had gathered at the front of the remaining crowd to witness the fallout of open regicide.

"DON'T LEAVE ME, PLEASE!"

"Let me through," said a voice. "Let me through!"

Anaburan appeared, pushing his way to the front. Chalimer stepped to meet him.

"We had nothing to do with this," said the champion of the people. "You have to believe me."

"A shame for you that I do not," Chalimer replied as Garonal appeared next to him. The Justicar turned to see a face red with fury. Behind the General, two university attendees appeared with a stretcher.

"He's dead. These bastards killed him."

"Then they will be executed," said Chalimer. "Parrin, take them to the cells."

One of the Gathire moved forward, barking orders for the Sons to move. Anaburan stood his ground for as long as he could, until a forceful shove to his chest sent him stumbling backwards.

"We're innocent, damn you!"

Disregarding Anaburan, Chalimer turned to the General. "We need to search the entire area for something we can use to find the assassin. Have your men go through every building and alley with even a remote view of this courtyard. Any evidence, no matter how small, should be registered and brought to me as soon as possible. Close the four gates, and do not allow anybody out of the city; including our own men. I also need two men to escort the Queen back to the House, and four more to cover and relocate Remelas' body. Fetch a carriage for the task."

"It may need more than two to convince Syllaine to leave," growled Garonal. "She's mad with grief."

"Then pick her up and carry her," was the cool reply. Chalimer motioned to the stage where Syllaine slumped, her face distorted in torment. "You cannot leave her here. She needs her chambers. But do not leave her alone. Summon the Prime Guide to watch over her."

"She needs privacy, man. She's beyond comfort, even from a Guide."

"Syllaine has lost her husband and both sons within two seasons. What she *needs*, General, is someone to ensure she does no harm to herself."

The words were understated, but cut through Garonal's anger. The man nodded, his teeth clenched, and whirled around to address the men nearest to him, assigning orders.

Chalimer started towards West Street, where the Gathire building stood. He would need to gather his thoughts and await news of the search. The interrogation of Anaburan was of top priority.

The matter had to be resolved as quickly as possible.

Chapter Eighteen

FERAGH TURNED TO look towards the sphere. He held out a hand, fingers spread wide, and closed his eyes.

Behind Sarene, something hummed. She turned to witness a thin ribbon of blue light emerging from the portal, snaking as though sentient through the air. The ribbon glided towards Feragh. Sarene stepped back, fascinated, as it passed her by a few feet. Then it touched Feragh, flowing into him with a shimmer. The man's hand glowed the same brilliant blue, before the ribbon reappeared and streamed into the sphere. The surface of the sphere rippled delicately, and then it was over.

The man staggered backwards and almost fell. Sarene ran forward to grab him under one arm and helped him onto the stool. He managed a weak smile.

"One of the Four required something."

"Oh." Sarene chewed her lip. "You have to do that every time?"

"No," said Feragh. "The soul contains enough power for the more mundane tricks. Only when they draw from the source, for a command of significance, must I replenish the deficit."

"Does it hurt?"

"Yes. Recently, at least. But I must maintain my post here, awaiting the moments when power is needed. And that is why I need your help, Sarene."

The statement made the hair on the back of Sarene's neck stand up. She gave an awkward laugh, throwing her arms up to her sides before slapping them against her hips. "I don't understand. I mean, I'm standing here in a dreamland talking to you, who could be a God for all I know, discussing how I might be immortal and watching thousands of spirits walk through a gateway to the source of all magic." She shook her head, running her hands over her face. "You're asking me for *help*? I'm nothing. I don't know why this is happening. Why me? If you know so much, why was I chosen to be different?"

Feragh accepted the girl's outburst. "Would it make you feel any better if I said you were not chosen at all?"

Sarene took a short, pointless breath. "What does that mean?"

"If you will indulge me, I can try to explain as best I can. I am not a God, or any other divine being. I was once mortal like you. In fact I was a magician. I used my abilities to heal the sick."

"What do you mean, magician? Only the Four can do real magic," said Sarene.

"Now, yes. When *I* lived, magic was much more common. The lands flowed with it, and there were many who could utilise that power for various reasons. Some, like myself, used it to cleanse the sick and heal the injured. Others used their sorcery for war and bloodshed. Such people were often highly valued by the many armies of the age, choosing to destroy rather than protect.

"Amongst these people – warlocks, sorcerers, mages; however you wish to call them – were five men who sought more. They were powerful in their own right, but ambition and greed are strong emotions. They sought each other despite the great distances separating them, each individual's reputation drawing their interest in one another. They studied and deconstructed the teachings, legends and folklore of every civilization in the known world with the goal of isolating which prevailing themes were present in each."

Sarene tilted her head. "When you say 'they'… You mean you."

Raising a brow, Feragh paused. "Hm?"

"These five men. Tyrrial, Corliani, Mubuto, Shigasi… And you."

The man chuckled. "Perceptive, aren't you. Yes. The Four as you know them were once Five."

"Why are you here, then?"

"If you allow me to finish, I shall explain."

"Oh," said Sarene. "Sorry."

Feragh inclined his head in forgiveness. "As I was saying, they… *We* saw one overarching constant in all the varying religions and mythologies established at that point, over five centuries ago. That was the idea of a spiritual existence. Most described it as a paradise or a reward for living a good life. Some saw a place of wretchedness. Others believed in rebirth.

However, the unifying fact was that every single study described the passing of the spirit from the body to an afterlife.

"The five of us decided that we had to find a way to tap into that realm. We believed that our magic came from the use of will. Our application of belief to make something happen. Conviction and faith are very similar, when one considers it. It became our sole objective; to somehow funnel the magic of the spiritual world into the physical one."

Sarene frowned, tugging at her thumb. "That's horrible. You might have ruined paradise for everyone."

Feragh nodded. "I agree… now. At the time, I believed I could use the potential gains to change the world for the better. I was a healer, after all. I imagined ridding humanity of plagues, fevers and cancers of all types with the increase in power our plans would afford me."

"What happened?"

"We developed a ritual which we believed would work. It involved focusing our gift internally in an attempt to connect our spirits to the afterlife while remaining within our physical bodies. Instead of simply casting our spells and conjurations outwards, we wanted to push *inwards* to the source of wherever our power came from in the hope of establishing a permanent link to this estimated source; a font of spiritual energy much greater than what residue ebbed through the world. Do you understand?"

"I think so," said Sarene after a brief hesitation. The man opposite smiled.

"Well, let us just say that the ritual worked. After years of meticulous preparation, we five completed our work and discovered a way to unite our individual powers, creating the link we needed. There was only one problem."

Feragh looked at Sarene, and she met beautiful blue eyes. He was waiting for her to ask what that problem was; she could see it. But the answer was standing in front of her.

"You died," she said.

"Yes. But my death was not an accident."

That surprised her. "What?"

"As you can now see, there is a separation between your physical realm and the realm of souls. As our spell grew in power, we reached this gateway. But the power beyond was too great for us to even hope to contain it. Indeed, even as we made the connection to the source of energy we craved, the gateway started to draw us in. Our souls were just as susceptible to its pull as all these others you see behind you."

Sarene turned her head at the mention, watching the myriad of shapes wander forwards.

"I do not know which of the others made the decision, but they were the first to realise there had to be a permanent buffer between the source and the physical realm. As such, they cast a spell directly upon the nearest soul to them, anchoring them to this interim plane of existence. That soul was mine."

"They killed you."

"Physically, yes."

"And you can't move on."

"No."

The girl turned to him. "You were just unlucky? How

awful."

"Worse than being purposefully betrayed?"

Sarene hissed through her teeth as the man smiled. "I suppose not."

"Allow me to therefore say that I sympathise with your own position, Sarene. For you were also selected by pure chance."

She allowed the words to sink in, giving a dumb nod without really knowing how to respond. The casual nature of his remark had caught her off guard.

"I preserved what tiny power I retained from my position here, and nurtured it until I could affect a soul for my needs. A single soul, protected from any outside energy, in the hope of standing against the Four and freeing me from my purgatory. That soul just happened to find its way to your mother's womb, ready for her newborn daughter."

"Is that why I can't talk?" asked Sarene suddenly.

"No. That was a rather interesting coincidence."

"Interesting is a funny choice of word," she replied with a smirk.

"Perhaps." Feragh's smile faded for the first time. "Will you help me?"

"How? And what's going to happen?"

"I am growing weaker. Every time I replenish one of the Four with power, my bond to this realm erodes further. I fear that there will come a time when I cannot maintain my control, and the energy I transmit will continue to flow down into the physical realm. Should the Four be unable to harness it properly the resulting current will surge like a waterfall. It may have catastrophic results."

Sarene stared at him. "How long do you have?"

"I do not know. It could be the next time a request is made. It could be centuries from now. But it *will* happen eventually, unless the Four's control is removed and the source is free to release its energy naturally into the world."

"How do I break the link?"

"One of the Four must pass through the gateway."

The girl blinked. "You mean I have to kill one of them?"

"Not necessarily. There are other ways."

She turned to look at the stream of spirits. "You said this is where the dead go. What other ways are there? Sur—"

Sarene paused. Amongst the rows of men, women and beasts, she saw a figure she recognised. Her eyes widened and she brought a hand to her mouth, taking several steps forward.

"*Remelas?*"

The ghost did not hear her. He continued his journey towards the gateway, his spirit just as striking as in life, oblivious to his unearthly surroundings.

"You knew him?" asked Feragh.

"Yes. He was with me when Tyrrial came for me."

"I see."

"Is there any way to reach him?"

"No. If you touched him he would not react."

"But how did he die?"

"I do not know. It is of no importance."

Sarene whirled around, annoyed by his flippant reply. "It's important to me!"

"Then return and find out."

Watching the King of Tamir walk forwards, following the lion before him and leading the young girl behind as simply another face in the endless stream of lost lives, Sarene felt entirely alone. That a man she knew personally now moved past her without any recognition of her unsettled her deeply. She tried to tell herself again that she was just a farmhand's daughter from Tamir, that this was all just a horrible dream, but the words didn't ring true anymore. Event after event eroded at her refusal to accept what she really was. Even now, in this fantastical place, speaking to the figure responsible for the flow of all magic, it all seemed impossible.

But she was here, and she was being asked for help.

To prevent what? The suffering of one man, or to avoid a cataclysmic disaster?

"I don't know if I can," she stammered as Remelas stepped through the gateway, the mercury surface rippling. The King of Tamir would now join with the source of all things, a release of energy which would never again be whole and yet would be so much more.

"You have exceeded expectations to get as far as you have, my dear." A hand closed around her shoulder. "I have tried to watch you, and what I have seen inspires even me, as jaded as I am. I have faith that you will find a way to not only save me, but to protect your people from ruin. If the Four's rule is not ended soon, the physical realm may be lost forever."

Sarene looked at her palms, before closing her hands into

fists. She whispered to herself.

"*Queen of the World.*"

"I beg your pardon?"

"Nothing," said Sarene. "I don't know if I can kill one of the Four."

"As I said, there are alternatives. Any one of the Four can willingly pass their soul to the next life."

"How do I convince them to do *that*?"

The hand on her shoulder squeezed for just a moment. "I have faith that you will find a way," Feragh repeated. "Are you ready to go back?"

"I think so."

"Good. Be prepared, for your physical body is still gravely wounded. I expect it will hurt."

"Thanks for telling me," she muttered, turning to face him.

"You are welcome. Oh, and one more thing you should know." Feragh placed his hands back inside the folds of his sleeves. "In all my time standing watch here, only one other soul has ever stepped aside from the stream and returned to the physical world." He gestured towards the sphere with a tilt of the head. Even this close, Sarene couldn't find any evidence that it was propped up by anything; it simply hovered in place at head-height.

"When?"

"As I said, time acts differently here. It could be days or years. But as it touched the surface of the orb I received a taste of that soul's contents. The energy beyond that gateway is in constant balance; the pure and the sinful mix in equal measures. This is why the world is filled with both good and evil."

Feragh sighed. "The other soul that was pulled back disturbed me greatly. There was malevolence within it which I fear may make itself known to you. Only the Four could have the power to draw something out of this realm. If you seek the Four out, you may encounter it."

Sarene nodded. "I'll remember that."

"Good. Are you ready?"

"Yes."

"Then reach into the orb, and wish it so."

NIALLYA STEPPED INTO the apartment, closing the door behind her. She leaned back against the slim wood, catching her breath. Outside was bedlam, with crowds of people charging from street to street, forming groups in their panic. From the snippets of conversations she'd heard, the people were convinced the murderous bolt which had slain their King had come from somewhere outside of the spectators to the debate. The slayer was in their midst, and so bands of vigilantes endeavoured to find them.

She was at a loss as to who had ended Remelas's life. Even with the view afforded to her, she couldn't tell where the bolt had come from. Had the Sons of Tamir set up their own assassin after all? Did Glaithe himself possess such skill with a bow? She'd seen no evidence of such. Perhaps an unknown party? Remelas had many enemies following Leithar Grove. That much was obvious. But who?

Replaying the event over in her mind, she recalled the misleading scene she had left in a stranger's home. The killings had shaken her, loathe as she was to admit it. The plan to frame Heiran as a lone assassin was always intended but Niallya had come to like the man, who spoke with manners and doted on his daughter.

Heiran never made the attempt on the King's life, yet Niallya had plunged her blade deep. Along with the owner of the home they'd invaded she sacrificed two lives to complete the scene of failed revenge. Never before, despite the many she had slain, had she ever taken a life without just cause. An innocent witness and a man who, while plotting to kill Remelas, had never gotten the chance. He left behind a young daughter; now an orphan.

According to Glaithe's plan, there was one more loose end to tie up.

Niallya looked towards the stairs ascending into the windowless gloom of the landing.

"Think of the reward, Nia," she whispered.

The mercenary moved towards the upper floor, her footsteps nimble. She eased open the door to her room and started to tug free the woollen clothes she wore, stripping herself bare. Then she redressed into her leathers and long coat, at last retrieving her curved sword. Niallya inhaled for as long as she could, until her lungs could expand no further and her chest felt tight.

Whatever happened next, her safety was by no means assured. If others *were* operating with Glaithe's knowledge, she had become a liability. It was possible that Agents were heading to this location already.

Exhaling sharply, she pulled up the broad hood and walked to the door opposite her own, turning the handle and stepping inside.

Sitting in the centre of the sparse room was Tillyan, holding on to her stuffed bear. She peered up, smiling through the mop of long, dark hair hanging in clumped strands over her childish face.

"Hello!" she said. "Where is daddy?"

Niallya moved forward, each step creaking upon the weak floorboards. Fingers flexed around the hilt of the blade.

"I'm sorry."

ETHANEI STUMBLED ALONG, removing himself from the throng of humanity swarming away from the scene of Remelas's death. He slammed a palm against the stone wall beside him and swore.

This wasn't how it was supposed to be. The Sons of Tamir were meant to stand for the people. They represented them; represented *him*. But instead they'd assassinated the King.

He pulled his hipflask from his pocket and unscrewed the cap with shaking fingers. Barely a mouthful inside. He knocked it back and then tossed the hipflask away, where it bounced off of a broken crate wrapped in rags.

The betrayal gnawed at him. He'd been telling anyone who'd listen about how Remelas was the traitor and needed to be removed from the throne. He'd put his stock in the

Sons, and they're repaid him with treason of the highest order. Not only was he now taken for a fool, but those others who'd dared to believe in Anaburan and his followers would lose further hope. If you couldn't trust your rulers *or* the people who spoke for you, who was left?

Tavern owners. Innkeepers. Bartenders. They were the ones you could always rely on.

Taking a deep breath, Ethanei took stock of the alleyway. The crowd still surged past at his end, but the opposite side seemed clear. He knelt down to pick up the hipflask and started to walk when something grabbed his ankle and made him yelp in a high-pitched voice.

An emaciated hand was latched against him. The wrist was red raw, attached to an arm reaching from beneath the rags. What he'd believed to be a collection of rubbish was actually alive.

"Help me…" it wheezed.

Ethanei considered walking away. Compassion held him in place. With another curse he knelt down, pulling back the hessian sack which clung around the strangers head. A mass of knotted hair spilled out over sallow shoulders. Ethanei met eyes lost within sunken sockets, staring up at him in fear.

He recognised the huge, hooked nose. That beak was famous amongst the Tamir. The Regent Nichai.

"Oh, bugger," he muttered.

"Help… Remelas…"

Ethanei grit his teeth. He didn't want the responsibility of being the man to find Nichai, six months after being declared *dead*. Not now, after what had happened. He'd be interrogated, no doubt. Probably for hours. All he wanted was to find a dark room and have a strong drink.

Instead he knelt down to lift Nichai from the ground, helping the boy to stand upright. He tried leading them forward but Nichai simply sagged against him, too weak to support his own weight. After some awkward cajoling, to which Nichai paid little heed, Ethanei hoisted the boy up over his shoulder. The Regent was nothing but bones. He'd carried sacks of horse feed that weighed more.

The House would probably be under lockdown, and the Kalethi barracks was a good hour's walk from where he stood. The Gathire headquarters were only twenty minutes away.

Ethanei hoped they wouldn't suspect him of any in-volvement as he stepped back into the main street, sticking to the edges as more Tamir ran past.

CHALIMER STEPPED INTO his office in the Gathire headquar-ters and closed the door behind him. Alone, he took a moment to collect his thoughts, eyes wandering as they often did to the singular window overlooking the streets of Tamiran. He could still hear the calls of citizens in the streets, yelling back and forth. The whistles of the Tamir guard *peeped* at each other, directing operations and signalling their whereabouts.

How could he have been so *stupid*? Allowing this debate to be held on a public forum, where anyone with a bow could take an open shot. He'd had Agents posted along all the alleyways and at the most likely vantage points. Two men had even been stationed on rooftops, directed to raise an alarm at the slightest sign of unusual behaviour. But it had all been for nothing. King Remelas was dead, and Chalimer was accountable for his demise.

The man hadn't stood a chance. Even if surgeons had been standing beside him, there was no way to stem the bleeding from such a grievous wound. Whoever took the shot, unseen and unheard, was either a master beyond peer or exceptionally lucky. To escape immediate apprehension suggested the former, but that left a *very* short list of known Tamir with the skills to carry out the assassination. None of them had been mentioned as travelling with the Sons of Tamir. Most likely the perpetrator was hired for the task.

Chalimer strode to his desk pulled open a drawer, and retrieved a bundle of blank parchments from within. A number of orders needed to be assigned to his best Agents. A full-scale search of the city was required. He reached over for the two items lying atop the desk; an ink bottle and a hawk-feathered quill.

A knock at the door behind him. "Come," he barked.

Someone stepped inside. "A note addressed to you, Justicar." The voice belonged to one of the clerks.

"Does it regard the assassination?"

"No idea, sir. The boy who brought it said it was to be delivered to you in person."

Chalimer turned around. The man before him stood with his back straight, but the way his eyes darted around the room suggested he was uncomfortable.

"Bring it here, then. When you are done, I need all available Agents gathered in the lecture hall. I shall be there in fifteen minutes to provide instruction." He took the note handed to him.

Turning the missive over in his hand once the clerk had departed, Chalimer examined the wax seal. His expression soured as he realised whose signet had made the impression.

The Regent of Tamir.

He opened the note, eyes scanning over the tidy handwriting.

Chalimer,

The Sons of Tamir were aided by several parties. They were funded by the underworld figure Kraye, currently stationed in Ghellei. You will find three gold coins marked with a blackened X stowed away beneath a chair in his mansion. These are used to identify payments made by him to Anaburan.

The two assassins bought with this money currently reside within Tamiran. They rent a shelf apartment in the south side marketplace, leased by a man named Dorste, situated immediately behind a stall with green fabric roofing. They, too, will likely possess a marked coin.

I am also involved, but you will never find me. I intend to leave Tamir forever. Do not try to locate me, for your Agents will fail at the cost of their lives.

Say hello to Nichai for me.

—Ulose

Chalimer closed the note. His mind raced, looking to recall the name. Ulose. Who would be brazen enough to openly taunt the Justicar of the Gathire like this? The name either belonged to a foreigner or was a code.

The last operative assigned a 'U'-five code had been…

"*Justicar!*" yelled a voice from the corridor. He calmly folded the note and slipped it into his pocket. "*You should come and see this!*"

Stepping from the room Chalimer found one of his officers marching at speed towards him. Heads popped out from doorways as other Gathire sought to find out the cause of such commotion.

"What is it?"

The other man came to a halt and bowed. "It's Nichai, sir. He's just been found in the eastern quarter of the city."

"Found…?"

"He's in bad shape but alive. The man who discovered him had to carry the lad over his shoulder. Two Agents are transporting him to the House as we speak."

Chalimer placed his hands behind his back. Whoever was playing games had impeccable timing. He couldn't resist an appreciative nod. "Well, well. Tamir has a King after all. You need to take a full squad and head to the marketplace. I will note down your destination."

"Yes, Justicar. What are my orders?"

"To apprehend two individuals guilty of regicide, it seems."

Chapter Nineteen

SARENE AWOKE TO a dull throbbing in her chest which swelled to overload her senses. Too tired to react other than to sigh, she finally managed to clench a fist against the pain.

A hand closed around hers. She realised her fingers were cold.

"Sarene. Can you hear me?"

Her vision swam as she opened her eyes, but eventually she formed a picture out of shapes and shadows. She turned her head to see Anthon sitting beside her, smiling. She tried to return it, but was already exhausted. Instead she gave the weakest of nods.

"You're awake!" Anthon's grin widened.

Another hand touched her cheek; much larger, it reached from her jaw to her scalp. A deeper voice spoke and she knew at once who it belonged to.

"Welcome back, lass. You had us worried."

Sarene closed her eyes, swallowing. Her throat was dry. Someone else was at the bed, but that didn't matter for now. Sleep returned to claim her. She felt weary to her bones, and it was a welcome release to darkness.

KANDERIL MOVED AWAY from the bed as the girl fell back to sleep. He exchanged looks with Anthon; the boy expressed a similar response as him. Relieved beyond measure.

"A marvellous sign," said Morwynn the Guide, rising from her seat at the foot of the bed. She moved to a bowl of water sat on a small table beside the wall, reaching for the folded washcloth next to it. Morwynn was a heavy-set woman with greying hair, clad in a fine white gown which hung from her frame in great folds of soft fabric. She dipped the cloth into the water before moving to Sarene, opening the girl's mouth and squeezing a few careful drops of liquid inside. "I believe we are out of the woods, so to speak."

"She still feels hot to the touch," said Kanderil.

"I expect she will be for a while yet," said the Guide. "The mere act of healing is taking a huge toll on her body. But she shows no other signs of fever, and the wound is producing less milky liquid. Sarene is recovering as well as could be hoped. She is lucky to be alive."

"So you keep saying."

"I will repeat the phrase until you believe it, Kanderil. Perhaps when you do you will consider getting some rest yourself." Morwynn smiled.

Kanderil did not respond. He had barely slept over the past week, choosing instead to stand watch while Sarene lay comatose in these spare quarters of the Shrine. The journey here had been tortuous, and Kanderil fully expected to arrive to find the girl dead. Even when he and Orlienn had learned that she still breathed, it seemed only a matter of time until her body gave out.

But with each passing day, there had been small improvements. Her pulse grew stronger. Colour returned to her cheeks. The wound sealed itself somehow, in a manner he had never before witnessed; a shiny film of thin skin had drawn across it and oozed a chalky white substance. He recalled how Jared and Sarene had recounted a similar occurrence when Spasmodic was healing from the vicious wound suffered at the hands of the Gathire months previous; how the two could be connected, though, remained a mystery. Spasmodic was a creation of the Four, while Sarene was immune to their talents.

Now the Guide had declared the girl was through the worst of it, Kanderil could focus on other matters.

"Excuse me. Anthon, wait here. She may wake again."

The boy nodded at him. Kanderil walked to the door and departed out towards the main hall. Just as in every shrine within Tamir, the interior of the building was stunning; decorated with gold leaf, stained glass and exquisite masonry. Rows of long benches, two abreast, ran from the altar at the rear to the large, arched doorway at the front. A domed roof sat overhead, giving an even broader sense of space.

Orlienn sat upon one of the benches, reading a book procured from the Shrine's modest library. Beyond, crouched in a corner and stuffing an oatcake into its mouth, was Spasmodic. It ignored his approach, but the ranger regarded him with an eager look.

"She woke briefly," said Kanderil.

"Oh, thank goodness. That's wonderful!" Orlienn closed the book and rose from her seat.

"It is a small step, but a positive one. She will still need plenty of time to recover."

"Absolutely. But at least now we can begin making plans for our next move. Once she's ready, I mean."

"Indeed," said Kanderil, rubbing his palms together. "Would you mind seeing if Morwynn needs anything?"

Orlienn nodded. "Of course." She side-stepped her way along the bench before walking forwards. As she passed Kanderil, she laid a hand on his arm. "Get some sleep, Kanderil. You look exhausted."

"So everyone keeps telling me."

The woman smiled, moving on towards the spare room where the others were. Kanderil glanced over his shoulder, waiting until she was gone.

Spasmodic slid itself up the wall, rising to its feet. Crumbs flew out as it spoke. "See, told you she'd be fine. A little scratch like that ain't gonna end our adventures."

Pressing a thumb over his nose, Kanderil approached the creature. "You did well to get her here in time."

"Yeah, well." It tilted its head to the side, the movement sharp enough to produce a dull *pop*. "What can I say? I'm better than you people."

"So it seems." He stood before it, placing a hand on Spasmodic's shoulder. "Without your talents she would never have survived. I appreciate it."

The dreadlocked thing peered up at him, grinning to

reveal piranha teeth. "What, you expecting a hug now or sum—?"

Kanderil snatched his huge hand across from the creature's shoulder to its throat, lifting it from the floor and slamming it against the wall. Immediately claws were against his forearm, the tips digging into skin.

"*You have a funny way of saying thanks…!*" it wheezed, ending with a shrill giggle of delight.

"They found her because of you," said Kanderil through gritted teeth. "You led them to her."

Blood beads swelled at the point where Spasmodic's talons pressed into his arm. "Let me… go… tear your arm o—*hkkk…!*"

The grip tightened. "Want to test if you can do so before I snap your neck?"

Spasmodic, its pale face growing a distinct shade of red, kicked out in response. Kanderil kept his arm straight, keeping distance between them. He used his other hand to tug something from his belt, shaking it out with two flicks of the wrist. A thin hide map was revealed, covered in tears and scratches.

"This is the map Sarene lost. I found it in the basement where the Dedicant had been holding her. How could it be there unless someone had given it to them?"

The creature forced air through its teeth, choking to draw fresh oxygen. It wavered between excited cackles and furious snarls, claws still at the Hunter's forearms. Over arteries.

"You departed the cabin before she was taken. You

showed up afterwards already knowing where she would be."

Its face turning purple, Spasmodic grabbed his arm fully, the edges of the claws slicing into his muscular flesh. Kanderil turned and hurled the creature with all the force invoked from his rage. It crashed through the nearest bench, splitting a huge crack through the wood. Spasmodic bounced off and landed in a heap over the next bench along, gasping for air.

"I waited to see if the girl would survive before deciding what to do with you. Now I want you to admit to me that *you* were responsible."

Spasmodic pressed at its throat with the back of a hand, breathing heavily. It rolled over onto its knees. "You… ow… you still don't get it…"

"I saw the bodies outside the monastery. You were supposed to frighten her captors off but you slaughtered them. Every single one who faced you died. That was the point, wasn't it? You just wanted an excuse for murder." Kanderil waited to see what it would do. If the creature chose to attack he would be at a huge disadvantage. Something warm ran along his arm and dripped from his fingertips.

It giggled again, shaking its head, chest heaving. "I'm not a pet… I'm not a companion… I'm not a…" It waved its hand. "Whatever *you* are…." It swallowed, standing upright in a single fluid motion… then staggered, grabbing the bench it had landed on for support. "I'm here for japes and jollies. Action. I wanna have *fun*, y'see? If I have to create that fun, then that's what I do."

Kanderil took two steps forward, the amusement in the

creature's voice infuriating him. He bellowed out in response.

"You almost killed her!"

The words echoed around the hall, reverberating between the marbled walls. Spasmodic, still panting, laughed.

"Yeah, and y'know what? She lived. Sarene's got some magical healing in her, just like me." It gestured towards the back room, emerald eyes sparkling. "So now we know she ain't quite so normal after all, is she? The whelp's better prepared to face whatever else she's gonna face. You keep trying to hide her off in this place or that forest, and for what? She belongs to the world, you idiot. It's impossible to hide her anymore. Might as well face what's comin' with a bloody charge instead of sneaking around hopin' to keep it at bay."

Kanderil shook his head, pointing towards the exit. Blood latticed across the weathered skin of his forearm like a spider web of gore. "You leave. Now."

"Heh. Gonna make me, big man?"

He looked up to that grinning face, framed by the red. "The only reason you are still alive is because you reached this place in time. Sarene may well recover. But I can no longer trust you."

"So you're asking me? Like a proper grown-up?"

"I'm telling you. Get out."

The two of them locked eyes, neither willing to back down. Spasmodic took a few steps towards him, leaning forwards with its arms spreading out by its sides, Kanderil recognised the posture it used before leaping and prepared himself to intercept. If the creature lunged he would have only seconds to end its life before those claws tore him apart.

But then Spasmodic swore, kicking the broken bench. "…rrrrRRR*GH*. Fine. But you wait and see, matey. All this smuggling her from place to place will leave you exposed. And then you'll find you're not as fuckin' good as you think you are. When that time comes, I'll be around to pick up the pieces. She'll see that killing folk is much better than just hoping they'll leave her alone."

Kanderil said nothing as he watched Spasmodic head towards the door. It sniggered, offering him a wave. Then it kicked the wicket gate open with a booted foot and lurched outside. Cold air swept in, the sudden breeze causing strands of Kanderil's hair to fall across his face.

After several minutes he moved to close the wicket gate. There was a thud as the door connected with the larger entrance.

"What in the Four's name was that about?"

He glanced over his shoulder to see Orlienn hurrying along the aisle towards him. "You're bleeding!"

"It had to leave," said Kanderil.

"So you fought it? Look at this place. It could have killed you!"

"No," he replied, turning to face her. "It could not. Fetch me a bandage."

Orlienn paused, taking in the aftermath of his confrontation with Spasmodic. She nodded without another word, heading back towards Sarene's room where the medical supplies were stored.

Kanderil moved to one of the other benches and sat

down. He inspected the wounds running along his forearm, grooves marking exactly where the creature's hands had been. He tensed his muscle, closing a fist, and watched the fresh blood pressed out of the cut trickle out and collect together in droplets which fell to the floor. In the silence, he heard the *tik* as each one landed.

He felt bitter at Spasmodic's words. Mostly because they held a degree of truth.

During the past six months he'd tried his best to hide Sarene away, to keep her safe until a solution could be found. During that time she had been located by Tyrrial and Corliani, Spasmodic, Glaithe, the Dedicant and the Gathire. The location of his childhood home was compromised as a result. He was becoming recognised by others due to his role as her protector. Jared was dead, with Sarene nearly following him to the afterlife.

Kanderil ran a hand over his face and stared at nothing.

"Don't give up hope just yet," said a voice behind him.

Over his shoulder, Kanderil saw Corliani of the Four standing inside the doorway. The ancient man leaned against his staff, smiling. "Your actions have led her this far, Windfury." he continued.

"I nearly got her killed," Kanderil replied, ignoring the meaningless term. Glancing towards the exit to the back room where Orlienn would be returning soon.

"And yet she lives."

"Thanks to the demon who arranged her abduction."

"A demon who has saved you both in the past. Spasmodic has a greater role to play in this than either of us realise, I feel."

Kanderil got to his feet, turning to face Corliani. The mage ran a hand through his whispery silver hair and shrugged. "Sarene has been somewhere quite incredible. I would wager she now further understands her place in the world. When she has recovered, no doubt she will share her plans with you."

"I hope so," said Kanderil. "I could use some guidance."

Corliani's forehead wrinkled. "I am surprised to hear you say so."

"If I cannot confide in a man who has observed humanity for five centuries then who else is there?"

"A fair point."

"Have I done the right thing by hiding Sarene away?"

"As I said, you have led her this far. If Sarene had not faced death she would never have learned of her capacity to cheat it. But you have saved the girl from those who would do her harm several times. Considering the difficulty of your task, I would say you have done just fine."

"And now?"

Chuckling, Corliani shrugged. "You either continue as you are, or you return Sarene to the world. Either way, the world will keep turning. I came here to warn you, however."

Kanderil said nothing, waiting for the man to continue.

"If I felt the ripple of Sarene's return to life, then my brothers likely did also. Tyrrial included. I fear what his response may be. You should be aware that he may come to see for himself."

"Tyrrial survived, then."

"Indeed he did, and I am grateful for it. But while he has kept his distance until now, Sarene's journey may incite another attempt to… shall we say, 'influence' the situation."

"He killed hundreds of my countrymen and Sarene's brother. If he shows up again I will make him wish he had not."

Corliani laughed; not in mockery, but with a gentle tolerance. "You have great ability, Kanderil, but do not overestimate yourself. I will seek to dissuade my brother from further involving himself. Just be mindful."

Looking across the main hall of the Shrine once again to the small corridor leading towards Sarene's room, Kanderil held a broad hand against the wound across his forearm, feeling the wet warmth there. He watched another drop of blood fall to the sacred floor. "I will do whatever it takes to protect her. This is the only time she will face death. I swear it."

"You care for her a great deal, don't you?"

Kanderil took a long time to respond. "She reminds me of a girl I once knew."

Corliani nodded. "Some say our past has the greatest influence on our future. I believe your companion is coming with a bandage now."

Kanderil lifted his head to see Orlienn appear, a wrap of bandage in one hand and a bottle in the other; a pin stuck out from between her teeth. He grunted. "I expect you will startle her."

"Who will?" said Orlienn through her tight mouth. Kanderil glanced to where Corliani had been, only to find the man had disappeared without so much as a whisper.

THE DOOR TO the hovel burst open, slamming against the wall behind it before shaking on its hinges. Footfalls on the creaking steps. At least three pairs of booted feet, close behind each other. Niallya watched the first man – the first Gathire – take the open door opposite; her room. Within a heartbeat a second Agent appeared, facing her with sword drawn.

Niallya sat cross-legged on the floor with Tillyan in her arms, the child's face obscured by matted hair. Her curved blade lay within arm's reach. Tilting her head back, she considered grabbing it.

The Agent must have seen her fingers twitch, for he gave a malicious sneer. "Try me, you murdering bitch."

A stirring in her lap. Tillyan raised her head, looking around with sleep creasing her eyes. "Who is it?"

With such a simple query, Niallya lost her will to fight. She wrapped her arm back around the girl's waist, laid her forehead against that small skull. "I'm sorry," she whispered.

The moment lasted barely a second before hands grabbed her arms and lifted her upright, sending the child sprawling across the floor. Something connected with her brow and her world became infinitely darker.

SARENE WOKE FROM time to time in the days that followed,

staring at those around her as though she were inside a glass cage. Nothing really connected with her; not when she was fed, not when she was cleaned, not when the others spoke to her. It was all a myriad of images and sounds which never stuck for long.

The only constant was the memory of her conversation with Feragh. Each day spent lying here, growing incrementally stronger each time she regained consciousness, was like a candle burning lower and lower.

When the flame went out, she would be forced to act.

Images whispered by her. Jared, smiling and handsome, speaking words she couldn't hear. Her parents, her triplet brothers, her younger sister, all back in the valley home she yearned to see again. Kanderil, both physically with her and a mirage of how she viewed him in memory; giant, indomitable, unwavering. Spasmodic, who had carried her to this place but had not been seen since. Anthon, holding her hand at all hours, still here for reasons best known to himself. The warmth of his grip was comforting and she enjoyed waking to realise it anew each time.

She should be dead. But her unique position within the world had saved her life. She had been given the chance to make a difference.

That last thought shimmered below everything else, whether her eyes were open or closed.

Sarene smiled one morning as sleep claimed her yet again.

Queen of the World.

Epilogue

GLAITHE RODE TO the north of Tamiran, cantering across grassland. A stream ran parallel to him, the water leading scores of miles towards the Horhai Lake beyond the Meadows. He felt as though he'd been smiling for the full two days since his escape from the capital.

Remelas was dead. Nichai had been delivered. Exactly as had been intended.

The horse continued onwards, beneath grey skies and through muted green fields, hooves churning through soft earth or clopping against hard, frozen dirt. Glaithe kept his cloak tight around him and his cowl drawn forwards, partially obscuring his vision. It was important to get out of Tamir first before focusing on the next stage of his plan.

It took a few moments to realise that someone was standing in the middle of the field he found himself in. Raising his head, Glaithe saw a grey-haired figure in a brilliant maroon robe of many woven fabrics. The stranger held a staff and watched his approach. Drawing closer and eventually to a stop, Glaithe realised that he was smiling.

The presence of the man radiated out like a beacon.

When he spoke, the voice carried over the winds without tarnish.

"Glaithe, I presume."

"Yes. Whom might you be?"

"Take a guess."

The former Gathire studied the man standing yards opposite. Slowly, gradually, a smile crept across his features.

"I had expected it would take a lot of work to find you," he said.

"Not at all. I have been observing you for some time."

"You should have introduced yourself."

"I wanted to see what you were made of, my boy." The man chuckled. "You passed with distinction."

"You saw what I did back in Tamiran?"

"Of course. Did you really believe you could use a crossbow so accurately and escape the city undetected *without* my aid?"

The words brought irritation from Glaithe, as though his great achievement had been cheapened somehow, but he retained his smile. Such selfishness was pointless in the face of a God. "I had marvelled at my own skill."

"Travel with me. We have much to talk about, you and I."

"I would be honoured. What did you have in mind?"

Tyrrial smiled, waiting for a kick of wind to pass between them before replying.

"I intend to start a magnificent war."

www.ingramcontent.com/pod-product-compliance
Lightning Source LLC
Chambersburg PA
CBHW061609210726
48287CB00001B/60